Curiosity got the better of Lady Verran...

Orange light thrust into the darkened room. Verran beheld a gigantic nest, a mass of woven branches, creepers, grasses, and reeds, packed with bodies: small, spiky, croaking little creatures. It was obvious they were only babies, for they squirmed and whimpered piteously. Verran knelt beside the nest, stroking the ugly little heads, and crooned to them. Her impulses were maternal, but the infants did not understand. They squealed in mortal fear.

A screaming dark form catapulted from the shadows. It was shrouded in coarse black hair, and a ridge of spikes bristled along the length of its spine. The mouth was open and snarling. Red eyes glared hideously in the dark visage.

Verran jerked back her hand, and sprang to her feet with a scream. The creature hissed and leaped for her, claws extended . . .

THE SORCERER'S LADY

PAULA VOLSKY

ACE FANTASY BOOKS
NEW YORK

This book is an Ace Fantasy original edition,
and has never been previously published.

THE SORCERER'S LADY

An Ace Fantasy Book/published by arrangement with
the author

PRINTING HISTORY
Ace Fantasy edition / April 1986

ISBN: 0-441-77533-0

Ace Fantasy Books are published by The Berkley Publishing Group,
200 Madison Avenue, New York, New York 10016.
PRINTED IN THE UNITED STATES OF AMERICA

The SORCERER'S LADY

Chapter One

It was with some trepidation that the household steward confessed that Dris Verras's daughter had escaped.

"I ordered you to lock her up." Dris Verras was of a tolerant nature, but his day had been taxing and his patience was at an end.

"We did so, your lordship."

"Then how did she get out? She couldn't have jumped from the bedroom window—it's four stories above the canal."

"Lady Verran appears to have knotted her bed hangings together, affixed them to the balustrade of her balcony, lowered herself to the window below, reentered the house, and made her way to canal-level, probably by way of the servants' staircase, my lord."

Dris Verras shook his head ruefully. "She's a clever girl. Why can't she be a little clever about the things that matter?"

The steward was respectfully mute.

"How long has my daughter been missing?"

"Certainly not more than an hour or two, my lord."

"How many know of this?"

"Six or seven of the household staff, my lord."

"Very well. See that no one else learns of it. Take particular care that Lord Grizhni's retainers learn nothing. I want Verran found immediately. Take the servants who already know and search the city through. Check the shipyards first—she may attempt to hire passage. Have someone watch the southern gate—perhaps she'll seek refuge with her mother's kin in Gard Lammis. Visit the homes of her friends, but do so discreetly.'' A new thought struck Dris Verras. ''And go to young Brenn Wate Basef's lodgings at the Shevellin Tower—she may be with him. When you find her, bring her back, and try to be as inconspicuous about it as possible. This entire humiliating affair is an affront to Lord Grizhni.''

''What if Lady Verran refuses to come with us, your lordship?''

''She would hardly dare to refuse. When I think of the honor conferred upon that foolish child, and her shameful ingratitude, her obstinacy, her folly—'' Dris Verras controlled himself with an effort. ''Use force if absolutely necessary. But it goes without saying that you're not to harm the silly chit.''

''And if we cannot find her at all, your lordship?''

Dris Verras contemplated the ordeal of informing the great Lord Terrs Fal Grizhni, Preeminent of the sorcerous Select of the city of Lanthi Ume, that his prospective bride had fled. Dris Verras turned pale at the very thought. ''If you fail to find her, I am ruined. In which case the girl may beg, starve, or walk the streets for all I care. I have never beaten her, never chastised her, and I see now that I was wrong.'' He encountered the inquisitive gaze of the servant and cut himself off. ''Find her. Do it now.''

Dris Verras walked from the room, silently cursing the fate that had burdened him with a recalcitrant daughter.

The steward's tongue was itching to spread the news. But who would dare to spread gossip offensive to the ears of Lord Terrs Fal Grizhni? Thus the servant sped in dutiful silence to perform his master's bidding.

It had been said that water filled the veins of Lanthi Ume, while the veins of her citizens carried fire. This poetic conceit simply referred to the city's arterial system of canals, and to the supposedly ardent nature of her inhabitants. But Lanthi Ume was a place that seemed to inspire poetry, if the richness of her literature could be taken as any indication.

Lanthi Ume—Princess Royal of all the cities of the great island of Dalyon, enthroned upon her famed Nine Isles—was guarded on three sides by the sea, and on the fourth, the mainland side, by the ancient Vayno Fortification. Since time immemorial a seat of power, wealth, beauty, and sorcery, she was to her proud sons and daughters the center of all the universe. The center of that center was the Lureis Canal, lined with fantastic mansions of the rich and powerful, crisscrossed with bridges of green marble and golden crystal. All manner of boats plied the Lureis: small crafts for hire, manned by professional watermen; privately owned dombuli, gliding about on their owners' errands; barges delivering produce and goods of every kind to the great houses and to the innumerable little market squares that dotted the city; here and there immense venerises, the pleasure crafts of the wealthiest nobles, with their fantastic carvings, their wildly luxurious appointments, their burnished oars and exotically costumed slaves.

One of the boats—a hired dombulis with polished black sides and a high, curving prow—carried a small, fair-haired girl attired in garments of exceptional quality. Her hands were twisted in her brocade lap, and her prettily immature face was streaked with tears. The dombulman glanced at her covertly. The girl was obviously of good family. Why would she be gadding about on her own, without so much as a maid to attend her? He noted the tears, the air of distraction. Could she be a runaway, and if so, would he endanger himself by assisting her? The dombulman's observations were sound. His passenger was the wayward Lady Verran, intent on fleeing her father's house.

Verran gazed upon the shore. Everywhere the people thronged: Guardsmen in their uniforms of green and gold; courtiers in their velvets; ladies in sweeping gowns of rainbow brocade; blue-clad tradesmen; beggars in their tatters; starveling apprentices and students; peasant farmers in from the country for a market day; Hurbanese rat-duckers; artists and vagabonds, slaves and thieves, green-veiled pilgrims from the inland regions, tall foreigners whose tattooed faces marked them as Strellian, soldiers of Gard Lammis, gilded priestesses of Ert, and even an occasional impressive figure whose robes bore the golden double-headed dragon insignia of the Select. Thousands upon thousands of people filled the streets and the boats, spilled through the alleys and squares, swirled over the waters in patterns of color and movement that never repeated themselves throughout all the ages of Lanthi Ume. Overhead the seabirds wheeled and called. Down below, the great city lay in the water like a queen in a silvery bath.

It was a stupendous sight, but Verran hardly saw it. "Stop

here," she directed the dombulman, thus solving his dilemma. He brought the boat neatly to dock at the foot of Shevellin Tower and assisted his passenger to the wharf. She paid—too much, she was obviously unused to handling money—and rushed into the gaily-tiled tower without a backward glance. For a moment the dombulman lingered. Would that pretty creature be safe on her own? She looked intelligent, but utterly inexperienced. Probably she had friends or kin in Shevellin Tower. In any case it was no concern of his. He shrugged and went his way.

Lady Verran sped lightly up a flight of carven stairs. No one might have guessed from the speed and certainty of her movements that she had never set foot in Shevellin Tower before. Presently she found the door she sought and pounded on it with both fists until Brenn Wate Basef answered the summons. It was obvious at once that Brenn was in the grip of one of his frequent, black despondencies. His pallor, shadowed eyes, sagging shoulders, all bespoke misery. "Verran—they told me you'd been sent out of the city. My messages were returned unopened, so I thought— Have you been crying?"

"They were lying to you. My parents have kept me locked up in my room for the past three days. Today I got away and came straight here. I need help."

"Come in and tell me." He stood aside to let her pass into his lodgings, but she hesitated. "What's the matter?"

"Brenn, I can't go in there. I'm alone, and . . ."

"And what would people say? Are you still such a child?"

Verran's chin came up. "I am sixteen years old, and no child." She walked into the room and paused, staring. The chamber was filled with hundreds of skeletons. There were skeletal birds, bats, grens, fish, dogs, sheep, a very large creature with tusks, and something that might once have been a horned sizbar. "How horrible—why do you keep these old bones?"

His eyes kindled. Moments earlier his mood had been leaden, but now he flamed with passionate enthusiasm. Brenn Wate Basef was like that. His lightning mood changes were excitingly unpredictable. Moreover, he was equipped with wavy dark hair, a pale complexion, chiseled profile, and burning eyes exactly like the noble hero of the poem *Zaniboono: The Doomed Emperor*. Verran had loved Zaniboono for years and was quite certain that she loved Brenn equally well.

"They're a part of my masterwork," Brenn explained, forgetting her troubles in his excitement. "With this, I shall become a member in full standing of the Select. They've kept me dangling as a candidate for years, but it will be different when they see this. Watch." A medallion on a twisted chain hung on his neck. It was one of those small artifacts frequently employed by the savants of the city to focus and enhance the power of their highly verbal Cognition. Brenn spoke certain soft words and the medallion glowed, although not more brightly than the young man's eyes. He finished speaking, and dozens of skeletons moved. Birds fluttered stiffly, cats prowled, snakes undulated. Lady Verran gave a faint exclamation of surprise and disgust. Brenn picked up the skeleton of a fish and dropped it into a glass tank of water. The white bones swam clumsily. "There." He turned to her in triumph.

Verran watched the twitching, jerking bones in bewilderment. "This is . . . interesting, Brenn. But what is it *for*?"

She had fired his gunpowder temper, and he glared. "You haven't bothered to consider the implications of this discovery. Just think—through this act of Cognition, I control the movements of bare, dead bones. But what if the bones weren't bare? What if they were still clothed in skin and muscle? And what if they weren't dead? Don't you see? Through this act, it may be possible one day soon to exercise complete control over the movements of other creatures, including men, while leaving the mind, the emotions, the conscious volition entirely intact."

"It sounds cruel."

"Now you're being silly. I suppose it could be put to perverted use by some unscrupulous person, but there's nothing inherently cruel in the discovery itself. The search for knowledge is essentially moral." It was one of those grand, idealistic sentiments of his that normally aroused her admiration, but somehow this one sounded flat. "It's an important discovery, and after this no one will presume to deny me my rightful place among the Select. I thought you'd be happy for me."

"Oh, I am, Brenn. I am, truly. Only . . ."

"What?"

"Can't you be content as an ordinary man? Why must you be a sorcerer?"

"Sorcerer? Don't use that term, Verran. It's vulgar. The members of the Select are called savants. Sometimes they're known as investigators, or experimentalists. But not sorcerers, and please, not *wizards* or *magicians*."

"Why not? They practice magic, don't they?" She wandered over to an armchair that was occupied by the palsied skeleton of a rat, or perhaps a squirrel. Brenn spoke and the creature lay still. Verran gingerly transferred the bones to a table and seated herself.

"To call it magic makes it sound unnatural. The savants of the Select investigate . . . possibilities. They understand the forces that govern the world, and therefore know how to use them. It's a noble life."

"I suppose so."

"I'd have been recognized as a savant years ago, if it hadn't been for—" Brenn broke off, his mercurial mood shifting toward bitterness. He did not need to finish the sentence. The Wate Basef family of Castle Io Wesha was the object of considerable popular suspicion and prejudice. It had been so ever since Brenn's ancestor, Staz Wate Basef, had led an unsuccessful rebellion against the Duke of Lanthi Ume. Staz's efforts won him slow death by torture, but in the eyes of Lanthi Ume, the Wate Basef debt had not yet been fully satisfied. "It's always the same, the world never forgets."

Brenn brooded darkly, much as Zaniboono was wont to brood, but this time Lady Verran remained unmoved by the handsome scowl. "Don't you want to know why I've come?" she asked quietly.

"Of course I do. I've longed for word from you."

Aware that she held his full attention and uncertain how long she would keep it, Verran did not waste words. "Father's kept me locked up in my bedroom because he knew I'd run away if I got the chance. I told him as much the day he let me know he plans to marry me off to—to—" She pronounced the name with an effort, "Terrs Fal Grizhni."

Brenn's reaction was gratifying. He literally blanched. "Are you telling me the truth?"

"Yes."

"You are to marry the master of the Select?"

"Unless you can help me to think of some way out of it."

"They can't mean to wed you to that old man! He must be fifty years older than you!"

"He's thirty years older than I."

"It's obscene!"

"I don't care about his age. It's worse than that. I've heard about Fal Grizhni all my life—who hasn't?—and I'm afraid of him. I can't marry him—I'm not even sure he's human!" Verran was trying hard not to cry, but she was losing the battle. Her voice shook and the tears were welling uncontrollably. "They say he's not really a man, but a son of Ert—where else could he have found such knowledge? They say he's in league with the White Demons of the Caverns who feed on unwary travelers. Well, I don't really believe that. But some folk claim he's made a compact with the powers of destruction, and that I *can* believe! I don't want to marry someone I'm afraid of. I'll be wretched all my life!"

"Have you told your parents how you feel?"

"They don't listen. All they think about is the advantages of allying our family with the House of Grizhni. When I told my father how frightened I am, he said I'm too young to know what's good for me."

"And did you tell them about us? Did you tell them that you're going to marry me?"

"I tried." She sighed. "That made Father very angry, Brenn. He doesn't like you much."

"I know." The young man stared out the window at the splendid panorama of the Lureis Canal. "Terrs Fal Grizhni, Preeminent of the Select. If it hadn't been for him, I'd have been a member in full standing years ago. But the Fal Grizhnis have always hated the Wate Basefs. And now this. His Preeminence may take any woman he cares to choose. Any healthy girl of good family, capable of bearing children, would probably do. But he must needs choose the woman *I've* chosen, just to assert his power. He's gone too far."

"What can I do to change Father's mind, Brenn?" Verran lifted her blue eyes to him in search of miracles.

"I'll tell you what you're to do. You are going to run away with me today, and we'll be married."

"We can't do that. Father would stop us."

"He won't stop us if he can't find us."

She reflected. "But what would become of my family? Lord Grizhni's wrath—"

"Why should you care what becomes of your family? They've proved that they don't care what becomes of you, haven't they?"

She did not agree, but remained silent. Experience had

taught her that flat contradiction was apt to provoke a temperamental outburst.

"Verran, do you love me or not? I thought you did."

"I think I do."

"But you'd rather marry Fal Grizhni because he's famous and powerful, is that it?"

"Unfair and untrue, Brenn."

"Then marry me. Today."

Lady Verran looked at him, sorely tempted. How handsome and impetuous he was, and what an adventure life with him would be! And the alternative— An assent hovered upon her lips, but was never spoken. Someone was knocking on Brenn Wate Basef's door.

"Don't answer it!"

Brenn ignored her plea and threw wide the door. Three of Dris Verras's servants, including the steward, stood on the threshold. "What do you want?"

"Master Wate Basef, Lord Dris Verras seeks his daughter," the steward announced respectfully. He caught sight of Verran. "You're to come with us, my lady."

"She's not coming with you. She's staying here with me. You can tell that to Dris Verras—and to Fal Grizhni, if you like." Brenn spoke evenly, but his eyes flickered oddly in a chalk-white face. His jaw, a little too finely cut for real strength, was set. Despite his youth, he looked surprisingly dangerous.

"Master Wate Basef, we have no quarrel with you. But we've received orders to bring the young lady back to her father's house."

"The young lady's father can sink in the Great Syan Ooze, and welcome. She stays here."

The steward perceived that argument was useless, and directed his appeal to Lady Verran herself. "My lady, this misbehavior of yours, if discovered, will cause a scandal that will smirch your family's good name for the next twenty years. Do your parents deserve that at your hands? Do not act as a child. Accept your responsibilities and come home." Verran wavered, and the steward took a step forward, closely followed by his two companions.

"Don't try to come into this room," Brenn advised tightly. "Verran, I don't want you listening to him."

Both Verran and the steward disobeyed. "My lady, in your

father's name I must insist—" The servant pushed purposefully into the chamber.

Brenn Wate Basef flushed violently. He spoke, and his medallion glowed. Something cracked, quickly and sharply. The steward howled and fell back, clutching a newly broken arm to his side.

"Brenn! Stop this—please!" Verran exclaimed.

He ignored her. "Take that answer back to Dris Verras—and to Fal Grizhni." The servants gaped at him. Two of them supported the stricken steward. "Now get out of here and don't come back." Lady Verran took an involuntary step toward her family's retainers. "Verran, you stay here." She turned on him, her eyes bright with angry tears.

The steward spoke painfully. "My lady, I ask you for the last time. It seems we cannot force you back to your father's house." He glanced at Wate Basef's medallion, took a deep breath, and continued, "But if you will not come, your family is disgraced, and Lord Grizhni's wrath will be terrible. Many lives will be affected by your decision this day. I beg you to think carefully and choose wisely."

"She does not care for her family's disgrace, for in me she has all the family she needs," Wate Basef proclaimed. "She does not care for Grizhni's wrath, for she knows I can protect her. Grizhni had best beware."

Lady Verran stared, astounded at the effrontery of this . . . *unbalanced boy*. Her eyes widened. The words had popped into her mind unbidden. It was inconceivable that she could apply such a description—unbalanced boy—to her beloved Brenn. But there it was, flitting around her mind like a black bat released from a cage. For the first time in days she paused to think, and rational thought led to certain unavoidable conclusions.

She walked to the door. "I'm going, Brenn."

"Verran, I thought—"

"I think it best, all things considered."

"Then what did you come here for in the first place?" he snarled. "To make a fool of me?"

"My father's dombulis is moored below?" Verran inquired. The steward nodded in profound relief. "Very well. We'll return home and see to that arm of yours." She bestowed a last unhappy look upon Brenn Wate Basef, thunderstruck amidst his prancing skeletons, then accompanied her father's servants out of Shevellin Tower, down to the waiting boat.

Verran soon arrived at her family home, where she endured
a terrible scene with her angry father. Despite the girl's prom-
ises of good behavior, Dris Verras decreed that his daughter
should remain in her room under constant surveillance until
the very day of her wedding to Fal Grizhni.

Chapter Two

❧❧❧❧

The wedding morning dawned as gray and grim as Lady Verran's mood. The sky would not remain overcast for long, she was certain, for surely the elements could not oppose the will of great Fal Grizhni. He possessed power to banish the clouds, or to call them if he would.

Verran's attendants arrayed her and she endured their twittering ministrations apathetically. In silence she donned the ivory gown, with its simple lines and intricate ivory embroidery; the silken slippers; and a few pieces of the most gracefully delicate jewelry. Fal Grizhni had made it known that the massive ornaments traditionally borne by brides of the old Lanthian stock were not to his taste. Thus Verran was deprived of her mother's blinding necklaces and jeweled girdle. In place of the towering golden headdress of her grandmother, she wore a misty veil sprinkled with minute diamonds set like tiny snares to catch the morning light. The comparative simplicity of this costume was vastly becoming, but Verran was indifferent, having little desire to please her fearsome groom. The women brushed her hair, but wisely did not meddle with it. The long, fair locks required no adornment. As a finishing touch, one of them stroked Verran's cheeks with rose-colored powder to disguise the pallor which followed an utterly sleepless night.

Verran examined her mirrored self. The exclamations of her attendants arose like matinal birdsong, but she scarcely heard them. She cared nothing for the gown, the veil, or even the first transformation of her prettiness to beauty. She stared intently into her own eyes, and in them she saw misery and anger, defeat and great fear. The girl straightened her back and tightened her lips. Whatever her new lord might be—savant, spirit, or son of Ert—he should not have the satisfaction of seeing her fear.

One of the servants pressed a bouquet of pale, cream-petaled lelia blossoms into her hand. Such blossoms were the traditional emblem of the bride's departure from her father's house. As she proceeded through the manse from tiring chamber to waiting dombulis or sendillis, it was the custom for a noble bride to scatter a trail of lelia petals to mark her passing. Verran did so mechanically, crushing the cool petals as she let them fall. She walked in a cloud of their cloying fragrance and the servants followed with measured tread. As she quitted her apartment for the last time, the musicians waiting outside her door struck up and joined the procession. For one moment it seemed to Verran like a children's game of make-believe, and then she thought it like a funeral cortege, and her step faltered.

Ceremoniously she descended and came at last to the canal portal where family members and household servants, all attired in their finest, were assembled. Verran distributed the requisite silver coins to the servants, and drank the traditional spiced freagh from the communal Verras chalice. She performed these duties in a courteous, detached manner, and received without apparent emotion the ritual embraces of her kinsmen.

Despite her air of abstraction, it did not escape Verran's notice that sundry aunts and uncles seemed perturbed, and several cousins looked unwontedly grave. One of the servant wenches was actually weeping. Her parents, however, were not thus afflicted. Lord Dris Verras and his lady glowed with pride or triumph—it was difficult to tell which. Dris Verras regarded his daughter with sentimental fondness. The girl was pretty and obedient, altogether a credit to her family. Now, by means of this brilliant marriage, she linked the noble House of Verras with the even more noble, and infinitely renowned House of Grizhni. Moreover, the wedding was to take place at the new Ducal Palace, and the marriage ceremony was to be performed by no less a personage than Povon Dil Shonnet,

Duke of Lanthi Ume. Duke Povon, it seemed, wished to of-
ficiate at an occasion marking the union of two of the city's
oldest Houses. The enormity of the honor drove Lord Dris
Verras nearly mad with delight. And to think that the groom
had intended to reject Duke Povon's kindness!

Fal Grizhni, who desired a small and quiet wedding, had expressed the cynical suspicion that Duke Povon's offer was
prompted by nothing more than a desire to display his splendid, ruinously expensive abode to all the world. Disapproving
of the taxes imposed upon the populace to finance construction of the palace, and even more disapproving of ostentation,
Fal Grizhni had initially sent word that the ceremony would be
performed upon the Select's privately owned island in Parnis
Lagoon. It was only the combined blandishments of Dris Verras and a number of the Duke's emissaries that had at last,
with infinite difficulty, persuaded Grizhni to reconsider. The
wedding would take place at the Ducal Palace after all, thus
crowning the House of Verras with unspeakable glory. And
little Verran? Doubtless she would adapt as best she could to
her new situation—it was her duty, after all. As the new Lady
Grizhni, she would be in a position to exert untold influence
on behalf of the House of Verras. Truly the child was worth
all the care and expense that had been lavished upon her!

Lord Dris Verras deposited a kiss upon his daughter's brow
and gently lowered her veil, which would now remain in place
until raised by the hand of her husband. This done, parents
and kinsmen, servants and musicians, escorted Lady Verran
out the canal portal to the Verras moorings, where eight sendilli waited to carry them all to the Ducal Palace.

The sendilli were glorious—new, shining, banked with flowers and brave with pennants. Above all waved the banners blazoned with the arms of Grizhni and of Verras intertwined. To
the sound of flutes and viols, Verran boarded her sendillis. As
she did so, a blade of sunlight sundered the clouds and struck
like a golden sword upon the silver waters of the Channel of
Ume. The spectators gasped at the magical sight. Their gasps
turned to shouts as the clouds rolled back reluctantly, back
even as far as the walls of Lanthi Ume. Directly above, the
skies were blue and clear. Without the city walls, the heavens
were dark and a great thunderhead loomed in menace. It
seemed that Fal Grizhni had chosen not to permit the clouds to
shadow his wedding day. The members of the wedding party

were agog with admiration, but Verran stared up at a sky that was blue by man's will alone and her very flesh turned cold.

The eight sendilli embarked. It was not a long journey, for the Channel of Ume opened directly onto the Lureis Canal, site of the Ducal Palace; but for Verran, time slowed to a crawl. Eager citizens thronged along the banks of the canal. Spectators by the thousands watched from the windows and balconies of bright-tiled domes and towers. The Lureis was alive with hundreds of boats. All of Lanthi Ume had turned out to view the grand event—the wedding of the greatest savant the city had ever produced, a wedding which served to reassure the populace that Fal Grizhni was but a man, after all.

Verran shut her eyes briefly, sickened by the scent of lelias, the bobbing of the boat, the oppressive stares of humanity, and above all, by the unnaturally beautiful sparkle of sunlight on water. Thank fortune for the diamond-spotted veil that raised a barrier of mist between herself and the world! She looked up as the sendilli passed beneath the facade of Shevellin Tower. The windows on the third floor, canalside, were closed. But perhaps Brenn Wate Basef watched the procession from behind the barred shutters.

The boats glided on. To the right arose the Shonnet Arena, a gigantic structure of black and green marble crowned with a bright froth of glass domes. The arena housed an indoor lagoon designed for the staging of boat races and mock sea battles. It was the opinion of some that the creation of an artificial lagoon within Lanthi Ume might be considered redundant, particularly in view of the cost. In response to these poor-spirited objections, Duke Povon pointed out that construction of the arena permitted all citizens to view the boat races in the worst of weather without suffering an instant's discomfort—surely a civilized amenity well worth the expense.

Verran's glance shifted to the left, to the half-completed Shonnet Theater, with its two hundred columns of porphyry. The theater was another pet project of the Duke's, and the massive taxes he had levied the previous year to cover building expenses had by some mysterious causality resulted in a forty percent increase in the price of fresh fruit. Popular outcry at the time had been loud and anguished. Now the complaints had ceased, but so had construction. The masons, who claimed they had never been paid, had abandoned their work and could not be induced to return. Now a group of the homeless had set up squalid camp inside the empty theater. Such sights had become commonplace of late.

Music, sunlight, rippling water, and bright colors almost hypnotized Verran. In all too short a time the eight sendilli arrived at the golden pier. The Ducal Palace presented a heavily ornate, gilded face to the Lureis Canal. The magnificence of the edifice was unquestionable, but its ponderous proportions somehow failed to please the eye.

An army of guests waited to greet the bride. Musicians piped her ashore and conducted her along the lily-strewn Ducal moorings and into the palace itself: through the cavernous, glittering entrance hall with its ceiling four stories high; up the broad stairway of rose-veined marble to a landing crusted with coral and mother-of-pearl; and thence to a reception chamber of almost ridiculous scale and grandeur. The procession wended its way in time to the stately music. Verran held her father's arm and from time to time looked at him as if still hoping for a last-minute reprieve. But Dris Verras's face reflected a satisfaction that promised no mercy.

The reception chamber was almost filled, despite its size, with hundreds upon hundreds of guests. Verran perceived them as a scintillant, featureless mob. The girl trudged forward as slowly as a prisoner approaching the block. Ahead of her she discerned a brilliant figure seated on a throne atop a dais; a number of equally resplendent figures grouped around the throne; a rainbow assortment of nobles and liveried servants; and one very tall, lean man clad in steel gray who waited before the dais—Terrs Fal Grizhni. Verran recognized him readily enough. She had seen him many times throughout her life, but always at a distance; always as an alien figure, sinister in his midnight robes, standing apart from all humankind.

Today Fal Grizhni did not wear black. In honor of the occasion he had abandoned his customary robe with its double-headed dragon insignia. But his gray surcoat, severe in cut and devoid of decoration, was almost incongruously plain in the midst of the finery of the wedding guests. Grizhni's posture was inflexible and the set of his head expressed arrogance; so much was unmistakable, even at a single glance. Verran did not wish to look more closely. She averted her eyes quickly and sought out the figure on the throne. It was the Duke

Povon Dil Shonnet, who was perhaps at that moment not in full command of his faculties. The Duke, a corpulent and epicene notable of middle years, slumped loosely in his great chair. His hair, moist with perspiration, had come completely out of curl, and his glazed eyes all but disappeared beneath their drooping lids. In his hand the Duke carried an embroidered handkerchief whose fragrance must have been pleasing, for he frequently raised the fabric to his nose and inhaled deeply.

Beside the throne stood the famous Lord Saxas Gless Vallage, a savant of accomplishment, senior member of the Select, and aristocrat of Lanthi Ume. It was said by sundry honorable men that Gless Vallage was ruthlessly ambitious, but his fine features and frankly humorous smile seemed to belie the rumor.

On the other side of the throne stood exquisite young Lord Beskot Kor Malifon, the wit and dandy, famous for his inspired extravagances, infamous for his libertinage. Kor Malifon's diamonds bid fair to outdazzle the sun.

Behind them stood many others of the highest and noblest of Lanthi Ume. These were the folk that ruled the destiny of all the city. There was Lord Cru Beffel, who advocated the use of slave labor forces comprised of criminals and enemies of the state to dig canals. There was Beffel's haggard daughter Lavenenla, said to have taken five hundred lovers, both singly and in groups of immoderate size. There was Commander Haik Ulf of the Ducal Guards, a burly lord whose personal servants often bore telltale scars. There was—

But Verran did not have time to complete her inventory of the great, for she had arrived at Fal Grizhni's side. She stole another quick sidelong glance at him through her veil, and spied a pale profile towering above her. Grizhni's features were strong and ascetic, his expression impenetrably cold, his bearing princely. The savant's dark hair was slightly streaked with gray, as was his short beard. His eyes she could not see clearly. He looked as if he could not know the meaning of human warmth or sympathy, and she shuddered. The Duke was speaking. The Duke himself was performing the marriage ceremony, and had she not been deeply distressed, Verran would have appreciated the honor. She might also have realized that the ruler's voice was oddly slurred and halting. But profound agitation did not permit her to take heed of such things. The Duke commanded the couple to join hands. Instinct warned Verran that Grizhni's touch would be cold, cold as a forgotten grave. She extended her hand reluctantly and felt it taken in a firm, warm clasp. Her own hand was icy.

The Duke intoned erratically. Although the text of the ceremony was written out on the parchment that lay in his lap, Povon encountered many difficulties. He seemed disoriented, but evidently found solace in the fragrance of his handkerchief, for he sniffed it frequently and appeared enthralled with the embroideries. The ceremony was a long one. Eventually Verran collected herself so far as to observe the extreme eccentricity of His Grace's behavior. She noted, too, that Fal Grizhni's responses were delivered in a deep and very sonorous voice, a voice whose beauty might have won its possessor much popularity among the common citizenry, had he stooped to employ it to that end. But he chose never to stoop.

It ended at last. They were husband and wife. Fal Grizhni turned to his bride, lifted her veil, and Verran encountered the full force of his dark gaze. She managed to meet his eyes squarely. Grizhni bent and bestowed a very brief and formal kiss upon her lips. The girl exercised self-control and did not flinch. Then the music struck up and she was instantly surrounded by clamorous well-wishers. Thus she was speedily carried away from her new husband, and did not regret it in the least.

Save for occasional brief exchanges of formal courtesies, Verran managed to avoid him throughout most of the festivities. During the banquet it was easy, for bride and groom sat at opposite ends of a table the length of a cargo vessel. Nor did she encounter difficulty during the dancing, for Grizhni never danced and the ballroom was so vast that she could almost lose herself in it. During the recitation of odes, encomiums, and congratulatory speeches, she was able to escape with a giggling band of girls her own age to the shelter of a canalside chamber where the Maiden's Last Rites were performed. Verran succeeded in prolonging these rites to almost unheard-of lengths, and while she was thus engaged, the wedding guests followed their Duke outdoors to the formal gardens where peacocks flaunted and the topiary was relentlessly geometric. It was early evening before she found herself seated beside her husband beneath the great silken canopy set up in the garden for the viewing of *The Masque of Marriage: An Exhortation to Virtue.* The choice of this particular entertainment was a matter of policy rather than taste. Its author was the Duke himself, who notoriously failed to follow his own precepts.

The setting sun provided a spectacular backdrop to *The Masque of Marriage.* The sky blazed and the air was balmy. Only a faint rumble of thunder reminded the guests of the storm clouds held unnaturally in check without the city walls. On Verran's right-hand side, Fal Grizhni watched the masque expressionlessly. On her left the Duke showed less interest in the pious production than might ordinarily have been expected of its author. His Grace's eyes were fixed glassily upon his handkerchief. His pupils were dilated, his breath came in wheezes and gasps. Verran watched in fascination.

The Duke felt her eyes upon him and looked up. "Eh, my dear," he observed blearily. "You disdain my masque? Yet it teaches a lesson in virtue every bride should take to heart."

"A most valuable lesson, even were its value less than its virtue. Valued all the more for the sake of its virtuous source no less than its own value intrinsical." The girl's convoluted response was only the product of her aristocratic training, but it pleased the Duke.

He wheezed with inane laughter. "Well said! A pretty bride with a pretty tongue! I should delight in playing the schoolmaster with you my dear, were that pleasant task not allotted to your husband, noble Grizhni." A hint of sarcasm or animosity sharpened the blurry edges of his voice. Verran heard it and had the sense to keep silent. "For who among us is so learned he cannot be schooled by Grizhni, Wisdom's true son?" The Duke's sloppy smile revealed too many teeth. He raised the handkerchief to his nose and inhaled.

"A special perfume, your Grace?" Verran inquired.

"Ah, you wish to change the subject. I am rebuked. A pretty bride with a pretty tongue should not be troubled. Yes, my dear, a very special perfume. This handkerchief was given to me by my friend Gless Vallage. A mere whiff of its fragrance soothes the spirits, promotes peace, contentment, contemplation. And here is the true wonder—one brief inhalation of these excellent vapors and you will see the embroideries of this handkerchief come to life. They assume a variety of animated forms—men and women, women and beasts, women and demons. Most amusing. Most stimulating. Here, child, breathe deeply." He extended the handkerchief.

"Do not touch that, Madam. I forbid it."

Verran turned, startled. She'd had no idea that Fal Grizhni was listening to the conversation. His manner precluded argument.

The Duke grinned. "You prefer to keep her ignorant, Grizhni? Perhaps it's best that women are so."

"Where false knowledge breeds pestilence, ignorance proves a sovereign cure. Your Grace is aware of my convictions," Fal Grizhni returned frigidly. Whatever the powers of his mind, he possessed no diplomacy.

"Only too well aware." His Grace sighed. "So intimate are we with our Grizhni's moral rigor that we hardly hoped to see him permit himself the luxury of marriage. Well, all's one for that, and I congratulate you upon a most charming acquisition."

Grizhni inclined his head briefly in a manner somehow devoid of respect, and turned back to the masque. Verran watched with great interest. It was plain that the Duke and her husband disliked one another, but she could not as yet divine the reason. Presumably the Duke's presence at the wedding was but an obligatory gesture in honor of the most powerful of his subjects. After studying Grizhni's hawk profile for some minutes, Verran gathered up her courage and leaned toward him. "Why did you not wish me to—"

She never finished the question, for at that moment there was a commotion in the crowd, a few shouts, and a man smashed through the ranks of the wedding guests to fling himself straight at the groom. The intruder, a ragged and wild-eyed hysteric of indeterminate age, brandished a dagger whose broad blade flashed red in the light of the setting sun. He was screaming at the top of his lungs, shrieking out invective, accusations, and curses against the House of Grizhni in general and Terrs Fal Grizhni in particular. It was difficult to make out much of what he said, for he was only semi-coherent and clearly deranged. He seemed to accuse Terrs Fal Grizhni of the vilest possible crimes. Fleeting phrases were intelligible: "Clouded my mind—tricked and cheated me—used me—" The grief and hatred were dreadful, but Verran did not have to listen long. With a scream the madman raised his blade and lunged for Grizhni's heart. Verran sprang from her chair and the other guests in the vicinity automatically recoiled.

Fal Grizhni did not stir. Rock steady in his great chair, he

uttered potent syllables in a voice too low to be heard. No
ring, medallion, or amulet customarily employed by the Select
to perform acts of Cognition was in evidence, but the words
were effective nonetheless, and in an instant the madman's
hands lost all their power. The dagger slid from a rubbery
grasp and landed on the ground. For a moment the man stood
staring at his own hands, then dropped to his knees to scrabble
for the lost weapon. His efforts were useless, and presently he
began to weep.

Fal Grizhni looked on inscrutably. He gestured, and cowled
figures leapt forward. Until that moment their presence had
somehow gone unnoticed by all. They wore long robes the
ghostly gray of dense fog, the color of the House of Grizhni.
Little of their faces could be seen beneath the deep hoods, but
Verran caught a glimpse of thick fur and white fangs. Her husband's servants did not appear to be human, but what they
might be was almost impossible to judge. Two of the am-
biguous attendants secured the sobbing lunatic and stood
awaiting instructions.

Then the Lord Haik Ulf barked out a command, and a
group of hard-faced men advanced. Evidently Ulf had
stationed his Guardsmen, disguised as wedding guests,
throughout the garden. Swords appeared in the hands of the
Guardsmen, and Ulf declared, "My men will take care of
this."

The sight of Lord Haik Ulf exercised a peculiar effect upon
the prisoner. He shivered spasmodically and his sobs gave way
to screams.

"Take him," Ulf commanded.

The madman whimpered and clutched at the loose gray
robes of his captors. Verran was torn between pity and disgust
as she watched.

Ignoring Haik Ulf, Fal Grizhni addressed the failed assassin
directly. "I do not know you. Who sent you here today?" Terrified silence greeted the inquiry. "I will question this man
personally. Remove him to Grizhni Palace. Do not harm
him," the savant directed his followers. They could not obey,
for Ducal Guards blocked the path to the dock. Low snarls
issued from beneath the gray hoods.

"This is Guards' business. We'll deal with it. What are you
waiting for?" Lord Ulf snapped at his men. The Guards
closed in, then halted as the uncanny snarls of their gray op-

ponents waxed in volume and intensity. "Go on, you needn't fear Grizhni's tame demons!"

In this Lord Ulf was mistaken, for one of the gray creatures struck suddenly with razor talons, laying a Guardsman's face open from eye to jaw. The Guard fell back, cursing. Ulf, his heavy face crimson with rage, turned on the savant. "Call off your demons, Grizhni, and let my men do what they have to do."

"It is my concern alone." Grizhni's eyes were fixed upon the prisoner. "I wish to hear who sent this man."

"Fine. As soon as we get him to talk, I'll let you know."

"I already know. I want confirmation before I take action. You understand me, my lord?"

The flush on Haik Ulf's face deepened, and his expression was uneasy. "You can think what you like. But it's my duty and my right to claim that prisoner. Anyone who tries to interfere defies the power of the state. Is that what you're trying to do, Grizhni?"

Grizhni did not deign to reply. His contempt for Ulf seemed too great to allow a prolonged exchange.

Verran saw Lord Saxas Gless Vallage whisper urgently into the ear of the Duke. His Grace was still woozy, but now found the wit to speak, albeit as if by rote. "Ulf is correct. This does not fall within the jurisdiction of the Select. Let it be known to all who are in danger of forgetting it that the Select do not rule in civil matters. Moreover, I have been reminded that it would look very ill, Grizhni, were the man who sought your life to be delivered into your keeping. It might be said that you will vent your wrath upon his person, and such an accusation impugns our ducal justice. Therefore Ulf must take the prisoner."

Fal Grizhni paused, and Lady Verran held her breath. Was it possible that her husband would defy the Duke's commands? Grizhni's face was unreadable, but his hesitation spoke volumes. To Verran's surprise, he glanced at her as if her presence were one factor that entered into his mysterious calculations. Then he gestured brusquely, and his servants released their captive, who was instantly pounced upon by half a dozen Guardsmen and borne away. Verran heard the frenzied shrieks, sobs and pleas for a little while, and then there was silence.

"You have made the right decision, Preeminence," Gless Vallage said in his light, cultured voice. A friendly observation and yet, Verran wondered, did it not underscore her husband's reluctance to comply with the Duke?

The sun had set, the gardens were gray, and the servants lit torches. For a time there was an aimless babble of excited conversation. Fal Grizhni stood alone, apparently lost in thought. Then the Duke gave commands and *The Masque of Marriage* resumed. The wedding guests, who had scattered far and wide in alarm, returned to their seats and sat dutifully through to the conclusion, after which the festivities came to a close.

Verran, who was exhausted and apprehensive, was forced to endure the slow transport by sendillis from the Ducal Palace along the great bend of the Lureis to the mouth of the Sandivell Canal, where Grizhni Palace stood. It was a most beautiful voyage. The palaces of Lanthi Ume illumined by torch and colored lantern were a gorgeous sight to behold, and overhead the skies displayed their finest jewels for the pleasure of Grizhni's lady. But Verran was blind to it all, for the thought of the night to come had paralyzed her perceptions. Fal Grizhni sat beside her. His behavior throughout the day had been irreproachably punctilious, but as yet they had exchanged few words beyond the formal phrases that the occasion demanded. The girl's nervous tension was growing unbearable. Her head throbbed and she felt she must speak or die. Without stopping to consider the propriety of the question, she turned to Grizhni and demanded, "Why did you wish to marry me?"

Fal Grizhni looked at her. For once his expression was readable, and it reflected faint surprise. When he spoke, his beautiful voice was quiet, as if he addressed a newly captured forest creature whose fears he wished to allay. "I am the last of my line, Madam, and the House of Grizhni must not end with me."

She considered. "Why so?"

He appeared yet more surprised. "Is it possible that a daughter of nobility has never had these matters explained to her?"

"Not in any way that makes sense. Is a family name, the descent of blood, a thing to be worshipped for its own sake? I'm told that it is, but no one has ever explained the reason for this."

"Your father has told you it is so. Is that not sufficient?"

"No," said Verran.

Grizhni examined her. He did not smile, but Verran thought she sensed amusement. "You are blunt, Madam," he said at last. "But I am not displeased. In answer to your question, the desire to perpetuate a dynasty is in the end based on self-love and the longing for immortality. Men fail to note that the immortality attendant upon great works is truer by far than that conferred by sons and daughters."

Verran digested this and then objected, "But most people aren't capable of great works. So they have to settle for the sons and daughters, don't they?"

"Your point is well taken, Madam." This time Grizhni actually smiled. His smile was very infrequent, but when it dawned, it completely transformed his face, and the intimidating coldness temporarily vanished.

"Take my father, for example," said Verran, encouraged. "He has never accomplished anything significant in his whole life, unless you count his renovation of the wine cellars at Verras House. I believe that may be one reason it was so important to him that his daughter should marry into your family."

"Possibly. Your observations are unconventional, Madam."

"Oh—do you wish me to stop, my lord?"

"By no means. Pray continue."

"You yourself have performed great works," Verran remarked. "All the world knows it. Your fame is assured, and thus by your own argument you have no need of offspring. Therefore my original question has not been answered. Why did you wish to marry me?"

"One day we must discuss the matter at leisure."

The response was not enlightening, but Verran had neither the courage nor the time to question him further, for they had arrived at Grizhni moorings. The accompanying fleet of sendilli dispersed, carrying a mob of noble guests off into the night. Only a few boatsful of Grizhni's household attendants remained. Verran watched in dread. Her fears, which had subsided briefly, rose up again more powerful than ever. What were these hooded creatures that served her husband? Demons, Ulf had called them. She recalled the dreadful screams and accusations of the madman at the wedding. She remembered, too, that Fal Grizhni was said to be a son of Ert, and her heartbeat quickened.

Before them towered Grizhni Palace, one of the greatest

structures of Lanthi Ume and one of the grandest, with its huge columns and its vast dome sheathed in beaten silver. They entered, and silent gray figures conducted Lady Verran to her suite of rooms. There were no ordinary human servants in evidence. Before the wedding Fal Grizhni had expressed willingness to accept as many retainers as Lady Verran cared to bring to his household. Despite a genuine fondness for their young lady, however, none of Dris Verras's servants had mustered the courage to accompany her to Grizhni Palace.

Her apartment was spacious and elegant. The bed was hung with pale blue silk and the tall windows had panes studded with faceted crystals that would paint the walls and ceilings with rainbows during the daylight hours.

Verran dismissed her weird attendants and prepared herself for bed without assistance. At length she blew out the candles and climbed under the silk coverlets. For a long time she lay corpse-rigid, half sick with miserable suspense. But Terrs Fal Grizhni did not appear. Verran strained her ears for the sound of footsteps, but heard only wind and rain. The storm clouds, released from bondage at last, now lowered upon Lanthi Ume. Wind and water lashed the towers of Grizhni Palace in vengeful fury.

Verran was deeply tired. Despite her fears, she drifted off to sleep, and slumbered undisturbed through the night.

Chapter Three

❧❧❧❧

Colors. Pure and brilliant colors everywhere. Verran watched in dreamy pleasure. Where did they come from? Curiosity banished the mists of sleep. She remembered where she was, who she was, and all the events of the preceding day. Lady Grizhni. She was now Lady Grizhni, mistress of Grizhni Palace, wife of— Verran sat up in bed abruptly. Morning sunlight was pouring into the room. The prisms in the windows trapped, bent, and shattered the light, flinging the gorgeous ruins across the vaulted ceiling. She looked around her—a beautiful, alien room.

Verran threw the covers aside, jumped from the high bed, ran to the window and looked out. Below her the waters of the Lureis Canal and the Sandivell Canal met and mingled. A spice merchant's great raft was moored at the junction, and the perfume of his wares rose to Verran's nostrils, together with the odors of fish, smoke, humanity, refuse—the characteristic scents of Lanthi Ume's humid air. She inhaled deeply. Had she still been unmarried, had she yet been a girl in her father's house, on a morning like this she would have been out on the canals with her young friends in small, quick boats playing Bump-Me, a game cordially detested by all mature citizens. But Lady Grizhni could not play Bump-Me. Lady Grizhni could hardly hire a tiny thimble-raft in which to shoot

the white water below great Vayno Bridge. What *could* Lady
Grizhni do? She sighed, turned from the window, and wandered toward the bellpull. It was time to dress, and she wanted
a maid's assistance. Verran reached for the pull, then stopped.
Should she ring, what sort of gruesome creature might answer
the summons? Fal Grizhni, she recalled only too well, employed inhuman servants—or were they slaves, or pets? Better
beware of the Grizhni servants.

Verran passed through the nearest doorway and found
herself in a richly furnished private audience chamber. It was
to be expected that a great lady, wife of His Preeminence of
the Select, might wish to grant audiences to various visiting
dignitaries and petitioners. Verran tried to imagine doing so.
Her tutor had once attempted to instruct her in the art of the
audience, the object of which was to destroy the self-assurance
of the visitor while maintaining an appearance of extreme
graciousness. But Verran had shown no aptitude. Her brow
creased dubiously.

She abandoned the audience chamber, passed through
another doorway, and discovered the tiring chamber, with its
mirrored walls, enormous lue-wood presses, gold-and-lacquer
jewel chests, and vanity inlaid with blue eglanite imported
from Taipel. Verran was amazed. Compared to Grizhni Palace, her family's Verras House was scarcely more than a cottage. She opened one of the presses and found her gowns
arranged in perfect order. Verran chose a dress that laced
down the front, that she might don without assistance. She
dressed herself with some difficulty and returned to the bedroom. On a table near the door lay a silver tray bearing a note.
Surely it had not been there a moment before? Verran
unfolded the parchment and beheld black, decisive hand-
writing. She read:

Madam:
    Certain matters necessitate my absence throughout the
morning. I shall return around noon, at which time I request your presence in the Great Hall. Until then, you
will find ample means whereby to entertain yourself.
    I must advise you to exercise caution in dealing with
the household servants, who are not yet acquainted with
you. Be assured I shall introduce you to my creatures at

the earliest opportunity, whereupon you will have no further cause to doubt their loyalty and service.

—Grizhni

His creatures? She read it again. Demons, did he mean? And what "means whereby to entertain" herself were there? She would have to investigate. Verran judged by the angle of the sunlight that she had over two hours to wait until noon, and she resolved to use the time to explore Grizhni Palace from attic to cellar. What matter that the place was huge, foreign, and overwhelming? She was its new Lady.

She commenced her explorations and soon realized that two hours would not suffice. Grizhni Palace was immense, vaster even than she had imagined. Moreover it was full of unexpected twists and turns, curving passages, spiral stairways leading nowhere, a wilderness of echoing galleries and hidden courtyards. In short, an easy place in which to get lost. The rooms were all furnished in great magnificence. The House of Grizhni was of the proudest and wealthiest aristocracy of Lanthi Ume. The name figured prominently in the city's history, and the Fal Grizhni line was considered by some scholars to be of older and purer nobility than the reigning Dil Shonnets. It had once been an extensive family, famed for its intellect and eccentricity. Grizhni Palace had sheltered a multitude of family members, guests, and retainers. Over the years, however, increasing eccentricity had smothered some spark of commonplace vitality, and the family dwindled until at last the only heir remaining was Terrs Fal Grizhni, undoubtedly the most brilliant and mystifying of all his line. And now the enormous Grizhni Palace, large enough to house a fair-sized village, was occupied only by its Master, his new Lady, and a collection of highly questionable attendants.

Verran roamed the endless corridors and was struck by the silence of the place. If she stood still and listened intently, she could hear the shouts of the bargemen and dombulmen outside. But no sound seemed to arise within Grizhni Palace itself. How different it was from bustling Verras House and all that was comfortable and familiar to her! At this moment the corridors of Verras House would be ringing with the voices of children, for at least a dozen of her small nieces, nephews, and

cousins were currently in residence. Servants would be joking
and quarreling, and—

But there was no point in thinking of all that now. Verran
sighed and wandered along a hallway of green marble with
green velvet hangings, as cool as an enchanted forest. From
time to time she encountered hooded, gray-clad figures. Mind-
ful of Fal Grizhni's advice, she did not accost them. The creatures, whatever they were, often turned to watch as she passed,
but made no move to hinder her. Only once a particularly tall
one stood squarely athwart her path and declined to move
aside. Verran drew near enough to catch the tiger-yellow flash
of eyes beneath the hood. She considered running away, and
dismissed the notion.

"What is your name?" she inquired at last. No reply was
forthcoming. It was impossible to judge whether the creature
understood her words. "Can you speak?" No answer, but a
faint hiss sizzled beneath the hood. Other grey figures hovered
nearby, as silent as clouds, and she could feel the pressure of
their eyes. "I am Lady Grizhni." It had an unconvincing
sound. "I am Fal Grizhni's wife." Perhaps they understood,
for they moved noiselessly out of her way. Verran marched on
with renewed confidence, which began to evaporate as she
realized that noon was fast approaching and she had no idea
where to find the Great Hall. Should she fail to appear as requested, her husband would imagine that she disobeyed him
willfully. It was said that the wrath of Grizhni resembled a bitter gale on the Sea of Ice, and she had no ambition to experience it.

Verran sped back along the green corridor the way that she
had come. She hurried past a knot of spectral attendants, took
à left turn, a right, another right, descended a spiral staircase,
ran through a sunlit gallery, climbed some stairs, and found
herself back in the green corridor. There were the same gray
attendants, observing her with what was probably curiosity.
One of the creatures drew near. "Where is the Great Hall?"
Verran inquired slowly and clearly. "Will . . . you . . . guide
. . . me . . . to . . . the . . . Great . . . Hall?" The gray figure
drifted slowly off to rejoin its companions.

She would have to find the hall herself, and she would have
to do it quickly. Verran searched in mounting anxiety. She was
going to be late, and Fal Grizhni might . . . he might— When

she stopped to think about it, she found she didn't have the slightest idea how Grizhni was apt to react.

The corridors went on forever. Verran eventually found herself in the nether regions of the palace, wandering among storerooms, through passageways damp with seeping canal water and furry with white mold. Her nostrils twitched. The odor was unpleasant, the atmosphere oppressive, and time spent in such a place was wasted. Ahead of her a narrow, slime-slippery flight of stairs led down to a cellar that must have been well below the level of the canals. The area was tolerably well-lighted. Lanterns cast their orange glow upon the oozing walls. At the foot of the stairs stood a door incised with angular runes. Curiosity got the better of Lady Verran. She descended and opened the door.

Orange light thrust into the darkened room beyond. Verran beheld a gigantic nest, a mass of woven branches, creepers, grasses, and reeds, all cemented with canal mud. The nest was packed with dark bodies. There must have been at least a dozen of them; small, spiky, croaking little creatures whose flat features were covered with wiry black hair. It was obvious they were only babies, for their eyes weren't open yet and they were toothless. Blind though they were, they felt the presence of an intruder, or perhaps the light troubled them, for they squirmed and whimpered piteously. Verran knelt beside the nest, stroked the ugly little heads and crooned to them. Her impulses were maternal, but the infants did not understand. They squealed in mortal fear.

A screaming dark form catapulted from the shadows. It was somewhat shorter than an ordinary-sized man, but proportionately broader and heavier. The creature was shrouded in coarse black hair, and a ridge of spikes bristled along the length of its spine. More of the same spikes formed a protective ruff around the thick neck and across the shoulders. The mouth was open and snarling. Red eyes glared hideously in the dark visage.

Verran jerked back her hand, sprang to her feet with a scream. The creature hissed and leaped for her, claws extended. A vicious slash ripped the air a whisper away from her eyes. She turned to run, felt the claws hook into the back of her trailing skirts. Rank breath teased her hair like a summer breeze and she could not move. Then she felt the heavy velvet rip like gauze and she was free.

Verran fled along a subterranean corridor with her enemy
raging close behind. She was aware that she should have run
up the stairs, she should have sought the daylight, but it was
too late for that now. She was being driven downward; down
stairways, down sloping passages, down to the bowels of
Grizhni Palace, where the air was perpetually dank, fungus
coated the walls, and the sounds of the outside world, of Sandivell Canal lapping overhead, could no longer be heard.

Verran threw a quick glance over her shoulder. Her enemy
was but a few yards behind, close enough for her to see the
steely sheen of its talons and the crazy rage in its red eyes.
Even in the midst of her terror, it flashed through her mind
that her parents would be sorry if they could see her
now—sorry they had forced her to marry a son of Ert or
worse, sorry they had sacrificed a daughter of the Verras line,
sorry and guilt-ridden. . . . The thought afforded surprisingly
little consolation.

The creature, which ran with an odd leaping gait, was gain-
ing on her. Its fierce, wavering cry rang in her ears. Verran
gasped and increased her pace, skidding perilously on the slippery floor. A useless effort, for she soon discovered that the
corridor along which she fled ended in a blank stone wall.

Several doors opened on the hallway. Verran tried three in
quick succession. All were locked. The fourth opened. Intense
darkness beyond, as black as a rip in the web of space and
time. She jumped through and slammed the door behind her.

Verran stumbled forward a few paces and stopped. She was
in utter darkness, supernatural darkness such as she had never
before experienced. The blackness pressed in upon her, close
and thick and foul. There was a strange odor in the air,
something like rotting vegetation, and it was hot with an ener-
vating warmth quite unlike the rest of Grizhni Palace. It was
Fal Grizhni's work, undoubtedly. Somehow or other he was
responsible for this horror, she was certain. Such a loathsome
phenomenon could only be the result of magic, or as a
member of the Select would have it, of Cognition.

Terror gnawed its way along her nerves. There was something about the quality of the darkness that killed courage,
that encouraged the overburdened heart to beat faster and the
sweat to gather like cold dew on throbbing temples. Verran

lurched forward, hands outstretched. Perhaps there was another way out, or a lantern, or a closet to hide in, or— She tripped over some object and fell sprawling. Something heavy hit the floor beside her with a crash, and she heard the sound of glass vessels breaking. Sticky fluid spread over the floor like lava, soaking the skirts of her dress. Another strange odor added itself to the vile atmosphere. Verran reached down and found her skirts partially eaten away where the liquid had touched them. She dragged herself to her feet, sobbing quietly. Her sobs ceased abruptly as the chamber door banged open.

There could be no doubt that the darkness of the chamber was extraordinarily resistant to the attack of light. The lantern-glow from the hallway scarcely penetrated beyond the threshold. To Verran, the doorway appeared as a very faint orange rectangle. Silhouetted in the rectangle was the broad, spiked form of her pursuer. She held her breath. Perhaps the creature would be frightened of the dark, perhaps it would give up and go away. Her optimism was unfounded. The dark figure bounded into the room with a croak, slamming the door behind itself. Once again the darkness was absolute.

Verran clenched her jaw to keep her teeth from chattering and stood absolutely still. If the creature would only move out of the way, she could get to the door and from thence to the upper levels of the house, where help might be found. Even better, she might escape the building altogether, find a dombulis, and flee Grizhni Palace forever. If her father wouldn't take her back—and he probably wouldn't—then she'd go with Brenn Wate Basef, which was what she should have done in the first place.

The creature was very near. She could hear its heavy breathing a few feet away. Perhaps the darkness was as foreign to the beast as it was to the girl, for the ferocity and energy of the pursuit seemed to be subsiding. Nevertheless, the creature was making a systematic effort to search the room, passing back and forth from wall to wall. Once she heard it tread on broken glass, and once she heard it thud against an obstacle, whereupon its croaks took on a note of heartfelt bitterness. Verran wondered that it wasn't able to locate her by the thud of her racing heart.

Very softly she started to edge away. Despite her care, the

creature sensed movement, perhaps a change in the quality of
the dead atmosphere, perhaps the ghost of a footstep. It
paused, and Verran could hear a snuffling inhalation as her
pursuer attempted to catch her scent. The stench of the darkness masked all other smells, and the creature croaked in frustration. When it resumed the search, Verran could bear no
more. She sprang for the door, but the hot darkness and her
fears served to confuse her. The door was not where she had
supposed, and she crashed against the stone wall. The creature
hissed and leaped for her, passing so close that the wiry fur
brushed her arm. Verran jumped aside and banged against a
piece of furniture that toppled loudly to the floor. An involuntary shriek escaped her. The creature knew exactly where she
was now, and howled in triumph. Verran backed away from
the sound, bumped again against the wall, turned and groped
desperately for the door. She never found it. But hinges
creaked close at hand, and the ghostly orange rectangle suddenly reappeared, just barely visible through the unnatural
darkness.

Verran jumped thankfully for the light and collided with Fal
Grizhni, who stood in the doorway. She would have fallen had
he not held her firmly upright.

"Let me go!"

"You are discomposed, Madam," Grizhni observed.

"We can't stay here! There's a vicious beast loose in this
cellar!"

"Indeed. I lodged him here. To call him a beast is perhaps
not entirely accurate, and might prove offensive to him."

"He takes offense easily, then. He tried to kill me!"

"Only because he failed to understand the situation. I
should have warned him of your presence had I foreseen that
your explorations would take you down as far as this level of
the building. I underestimated you, Madam. I will now correct
my error." Grizhni clapped his hands sharply. "Come forth,
Nyd. Come forth! Remain here, Madam," he added as Verran
started to edge away. She paused reluctantly.

Nyd emerged. His hirsute face reflected wrath and suspicion.

"This woman is my wife. You have dared to assault her."
Fal Grizhni addressed the creature in the coldest of voices.
"Wife and husband are as one, or so it is claimed. Thus in at-

tacking her, you have attacked me. Am I then to assume that you desire to sever all bonds of mutual friendship? Are we henceforth strangers?''

Nyd wriggled and croaked. No spoken words could have conveyed his distress more clearly.

''You wish our association to continue?''

Nyd gestured an emphatic affirmative. The scarlet glare had faded from his eyes, which were now wide with anxiety. He beat his talons nervously upon the stone floor.

''Very well. Then learn here and now that this is Lady Grizhni and she is mistress of Grizhni Palace. You will accord her the same respect and devotion you have given to me. You will serve her, you will smooth her path, and if need be, you will lay down your life in her service. Do you understand?'' Nyd croaked, somewhat tremulously. ''Am I assured of your allegiance to this lady? Answer.'' Nyd croaked with increased assurance. As if to demonstrate his good faith, he crouched at Verran's feet and performed a gesture of clumsy obeisance. ''Do you accept the homage of Nyd, Madam?'' Grizhni inquired.

Verran had no idea what to say. ''I am grateful,'' she replied uncertainly, ''and I hope we shall be friends. I am sorry to have disturbed his young ones. I meant no harm.''

Nyd peered keenly into her eyes. He could not speak with a human tongue, but assuredly he caught the sense of her words. Was he intelligent? It was unclear. He looked from Verran to Grizhni and back again, as if to fix the connection in his mind, and croaked softly.

''Nyd will henceforth perform your bidding faithfully, Madam,'' Fal Grizhni promised. ''I will introduce you in a like manner to the rest of my creatures. Now come away.'' He guided her expertly up the stairs and through the maze of passageways, with Nyd leaping in their wake. If his young wife's near-disastrous intrusion into the cellars had alarmed or angered him, he gave no sign of it.

Excitement and curiosity loosened Verran's tongue. ''What are these creatures that serve you?''

''That would require a long explanation. Suffice it to say they represent a blending of diverse species, a blending made possible by Cognition. They are faultlessly loyal servants, as you will see. Above all, they possess one great virtue—they cannot speak. Among these creatures Nyd is the most courageous and devoted. It is my desire that you come to trust in him.''

Verran threw a reluctant glance over her shoulder at the hopping, hirsute creature. "I'll try, my lord. But have you no human servants?''

"None.''

"You don't trust human servants?''

"They do not trust me. But that is of little consequence. I do not trouble myself with the vagaries of peasants.''

"Do you trouble yourself with the vagaries of the quality?''

"Infrequently.''

"Then you care nothing for other human beings?''

Fal Grizhni considered the question. "Man is a creature most remarkable for cleverness and invention. He is therefore of some interest to me, although the species as a whole is repellent. His cleverness is used to perfect his vices, and his inventiveness used to refine his cruelties. Occasionally I have found exceptions to this rule, but only occasionally.''

"That's curious, my lord. It's been my experience that people are usually kind and good.''

"So I believed, when I was your age.''

"But . . . have you no friends?''

"I have had three friends in my lifetime. One died in childhood. One was murdered by an angry city mob not six months ago. Only one remains.''

It was hard for Verran to understand, for she had dozens of friends and much enjoyed their society; or had done so prior to her marriage. She stole a glance up at her husband's face. His expression was more somber than ever, and it occurred to her to wonder that great Fal Grizhni should consent to answer her queries. Presumably her position as his wife conferred certain privileges. It did not enter her mind that it might be a luxury for him to express himself freely, albeit to a member of the repellent race of Man.

"The one who was murdered—would that have been Rev Beddef?'' Verran asked cautiously. Rev Beddef was a savant high in the Select who had been attacked by a crowd of enraged commoners, bound in iron chains, and flung from Vayno Bridge to drown in the Vayno Wash.

"Yes.''

"That was a shocking thing! I never understood how it

could have happened. Why was he so hated?"

"He was hated because the rumor had been systematically circulated that Rev Beddef and sundry others of the Select employed Cognition to influence Duke Povon to increase taxes. The Commons were particularly restive at the time and required a victim on whom to vent their dissatisfaction. Rev Beddef served that purpose admirably. Thus the popular anger was deflected from its appropriate target."

"But it makes no sense—what could the people have been thinking of?"

"The people, Madam, do not think at all. From time to time they act, usually at the behest of the individual who has gained ascendancy over them at any given moment. In this particular case the mob was incited to violence by Rev Beddef's enemies—who are also my enemies."

"You mean that it could happen to you, my lord? An attack in the streets?" It had never before occurred to her that Grizhni might be vulnerable in any normally human way. He exuded invincibility.

"It is possible," he replied indifferently. "But unlike Rev Beddef, who expended his creative energies upon the development of self-replicating pyramids, I have provided myself with means of self-defense."

"What means, my lord?"

"Many. You have already encountered one." In response to her uncomprehending look, he added, "In the Black Chamber —that is, the the room in which I found you just now—"

"It was horrible! Ghastly! I've never seen or felt anything like it!"

"I hope you have not. The darkness in the Black Chamber—"

"So hot! So sickening! I can't tell you how dreadful it was!"

"That darkness," Fal Grizhni continued with unwonted patience, "which is associated with the death and poisonous decay of light, is of my own devising, and its properties are highly malign. It is a powerful weapon, should I ever choose to loose it upon my enemies. There are other resources at my command. If necessary, my Shield of Ice can enclose all of Grizhni Palace. Be assured I am capable of protecting myself and my own."

"Protecting yourself against whom, my lord? Whom have

you offended?'' She hesitated. ''The man who attacked you
yesterday—''

''Was an unfortunate whose mind was not his own. Clearly
he hardly knew what he did, nor was he responsible for the attack. I trust he caused you no undue alarm, Madam.''

''Oh, no. None at all, my lord. When a screaming lunatic
with a knife suddenly pops up in my vicinity, I scarcely give it
a second thought.''

Grizhni regarded her with distinct interest. ''You have
nothing to fear from such a one. But as my wife, you would be
well advised to beware of Gless Vallage and Haik Ulf. They
are now your foes. Nor is the Duke cordially disposed.''

''I saw that yesterday. But why should his Grace dislike
you?''

''He knows that I have recognized his weakness and his in-
competence. Moreover, he is at once dependent upon and
fearful of the Select. He should be neither.''

''Surely you have not *told* him so!''

''Not directly, but I have made the man aware of my opinions. I am no courtier.''

You certainly are not, Verran thought. Descendant herself
of a line of honey-tongued diplomats, she was dismayed at this
evidence of her new lord's fearless arrogance. Honesty was
one thing, but this. . . ? Aloud, she asked, ''And Gless
Vallage?''

''Desires Preeminence and the favor of the Duke. Intelligent, subtle, and treacherous as a mirage.''

''Haik Ulf?''

''Fears and detests the Select and their influence in civil affairs. A soldier and aristocrat who believes that matters of
state should rest in the hands of the aristocracy and the
military. Barren of vision and devoid of intellect, I hold him
of no account,'' Fal Grizhni concluded contemptuously.

Verran did not share his confidence, but kept her misgivings
to herself. ''I know where we are now,'' she observed. ''My
rooms are at the end of this hall.''

''You will wish to refresh yourself,'' Grizhni observed, with
a quizzical glance at her mutilated clothing, ''before proceeding to the Great Hall, where the household staff will greet
you. Nyd will guide you to the hall. You are not afraid to be
left alone with him?''

Verran turned and scrutinized the hybrid creature. ''Nyd,''

she said at last, "I think I may trust you."

Nyd wriggled vehemently.

"Your judgment is good, and you are no coward. Your conduct has pleased me, Madam."

Without awaiting acknowledgment of the compliment, Fal Grizhni turned and strode off down the corridor, leaving Lady Verran to ponder the singularity of her new husband's disposition.

Chapter Four

The hybrids needed supervision. They were hardworking and tireless, but a little clumsy in the performance of the more exacting household tasks. An exception lay in the creatures' ability to weave, plait, and to tie complex knots. Apparently their nest-building instincts aided them in this. It was Lady Verran's intention to take advantage of her servants' skill.

Verran stood in the great stone kitchen of Grizhni Palace. Around her the hybrids toiled. They had worked that morning to concoct an elastic flour dough. The dough had been kneaded, cut, and drawn into strands of great length and fineness. The strands had been boiled to the appropriate consistency and tinted a variety of colors. The hybrids were now weaving the colored strands into a large, edible tapestry. The creatures did magnificent work. She watched them with affection, for after six weeks of life at Grizhni Palace, they no longer seemed at all strange to her. Indeed, they demonstrated capacities for devotion and self-sacrifice that their human counterparts were unlikely to possess. And their appearance? Now that they were accustomed to her presence, the hybrids no longer wore their hoods pulled forward over their faces. Verran found that the dark, hairy features reflected an almost-human variety of expressions. The eyes that could glare so fiercely were usually mild, and the talons that could rip a man's face open at a single stroke made excellent gardening tools. Their looks were not so bad, after all.

"Do you need any more blue strands?" Verran inquired. "Have you enough?"

They answered her with reassuring croaks. It was amazing what a range of feeling those hoarse voices could express. She had discovered that it was possible to hold conversations with the servants. The longer she listened to them, the more she realized the subtlety and complexity of their inflections.

Verran inspected the work in progress. "It's going to be beautiful!" she exclaimed, and the hybrids hissed in gratification. The praise was deserved, for the tapestry was a wonderful creation depicting Grizhni Palace with its columns and dome, surrounded by a border of curling wavelets that represented the waters of Sandivell Canal; every bit of it edible and savory.

The hybrids' culinary excesses were committed at Verran's behest in anticipation of a special guest. Gaerase Vay Nennevay was coming to dinner.

Vay Nennevay was a savant, one of the few female members of the Select, and the only female senior member. It was a tribute to the magnitude of her powers of Cognition that she had attained her position despite her sex. Had she been male, it was not impossible that she might have aspired to Preeminence. A woman of great force, she was the last remaining personal friend of Terrs Fal Grizhni, and for that reason if no other, Verran wished to honor her. The special preparations were designed for the pleasure of Fal Grizhni no less than Vay Nennevay. And they would please him, she was sure. He would not say anything, most particularly not before a guest, but the lift of his brows and the lightening of his dark eyes would signal his approval. No one else might see it, but Verran would. As she had learned to translate the croaks and hisses of the hybrid servants, so had she learned to read the very slight changes in expression that communicated the sentiments of Fal Grizhni.

Verran thought of her husband and frowned. It was true that she could often read his facial expressions, but after six weeks of marriage, he remained a mystery to her. Always he treated her with detached and formal courtesy, and he had never set foot within her suite of rooms, nor she in his. She would have thought that she failed to please him, but for the fact that he requested her company often, far more often than

strict convention demanded. Moreover, Terrs Fal Grizhni was
unmoved by the opinion of the world and in no wise influ-
enced by convention. If he demanded his wife's presence, it
was surely because he wanted it. Verran's fears concerning
him had been lulled, but not banished. She was not altogether
sure that her husband was not a son of Ert, and yet there could
be no denying that she enjoyed his society. No one could talk
as Fal Grizhni when he was in one of his communicative
moods. No one owned such depth of knowledge and breadth
of vision. When he spoke of his hopes for Lanthi Ume, it was
as if the city's future glittered as brightly as sunlight on the
surface of her canals. More often, however, far more often,
Grizhni spoke of corruption, degeneration, and the approaching fall from greatness. But if his wisdom was often edged
with bitterness, that bitterness was never directed at her. She
had the distinct impression that she often amused him, and
was glad of it, for she welcomed the chance to divert his mind
from dark thoughts. Fal Grizhni's gloom was something icy
and tenebrous, product of the unknowable frustrations of a
man unlike others.

Lady Verran could not hope to fathom his moods, and only
knew that when she managed to banish the cold shadows from
his eyes, her own spirits brightened.

"Lord Grizhni meets with the Duke," Verran informed the
hybrids. "This evening he returns with an important guest.
When he sees the work you've done, he'll be proud of you."

The creatures wriggled appreciatively and redoubled their
efforts.

The new venerise had green silk sails embroidered with
golden lilies and roses. Her rigging and oars were likewise
golden, and the mainmast was inlaid with sculptured jade. It
was her maiden voyage. Her name was *Sublimity* and she was
unique among her kind.

Aboard *Sublimity*, the Duke and a clutch of his subjects
lounged beneath green canopies set up on the parquetry deck.
Around them rose all the splendor of Lanthi Ume, which they
disregarded. Ostensibly a meeting was in progress, wherein the
Duke would discuss issues of civic significance with the lords
and with representatives of the Select. In actuality the main
topic of conversation was the boat, and the air was filled with
congratulatory babble.

"Superb, your Grace! I have never seen a more magnificent venerise."

"A miracle of luxury and beauty, your Grace."

"His Grace sets his slow subjects to school. He raises extravagance to the level of an art."

"She reminds me of a Zellanese dancing girl, your Grace," observed gorgeous young Beskot Kor Malifon. "The same languid grace, the same opulence!"

"A just comparison, Beskot," Povon Dil Shonnet responded with plump satisfaction. "For the languor of *Sublimity*, like that of the fair Zellanese, sometimes gives way to activity of the most interesting kind. I will show you."

The Duke clapped his jeweled hands and a green-and-gold-clad deck attendant was instantly at his side. A command was conveyed to the helmsman. *Sublimity* shuddered and gave a hitch that lifted her partially out of the water. Then she leaped forward at impossible speed, skimming along the surface of the canal as a pebble skips over the surface of a pond. The passengers cried out in amazement and delight. *Sublimity* whizzed over the water, and the small boats and barges made way in haste to let her pass. One little craft, piled high with fruit, was not quite fast enough and capsized in the wake of the speeding venerise. *Sublimity* also clipped the edge of a barge in passing, and sent the bargeman and most of his wares flying through the air to hit the water with a gigantic splash. The bargeman's imprecations mingled with the exhilarated shouts of *Sublimity*'s passengers, while the citizens on the banks watched in dismay. Past the Ducal Palace they sped, past Fennahar House, Ka Nebbinon Bell Tower, and Beffel House, then on at headlong speed toward the statue of Croino Deth, with green sails spread and pennants flying; and they left destruction in their wake. It was not until they rounded a bend and hurtled under the old Bridge of Eatches that the Duke, amidst breathless hoots of laughter, commanded the helmsman to reduce speed.

"Miraculous, your Grace!"

"How is it possible?"

"As this venerise is the gift and creation of my very generous friend Saxas Gless Vallage," the Duke replied, "I'll leave all explanation of its mechanics to him. Saxas?"

Gless Vallage responded with his winning smile. "Upon beholding a fine painting, does a noble company wish to ques-

tion the artist and learn the source of his inspiration? Alas, the
artist cannot speak of such matters! Being little more than a
common mechanical, he will talk of the colors he has ground,
the oils with which he mixes them, of his bristle brushes and
similar dreary irrelevancies. He wearies the listener and may
even go so far as to spoil the glamour, the illusion, of the
finished work—which destruction all but cancels any credit
due the wretch's creation. In short, your Grace, an explanation of my work is fraught with double peril—tedium to a noble audience, and relegation of *Sublimity* to the ridiculous."
He finished with a lightly self-deprecating bow.

"Bravo, Vallage!"

Sublimity echoed with laughing applause in which Terrs Fal
Grizhni did not join. Grizhni stood apart from the chattering
group. In his black robes he resembled a raven alongside iri-
descent hummingbirds. With him stood his friend and ally,
Gaerase Vay Nennevay.

"The motion of the vessel can be explained in simple
terms," Fal Grizhni remarked, and his companions turned to
him in surprise. "I will do so because I think it best in this case
that you understand the source of your amusement. The venerise is equipped by Cognition with a multitude of nervous
fibers capable of absorbing the vital emanations and humors
of Man. Such emanations provide intangible nourishment and
thus a source of life to the vessel. The men confined below,
from whom the emanations are drained, grow faint and listless. Presently they will die of exhaustion, whereupon they will
be replaced with others of the same ilk—presumably condemned criminals. There is little danger of running short of
human fuel with which to feed *Sublimity*. Given the ferocity
of the city law and the frequency with which the death penalty
is pronounced, the supply of condemned felons should prove
limitless. In the unlikely event that such criminals become
unavailable, our excellent civic institution of slavery ensures
an alternate supply of bodies. Therefore be at ease—*Sublimity*
shall never lack for nourishment." Grizhni's voice cut like the
northern wind. The Duke and the others listened in resentful
discomfort. Fal Grizhni always managed to cast a pall over the
most enjoyable occasions. "Having satisfied your curiosity
concerning the venerise," the savant continued, "perhaps this
assemblage will consent to discuss the question of the Gard

Lammis debt, which as I understood it, was the objective of this meeting.''

"The news is good," the Duke explained shortly. "The Keldhar of Gard Lammis has offered favorable terms. In exchange for temporary and conditional transfer of title of the Vayno Fortification to the City of Gard Lammis for a term not to exceed twenty years, the Keldhar will grant a fifteen-year extension on the present loan.''

After a moment's awful silence, Fal Grizhni inquired with restraint, "That is what your Grace regards as favorable terms?''

"The Keldhar intimates the possibility of an advance of additional funds.''

"In exchange for what concessions?''

"He has not specified. But I have no reason to doubt the good faith and good will of our brethren of Gard Lammis.''

"They are not our brethren.'' Grizhni spoke in low and bitter tones. "They are rivals, and given the opportunity, our enemies.''

"It seems his Preeminence is quick to see enemies, perhaps where none exist. We appreciate his concern.'' The Duke spoke calmly, but did not succeed in disguising his annoyance. "The hostility of Gard Lammis is questionable. Our current needs are not.''

"Needs?'' Grizhni did not trouble to hide his contempt. "The need for expensive toys—like this one?'' His gesture took in all of *Sublimity*. "Need for theatres, arenas, and senseless displays of empty public glory? Need for grander palaces, larger estates, brighter jewels, trifles and knickknacks for yourself and your favorites? Are those the needs to which you refer, and are they worth the price of the Vayno, our chief means of defense against a mainland attack?''

The courtiers regarded him with concerted hostility. It was the savant's attitude, his stance, the twist of his lips and the poise of his head, that were even more objectionable than his words. Gless Vallage watched alertly.

"But we are in no danger of a mainland attack, Preeminence,'' Beskot Kor Malifon ventured. "Such a thing has never occurred.''

"And never will, as long as we hold the Vayno.''

"Well, we will hold it.''

"With soldiers of Gard Lammis garrisoned therein?"

"Preeminence, always you anticipate the worst—"

"And with good reason. You courtiers and you of the Select, listen to me. Too long has this city employed dishonorable methods to raise money for unworthy purposes." Fal Grizhni's dark eyes rested deliberately upon the Duke's face. Gaerase Vay Nennevay, who remained at Grizhni's side, raised her hand slightly as if she would caution him, but held her peace. "For many years the Commons and the aristocracy have been taxed with increasing severity, and now their resources and their patience are all but spent. The provincial subjects without our walls have been exploited beyond endurance, and death duties bid fair to deprive heirs of their patrimonies. The nobles are virtually united in their hostility toward the present regime." The Duke looked shocked, but Grizhni continued remorselessly, "The Commons are enraged to the point of desperation, but have been deliberately prevented from perceiving the true source of their suffering. Eventually they will learn, and armed rebellion may well ensue.

"Having all but exhausted our supply of domestic revenue, the administration has turned to foreign sources. In exchange for stolen gold, sanctuary has been granted to fugitive criminals from other lands. Harbor rights have been sold to strangers and bribes have been accepted from foreign ambassadors in payment for trading concessions. Lately we have accepted vast foreign loans at usurious rates of interest. These acts have been despicable, and they have weakened us in ways that are not apparent as yet. But sacrifice a military fortress—permit alien forces within the walls of Lanthi Ume—and our growing debilitation is revealed to all the world. We proclaim our city a target ripe for conquest, and such a proclamation will not go unheard. It is too high a price to pay for . . . glittering toys. I speak both personally and as leader of the Select in advising you that foreign occupation of the Vayno Fortification must not and shall not be permitted."

"Must not? Shall not?" All traces of good humor had fled the Duke's face. "The decision is hardly yours, Grizhni."

"Does his Grace despise the counsel of the Select?" Fal Grizhni inquired dangerously.

"The Select may counsel. They do not command."

"Is it not a reflection upon our present situation that such a question should arise at all?"

"It is a reflection upon the Select and its current leadership. In my grandfather's day, let me remind you, it was not thus. The Select performed their own work and did not meddle in affairs of state—"

"In your grandfather's day, the Select had no cause to meddle."

The Duke's face suffused. "I will not tolerate interference! The Select are not omnipotent, nor are they beyond the power of civil law—"

"The Select are your Grace's loyal servants," Saxas Gless Vallage interjected smoothly, "who desire only what is best for Lanthi Ume and its master. If we speak overzealously, it is only through our excessive concern."

"Zealousness I might overlook, Saxas," the Duke complained, "but a deliberate affront, never."

"No affront was intended, I warrant your Grace," Vallage soothed expertly. "His Preeminence was perhaps led away from his path, and no doubt regrets the offense as I do. He intended only to speak of the city's interests."

"I intended to speak of the Gard Lammis debt. The question has not been adequately addressed." Fal Grizhni stood like a personification of inflexible pride. "I am firm in my resolve that the Vayno shall not be offered as security for another loan, even to the extent of employing the resources of the Select to oppose such an action."

It had come at last. Fal Grizhni had finally verbalized the courtiers' greatest fears. They stared at him in outraged silence.

The Duke's face darkened from red to purple. "It has come to this?" he choked. "You threaten retaliation if we fail to accede to your demands?"

"I promise opposition."

"You and your fellow sorcerers would dictate policy? Perhaps you would rule in my place, Grizhni? Do you look so high?"

"His Grace strays from the subject of discussion," Fal Grizhni remarked icily.

"And we are all of us in danger of giving way to anger," Gless Vallage broke in. "Surely there is no need for that, my honored lords! Nor is there any need to carry on this conversation in the open air, under the eyes of all Lanthi Ume. *Sublimity* is equipped with a council chamber wherein we may speak in privacy and comfort. The room is hung in perfumed green damask and furnished with cool golden wine and essences whose fragrance soothes the spirits.''

The courtiers murmured in admiration.

"My spirits are troubled, Saxas," the Duke sighed. "I long for peace."

"Then come with me now, your Grace, and do not fear that the Select are united against you. Among us you have many loyal friends. Allow me to show you the way."

Gless Vallage steered the Duke along the deck and the courtiers followed close behind. For a moment Fal Grizhni and Vay Nennevay lingered. Nennevay was a remarkably tall woman, almost as tall as Grizhni himself. Her height was accentuated by erect carriage and by a great hennin of antique design, under which her gray hair was entirely concealed. The strong, aged face beneath the headdress now reflected concern. "You do more harm than good, Terrs." She spoke with the freedom of very long friendship.

"I had thought that you supported me in this, Gaerase."

"Your motives, yes. But not your methods, which are unproductive."

"Indeed, Madam?" he inquired frostily.

"There's no reason for you to take offense. I speak the truth. You antagonize the Duke and his nobles. In doing so you undermine your own purposes—which are mine as well— and you play into the hands of your enemies. You must find other methods, or you work against yourself."

"What do you advise? Shall I smirk and bow, flatter, cozzen, and play the courtier? Shall I be another Gless Vallage?"

"No, indeed. You could not, even if you wished it. But you must not use the Duke with such contempt, nor should you underestimate your enemies. They are numerous, and your public behavior strengthens them."

"I have no patience with Dil Shonnet's stupidity and vanity."

"You must disguise your impatience."

"In private and in public I state my true opinions. I will alter that for no man," he returned.

"That is more pride than honesty. There are many ways of stating opinions."

"I know only one."

Vay Nennevay recognized the futility of pursuing the matter. She sighed and changed the subject. "Who was the young man standing next to Cru Beffel who watched you with such anger? He made me think of Zaniboono—you remember the poem—with those burning eyes of his."

"That's Trel Wate Basef's youngest son. He aspires to the Select."

"Has he ability?"

"Considerable ability, but little discipline and less method. In a year or two he may be ready, and then I will sponsor him. In the meantime I have not supported his candidacy."

"Ah—that would explain the look he gave you, although I should have thought there was more to it than that." She examined the grim set of his jaw and asked casually, "And how is your bride? I didn't speak to her at the wedding, but she seems a charming child."

His face relaxed slightly. "She is well. You will meet her this evening."

"The marriage goes well?"

Fal Grizhni gazed off at the towers of Lanthi Ume. "It is too early to say." He would not speak of such matters, even to his best friend.

"Have you stopped to consider the possibility that your actions place your young bride in some danger?" Vay Nennevay inquired deliberately.

He turned to face her. "I do not understand you."

"You understand me very well, Terrs." His brows rose, and she continued, "You've angered the Duke and his powerful friends to the extent that there already have been attempts on your life. If such ostentatious self-assertion is the only means whereby your sense of integrity may be preserved—why that, of course, is your own affair." She noted that he appeared more surprised than angry. "But now I fear you go too far. You threaten systematic Selectic opposition to the ducal policies, and such a course will be called treasonable by your enemies."

"I do not doubt it," Grizhni replied. "Do you fear for the Select?"

"Not really. The Select are able to protect themselves."

"As I am able to protect myself and my household."

"You're overconfident. You may despise your enemies, but don't make the mistake of underestimating them. Should you be judged a traitor, you are in grave danger."

"You exaggerate."

"I don't think so. And remember—if you die a traitor's death, then the young girl you married quite possibly dies beside you."

"There is no possibility of that," Fal Grizhni told her. "In the event of an attack, Cognition will serve me. But I do not anticipate such difficulties. The danger of which you speak will never materialize."

"It's still within your power to see that it doesn't."

"I value your friendship and advice, as always. In this case, however, your misgivings are groundless."

There was nothing more to be said. Vay Nennevay and Fal Grizhni proceeded to the green damask council chamber, where they found Duke Povon and the rest. The Duke had been suitably soothed and cheered by means of Gless Vallage's perfumed essences. The ducal pupils were dilated, the ducal spirits greatly improved. Nonetheless, the rest of the afternoon passed in acrimony. Fal Grizhni was relentless in his insistence upon reform, and his icy, uncompromising manner infuriated his opponents. Before the end of the afternoon he had succeeded in unifying his foes, and even the diplomacy of Gaerase Vay Nennevay could not repair the damage.

At the close of the meeting Fal Grizhni announced that the services of the Select in matters of divination and prophecy concerning births, deaths, marriages, investments, wagers, and the like should no longer be made available to the aristocracy of Lanthi Ume until the matter of the Vayno Fortification had been satisfactorily concluded. Moreover, Selectic protection should no longer extend over the city's maritime trading routes.

This decree sent Povon Dil Shonnet into a fit of wheezing, stuttering rage. Fal Grizhni observed his ruler's transports without emotion for a time, then rose and stalked wordlessly from the chamber. It took a massive application of fragrant essences to tranquilize the Duke. And even then, his spirits were not truly restored until *Sublimity* had completed a lightning circuit of the largest canals, to the consternation of all who beheld her.

Fal Grizhni came home at last. Verran could see at once that her husband was angry and that his anger was not directed at her. She could only surmise that the meeting with the Duke and nobles had not been a success. With Grizhni came Gaerase Vay Nennevay, whose intelligence and urbane manner possessed charm.

Dinner was a congenial occasion, and the savant's mood appeared to improve. His wintry eyes slowly thawed, and when he beheld the tapestry, his amusement was unmistakable. Verran herself was in excellent spirits when Vay Nennevay finally found the chance to draw her aside for a private conversation. They spoke at some length, and their closing remarks lingered in Verran's mind for months to come.

"I think Terrs has done well in marrying you, my dear. You are very young, and yet I believe it may prove a good match. Am I correct in assuming that you would do your husband a great service?" Verran nodded a little warily. "Then use your influence to persuade him to moderate his public attitude toward his opponents. Teach him discretion if you can."

"Teach Lord Grizhni—I?" Verran was amazed at the thought. "How could I? He is so wise."

"Wise—yes. You have wed the greatest savant that ever was or ever will be. But extraordinary wisdom, and pride in that wisdom, have set him apart from other men. I've known him since his early youth, and it has always been so. All his life has been solitary, and therefore, despite his knowledge, he has no understanding of other men, and little tolerance. He will draw great misfortune upon himself if he does not change. You must urge him to it."

"But *I* have no influence over Lord Grizhni!"

"Oh, but you do, my dear—far more than you realize. Take my advice and use it."

Chapter Five

Two days later the Duke proclaimed that all real property belonging to the Select should henceforth be subject to taxation. Preeminence Terrs Fal Grizhni promptly replied that the Selectically owned island called the Victory of Nes, being the artificial product of a great savant's Cognition, did not fall under the jurisdiction of the Duke of Lanthi Ume and was therefore exempt from such taxation. The Victory and its buildings composed the major portion of the Select's holdings. The Duke's response, obviously the work of tame scholars, hinted at the possibility of major revisions in the Select's existing charter. Fal Grizhni immediately called for a meeting of the Council of the Select. Verran surprised herself with her own boldness in asking to attend the meeting with her husband.

Fal Grizhni's brows arched almost imperceptibly. "Why do you wish to go, Madam? To what purpose?"

"Because I'm interested," Verran replied. "After all, the Select form one of the most powerful organizations in this city. And now, with the new proclamation about the taxes, it looks as if there may be trouble between the Select and the Duke. What happens next could be important. Besides, I don't know much about the Select and their ways. Now that I'm your wife, I ought to learn."

"That is sound reasoning." Grizhni nodded in approval. "Your interest pleases me greatly. You are welcome to attend."

"Good! I've always wondered what the savants do at their meetings. Do they make sacrifices to Ert? Do they conjure up demons?"

"Hardly, Madam." Grizhni's lips twitched, a sign that he repressed a smile. "I fear the proceedings may not live up to your expectations."

"Oh, I'm sure they will! Only, are you certain it will be all right?"

"All right?"

"With the others, I mean. Will they mind that I'm there? Will they let me in at all?"

"That is for me to say. If I choose to admit a guest, who is also my wife, to the Council, no member will presume to question me."

Verran looked up at the haughty, austere face. "Perhaps no one will question you aloud, but won't they be offended?"

"That does not signify. Prepare yourself, Madam. We leave within the hour."

The meeting was to take place upon the Victory of Nes. The Victory was a small island set like an improbable emerald in the middle of Parnis Lagoon. Generations earlier, following the expulsion of the primitive Eatchish magicians from Lanthi Ume, the savants and the wise of the city banded together under the cognomen *Select* and appealed to the Duke Jeenisch Dil Shonnet for a charter legitimizing the formation of a new order. Duke Jeenisch was understandably reluctant, and granted only conditional authorization. He decreed that the signing of the charter must take place on Parnis Lagoon, but use of a boat, raft, or similar floating contrivance was prohibited. The leader of the savants at that time was one Nes, surnamed "The Eyes," a brilliant experimentalist of common origins. Aware of the necessity of a charter were the Select to thrive, Nes accepted perforce the Duke's sardonic proviso. On the eve of the first black moon in the seventh year of the reign of Jeenisch Dil Shonnet, Nes the Eyes labored alone throughout the night. When the sun rose on Lanthi Ume the next morning, a green isle lifted from the waters of Parnis Lagoon. The charter was duly signed. The Select came into being, to the sorrow of the nobles, of the traditionalists, and of many others. The island became known as the Victory of Nes, and was in times to come the site of numerous private functions of the Select.

Lord Terrs Fal Grizhni and his Lady went there by dom-

bulis, with Nyd in attendance. Verran had clothed herself in
the rich but subdued style that Grizhni preferred, for she
wished to make him proud of her. The day was overcast and a
silvery haze veiled the towers and domes of Lanthi Ume, soft-
ening their outlines and muting their bright colors. Sound
seemed muted as well, and the calls of the merchants scarcely
carried over the water. When Ka Nebbinon Bell sounded the
hour, its deep notes were muffled. The air was cool and gray,
and fresh with the scent of the sea.

Verran gazed around her with delight, as if the city sights
were new to her eyes. It was the first time she had been abroad
in days. There had been many invitations, but Fal Grizhni
refused to socialize beyond the extent of absolute obligation.
He had made it clear that his wife was free to attend such functions as she desired, provided that hybrid bodyguards accompanied her. She accepted a number of invitations, but found
that the friends of her girlhood treated her with unwonted
deference now that she was Lady Grizhni. Moreover, their
conversation seemed childish and inconsequential to ears accustomed to the discourse of Fal Grizhni, and upon such occasions Verran found herself missing her husband.

The dombulis bumped Victory Pier. Nyd lashed it to a post
and assisted his master and mistress to land.

At the heart of the Victory of Nes stood the Nessiva, an
overpowering edifice housing a complex of audience chambers, council chambers, workrooms, and private accommoda-
tions. The Nessiva was shielded from view by trees. Around
the perimeter of the island, parks and gardens flourished.
Those gardens camouflaged a multitude of traps and pitfalls
that had eliminated many a trespasser.

The gardens were silent and empty. Verran, Fal Grizhni,
and Nyd made their way through the quiet park, passed under
an archway in the event of an attack. Its outlines were simple,
its windows narrow, its walls enormously thick. No guards
were stationed at the entrance, for the savants of the Select
had no need of human guards. The great door was ringed with
staring glass eyes that shone with odd brilliance. As the little
party approached, the glow increased. Verran paused to stare.
The soulless eyes returned her gaze. She thought she saw one
blink. Imagination? Fal Grizhni and Nyd were drawing ahead.
Verran hurried to catch up.

Within the Nessiva the halls were dim and narrow. Weak

gray light fought its way in through small windows deep-set in massive walls. The floor was mottled with patches of shadow. Through the shadows the savants walked, impressive in their dire robes. They greeted their leader with guarded respect and observed his young wife with curiosity. There was little conversation. All moved toward the Council chamber, which was located beneath the central dome. The faces around her seemed grim and preoccupied. Tension hung in the air like a noxious gas, and it crossed her mind that she had chosen a poor day to visit. Of course, her husband could easily have refused to bring her. Had he failed to consider the reactions of his peers? Or was this gesture meant as a deliberate assertion of authority over them? With Fal Grizhni it was impossible to say.

The Council chamber was an enormous circular room with a domed ceiling supported by a triple row of columns. The coffered dome was gray granite, and the giant columns were of plain black basalt. In the middle of the veined black marble floor, upon a raised dais, stood a long table and chairs to accommodate the ten members of the Council of the Select. Ranged about the dais were curving rows of seats. The first couple of rows were reserved for the use of the forty senior members. The rest were used by all remaining members, of which there were some one hundred sixty or so, most of whom seemed to be in attendance. The group was surprisingly small, in view of the influence it exerted, and additionally dwarfed by the scale of the room.

Fal Grizhni and his party were among the last to arrive. Verran had hoped to remain inconspicuous, but Grizhni conducted her to the front row of seats and left her there with Nyd at her side before joining his colleagues on the dais. Several grave savants regarded the young girl in surprise, and Verran felt her face redden. She kept her eyes fixed resolutely on the ten Council members seated before her. Her husband, his Preeminence, was one of the youngest of the lot, she noted with surprise. Fal Grizhni seemed infinitely wise and experienced to her, but most of the others were years older than he. How, then, had he achieved Preeminence? How had he supplanted Lekkel Dri Vannivo, Preeminent before him? She had spoken truly in confessing that she knew little of the Select.

With a swish of dark draperies, a tall woman seated herself beside Verran, who turned to exchange greetings with her husband's ally, Gaerase Vay Nennevay. Aside from Vay Nennevay, Verran recognized two Council members. There was Saxas Gless Vallage, the Duke's particular friend. At the end of the table sat Bon Dendo, whose allegiances shifted as expedience warranted. The other seven men were vaguely familiar. Verran guessed that she had seen several of them at the wedding, weeks earlier. Their expressions were now grim.

Fal Grizhni rose to his feet and stood motionless at his place of honor. The great room fell silent and remained so for a long moment. Then Grizhni started to speak unintelligibly. Verran started. Her husband's beautiful voice rose and fell in measured cadences, but she could not understand a single word. He was speaking Old Umish, an archaic dialect that had continued in wide use for a few generations following the unification of the ancient Lanthian and Umish island-cities. Old Umish was the language of the early savants. An invocation in this tongue had opened each congress of the Select since the days of Nes the Eyes.

Just as Verran was beginning to wonder if the entire meeting was to consist of nothing but gibberish, the invocation ended. Fal Grizhni remained standing and spoke in Lanthian. Verran perked up. Here was something she could understand, or so she thought. But Grizhni's Lanthian was scarcely more comprehensible than his Umish had been. He spoke at length of Selectic rule and procedure, and his discourse was filled with references understandable only to those familiar with the mechanics of high Cognition. It was the highly ritualistic prologue that custom demanded, and Verran found herself losing interest again. She gazed up at the ceiling, with its round skylight fitted with a great pane of glass, curved to follow the line of the dome. Overhead a seabird wheeled in a silver sky, and for a moment she envied the creature. So far Fal Grizhni had been right: the meeting did not match her expectations. It was all very dry. She glanced covertly at the senior members seated near by—mostly gray-haired, black-clad men whose appearance hardly hinted at their unusual talents; native talents refined and sharpened by decades of training and study. Why would volatile Brenn Wate Basef be so eager to join them? At her side sat Nyd. His hood was thrown back from his face, for none of the Select would find him fearsome. The hybrid's eyes were fixed upon his master and his ugly face glowed with devotion. Verran followed Nyd's gaze back to Grizhni's countenance. She paid little heed to his confusing utterances, preferring instead to luxuriate in the resonant tones of his voice. With such a voice, did it matter what he actually *said*? He would not like that, she knew. He had brought her to this place in order to learn, to increase her store of knowledge, for he counted knowledge a truer friend than power, love, or wealth. Verran shook her head to clear away the dreamy mists. It was well that she did so, for at that point Fal Grizhni concluded his introductory remarks and his address suddenly became comprehensible. Grizhni was renowned, in fact, for the pointed brevity of his speech.

"You are all aware of the situation that we now face. The Duke has imposed heavy taxes upon Selectic property, including this island stronghold, which arguably does not fall within his dominion. That he has done so is an indication of the severity of his predicament. He is in desperate need of money. His reckless and shortsighted policies have led to this desperation. He displays animosity toward those who advise him in any manner contrary to his own inclinations. He has received such unwelcome advice from the Select in response to his proposal to mortgage the Vayno Fortification to the city of Gard Lammis, and the tax levies upon the Victory are the result. This being the case, several possible courses of action are open to us.

"Imprimis, we may placate his Grace by simultaneously paying all levies and withdrawing all opposition to his plans. In this manner we will regain his favor temporarily. Secondly, we may decline to pay and withdraw our opposition, in the hope that such withdrawal will be sufficient to sooth our ruler's anger . . . and his fear." Grizhni's minimal hesitation provided all the emphasis necessary. "Thirdly, we may pay as required and continue to advise as we see fit—which course will lead to additional official reprisals. Finally, we may refuse to submit to taxation and at the same time increase our opposition to the Duke's current policies. It is this last course that I favor, for two reasons.

"It must be recognized that the Select form a self-governing body which, due to our unusual abilities, exists as an independent power within the city-state of Lanthi Ume. Although the fact of our power is self-evident, it has throughout Lanthian history been officially ignored. For various reasons of policy, we as an entity have chosen to accept in all aspects and without limitation the authority of the successive Dukes of Lanthi Ume. Whether it is necessary or even desirable for us to continue to do so has now become open to question. The Duke's tax levy upon Selectic property amounts to political coercion, and as such should be resisted.

"In addition, and quite unrelated to financial considerations, exists the question of Selectic obligation to ensure the city's welfare. There can be little doubt that Povon Dil Shonnet's present course of action weakens the state, perhaps to disastrous extent in times to come. Is such a matter a concern of the Select? In my opinion it is, for the Select are bound to Lanthi Ume by ties of tradition, blood, sentiment, and history. We could not hope to break those ties without altering the very nature of our organization. For that reason, our interest in the continuing health and prosperity of this city is indistinguishable from self-interest. We have great strength. For the common good, it is now time to use it. Therefore it is my intention to increase Selectic opposition to the Duke's proposal concerning the Vayno Fortification and to all other schemes that I perceive as similar in nature. It is within my power as Preeminent of the Select to undertake this decision without consultation. However, as it is a decision of some significance which may result in ducal retaliation affecting all members of this order, I consent to open the matter to discussion. If there are those among you who would present opposing arguments, I will hear and consider them today." Having concluded his remarks, Grizhni raised his left hand in the traditional gesture that signaled the opening of the floor, and resumed his seat.

Verran was wide awake now and astonished at the paradoxically cool manner in which her husband expressed incendiary sentiments. The savants seemed equally perturbed, for they stirred and whispered in an uncharacteristic manner.

Saxas Gless Vallage, blessed with great presence of mind, was the first to formulate a reply. As he rose to speak, his face expressed thoughtful concern. "Preeminence Fal Grizhni speaks with an impetuosity that momentarily takes us aback. Some little time will be required to consider the implications of the matter he has set before us and to devise an appropriately rational response. I will therefore request that a committee be established to investigate the probable effects of his Grace's current fiscal policies and to formulate a recommendation to the Council based upon their findings. Such an investigation will require several months to complete, and I can but hope that Preeminence Grizhni will control what can only be regarded as reckless impulses during that period."

Nyd uttered a soft hiss. Verran turned to look at him in surprise. The hybrid's lips were drawn back over his fangs. It was impossible to tell whether he understood Vallage's words or whether he merely reacted to an insinuating undertone to the savant's cultivated voice. She looked at Fal Grizhni. His face was coldly expressionless, utterly unreadable. For some reason, Verran shivered.

"There are certain points," Gless Vallage continued smoothly, "so obvious that prolonged reflection is not required to note them, that may be raised here and now in opposition to his Preeminence's opinions. In the first place, Lord Fal Grizhni has set forth as a statement of fact his personal conviction that our ruler's decisions are actively harmful to the state. Has this fact been proved? Our city-state is the proudest, the strongest, the wealthiest of all Dalyon. So it has always been, so it will always be. What reason have we to think otherwise? Is the proposed mortgaging of the Vayno Fortification the sign of a collapsing economy? Who is to judge such matters? Duke Povon, scion of our ruling house and born to the position he holds? Or Preeminence Grizhni, whose powers of Cognition are great, but whose qualifications as a statesman are perhaps open to question? I leave it to this company to decide."

He permitted himself a smile of intelligent skepticism before continuing. "Lord Grizhni postulates that this island, the Victory of Nes, does not fall within the Duke's jurisdiction and is therefore not subject to taxation. To this I can only point out the obvious: the Victory stands at the heart of Lanthi Ume. That it has been exempt from taxation for so long has only been the result of the continuing good will of the Dukes of Lanthi Ume. But now it seems that good will is diminishing. His Preeminence has rightly noted that the Duke's actions appear to be motivated in part by personal animosity. But animosity toward whom? Surely not toward the Select in general. It is no secret, hence there can be no harm in remarking, that relations between his Grace and his Preeminence are far from cordial. His Grace eyes askance the aspirations of Fal Grizhni, and it would appear in light of what we have heard here today that his Grace perhaps has cause. Were Duke Povon secure in the knowledge that the leadership of the Select harbors no hostility toward him, then his own defensive enmity, and all substantive manifestations thereof, would doubtless vanish." He did not discuss the mechanics whereby this desirable effect might be achieved. It was not necessary.

"His Preeminence's final argument," Gless Vallage continued, "touched upon Selectic obligation to involve ourselves in affairs of state. How shall I answer? How shall I deal with a deliberate perversion of the principles upon which our order was founded? My colleagues, are we politicians? Or are we savants, whose function it is to solve the mysteries of the universe? Do we intrude where we are unwanted and worse than useless? Or do we continue with our own work, do we fulfill the purpose of the Select? My friends and peers, I have searched my heart for answers to these questions. I now leave it to your wisdom to find answers of your own." Vallage concluded on a grave and melancholy note, then took his seat.

Lady Verran was startled to the point of forgetting her shyness. Turning to Vay Nennevay, she inquired, "Can all savants speak so well extempore?"

"If I know Gless Vallage, he's been prepared for weeks," Nennevay replied. "My dear, your husband takes grave risks."

Council member Jinzin Farni now rose. Farni's appearance reflected his peasant ancestry, and for this reason he owned much popularity amongst the Commons of Lanthi Ume. His face was blunt-featured and low-browed. Behind the dull facade lay both educated intellect and a practical shrewdness. "Gless Vallage speaks with his accustomed caution and consistency. But if we take him at his word, then the only conclusive proof of Fal Grizhni's theory would come in the form of a major disaster. I, for one, do not require a disaster to convince me. I observe the present situation in light of my knowledge of our city's history, and my observations lead me to conclusions similar to those of his Preeminence. For the sake of us all, the Duke must be diverted from his present course without delay."

Farni was held in much esteem, and his words exerted considerable influence. Drervish Day Leemit rose to speak in Grizhni's favor. So too did Ches Kilmo. But the cautious savant Lej Rom Usine supported Vallage's conservative stance, as did two or three eloquent others. Bon Dendo did not commit himself.

Lady Verran looked around her. The savants in the audience, both senior members and those of lesser ilk, exhibited signs of unease and confusion rarely visible to those outside the exclusive order. She had never dreamed that those sage and somber figures could seem so indecisive. Now they whispered and disputed amongst themselves for all the world like ordinary mortals.

And her husband? Verran glanced back at the dais. There he sat, apparently at ease, observing his colleagues inscrutably. She remembered that he had said it lay within his power as Preeminent to undertake the decision without consultation, and it occurred to her to wonder whether he had opened the floor to discussion as a gesture of purely perfunctory courtesy. Perhaps he meant to listen politely to all the arguments, then go ahead and do exactly what he wanted. Evidently a number of savants thought so, for the whispered conversations here and there throughout the room were staccato with indignation. At that time Fal Grizhni turned his face slightly, and Verran caught his eye. He looked straight at her and his face did not change by so much as the twitch of an eyelid, but she felt some current of . . . what? Reassurance, she thought.

Several rows back, a plump and truculent young man, identifiable by the green band edging his dragon insignia as a newly admitted savant, rose to his feet.

"Ah, now we'll come to it," Vay Nennevay muttered. "Earlier than I thought."

Verran looked at her inquisitively.

"That fat fellow there is Nyro Lis Deddelis, Gless Vallage's creature. Vallage always has several such young men whose candidacy to the Select he sponsors. Once admitted, of course they're in his debt. Deddelis wishes to repay, but he's trying a little too hard, I think."

Verran didn't know what Nennevay meant. She twisted in her seat to face Lis Deddelis.

"What we have heard here today verges on treason!" Deddelis blazed with convincingly righteous anger. The effect was spoiled by an unfortunately high-pitched voice. "It angers me, it sickens me, that there are those among us who believe themselves so firmly ensconced in positions of power that they will set themselves beyond the bounds of all legal authority!

We are Lanthian, yet our fellow citizens regard us with fear and suspicion, and yes, even hatred among the ignorant. I could almost go so far as to say I do not blame them, for I, Nyro Lis Deddelis, hate all traitors! Thus I urge my colleagues to demonstrate once and for all that the arrogant authority of one man cannot make traitors of us all! We must resist this tyranny within our own order, and therefore I demand a vote! Before the eyes of all, I demand it!'' The fury of his gestures matched the fury of his rhetoric.

"Why is he yelling?" Verran inquired.

"He's young," Nennevay shrugged.

"What's happening?"

"I think Vallage's protégé has just committed a major blunder. That vote he's calling for—ninety percent of the Select's entire membership would have to concur in order to overturn any decision of his Preeminence. There's no possibility of such accord in this case. The vote, if it takes place, will only strengthen your husband's position."

"Oh." Verran began to relax. She glanced at the dais where Grizhni and Jinzin Farni conferred quietly. The Vallage partisan Lej Rom Usine wore an expression of utter disgust. Vallage himself had the regretful look of a man whose lapdog has just overturned the chess board. There were many overtones that Verran could not hope to catch, but she was certain of one essential point—her husband had nothing to worry about—and she watched the proceedings with interest.

"Cognizance Nyro Lis Deddelis, scholar and savant, you have the floor." Fal Grizhni employed the traditional language of formal Selectic proceedings.

"Preeminence, by my rights as a savant of this order, I demand a general vote on the issue of Selectic opposition to his Grace's policies," the young man answered with equal formality and a hint of defiance.

If Grizhni noted the defiance, he ignored it. "Then it is so ordered. Let the tally be taken and counted without delay, that we may proceed to other matters." Clearly he attached little significance to the vote.

Close beside her Verran heard a murderous snarl. She turned to Nyd, whose baleful eyes were fastened upon Lis Deddelis. The hybrid's talons flexed. He started to rise from his seat and Verran laid a restraining hand upon his shoulder.

"Stop that! Just stop that, Nyd!" Her voice was unusually peremptory. "If you create a disturbance here, Lord Grizhni will be sorry that he brought you. He'll be ashamed of you— yes, very ashamed!" Nyd subsided with a croak of dissatisfaction.

The Select were well-equipped for impromptu votes. Attached to the arm of each chair was a small box containing a black tablet and a white tablet. Now the overworked Scribe of the Order passed to and fro carrying a widemouthed jar. Into the jar each savant dropped a token.

"A white token signifies an affirmative vote, or support of your husband's intentions," Vay Nennevay explained. "A black token indicates opposition."

Verran watched attentively. As far as she could make out, most of the savants were dropping white tokens. As the Scribe passed, Vay Nennevay tossed a white token into the jar, then leaned back in her seat with a thoughtful frown.

"He's going to win," Verran opined.

"Oh, obviously. So obviously that I can't help but wonder why this is taking place at all."

"But you said that disagreeable-looking young man who speaks so melodramatically had made a mistake of some kind."

"That may be the case. I can only hope there's nothing more to it than that."

"What more could there be?"

"Don't look so uneasy, child. There's probably no cause," Nennevay advised. "Surely you know by now that Terrs is able to protect himself."

"Protect himself from what?"

"From plots among his compeers, for one thing."

"Who would wish to plot against Lord Grizhni, Madam? Is his leadership of the Select considered inadequate?"

"He's a very strong Preeminence and therefore has his enemies. A leader who has offended no man is necessarily indecisive. Fal Grizhni is most decisive. Even his greatest enemies must admit this."

"What qualities of leadership does he lack, then?"

"Diplomacy. Tolerance. Patience. Flexibility. And what must be called craft or guile. Fal Grizhni possesses none of these traits."

Verran was a little insulted. "If so much is wanting, then why did you people choose him for his position at all?" Frowning, she looked away.

Seated at a small table off to one side of the room, the Scribe counted tokens in the presence of the requisite three witnesses. A host of savants conferred in sundry funereal clumps. Lis Deddelis stood at the center of a large group. He talked and gesticulated a great deal. Verran watched and decided that he did not look like a young man who had just committed a major blunder.

"Terrs was not chosen for Preeminence. He won it," Vay Nennevay said, and Verran turned back to her in surprise.

"You mean in a lottery of some kind?"

"Certainly not."

"I must apologize for my ignorance."

"You are no more ignorant than most citizens. It's our policy to speak little of Selectic procedures to outsiders. Preeminence is the property of the savant possessing the strongest power of Cognition. So it has been since the days of Nes. In latter years it's been suggested that other qualifications should be taken into account, but for now the old rule still stands. For years Fal Grizhni's Preeminence has gone unchallenged, for it's acknowledged that his power of Cognition is unequalled. Therefore I am puzzled."

"About this voting, you mean?"

"Yes. Grizhni's decision won't be overturned. However, should his opposition amount to a quarter of our total membership—and it may perhaps do so—that is considered sufficient grounds upon which to issue a formal challenge to Preeminence. In the face of such a challenge a Cognitive competition called the Droyle ensues, and the ultimate victor is Preeminent. But it's unthinkable that the puppy Lis Deddelis would presume to issue such a challenge to Fal Grizhni. Deddelis would emerge from such a contest with a permanently injured mind, and surely he must know it."

"Maybe he doesn't mean to challenge Lord Grizhni. Maybe he's only showing off."

"Very dangerous bravado."

The votes had been counted. The Scribe stepped to the dais to announce the results. The total membership of the Select amounted to 203 savants, of which 199 were present. The Scribe had counted 53 black tokens.

Nyro Lis Deddelis leaped to his feet. "No confidence! No onfidence!" he brayed triumphantly. "The support of the nembership falters! The authority of Preeminence Grizhni is hallenged!"

"What possesses the fool?" Verran heard Vay Nennevay nutter. All over the room the savants watched and wondered.

"Challenged by whom, Cognizance Lis Deddelis?" Fal Grizhni inquired expressionlessly.

Dead silence fell. Lis Deddelis was not dismayed. "I issue he challenge, Preeminence!" he proclaimed. "By my rights inder the law that governs us all, I challenge you!"

Fal Grizhni studied his youthful opponent. "Let me assure myself that I understand you correctly. You issue a challenge and you demand the Cognitive competition of Nes. You have been a member of this order for some six months and you aspire to Preeminence?"

"That is correct, Preeminence."

"You possess abilities of which we have been hitherto unaware, Cognizance Lis Deddelis?"

"My powers are what they are. I do not claim to be worthy of Preeminence. Yet my convictions are such that it is my duty to oppose those actions that represent a danger both to the city and to the Select. Whatever the personal cost, it is my duty as a savant of honor."

"Oh, this is absurd," Vay Nennevay remarked more to herself than to Verran. "The young fool's brain will be blasted clear out of reason. And I'm certain Terrs doesn't want to do it."

"Then why doesn't he refuse?"

"He can't refuse a formal challenge. Refusal would be equivalent to concession of victory, in which case Deddelis becomes Preeminent by default."

"*He* Preeminent? But he's so—so—undignified," Verran finished lamely.

"To say the least."

Following brief thought, Grizhni spoke. "I do not refuse your challenge. However, I am granting you a period of time in which to give careful consideration to the consequences of your actions—"

"Contrary to your belief, Preeminence, I do not fear the consequences of my actions and I do not require additional time. All I require is an answer."

"You shall have one," Grizhni replied. "As you cite the rule of Nes, I will for your own benefit remind you of an additional ruling. The challenge stands until it has been met or withdrawn. But it is within the power of any savant here with standing superior to yours to exercise precedence." Lis Deddelis was silent. "Does any qualifying member wish to do so?" Nearly two hundred savants whispered feverishly among themselves.

"What does he mean, 'exercise precedence'?" Verran asked.

"Someone of superior standing may take Deddelis's place in the Droyle, whether Deddelis likes it or not," Nennevay returned. "If the young fool is fortunate, some friend may stand in for him."

It seemed that Deddelis was indeed fortunate, for Gless Vallage spoke. "Preeminence, friends and savants, the intense idealism of the Cognizant Deddelis places us all in a difficult position. My young friend's convictions oblige him to issue a challenge promising consequences undesirable to us all." Vallage's smooth voice held the merest hint of apology. "As the Cognizant Deddelis entered this order under my sponsorship, the responsibility for this situation in a sense belongs to me. I therefore exercise my authority to undertake the challenge on behalf of Lis Deddelis." Deddelis stared at him, apparently stricken. There were murmurs of relief amongst the savants. Fal Grizhni's inscrutable black gaze was trained steadily on Vallage.

"I agree to the substitution," Grizhni said. "And it is my decision that the competition will take place here and now. Cognizance Gless Vallage, is that acceptable to you?"

"Quite acceptable, Preeminence," Vallage replied easily. "I regard the Droyle as a formality only."

"In that case, have you any preference as to the method?"

"Old ways are best, it's said. Shall we have the Droyle of Nes?"

"What does he mean?" Verran inquired of Nennevay. "What's the Droyle of Nes? Are Vallage and Lord Grizhni actually to *fight* one another? Please stop that, Nyd." Beside her the hybrid had started to snarl again. At her command he grew silent, but continued to twist restlessly in his seat.

"Your husband and Vallage do not actually fight one another, they merely test the relative strength of their Cognitive powers. Neither will be in any physical jeopardy. Were Grizhni to Droyle with Lis Deddelis, the inequality of their abilities might well prove hazardous to Deddelis. With Vallage as challenger there's no such danger, for Vallage is a savant of great accomplishment."

"Then he might win?"

"Unlikely, unless—" Nennevay changed the subject abruptly. "There are many different methods of Droyle. When Vallage asked for the Droyle of Nes, he requested the oldest, original form of competition, named after the apparatus invented by Nes."

"What apparatus?"

"Watch."

Atop the dais a number of savants toiled. The Select employed no servants, for they wished to guard the secrecy of their congresses. Even the most menial of tasks were performed by members of the order. Now a couple of black-robed figures carried the table away while the Council members dispersed, save for Vallage and Grizhni. Somewhere a savant set machinery in motion or else performed Cognition. Two panels set in the floor slid away. With a whirring of ancient machinery and a grinding of rusty gears, the Droyle of Nes slowly lifted into view.

To Verran it resembled only a couple of fair-sized booths, stoutly constructed and enclosed on all four sides. The walls appeared to be made of some dark, moderately lustrous substance; perhaps metal, perhaps tinted glass. "It doesn't look like much. What does it do?"

"Engraved upon the inner wall of each booth are symbols and patterns enabling a savant of the Order to focus and concentrate his thoughts to the degree necessary to create a projection," Nennevay replied. "You don't know what a projection is? Never mind. You'll see for yourself in a moment."

Fal Grizhni and Gless Vallage entered their respective booths. The doors were shut and bolted from the outside, imprisoning the two savants. No sooner had the bolts slid into position than soft light glowed within the booths. Vallage and Grizhni were both clearly visible to the audience. Each man was seated, each man studied the wall before him with concentrated attention.

"Won't all these people watching disturb them?" Verran asked.

"They can't see us. To them, the walls appear opaque. Nor can they hear us, for the material of the Droyle excludes all sound. Each man feels himself to be cut off from all the world, alone with the symbols that will enable him to achieve Cognition."

"And when they do?"

Gaerase Vay Nennevay did not answer. Her attention was fixed on the Droyle. Verran glanced around the room. The savants in the audience were completely absorbed. Nyro Lis Deddelis leaned forward in his seat, eyes fixed intently on his mentor Vallage. Verran felt a clawed hand descend upon her wrist. She turned to face Nyd, who whimpered anxiously. "It's all right, Nyd. He won't be hurt. Madame Vay Nennevay says there's no danger." She hoped she sounded confident. Nyd was unconvinced, and turned away with a hoarse whine.

The savants sat within their booths of Droyle and their expressions were identical. Their eyes were shut, their faces blank to the verge of unconsciousness. They might almost have been asleep. Verran studied her husband. He looked pale, but then he was of a naturally pale complexion. There might have been a crease of concentration between his brows, but at that distance and in uncertain light, it was difficult to tell. Uncertain light? Did the gray daylight not pour through the skylight in the dome? She looked up. The skylight was unobstructed, but surely the light in the Council chamber was waning. It grew dimmer by the moment. The savants at the back of the audience were already lost in shadow. Simultaneously the air grew cold, cold enough to raise gooseflesh on her arms. She groped for Nyd's paw, found it, and held on tightly. Darker and darker the chamber grew, while the light within the Droyle intensified, illuminating the booths, their occupants, and the surrounding few feet of the dais.

Then Verran saw what Vay Nennevay meant when she spoke of projections. At the opposing ends of the dais two figures took shape; vague and amorphous at first, then increasing in substance and solidity as she watched. Soon they became identifiable as men, misty and insubstantial, but unmistakable in outline. The shapes darkened, the blurred faces cleared slowly, the details of feature and costume became apparent and the wavering forms resolved themselves into simulacra of Fal Grizhni and of Gless Vallage. The figures were a little smaller than life-size and a trifle transparent,

but clearly recognizable. Verran gazed from her husband
seated within the Droyle to her husband standing in his black
robes upon the dais, and wondered. Fal Grizhni within the
booth sat with closed eyes and blank face. The eyes of the
simulacrum were open and aware. The face was set in an expression that chilled Verran. She had never seen him look so,
but it was a face with which his enemies were not unfamiliar.
By contrast, the figure of Saxas Gless Vallage seemed ineffectual—shorter, less distinct in outline, the aspect cunning
rather than forceful.

The two figures inspected one another. Neither was armed,
so it seemed unlikely to Verran that they would fight. In this
she soon found herself mistaken.

The Grizhni-projection floated toward its opponent. Its motion was slower than a man's, silent as the mist riding a breeze,
and unsteady, as if the pressure of the atmosphere created a
major impediment. The projection looked as insubstantial as
smoke. Its greatest vitality seemed concentrated in its eyes,
which glittered strangely even in the subdued light of the
Council chamber. The Vallage-projection retreated a step,
then held its ground. The Grizhni lifted its arm like a man attempting to swim through glue. Its wide black sleeve billowed
slowly on almost imperceptible currents of air. From its
spread fingers issued five tendrils of dense, dark vapor. In
midair the tendrils condensed to serpents, and the audience
murmured.

"Terrs is in good form," Vay Nennevay remarked.

The snakes settled upon the shoulders of the Vallage-projection and twisted themselves around its body. Soon the Vallage
was enmeshed from throat to ankle in smoky, undulating
forms. Inside the booth, the real Gless Vallage drew his breath
with difficulty, panted, and could be seen to compose himself
for an effort. The Vallage-projection bowed its head, stood
for a moment lapped in snakes, then slowly spread wide its
arms. The snakes slid away, hung writhing in the air for a moment, then dissolved to formless mist that wafted upward to
hover beneath the dome.

Encouraged by its success, the Vallage-projection counter-
attacked. Swiftly it spewed forth strands of mist and wove
them together to form a net, which swam through the air
toward the waiting Grizhni. The Grizhni raised both arms. To
Verran's amazement, the misty fingers lengthened, stretched,

flattened and sharpened along the edges, finally becoming ten
knifelike blades of improbable solidity. With these blades the
Grizhni cut the descending net again and again until nothing
remained but ragged shreds of smoke.

Once more the Grizhni floated forward, its ten blades questing thirstily. The Vallage-projection bounded aside slowly and
hung suspended for a moment before settling to the floor. Five
daggers clawed the Vallage's shoulder, shearing through the
black robe and whatever lay beneath to sever the projection's
left arm from its body.

Verran gasped. Excitement stirred the watching savants, but
they did not speak. Within the Droyle, Saxas Gless Vallage's
face contorted, the lips pulled back in an agonized grimace
and the eyes squeezed violently shut. He might have been
screaming, with head thrown back and throat cords straining,
but if he was, the substance of the Droyle permitted no sound
to escape.

The severed arm floated above the ground. The wide black
sleeve trailed along the floor, the hand clenched and un-
clenched repeatedly, spasmodically, as if it would never die.
Verran choked and nausea seized her. She looked away
quickly, clutched Nyd's paw in both hands, and took a deep
breath. Nausea receded. "It's only a projection, not a man.
Not a man," she reminded herself, and looked again at the
dais.

The arm had melted away. In its place hung a smudge of
dark vapor. The Grizhni advanced upon its foe. The Vallage
drew back, took a deep breath and expelled it. Torrents of
dense, opaque vapor issued from its mouth and nose. Strands
of the black stuff wound themselves around the Grizhni's
finger-blades, dulling the points and edges. Black puffs clustered over the Grizhni's face and eyes. The projection fell
back, obviously blinded. Within the Droyle, Terrs Fal Grizhni
could be seen to pass a hand swiftly before his face. As he
did so, his projection wavered and lightened for a moment.
Then Fal Grizhni regained full concentration and the projection waxed in substance. Its face was clear, but its blades
had shrunk back to normal finger-size. During this time, the
Vallage-projection succeeded in partially regenerating its
severed arm. A shadowy stump, bereft of its hand, now protruded from the Vallage's left shoulder.

Once more the Grizhni attacked. Now it sent a volley of neb-

ulous projectiles drifting toward its foe. The missiles moved
slowly by objective standards, but in the context of the battle
they hurtled. The Vallage raised its arm. Its billowing sleeve
expanded, became a great foggy shield against which most of
the projectiles launched themselves in vain. One or two got
past the shield, encountered their target, and exploded darkly,
ripping large chunks of the Vallage's substance away. Within
the booth Gless Vallage stiffened and his eyes flew open. The
Vallage-projection lightened and its transparency increased
noticeably. The outlines quivered, and for a moment the entire
projection seemed to waver on the edge of dissolution. The
Grizhni launched another volley and the Vallage, now ghostly,
floated backward to the very edge of the dais.

The Grizhni-projection grew. Before the eyes of the assembled Select, the projection darkened, solidified, and enlarged
until it was half again the size of a normal man—an extraordinary manifestation of Fal Grizhni's Cognitive powers. The
icy, relentless face might have been carved in white marble,
so solid did it seem. The robes were black without a hint of
transparence, and when the figure slowly raised both arms, it
seemed like early nightfall.

But Gless Vallage wasn't finished yet. Within the Droyle,
his face assumed an expression of increased concentration, a
determination not often displayed openly to the world. The
faltering Vallage-projection now exploited its waning solidity,
surrounding itself with a cloud of roiling vapor into which the
quasihuman figure vanished altogether. The Vallage-projection was nowhere to be seen. The dais was covered with cot-
tony fog through which the towering figure of the Grizhni and
the outlines of the Droyle apparatus were all that could be
discerned.

For a few moments the Grizhni hunted through the swirling
clouds for its vanished opponent. Then, as if in caution, the
tall figure slowly dwindled, shrinking back to its original
height. It was well that Terrs Fal Grizhni chose that careful
move. A split second later a brilliant bolt of light and force
streaked out of the fog to cleave the space lately occupied by
the Grizhni-projection's head. The bolt did not drift like mist,
but struck with the speed and power of the miniature lightning
it resembled. Every savant in the audience gasped or exclaimed, for such a thing had never been seen in a Droyle before. Almost immediately another bolt blazed out of the mists,

lower this time, and struck the Grizhni full in the chest. It rent a jagged hole from breast to back, and black mists spilled out over the dais.

Verran gave an involuntary cry and beside her Nyd whimpered in anguish. The Grizhni-projection foundered like a ship struck by a cannonball. The dense gray fog was starting to disperse now, and the Vallage was once more visible, a dim gray figure with fire at its command. The Vallage had completely replaced its ruined left arm. Another bolt sped from its outstretched hands, struck and carried away most of the Grizhni's right shoulder. Verran looked to the Droyle. Her husband's face bore a look of pain that horrified her, and he was visibly swaying in his seat.

A crackle, a flash, and another direct hit cut through midnight robes to amputate the Grizhni's lower leg. The severed member retained its shape for an instant before it softened and spread into formlessness. Deprived of support, the Grizhni-projection sank to one knee.

Verran's hands clenched as if she felt the pain through her own body. "This is hideous!"

To her surprise, Vay Nennevay agreed. "Vallage's conduct is unethical," the savant replied. "It may even be illegal under the Code of the Select."

"How, unethical?"

"He uses a form of Cognition not customary to the Droyle, and it gives him the advantage. He trained himself to perfection in a new technique, and then, having carefully prepared himself, instructed his creature Deddelis to engineer a general vote in the hope of catching Fal Grizhni unaware. That is Gless Vallage's way, and it doesn't surprise me. But make no mistake, I'll challenge a victory won by such unscrupulous means."

The next bolt sent the Grizhni simulacrum toppling slowly to the floor. It landed noiselessly and for a moment lay still while its outlines softened. The face of the real Fal Grizhni was empty to the point of extinction.

The Vallage-projection wafted near its rival and launched another brilliant missile. The bolt struck a glancing blow that ripped nearly half the Grizhni's skull away, and the audience murmured.

Vay Nennevay sighed. "That finishes it. I will protest."

For a moment Verran regarded the simulacrum in horror.

Half the face remained. Part of the head had softened to a shapeless mass of dark vapor and part was completely gone. Quickly she turned her eyes to the Droyle where her husband sat pale as a corpse, but whole and sound.

The mutilated figure stirred unexpectedly and sent a thin stream of mist curling along the floor. Fal Grizhni evidently owned reserves of willpower undreamed of even by his staunchest allies. The mist wound itself around the Vallage-projection, swiftly ascending to chest level. The Vallage simulacrum and the real Vallage in the Droyle bore identical expressions of surprise.

What was left of the Grizhni dragged the Vallage-projection near, and a confused mutter arose in the audience.

Terrs Fal Grizhni raised his head, his face changed, and he stiffened as if to brace himself for an effort. At that moment the Grizhni-projection exploded silently, flying apart into a thousand sharp-edged fragments that sliced through the air at surprising speed. A barrage of flying fragments caught the Vallage-projection, cut through its smoky substance, and reduced the human figure to shapeless rags of fog.

Saxas Gless Vallage sagged against the wall of the Droyle. His eyes were wide and glazed. Above the dais hung a bank of small black clouds, all that was left of the two projections. For a short time the clouds hovered. Then, as if stirred by imaginary winds, some of them drew together, darkened, coalesced, and slowly the figure of Fal Grizhni reformed itself out of the restless vapor. The Grizhni-projection waved its hand, and the remaining patches of mist, all that remained of the Vallage, dispersed and floated out over the heads of the spectators. Verran reached up to touch a cloud as it passed. It was warm as blood, and she snatched her hand away.

Presently the clouds lightened, then faded from view; whereupon the Grizhni-projection, now clearly the victor, stood alone on the dais and voluntarily discorporated. The Droyle was over. The Council chamber gradually warmed and lightened.

Fal Grizhni unfastened the door somehow and emerged from his booth. His carriage was erect and his step was firm. By no sign was it evident that he had just undergone an ordeal. Forgetting their customary reserve, the savants of the Select broke into spontaneous applause.

Grizhni acknowledged the ovation with a slight inclination

of the head. "Attend to the Cognizant Vallage," he commanded in a perfectly even voice, "and remove the Droyle."

His orders were obeyed at once. A couple of underlings extracted Gless Vallage from his booth and bore him from the
dais. Vallage's eyes were open, but he appeared unconscious.
By unseen methods, the Droyle was made to descend.

Terrs Fal Grizhni brought the meeting to a swift close.
Evidently he assumed that the outcome of the competition had
confirmed his judgment beyond further question, for he announced that such Select-crafted devices designed to prevent
the nocturnal intrusions of assassins, rapists, thieves, and kidnappers should henceforth be made unavailable to the Duke
and his supporters.

No one presumed to object.

During the dombulis ride home Grizhni was silent and Verran hardly ventured to address him. The savant sat in the bow
of the boat, staring out over the water. The sky had cleared
and sunlight beat down on his face, throwing every line into
sharp relief. Verran sneaked frequent surreptitious glances.
Her husband was unnaturally pale. There was a network of
fine wrinkles around his eyes which had never seemed noticeable before, shadows that could have been applied with charcoal, and a deep, vertical crease between his brows. She saw or
sensed that he was mortally tired and perhaps in some pain. It
occurred to Verran that he might pass her hand across his
forehead to smooth the lines away, and almost she raised her
hand, but did not dare.

They reached Grizhni Palace. Grizhni excused himself with
his customary formal courtesy and sought his own apartment,
where he remained in seclusion for the rest of the day. He did
not state his intentions, but Verran suspected that he wanted
sleep.

The day was long, lonely, and tedious. Verran loitered for
a time in the gardens, but soon the beauty bored her. She
attempted to write letters but could not concentrate, for the
events of the morning preyed upon her mind. She visited with
the hybrids briefly and found she was not in the mood to listen
to croaks and hisses. Finally she wandered into the great library, with its racks of manuscripts, maps, charts, and hand-
lettered volumes. She chose Rev Beddef's *History of the Select*
and settled herself to read. Rev Beddef had evidently been a

savant of extraordinary erudition. He had also been one of Fal Grizhni's very few personal friends. What was Fal Grizhni doing now? Had the Droyle weakened or sickened him? Impossible—was he not invincible? Then why had he looked so pallid and exhausted? There was no point in sending any of the hybrids to check. None of the creatures, not even Nyd, would dare to cross the threshold of Grizhni's chambers unless summoned.

Verran read throughout the afternoon. By the time evening fell she was considerably less ignorant of the Select. At last she sat down to a solitary dinner which she consumed without appetite.

After dinner it was impossible to concentrate on *History of the Select*. Verran did her best, but failed. She put the book aside, got up and roamed from room to empty room, worried and unaccountably wretched. For hours she paced, far into the night. The candles had burned low in their sconces before she finally betook herself to bed.

It was a cool night, but the silk coverlets seemed stifling. Verran tossed, fidgeted, and twisted the sheets into knots. It was clear she was not going to sleep. After an hour or so, she gave up trying. She flung the covers off and jumped down from the bed. Through the moonlit bedchamber she glided like a barefoot ghost in her trailing white nightgown; through the receiving room and the antechamber, out into the hall.

The candles had all burnt out. White moonlight poured through the windows and chilly breezes swept the floor. Before her the corridor stretched like a dark-gleaming highway. Verran proceeded on tiptoe to minimize contact with the icy marble floor. Along the corridor she stole in utter silence, through splashes of moonlight and pools of blackest shadow, past open windows where the sweet breath of the garden fanned her cheek, past occasional gray-clad, flame-eyed figures that acknowledged her presence with quiet obeisances.

On she went, a white wraith with a racing heart, step slowing as she neared her destination. She stopped before a black portal and listened intently. Outside in the garden crickets chirped, insects buzzed, and leaves rustled; those were the only sounds to be heard. Verran opened the door and slipped into Fal Grizhni's apartment, where she had never before set foot.

She stood in a moonlit antechamber, chilly and deserted. None of the hybrids were in attendance. There was no sound

and no sign of life. She tiptoed across the antechamber and
passed to the chamber beyond. Her bare feet were freezing on
the stone floor and her hands were icy. She quickened her
pace, now rushing through the unfamiliar rooms until she
came to the one she sought.

It was large, but sparsely furnished, containing little more
than a few carved wooden chests and a tall bed with a massive
tester and gray hangings. The curtains around the bed were
drawn nearly closed. Only a narrow opening had been left,
and it looked as dark as the entrance to a cave wherein Fal
Grizhni lay sleeping. Quite suddenly and with utter certainty
Verran knew that he was not sleeping at all, but awake, wide
awake. In silence she glided forward to the bed, climbed into
the cavelike place, and for the first time lay down beside her
husband.

Chapter Six

❧❧❧

Close beside the Lureis Canal the walkway known as the Prendivet Saunter extended for the distance of half a mile, and there the fashionable strolled in the sunlight. On a terrace overlooking the Saunter sat the Cognizant Saxas Gless Vallage. It was the first time in the weeks following his defeat at the hands of Fal Grizhni that he had been strong enough to venture abroad, and the effects of the Droyle were still visible. The savant was drawn and haggard, a look unbecoming to a face that seemed to be sliding from boyishness directly into middle age. He had set aside his black robes and dragon insignia for ordinary street garb, perhaps to avoid attracting unwanted notice. A goblet of sparkling wine and a dish of poached winkles sat untouched on the table before him.

Vallage scanned the crowd upon the Saunter. Presently he picked out the figure he sought; a hulking form attired in the uniform of the Ducal Guards. The savant leaned forward over the terrace railing. "Commander," he called. "Over here, Ulf."

Lord Haik Ulf looked up, caught Vallage's eye, and stopped reluctantly. "Yes?"

"Will you join me, Commander?"

Ulf's eyebrows arched in open surprise. He had no use for Gless Vallage, or any other savant, for that matter. It was no secret that Haik Ulf loathed the Select—that close-knit, close-

mouthed band of meddlesome magicians who had not even
the honesty to own their own calling. *Savants,* they preferred
to call themselves, and disavowed all knowledge of the supernatural. *Scholars,* they chose to call themselves, or *investigators*—anything to avoid admitting what they really were! To
hear them tell it, their group was nothing more than a harmless gaggle of academicians who sometimes gathered to discuss
questions of natural philosophy. Lord Ulf smiled grimly at the
thought. He knew better—everyone knew better. Those so-
called savants had forces at their command far beyond the ken
of normal, decent men.

Certain it was that the knowledge of the Select would enable
them to exercise untold influence in the council chambers and
in the throne room itself, should they care to do so. It was not
impossible that they might even aspire to take the reins of
government entirely into their own hands. A bitter expression
twisted Lord Ulf's features. It was hateful to contemplate
the possibility of a group of incomprehensible—*alien* was the
only proper description—sorcerers controlling affairs of state.
Such matters as the disposition of taxes and tribute, the pre-
ferment of generals and courtiers, the negotiations with foreign princes and the declarations of war—these were all things
that should be left in the hands of the hereditary nobility of
which he, Ulf, was a member. The nobility, and of course, the
military. That was the way things were meant to be.

Fortunately the initiates of the Select were traditionally too
involved in their arcane rituals and their secret congresses to
involve themselves in government matters to any great extent—although any involvement at all was too much, in Lord
Ulf's opinion. So it had always been until the advent of Terrs
Fal Grizhni, who was regarded by Lord Ulf with inexpressible
detestation. Fal Grizhni was arrogant and ambitious. Fal
Grizhni demonstrated unbecoming interest in affairs of state,
and Fal Grizhni was too powerful by half. Lord Ulf was not a
passive character, and it was not his way to accept an objectionable situation if it lay within his power to effect a change.
All efforts directed toward the removal of Fal Grizhni had
hitherto been failures. But now this man Vallage, this slippery,
always-at-his-ease magician wanted to talk to him, and it was
whispered that Vallage sought the downfall of Grizhni. Perhaps the fellow could be of some use.

Haik Ulf approached and eased his large frame into the chair facing Vallage. "At your service, Cognizance," he said, the courtesy of his address belied by the negligent tone of his voice.

They ordered a fresh pitcher of wine, of which Haik Ulf partook hugely. Gless Vallage studied his companion. Ulf was notoriously crude and surly, but not altogether a fool. Perhaps the fellow could be of some use.

While Vallage deliberated upon an appropriate opening, Haik Ulf jumped into the conversational breach. "Recovered from your trouncing, have you?"

Gless Vallage repressed a start of surprise. "I beg your pardon, Commander?"

"I heard you got into a tangle with Grizhni a while ago, and he just about left you for dog's meat."

How could Haik Ulf know what went on at a congress of the Select? Was Fal Grizhni's chit of a wife spreading gossip? "Where could you have heard such rumors, Commander?"

"Never mind, I have my sources. I hear a lot of things that might surprise you, Cognizance."

"I don't doubt it. All of Lanthi Ume recognizes that little escapes the attention of Haik Ulf of the Guards." Vallage employed his winning smile. "It would please me to be addressed by my given name, rather than my title."

Ulf folded his big arms. "It would, eh? I thought you magicians want to make sure the whole world knows what you are."

"Some of us do, no doubt. As for me, I feel that possession of a noble name carries greater honor than any title conferred by the Select."

It was difficult to judge whether the appeal to Ulf's patrician sympathies exercised any effect. The man merely grunted and lifted his goblet to his lips.

"You must not imagine," Vallage continued, "that his Preeminence and I engaged in anything so crude as physical combat. I assure you nothing of the sort transpired."

"Whatever transpired, your efforts did you no good." Ulf drained his goblet. He appeared to be losing interest.

Gless Vallage studied his companion. It was clear that subtlety of approach was wasted on this oaf. Only the most brutally direct of methods might prevail. "Your own efforts have been equally ineffectual," he observed.

Ulf did not blink. "What d'you think you're talking about?"

"I've noted that you have been responsible for several attempts on the life of Preeminence Grizhni in the last year, Commander. The most recent occurred at his wedding. It was a clumsy plan and poorly executed. You hadn't a chance of success."

"I don't know a thing about that," Ulf replied without rancor, and poured himself out more wine. "You're dreaming, magician."

"Ah? You interrogated the assassin, I believe?"

"A poor loony that should have been kept locked up."

"As he is kept now?"

"No," Ulf replied easily. "He died under questioning."

"A pity. Was he of a singularly feeble constitution, or were your methods of interrogation singularly harsh?"

"As for that, I couldn't say. Anything else you'd like to know, Vallage?"

"Yes. I'd like to know why you persist in these useless and ill-conceived schemes. What good do you think it does you to send lone assassins against his Preeminence of the Select? Such attempts are childish. Why do you fail to use the one powerful weapon at your command?"

"And what would that be?"

"Your guardsmen, obviously."

"Just like that, eh? Listen, Vallage, I'm telling you I'm not responsible for any attempts on Grizhni's life. He's got plenty of enemies, you know. Why single me out?" Ulf took a swig of wine, eyed the savant, and continued deliberately, "But just for the sake of curiosity, let's suppose I was after Grizhni. You don't think I can sic a squadron of my guards on someone that important whenever I feel like it, do you? You've got to be smarter than that. I'd be exceeding my authority, and there's the Duke to consider."

"What if you knew the Duke would not be displeased?"

"I'd need more than your word for that."

"What would you need?"

"Direct orders from the Duke's own mouth, or else something in writing."

"You make difficult requests."

"Why not?" Ulf shrugged. "We're only supposing, aren't we? And while we're supposing, let's suppose we find out why a magician like you is discussing the removal of Fal Grizhni, his leader. His illustrious leader."

Gless Vallage toyed thoughtfully with his goblet. Much as he disliked the barbarity of blunt conversation, it seemed to be the only way of making an impression on the primitive intellect of Haik Ulf. "I'll deal plainly with you. I think we are alike, Commander, in viewing Fal Grizhni as a danger to the city of Lanthi Ume. His unwarranted meddling in affairs of state poses a danger to all of us, do you not agree?"

"That's what I've been saying all along, but I never thought that any of you magicians of the Select would have the brains to see it. Or the guts to do anything about it."

"My loyalties to the city and to my peers take precedence over my allegiance to the Select. But in this particular case they do not conflict, for the truest service to the Select lies in the elimination of irresponsible leadership." Vallage might also have mentioned that Selectic Preeminence had been a private ambition amounting to obsession for many years, but there was little point in discussing such matters with Ulf.

Ulf reflected. Gless Vallage was an oily liar, an effete milk-sop, and a magician to boot. But surely the man was a true enemy of Fal Grizhni, and worth listening to for that reason if no other. "Elimination, eh? And just how would you go about doing that? You didn't have much luck the last time you tried it."

"It's quite certain that he won't be displaced by a savant of the Order using traditional methods. Nor will a lone assassin bring him down. But an organized attack by your Guards, with the authority of the Duke behind them—that might suffice."

"Oh, my men could take him, all right."

"Don't underestimate Grizhni, Commander."

"Don't underestimate my Guards, Vallage. I'd stake them against a magician any day. But I wouldn't order them to it without a command from the Duke. And me, I don't think the Duke's about to give any such command."

"He'd need a good reason," Vallage murmured. "But I think we might discover one."

"How?" Ulf looked hungry.

"I'll attend to that. In the meantime, there's much that can be accomplished if I may rely on the cooperation of the Ducal Guards."

"You move too fast, magician. I haven't agreed to anything."

"I thought you had agreed that we have a common enemy."

"What of it?"

"I assume that a man of your energy would actively seek the downfall of his enemies."

"I'll think about it."

"Good. Then think about this as well. The man who assists in freeing Lanthi Ume of Fal Grizhni will earn the gratitude of the Duke and of the next Selectic Preeminence. Such a man may expect advancement."

"Don't try to buy me. You're overplaying your hand." Ulf spoke with some contempt. "I said I'd think about it. You'll hear from me." Without awaiting reply, he rose and strode away in a purposeful manner that set him apart from the aimless strollers on Prendivet Saunter.

Vallage watched him go. Haik Ulf was a necessity at the moment, but some happy day in the not distant future, it would be possible to dispense with him. Ulf would make a fine military governor, Vallage reflected. He possessed just the right combination of caution and brutality. It should not be difficult to find a suitable position for him, perhaps on some small and very remote island in the Sea of Ice. There were more immediately pressing matters to consider, however, and one of them was now approaching.

Brenn Wate Basef advanced along Prendivet Saunter. His dress was careless, his manner indefinably agitated. He soon joined Gless Vallage, with whom he had an appointment.

Vallage greeted the young man cordially. Brenn seated himself and regarded the savant with a mixture of respect and bewilderment. He had no idea why he had been summoned by the famous Gless Vallage.

"I've invited you here today to discuss the matter of your candidacy to the Select," Vallage announced with apparent candor.

"I didn't know you were aware of it, Cognizance."

"Indeed, yes. I've been forced to witness your exclusion, which I regard less as an error than an injustice."

"Injustice?" The sudden fire in Brenn's eyes revealed that Vallage had touched a nerve.

"When a young man of your ability and promise is denied membership in the Select, it's a great injustice."

Brenn shrugged with assumed indifference. "You are kind, Cognizance. As for my exclusion, I hope the situation will change, in time."

"Perhaps." Vallage smiled sympathetically. "But it seems you have enemies in high places. Preeminence Fal Grizhni does not favor you."

"I hope to convince him of my quality." The young man was inept at disguising his emotions. He spoke with false tranquility, but the underlying intensity was obvious.

"An impartial judge would have been convinced of your quality long since, Master Wate Basef. I'm almost tempted to question his Preeminence's objectivity."

"Fal Grizhni and I are not friends. I know him to be deeply prejudiced. In fact, he—" Brenn became aware of the transparency of his bitterness, and cut himself off. He eyed his companion warily.

"In fact, he. . . ?" Vallage prompted without success. "Has it ever occurred to you that a man ruled by personal prejudice may be unsuited to Preeminence? Fal Grizhni is a great savant —never hear me deny it! But Preeminence is an office that demands abilities beyond mere mastery of Cognition."

"I agree. Perhaps some day the Select may hope for a Preeminence devoid of arrogance and malice. For my part, I can only wait for time to soften Grizhni's attitude toward me."

"Granite will soften sooner than Grizhni. If you wait for that, then you'll wait forever. Fortunately there's another way."

Brenn's expression reflected undisguised curiosity. His eyes were laughably eager.

Vallage took a thoughtful sip of wine, studied the boats on the Lureis, and enjoyed the luxury of power. At last he answered, "It's possible that you might enter the Select despite his Preeminence's malice. If a member of the Council sponsors you, and at least half our membership supports you, then Grizhni's opposition may be overruled."

"I know it. But is it likely that a member of the Council

would oppose the will of Fal Grizhni?''

"It's not an impossibility. Such a member would naturally require belief in the absolute loyalty and support of his protégé.''

"Let me understand you, Cognizance. Are you offering to sponsor my admission to the Select?''

"I? No. All things considered, I think it better that my comrade Lej Rom Usine officially sponsor you. There's no reason for all the world to know who Cognizance Brenn Wate Basef's best friends are.''

The interview concluded shortly thereafter, and Brenn departed. For a time Gless Vallage remained seated in the sunlight, replete with an agreeable sense of accomplishment. His fine features took on a look of such infectious affability that the passersby could scarcely forbear smiling in return. Some friendly salutations were exchanged, for it was believed by most Lanthians that for a savant, Saxas Gless Vallage was the best of good fellows.

Events of the following weeks were not calculated to improve Fal Grizhni's temper. Duke Povon concluded his negotiations with the Keldhar of Gard Lammis, and the Vayno Fortification was duly mortgaged to a foreign power. Shortly thereafter, soldiers of Gard Lammis appeared on the Vayno ramparts. It was the opinion of the Keldhar, in view of the cordial relationship between the two city-states, that Lanthian harbor duties should be waived in favor of the ships of Gard Lammis. Following the garrisoning of the Vayno, the Keldhar formally requested the Duke to extend this favor as a gesture of goodwill, and Povon found it expedient to agree.

Fal Grizhni's resulting contempt was corrosive. The savant had already made public his unwillingness to pay taxes upon the Victory of Nes. He now announced his refusal to submit to taxation upon any Selectic property, regardless of location. In addition, his Preeminence proclaimed that Selectic Cognition should no longer ensure the hitherto salubrious cleanliness of the Lanthian canals, or the resistance of dockyard pilings to the attack of various marine worms.

Duke Povon angrily refused his Preeminence's next demand for a parley whereupon Grizhni conveyed his grievances to the great nobles of Lanthi Ume, requesting their support in the conflict. It was Grizhni's belief that a combination of Selectic and aristocratic influence might exert pressure sufficient to force the Duke to compliance. The savant did not, however, attempt to carry his suit to the commoners of Lanthi Ume. Such an idea did not occur to him.

On a less exalted plane, his Preeminence's wishes were thwarted by the admission of Master Brenn Wate Basef to the Select under the sponsorship of the Cognizant Lej Rom Usine. Having questions of far greater import to occupy his mind, Grizhni paid the matter of Wate Basef very little heed. He mentioned the incident in passing to his wife one evening, little dreaming that it held any particular significance for her.

Chapter Seven

✷❧✶❧✷

In the summer came the Water Games and Festival. This most
beloved and characteristically Lanthian of celebrations lasted
for five days, during which the canals were crowded with
floating booths, music filled the air day and night, and young
folk danced on the huge barge that sprawled over Parnis
Lagoon. Throughout the five days the games continued, and
they included boat races, swimming and diving competitions,
aquatic acrobatics, water wrestling, bouts of the team sport
dravendo, the Human Flowers contest, gorgeously dangerous
fire-on-water duels, and much more.

Verran visited the games with Nyd. She would have preferred the company of her husband, but no human power
could lure Terrs Fal Grizhni to a public festival, where the
press of the common multitudes offended his sensibilities.
Moreover Fal Grizhni had for some weeks past been deeply involved in arcane experimentation, the object of which he
seemed disinclined to discuss, and he was reluctant to leave his
workroom for purposes other than eating or sleeping. Verran
suspected that Grizhni's periodic emergences were for her
benefit alone. Saving her presence, he would probably have
dispensed with both food and rest, for he was capable of func-
tioning for extended periods on Cognition alone.

Verran wondered what he was up to. Several times she had
paused outside his workroom door without daring to knock.
On such occasions she had heard voices within; inhuman
voices, strangely melodious. They might have been singing, or

perhaps an infinitely musical conversation was in progress. There were several voices—as many as four or five—among which Grizhni's bass tones were distinguishable. Once Verran had plucked up sufficient courage to open the door and peek inside, but her daring availed her nothing. She had been met with intense, unnatural darkness, which she recalled only too well. She had encountered it once before in the depths of Grizhni Palace. Out of the darkness the musical voices warbled. Verran had shut the door hastily and gone away. She had never asked her husband what it all meant. But certain it was that the owners of those mysterious voices now claimed most of Fal Grizhni's attention.

Thus Verran found herself together with Nyd in the midst of a mob of merrymakers, and she made the best of it. She bought trinkets from the merchants for Nyd and the other hybrids; lost money playing the Green Octagon; bought paper cones filled with fried gantzel puffs; watched Nyd devour most of the gantzels and all of the paper; wagered successfully on the sendillis races; and laughed at the ridiculous antics of the clowns as they staggered about on the water, buoyed up by their huge, inflated footgear.

It was late afternoon when Verran and Nyd made their way by dombulis to the Sunburst Float, a large raft bright with orange and yellow rosettes. It was here the Lanthian crowd gathered to watch the Bubble-drubbing competition.

Originally a harmless pastime, Bubble-drubbing was played by a host of drubbers balanced very precariously upon inflated floats known as bubbles. The object of the game was simply to belabor opponents' bubbles with flails, causing rival drubbers to topple into the canal. The one drubber left afloat at the conclusion of a general melee was considered the victor. During the present Duke's reign this sport had been enlivened by the introduction of spiked flails used to puncture rival bubbles and bodies.

Nyd secured them a good position near the edge of the raft, with a clear view of the competition. Verran soon found she wasn't enjoying it. Several of the drubbers carried flails equipped with particularly vicious spikes, and the contest was a bloody one. The girl averted her eyes. Rather than watch the drubbing, she preferred to study the faces in the surrounding crowd, and soon picked out a familiar chiseled profile—Brenn Wate Basef's.

Verran thought of their last unhappy meeting and wondered

if she should approach him. He did not appear to have spotted her—perhaps it would be best to leave unobtrusively? Nonsense, she decided. It would be childish to run away from Brenn Wate Basef. She waved to attract his attention and deliberately caught his eye. Brenn looked startled, then uneasy. For a moment he seemed to contemplate rapid retreat. Verran smiled and beckoned. The young man drew near, but did not return the smile.

He looks so young! she thought incredulously. *He looks like a boy*! She greeted him.

"Good afternoon, Lady Grizhni," he replied stiffly.

There was an awkward pause while she cast about for something to say. He wore a black robe and dragon insignia, she noted. "Congratulations on your new Cognizance, Brenn. I know how much it means to you."

"Your ladyship is kind."

"Is it everything you'd hoped for? The Select, I mean."

"I study, I learn, and I believe I improve."

"Then you are content?"

"Wisdom breeds contentment, or so I must hope. It is good of your ladyship to inquire."

"Can't you use my name, Brenn? We're hardly strangers."

"Aren't we? I am hardly the intimate of Lady Grizhni, wife of his Preeminence."

"I'd like to think that neither of us bears the other a grudge."

"I am sure you would like to think so."

"You're still angry. But we musn't be enemies—surely that's not what you want?"

"I was not aware that my wishes were of any consequence to your ladyship." Brenn's excitable temperament was getting the better of him. His voice rose and his eyes ignited. "I was forced to conclude that my wishes were of no importance on the day you sold yourself in a loveless marriage to a vicious old man."

Nyd uttered a warning croak and Verran shushed him. The diversion gave her time to curb her annoyance. When she spoke, her voice was cool. "You've been misinformed, Brenn. I did not sell myself. Lord Grizhni is neither old nor vicious. He is a good man and a very great one. My marriage is not loveless, and I am happy."

"Happy?" Brenn sneered. "You expect me to believe that?

You couldn't be happy with a man like Grizhni! At best you only imagine you are, and your so-called happiness is illusory, not real!"

"There's a difference?" she inquired with a self-possession that infuriated him.

"There's a difference if he's used his Cognition to cloud your mind. And knowing Grizhni, he probably has."

"That's enough. I won't listen to any more of this. You don't know anything about him. I'm leaving."

She turned to go and Brenn laid a restraining hand on her arm. Nyd snarled horribly and gathered himself for a spring. She halted the angry creature with a gesture.

"Wait—don't go yet. I apologize." He looked genuinely contrite. "I spoke too harshly, out of concern for you."

She forgave him at once. "But there's no need for concern. Believe me—"

"I'm fearful for your safety. Listen, Verran. You're the only woman I'll ever love. The fact of your marriage hasn't changed that. I intend to remain faithful to you all my life."

"But Brenn, you're only twenty-one years old—"

"It doesn't matter. I'll never look at another woman." She didn't believe him, but there was little point in arguing the matter. "Your happiness and safety concern me, and I'm certain that both are in jeopardy as long as you remain in Grizhni's household."

"I don't think you understand—"

"It's you that doesn't understand what kind of a man Fal Grizhni really is. I have friends in the Select—highly-placed friends—and they've told me things about your husband that would sicken you to hear!"

"Then your friends are liars, or ignorant, or both," she snapped, her own temper beginning to fail. "Who are they?"

"I tell you they're savants—men who know of Grizhni's deeds and character."

"Know more about him than his own wife?"

"Oh, I daresay he's been kind to *you*. No doubt he's presented his best face to you. A young girl's admiration must seem sweet indeed to an aging autocrat. But tell me, Verran—what do you actually know of Fal Grizhni? What do you know of his past life? What do you know of his crimes, his malignity as Preeminent of the Select? Do you know anything of his ambition and his ruthlessness? Do you know anything of his experiments? Or of the ends to which he perverts his great powers of Cognition? What, for example, is he working on today? Do you even know that?"

She was silent.

"You see? He's revealed very little of himself to you—understandably so. Thus it's left to me to warn you of your danger and to urge you to break off all ties with Grizhni while you can. Be warned, Verran—his outrages will not continue unopposed forever."

"Warn me of what danger? And what outrages? You speak wildly."

"I speak the truth. Fal Grizhni cannot conceal his crimes indefinitely. One day he must face judgment. When he does, it mustn't be said that you, his wife, are also his accomplice."

"I know you're not a liar, so I must believe you're deluded. But don't you see how ridiculous this is? You come to me with wild tales about my husband and no proof at all. You listen to the slander of his enemies, men whose names you can't or won't reveal. You come to me with poisonous accusations and expect me to take your unsupported word for their truth. You blacken my husband's name and you try to destroy his marriage." She had worked herself into a fine rage. "I despise you for it, Brenn Wate Basef, and tell you to your face that you should be ashamed!"

"You cannot anger me, my Verran, for I know you're not responsible for what you say. Fal Grizhni speaks through your lips." She started to answer furiously, and he forestalled her. "But I will save you despite yourself. You needn't take my unsupported word for anything. All of Lanthi Ume is awakening to the danger, and I can prove it. I have something to show you."

He opened the leather pouch that hung at his waist, withdrew a piece of paper, unfolded it and handed the sheet to Verran.

It was a large broadside. The first thing that caught her eye was a crude woodcut portrait of Fal Grizhni, wherein the savant wore an expression of lupine ferocity. Winged, demonic figures hovered about his head. There was printing below the picture and Verran read:

Lanthi Ume Preserv'd; A Plot Discovered

Let it be known to all Men that Lanthi Ume is threatened

with grave Peril. It has been discovered and proved beyond all Question, upon sound Evidence, that the wicked
and bloodthirsty black Sorcerer of the Select, the Lord
Terrs Fal Grizhni, together with divers other Magicians
and the Witch Gaerase Vay Nennevay, plot against the
public Weal. Already the Sorcerers live in Splendor purchased at the Price of human Misery, for it has been
disclos'd that the Silver of the Commons now reposes in
Lord Grizhni's Vaults, whither our tax Monies are trans-
ported by magic Art. This stolen Wealth has but whetted
the Greed of the Traitors, who now plot to murder the
Duke and all his Family, and set themselves up as Kings
and Princes.

Further it is revealed that Terrs Fal Grizhni has enlisted
the Aid of the White Demons of the Caverns to assist him
in his Endeavor. This he has done by undertaking to
promise the Demons they shall have human Babes to feed
upon. Thus will Fal Grizhni and his Cohorts demand a
human Tribute of the Commons of Lanthi Ume, and our
Children shall nourish the devilish Appetites of hideous
Monsters.

Be assured this will come to pass, if the brave Commons
of Lanthi Ume do not take arms against Treachery.
Therefore heed this Warning, all among you with the
Spirit to resist Tyranny and unnatural Cruelty.

The League of Patriots

Verran read it at a glance. "Where did you get this thing?"

"They've been posted all over the city for the last day or
two," Brenn replied.

"All over the city? But why? It's vile, it's filled with lies—"

"Is it? Are you certain?"

"Yes, I'm certain! I know Lord Grizhni, and none of this is
true!"

Brenn looked at her pityingly, but said nothing.

"How could any sensible person believe such nonsense? The
White Demons of the Caverns are only a legend, everyone
knows that! They don't even exist!"

"Yes they do. They're real."

"What's the League of Patriots?"

"What the name implies, I imagine."

"Well, they're filthy liars and they should be stopped from spreading such stories! The Duke ought to find them and lock them up."

"It's not easy to stifle the truth."

"This is not the truth! For the first time in my life I'm glad that so few people know how to read."

"Information has a way of spreading, Verran. Look." Brenn pointed. At the far end of the Sunburst Float a crowd of citizens clustered around a man who was reading the broadside aloud.

"This must stop right now. I'm going over there to talk to them."

"Don't try it," Brenn advised. "If those people learn that you're Grizhni's wife, even your hybrid servant won't be able to protect you."

"I don't care. I want to hear what they're saying." Without pausing to await his reply, she turned and approached the rapt citizens. Brenn and Nyd followed. They drew near just as the reading concluded. For a moment there was silence and then a blue-smocked tradesman with a clever plump face observed concisely, "Rat turds."

Several listeners nodded, but many seemed doubtful and some looked frankly appalled. One hungry-eyed fellow inquired, "What makes you so sure about that?"

"Common sense. For one thing, it's not the Select who keep raising our taxes. If you want someone to blame for that, then blame our Duke and his fancy favorites. As for the business about feeding babies to the White Demons, that's a tale to frighten children and idiots. Which are you?"

"Neither, Master Know-All. Since you're so wise, please tell me how ordinary men can know what the Lord Grizhni might not do? Tell us all how *you* know *that*!"

"At least the Duke and his nobles are human, and everybody can be sure of it. They don't practice magic and they don't hobnob with demons. Can you say as much for the Select?" demanded an uneasy apprentice.

"Most of the Select are human enough. But Preeminence Fal Grizhni is Ert's son. This is a fact." The speaker was a laborer with a slow voice and an air of absolute certainty.

Verran held her tongue with difficulty.

"The Select have no reason to plot against the Duke or against the Commons."

"What reason would a son of Ert need? His natural malignity would suffice."

"There's no proof."

"The League of Patriots says there is."

"Where is it, then?"

"And what's this League of Patriots?"

"Very brave men, that's what."

"I don't know about plots," a querulous new voice chimed in. "But I do know that things in this city are getting worse and worse for the Commons, what with the taxes and the high prices on food these days. But the Duke, the nobles, and the Select are all thriving. We're hungry, and they're all fat. If there's any plot, then they're all in it together, against us."

This sentiment appeared to strike a responsive chord, and a babble of angry assent arose.

"Things will get worse yet unless we fight back."

"Good, but fight back how? Fight who?"

"Our enemies—"

"The tax collectors."

"The greedy merchants."

"The Ducal Guards."

"The fat nobles."

"The Select."

"Fal Grizhni—son of Ert."

"Fal Grizhni—King of Demons."

"Wait—" Verran begged, goaded beyond endurance. "Listen—"

Around her the debate continued and no one heard her pleas save Brenn Wate Basef. "You see, Verran? You see how they feel about Grizhni? And with good reason. Come, this isn't a safe place for you. If you wish, I'll escort you home. But if you're wise, you'll never return to Grizhni's house. You'll seek refuge with your father. Or better yet, you'll come away with me this instant and both our lives will be as they were meant to be."

"Meant to be?" She could barely contain her rage and fright. "Let me tell you something, Brenn. If I ever believed that I cared anything about you, our meeting has destroyed that illusion once and for all. My marriage to Lord Grizhni is the best thing that ever happened to me, and—"

"He *has* done something to your mind!" Brenn exclaimed. "You must be rescued!"

"And I'll be happy indeed if I never set eyes on you again!

Come on, Nyd." Verran whirled and stalked away, leaving
Brenn to gaze after her in pained confusion. Soon a hired
dombulis bore her over the water toward Grizhni Palace. She
still clutched the broadside in one hand. As it became spat-
tered with canal water the printing blurred, but not so badly
that she couldn't read the outrageous text again and again.
With each reading, her anger deepened. "Brenn's a fool," she
muttered between clenched teeth. "A stupid, bigoted, credu-
lous, irresponsible fool." Nyd croaked in agreement and the
dombulman regarded both passengers curiously. "Always attacking what he doesn't understand," she continued bitterly,
then paused as she recalled Brenn's question: What do you actually know of Fal Grizhni?

"I know enough," she told Nyd. "I know enough to be sure
that this paper is full of lies. Lord Grizhni isn't evil, he's just
different. His enemies are scared and jealous. It would be better if he let the people meet him and know him—then perhaps
they'd understand. But he'll never do that. He'll say he hasn't
the inclination. Do you think he might be doing himself harm,
Nyd?"

Nyd croaked reassuringly. He did not understand her, but
caught the worry in her voice.

The dombulman strained his ears in vain. His interest was
piqued by the fair-haired girl who muttered so earnestly to her
gray-shrouded companion.

"Perhaps I should show him this broadside," Verran went
on. "The lies would anger him, though. Maybe I should hide
it and say nothing. But if they're posted all over town, he's
bound to see one before long, no matter what I do. But I must
speak to him, Nyd. And soon."

The dombulis touched Grizhni moorings. Verran dashed
into the palace with Nyd trailing in her wake. For a time the
hybrid shadowed her as she roamed the halls in search of her
husband, and finally she sent him away. Having failed to locate Grizhni elsewhere, Verran reluctantly approached his
workroom. Ordinarily she did not like to disturb the savant at
work, but today there was just cause.

The girl pressed her ear to the workroom door. She heard
voices within; musical, harmonious voices that unnerved her
—inhuman voices. Verran took a deep breath and opened the
door. Before her towered Fal Grizhni, and with him stood the
White Demons of the Caverns.

There were four of them—tall, emaciated, pallid figures. They resembled men in outline, but they surely were not human. Their huge, brilliant eyes were utterly alien. Their flesh, Verran noted with revulsion, was luminous. It radiated a faint, weird glow, clearly visible in the dimly lighted chamber.

She gave an involuntary cry. The noise attracted the attention of the Demons, and their reaction was incomprehensible. Their great, uncanny eyes flashed in her direction and their voices blended in strange harmony.

Fal Grizhni came forward swiftly and stood before her, blocking her view of the Demons. "What is it, Madam?"

"I'm . . . sorry to interrupt your work," Verran stammered. "I must speak to you. It's important."

Grizhni looked closely at her, nodded, and stepped out of the workroom, closing the door behind him.

"What are those *creatures*?" Verran whispered.

"Nothing to fear. You are troubled. What is the cause?"

"This." She handed him the broadside. "I got it from Brenn Wate Basef this afternoon. He says they've been posted all over town."

Grizhni perused the text with his customary impassivity, studied the woodcut portrait, and observed at last, "It is not a good likeness."

"The picture? Or the words?"

"Either."

"They *are* lies, aren't they?"

"The information printed here is inaccurate. Did you fear otherwise?"

"Not at first," she replied uncertainly. "I told Brenn that it was nonsense, especially the part about the White Demons of the Caverns. They're a myth, I thought. But Brenn says they exist."

"In a sense he is correct."

"I believe it now. Those—*things* in there." She pointed at the closed door. "It's true. There are White Demons here in this house. If the broadside is full of lies, then why are the demons here?" He did not answer at once, and she added, "My lord, I trust you. But will you not explain?"

"I see by your face you fear to offend me. Set your mind at rest. Your curiosity is not unreasonable and I am not displeased. Be assured I have no designs on the life of the Duke or his family members. He is an incompetent ruler whose removal

would benefit the state, but I would not resort to murder to effect such removal, nor do I aspire to his place. As for the
'White Demons,' the creatures sometimes referred to by that
title are for the most part harmless unless threatened. Four of
them now are present in this house as my guests, and they are
by no means demonic."

"But what are they, my lord?"

"They are Vardruls, native inhabitants of the caves of Dalyon. They are shy, retiring, and intelligent—altogether more
appealing than humans, to whom they are closely related."

"Those monsters are related to us?"

"Obviously. Did you not note their similarity to men?"

"They're like ghastly caricatures. The similarity to men is
just what makes them so horrible."

"They are not at all horrible, Madam. In fact, in most essential areas we humans suffer by comparison. The Vardruls
lack our courage and ferocity. Their fears confine them underground, but I have so far prevailed with them that a delegation
has consented to enter this city under my protection. I have
guaranteed their anonymity and expect your cooperation in
guarding the secret of their presence."

"But somebody's already seen them," Verran objected.
"The League of Patriots, whoever they may be, must somehow have glimpsed the white creatures, the . . . Vardruls, mistaken them for demons as I did, and assumed the worst. If
only you could find this League and convince them of their error, then maybe they'd stop spreading lies about you—"

Fal Grizhni's smile was sour. "You are an innocent,
Madam. There is no League of Patriots. The publication that
has caused you such distress is a thing devised by my enemies,
who perceive my present conflict with the Duke as an opportunity to work my downfall. They hereby give me notice of their
intentions and their methods."

"Then you are in danger?"

"Perhaps, but theirs is greater," he replied dryly.

"Shouldn't the Vardruls leave? If they're seen, it will make
people believe that the stories are true, won't it?"

"The Vardruls will leave at their own discretion. They are
my guests and their presence honors my house. I do not believe them to be in jeopardy. But I am not sure the same can be
said of you. The conflict to come may prove unpleasant. Your
position as my wife places you in some peril. It might be best

that you retire to one of my country estates for a time."

Verran felt her face go hot, as if she had been slapped. "Leave my home? Leave *you*? No. I won't do it."

"As your husband and your lord, I am responsible for your welfare." Grizhni's voice was chill and precise. "I expect my decisions on your behalf to be accepted without argument."

"But I don't want to go, my lord! I'm your wife and I belong here!"

"You belong where I choose to send you."

"*I don't want to leave!*" Her voice broke. Tears gushed out of her eyes and she began to sob miserably.

Fal Grizhni appeared taken aback. "There is no need for this outcry. Try to control yourself, Madam," he advised in a softened voice. "You must realize that I act in your best interests—"

"You don't understand," Verran sobbed, "or you'd never talk of sending me away at a time like this! Not now!"

"We may negotiate the matter if you will stop crying. I urge you to cease, Madam. Please."

She did not comply. "Of all the times that I ought to be here with you, this is surely the most important—now that I'm with child." She had intended to find some graceful means of introducing this topic, but the present moment seemed too propitious to waste.

"You are with child? You are certain?" he asked in surprise. She nodded. "How long?"

"About six weeks, I think."

Grizhni was not given to displays of sentiment, but his rare smile shone and his eyes lightened wonderfully. It was extraordinary how youthful he suddenly looked. "I am gratified, Madam. I am most pleased."

"Are you, my dear lord?"

"I am"—he searched for the right word and pronounced it with faint astonishment—"happy."

Verran's eyes still brimmed with tears. Grizhni drew her close and kissed her, as she had hoped he might. He spoke no more of sending her away.

Chapter Eight

❧❧❧❧

Autumn brought unrest to Lanthi Ume, and Duke Povon found himself vexed. In the first place, there was the matter of Cru Beffel's ships. Three vessels belonging to Beffel had been wrecked in a fearful storm off the coast of Strell, and their valuable cargoes lost. It was Fal Grizhni's doing, of course. Such a thing could never have happened had his Preeminence not deliberately discontinued Selectic protection of maritime trading routes. Grizhni was practically a murderer. But instead of placing blame on the savant, who clearly deserved it, Cru Beffel chose to believe that the Duke's actions had caused the tragedy. Now the aggrieved lord's complaints and reproaches made Povon's life miserable. And Beffel wasn't the only one. There were at least half a dozen prominent nobles engaged in exactly the same kind of tiresome misbehavior, at Grizhni's instigation without doubt.

There had been an outbreak of burglaries in the palaces of the great, chiefly owing to the failure of Selectic guards against intrusion. Voracious marine worms had recently attacked the dockyard pilings and the wharfs had weakened. This, too, was the result of Grizhni's malice.

It was a terrible thing, Povon reflected, to deal with a destructive, malignant Preeminence. What a pity it was that a savant of understanding and sympathy, a man like Saxas Gless Vallage, couldn't lead the Select! How much more agreeable life would be! Saxas, for example, would understand the necessity of maintaining cordial relations with the Keldhar of Gard Lammis. The Keldhar had proved a little demanding of late, it was true; but his continuing goodwill was essential to the well-being of Lanthi Ume. The Keldhar was offering a generous loan in exchange for unlimited toll-free access to the Straits of Wythe, which were guarded by a Lanthian fortress perched like an eagle on the Cliffs of Wythe. Povon had found it expedient to agree, and now Fal Grizhni marshalled the forces of the Select in opposition. Such concerted defiance verged on treason, the Duke concluded. In fact, Saxas had informed him that a sizable party among the city Commons regarded Grizhni as a public menace. The League of Patriots —concerned citizens, all of them—regularly printed and distributed denunciatory broadsides, the most recent of which demanded Grizhni's immediate arrest and execution. If only it were as simple as that, how happy Duke Povon would be to comply with his good subjects' wishes! Alas, it was no easy matter to dispose of a savant of Terrs Fal Grizhni's power, for the man's malevolence was boundless, and an attack upon him was bound to provoke retaliation of some unpleasant variety. Moreover, the Select were arrogant and might well venture to protest the removal of their leader. Such opposition could prove troublesome, and Povon loathed discord. Why did life have to be so difficult? Why couldn't he be left to rule in peace and justice, as he desired above all things? Why couldn't his subjects offer him a little loyalty, support, gratitude, and appreciation for a change? Why couldn't some useful citizen plant a knife between Fal Grizhni's ribs, where it would do the most good? Why?

Duke Povon pondered these questions at length, but reached no satisfactory conclusions. Fortunately, young Beskot Kor Malifon was holding his Emerald Masquerade that very night. The Masquerade was to be highlighted by a grand ball and pageant, wherein Zellanese dancers would parade before the guests in costumes literally encrusted with emeralds. It was rumored that Beskot had sold two of his finest country estates to finance the pageant, but it would have been vulgar to inquire closely into such matters. Beskot was too great an aristocrat and too fine an artist to count the cost.

Duke Povon contemplated the festivities soon to come, and his oppressed spirits lightened.

•   •   •

The weeks that brought such a burden of care to Duke Povon were kind to Lady Verran. The encounter with Brenn Wate Basef faded from her mind. Her pregnancy was healthy and progressed with minimal discomfort. Her husband was attentive. She neither saw nor heard anything more of the White Demons. Much of her time was spent in consultation with female friends and relatives, all of whom had advice to offer concerning the delivery and care of infants. The women clearly regarded her with warmth. They spoke much of children, but whenever Verran mentioned her husband, they invariably changed the subject. Verran wondered why, but did not let it trouble her. It was necessary at that time for her to pay many visits, for her friends refused to set foot within Grizhni Palace. She half expected that Fal Grizhni might be reluctant to permit her to travel about the city. He favored the feminine companionship for her, however, and consented to the visits on condition that no less than three guards accompany her at all times. Similarly Verran had believed her husband might forbid her the long walks along the canals that she so enjoyed, for it was well known that pregnant women should avoid all forms of exertion. To her surprise, Grizhni encouraged the exercise.

Thus it was that Verran strolled the Sandivell Path on a golden afternoon in autumn. Nyd walked at her side and three other hybrids followed close behind. The sunlight was soft on her face and gentle on the canals. The sights of the city were absorbing, as always, and Verran was content—until she spied the paper fastened to the base of the statue of Zin Greevis. She knew what it was at once, on instinct. Another broadside, another outpouring of lies and filth. They were all over the city now, tacked up on public buildings, on statues, on fountains; posted in the taverns, inns, and market squares; plastered over the wharfs and dockyards; everywhere. There were new ones every day. The League of Patriots was nothing if not prolific. Verran had begged her husband time and again to destroy the broadsides. His powers would easily have enabled him to do so, and he would have been entirely justified. But Fal Grizhni did not deign to note the effusions of his enemies. He ignored all libel and urged Verran to do the same; advice she could not follow. Now the girl and her entourage hastened to the statue for a closer look.

The broadside was torn and stained. Evidently it had been

posted for some time. It bore a sinister portrait of Fal Grizhni and its message was succinct:

Treachery Reveal'd

It has lately been disclosed by nameless Sources that the Servants of the loathly Lord Terrs Fal Grizhni are Demons snatch'd by magic Art from the Underworld, and Fal Grizhni himself is no less than King of Demons. The Presence of these evil Spirits within our City Walls is a Danger to us All, and so let the Brave and Free among us heed the Warning of

—The League of Patriots

Verran ripped the broadside off the statue, crumpled it into a ball, and flung it into the Sandivell Canal. Her action was observed by a band of university scholars. The young fellows drifted near. Their interest seemed harmless. They ogled Verran with forgivable impertinence and eyed the hybrid servants with curiosity. The hybrids were well-muffled. Their voluminous hoods and robes completely shielded them from view. The scholars wanted a closer look. When Verran and her companions moved off along the walkway, the young men followed.

At first Verran wasn't worried. The scholars stumbling in her wake were mildly embarrassing, nothing more. But soon their comments, which she was clearly intended to overhear, began to trouble her.

"She's handsome. Very handsome."

"Too pretty to be wandering around alone."

"Frakki, you nincompoop, she's got four servants with her. That's not exactly alone."

"Servants don't count. She'd be much happier in the company of scholars and gentlemen. Do you think the pretty lady might take a glass of wine with us?"

A voice with a touch of warning in it replied, "No, I don't think she would. You wouldn't ask if you knew who she is."

"Oh, and you *do* know, I suppose?"

"Yes, as it happens, I *do* know."

Verran's cheeks began to burn. She frowned and quickened her pace. The inquisitive students hurried to keep up.

"You're bluffing, Reedo. A hundred dakkles says you don't know her."

"You're on. Anyone else care to wager?"

A joyous babble of voices arose behind Lady Verran. By this time the little parade was attracting the amused attention of numerous spectators. She turned to Nyd. "This is embarrassing, and Lord Grizhni won't be pleased if he hears about it. Let's go home."

Nyd croaked in assent. The other three hybrids drew near to surround their mistress closely.

The students had arranged all bets to their satisfaction. "All right, Reedo—now we're for it! Speak up or pay up!"

"Willingly. Gentlemen, brace yourselves for a thunderbolt. That pretty little lady is none other than Lady Grizhni, wife of his Preeminence himself. Frakki, you owe me one hundred dakkles."

But Frakki was unready to admit defeat. "Preposterous. Your head's full of feathers if you think I'm going to swallow that. Lady Grizhni indeed!"

"Well, she is. Look at that badge the servants wear—it's got the Fal Grizhni arms. You'll make good your wager if you're a man of honor."

"I'll pay when I'm convinced I've lost, and I can tell you I'm not half convinced. But we can settle this easily enough."

Verran made swiftly for the Grizhni dombulis, which was moored not far away. The surrounding gray forms of the hybrids nearly hid her from public view. It was her hope to withdraw as unobtrusively as possible, but in this she was unsuccessful.

Frakki, a pleasant-faced lad with an abortive moustache, ran to intercept her. "Your ladyship, if I might be so bold—" He caught the warning flash of her blue eyes but refused to be discouraged. "If I might inquire—" She did not slacken her pace, and the young man stretched out a hand to detain her. A violent shove from one of the hybrids, an inexperienced creature named Glys, sent him sprawling. His companions roared with laughter. Frakki bounced to his feet.

"Glys, you needn't be so—" Verran began.

Frakki planted himself athwart their path. "Your ladyship's attendants are zealous, but I must learn the truth of—" This time the talons of Glys raked the unfortunate student from elbow to wrist. Frakki yelped and fell back, his sleeve bloodied.

The fracas attracted an audience, and the crowd gathered quickly. It was composed of scholars, apprentices, tradesmen, beggars, marketwomen, quick-darting ragamuffins—a fair sampling of the diverse Commons of Lanthi Ume. Being Lanthian, they were both curious and intensely volatile. Questions and comments swarmed through the air like locusts.

"Did you see that? One of the servants pulled a knife."

"It wasn't a knife—he used his claws."

"What are you talking about? Men don't have claws like that."

"I've got news for you—that isn't a man."

The scholars conferred for a moment, then advanced en masse on the hybrids.

Verran cast an alarmed glance at the young men and spoke urgently to Nyd. "Get us out of here. Right away!"

Nyd croaked imperatively to his fellows, but it was already too late. Glys leaped forward with a scream, seized a struggling scholar, lifted and flung the astonished young man into the Sandivell Canal. His colleagues rushed forward, the crowd cheered, and someone shouted, "Summon the Watch!"

Reedo struck Glys like a stone from a slingshot and the force of the impact carried the hybrid backward several paces. For a moment the two figures grappled, pounded and tore each other before toppling to the ground. It soon became clear that Reedo was hopelessly outmatched. The claws of Glys flashed in the afternoon sun, and instantly the young man was streaming blood from a dozen wicked cuts. Reedo yelled and struck out violently. One of his random blows caught Glys in the midriff. Glys uttered a furious snarl and seized his opponent by the throat. His talons sank deep into the flesh, and Reedo's cries dwindled to feeble moans.

Shouting students now threw themselves upon Glys. The hybrid hissed and released Reedo, who dropped to his knees and crawled away. The remaining hybrids leaped into the fray.

Fal Grizhni's servants were deadly, particularly Nyd. Within seconds three scholars lay groaning upon the soil and a fourth had taken to his heels. Nyd's wavering war cry arose in triumph, but too soon. Another cry from young human throats arose and surpassed it.

"Scholars—friends—'Ware Cits! Ward the University!" It was the students' ancient call for assistance, and never in the history of Lanthi Ume had it been raised in vain. Within sec-

onds a gang of scholars had converged upon the spot, and
more were arriving by the second. Close behind them came
a party of Ducal Guards, together with scores of interested
citizens.

"Glys—Nyd—stop it!" Verran commanded uselessly. They
could not or would not hear her. Lord Grizhni, she realized,
would be enraged. Beside her stood the post to which her dombulis was lashed. She turned to the mooring line and struggled
frantically with the knot.

By this time dozens of students had arrived upon the scene
and their combined numbers proved overwhelming even to the
ferocity of Fal Grizhni's creatures. Somebody had a stick, and
a well-directed blow took Glys soundly across the shoulders.
The hybrid staggered, recovered himself, and sprang forward
with a hiss. As he leapt his hood fell back, exposing the hairy,
flat-featured countenance. Instinctively the crowd pulled back
and two or three people screamed. And truly Glys was a terrifying sight, half crouching in the sunlight with lips contorted,
fangs exposed, and facial hair bristling as he faced a host of
enemies.

The cry arose spontaneously. "*Demons!*"

Somebody recognized the badge and called out, "The demons of Fal Grizhni! Grizhni's demons!"

"The King of Demons sends his children! Brothers, we are
attacked!"

Shrieks of terror arose, and hoarse roars of execration.
Many citizens fled, but the braver and angrier among them remained.

"That's not true!" Verran cried. "Listen to me!"

They did not heed her. There was sudden hysteria there;
rage, screaming fear, confusion, and the promise of incipient
mass panic. A thick-armed, thick-necked laborer strode forward and thrust the young students from his path. He wielded
a pickaxe. When he spoke, his voice was harsh with fear. "I'm
not afraid of a sorcerer's demons. I'm not afraid of Grizhni
himself. Here's how I handle demons." He swung the axe.

Glys dodged—not fast enough. The point of the axe plunged
into his neck. Blood spurted impossibly high, to fall like a
ghastly rain upon the crowd. Glys fell without a sound. He
was already dead, but the excited Lanthians kicked and beat
and stabbed the prostrate form as if to assure themselves that
even a demon could be vanquished.

The remaining hybrids, nestmates all of the slaughtered Glys, howled in grief and rage. The desolate harmony froze the Lanthian crowd for a single instant, and in that instant Grizhni's servants hurled themselves upon their brother's killer and rent him fatally with fang and claw.

The dying man's groans awakened the full fury of his comrades. Someone shouted "Kill the demons!" and the crowd took up the cry.

"Kill them!"

Cudgels and staves appeared. Sticks were clenched in sweaty fists. Many men carried daggers and some owned swords. The neediest citizens did not go weaponless, for there were rocks to be had for free.

"Kill Grizhni's demons!"

Verran watched in terror as a dagger sank to the hilt into the back of a hybrid. The creature gave a rasping cry and fell. The crowd roared and eager hands tore the gray robes away. When the spiked and alien form of Fal Grizhni's servant was revealed to view, general hysteria mounted to the level of madness. Merciless blades ripped the dying creature's flesh and equally merciless hands plunged into the wounds to tear organs from the outraged body.

Similar treatment was swiftly meted out to a third hybrid, despite its fierce resistance. Of Verran's four companions, only Nyd still remained on his feet. Nyd had discarded his gray robe to permit himself freedom of movement, and it was not difficult to see how he might be mistaken for a demon as he leaped, dodged, and spun with a speed that seemed supernatural. Blood dripped from his teeth and claws, his eyes flamed, and two human corpses already lay stretched at his feet. So terrifying was his aspect that there was a momentary lull in the conflict as his attackers instinctively retreated before him.

Verran realized that the respite would be brief, and she seized the one moment in which her light voice could possibly make itself heard. "Nyd—over here! Come to me!"

Nyd heard her. He could not see above the heads of the crowd that separated them, but he sprang straight for the sound of her voice. So high and so swiftly did he leap that he seemed to fly like the demon they mistook him for, with glinting fangs and flickering bright talons to complete the illusion. Citizens drew hastily aside to clear his path, and those that did not do so were flung to the ground. Verran continued to fight

with the line that bound the dombulis. The knot was tight and
damp. By no means could she undo it. For a moment she
struggled, breaking her fingernails on the hard rope. The
broken nails reminded her of the nail file carried in the pouch
at her waist, and she quickly withdrew it. The tiny, jeweled
object had no edge, but its point was fairly sharp. Verran
jammed the point of the file into the knot, which gradually
loosened.

Nyd's leap carried him halfway to his mistress. The shock
and fear that temporarily paralyzed the crowd soon dispelled,
savage shouts arose, and several of the boldest Lanthians came
at Nyd with lue-wood sendillis oars. Blows rained down upon
the hybrid's head and torso. Nyd snarled, slashed blindly, and
where he struck, blood flowed.

Rocks began to fly. Some thudded into the hybrid's body,
while others missed their target and slammed straight into the
thick of the mob. A stone grazed his cheek and Nyd instinctively threw an arm up to shield his head. He staggered, and
for a moment it seemed he must fall—in which case he would
never get up again.

"This way, Nyd!" Verran cried, and once again he heard
her.

Her voice lent him fresh courage. It might have been the
knowledge that Fal Grizhni's lady must be protected at all
costs that gave Nyd the strength to battle his way through the
homicidal mob. He arrived at Verran's side just as she succeeded in loosing the last knot and freeing the dombulis.

Verran jumped down into the boat and Nyd followed. The
little craft pitched perilously, nearly capsized, and Verran held
her breath. Nyd grabbed the oars, plied them furiously, and
the boat drew away from the pier.

New shouts arose.

"Who's the woman?"

"A witch consorting with Grizhni's demons!"

Flung rocks splashed into the Sandivell Canal in the wake of
the fleeing dombulis, but all fell short of their mark. Verran
wondered if they would be pursued. The mob was enraged to
the point of recklessness, and there were plenty of boats to be
had. She glanced back fearfully. Behind her the crowd seethed
fiercely, but there was no sign of pursuit. She turned to Nyd.
He was bleeding freely from a profusion of cuts. One eye was
already swollen shut, he had lost large patches of fur, and two

of the spikes of his ruff were broken and dangling. Nevertheless the poor creature rowed indefatigably. Verran found that her eyes were wet with tears, and she dashed them away. "I don't understand," she whispered. "They must be mad."

In due course they reached the junction of the Lureis, and Grizhni Palace. Verran entrusted Nyd to the care of his nestmates and ran in search of her husband. She soon discovered that Grizhni was not at home. No one knew when he would return. She curbed her frustration with difficulty, for she was desperate to tell him what had happened.

She rejoined the hybrids and assisted in bandaging Nyd's wounds and setting his broken spikes. The creatures were sunk in gloom. Quite obviously they understood that three of their nestmates had been slain. Verran sang to them, choosing plaintive melodies, and the hybrids took comfort. Presently they joined in with mournful croaks. Thus they were engaged an hour later when Fal Grizhni returned.

One look at her husband's face told Verran that he already knew what had happened. The steely quality of his expression was unfamiliar to her, and for a moment she was frightened. So menacing was his appearance that once again she wondered if the stories about him could be true. He looked capable of violence or worse, and as Verran slowly stood, she was conscious of a certain sick feeling in the pit of her stomach.

He came across the room to her and asked, "You are unhurt?"

She nodded, and the tears rose to her eyes. "I'm all right. But the servants—Jatsil, Mor, and poor young Glys—they're dead. The people on the Sandivell Path saw Glys and were frightened, and a fight started—and—" She swallowed and continued with difficulty, "And all of a sudden there was shouting and confusion and—and blood all over the place, and three of your creatures were dead. Nyd and the others went wild when they saw Glys slaughtered. They killed the townsman who did it, and during the fight Nyd killed at least two more. There were guardsmen there and they didn't even try to help. But what will happen to Nyd now? He's killed men and he must flee the city."

Nyd greeted this suggestion with whimpers and croaks. His reddish eyes widened and he wriggled.

Fal Grizhni turned to his servant. "Do not fear. You will not go." Nyd subsided in obvious relief.

"But how can he stay, my lord?" Verran inquired. "He's taken human lives. No matter what the provocation, the vengeance of the townsfolk will—"

"The townsfolk have greater cause to fear my vengeance, Madam." She did not answer at once, and he added, "You do not seem to realize that you yourself might well have been injured or killed. They hurled rocks at you, did they not?"

"Only at the very end, when I was in the boat with Nyd. And none of them even came close to hitting us. They were—"

"A murderous rabble attacked my wife. *My wife.*" The look on his face made Verran flinch.

"They didn't know I'm your wife, I think," she replied quickly. "It was the hybrids that frightened them. They actually believed that Nyd and the others were demons. It's because of those lying broadsides that have been—"

"I do not heed the broadsides. They are beneath contempt. What is of concern to me is the violence these peasants have dared offer you."

"I'm well, my lord—quite well. But what of Nyd? It's certain that the Commons will demand justice—"

"And they shall have it," he replied with ominous significance.

"My lord, I don't know what you intend, but I must beg you not to—"

Verran never finished her request, for at that moment a rock came flying through the open window, whizzed past her head, and spent its force against the opposing wall. Nyd hissed and leaped to his feet, despite his wounds. Fal Grizhni seized his wife, swung her out of the way, and interposed himself between the girl and the window.

"Who is it?" she cried. "Did the crowd follow us home?"

Another rock came flying in, and another. Shouting could be heard outside. Something dark and furry arched through the window and thudded softly to the floor. It was the decaying carcass of a rat. A strangled sound escaped Verran.

"Nyd, Kevyd, and the rest of you," Fal Grizhni addressed the hybrids deliberately. "Escort Lady Grizhni to her apartment. Lock the door from within, shutter all windows, and remain with her until I give you leave to depart. Should strangers attempt entry, kill them. You understand?"

There could be no doubt whatever that they understood.

"Please, my lord, I'd rather remain with you."

"Madam, obey me!" Grizhni signaled his servants, who gently shepherded her from the room.

Verran didn't try to resist. With some resignation she accompanied the hybrids back to her apartment, where the outer door was barred in accordance with Grizhni's commands. Verran sought the sanctuary of her bedchamber. There the shutters were drawn, but she was able to squint through the chink between them to the canal below. What she saw was disheartening. There was a crowd gathered down there—far larger than the crowd on Sandivell Path, and just as hostile. Their shouts and curses were clearly audible to her where she stood. Angry citizens milled on Grizhni moorings. Many of them carried rocks, dead rats, fish, and refuse with which to bombard the palace. A host of dombuli had gathered at the junction of the Lureis and Sandivell. They formed a blockade that would effectively prevent departure from Grizhni Palace by boat.

A random stone crashed against the bedroom shutter. Verran instinctively jerked her head back, then reapplied her eye to the chink. The yelling had grown louder, and the language was vile. "What do they want?" she whispered more to herself than to her hybrid bodyguard. "Have they a definite purpose? What is it they're trying to do?"

It was doubtful that the mob had any clear-cut objective in mind. The same could not be said of Terrs Fal Grizhni.

A slight tremor shook Grizhni Palace and its environs. Verran put a hand against the shutter to steady herself. Had the building actually shivered, or had she suffered a dizzy spell? She looked back over her shoulder and saw the hybrids wobbling. Another tremor hit, this one unmistakable.

Down below on Grizhni moorings the shouts of rage dwindled to cries of alarm. Black clouds materialized in a blue sky and veiled the face of the sun. The world darkened. A breeze sprang up, a dank, cold, carrion-stinking breeze like the breath of a mausoleum. Swiftly the breeze gathered force and speed. A mighty wind was born, a foul and freezing gale that carried darkness with it. The city was shrouded in shadow. Gray twilight reigned. The Lanthians on the moorings staggered under the sudden onslaught of the wind. Their hair and garments streamed wildly. The flying grit and debris scourged them all.

"Lord Grizhni," Verran said very softly.

The waters of the canal were lashed to foaming frenzy. The dombuli pitched, veered, collided. The little boats began to capsize, despite the best efforts of experienced oarsmen. Scores of terrified Lanthians were plunged into the canal and found themselves unable to swim to shore.

The riot had been aborted, and the citizens sought to flee. But Grizhni was not yet satisfied. The thunder roared, the heavens split, and riding the wings of the howling wind came gigantic bat shapes, tangible manifestations of the wrath of Fal Grizhni. The shriek of the gale overwhelmed the screams of the populace as the horrific creatures descended. Then the world was lost in darkness, confusion, and sick terror. Vast wings blackened the air, blotted out the sky, beat in frightful concert with wind and water.

It did not last long. Having utterly demoralized their victims, the bat shapes departed, bearing the darkness with them. The wind died and the waters quieted. Almost before the skies had lightened, the place was deserted. The moorings were empty. The canal was littered with the floating wreckage of dombuli, but there was nary a human to be seen on the water.

It was believed at first to have been a great and terrible massacre inflicted by Preeminence Grizhni upon his foes. For a night and a day men spoke of the carnage in hushed tones. But finally it became apparent that despite the violence of the disturbance, not a single human life had been lost. Even those flung into the canals had amazingly escaped destruction. Survivors were puzzled by this, discussed it at length, and reached various conclusions. No one requested an explanation of Fal Grizhni himself. No one ventured to approach him at all. For days the canals and walkways around Grizhni Palace remained eerily silent, as befit the realm of the King of Demons.

Chapter Nine

❧❧❧❧❧

The first visitor Verran received following the incident on the Sandivell Path was her father. She chose to meet with him in her private sitting room, for somehow it seemed unfilial to subject a parent to the rigors of the Audience chamber. When the purpose of Dris Verras's visit was revealed, however, it became clear that the Audience chamber would have been the appropriate setting after all.

Dris Verras did not waste time. "Daughter," he announced, "I have committed an injustice. I have wronged you, and I am mightily sorry for it." He regarded her attentively.

Verran scrutinized her father with equal care. She noted the blandly familiar features, the plump hands neatly clasped, the air of spurious penitence. And she recalled with an unpleasant sensation that Dris Verras was but a scant five years older than her husband. Verras had chosen to visit on a day that Fal Grizhni was absent from home. Verran had some inkling of what was coming, but nonetheless inquired dutifully, "What do you mean, Father?"

"My dear child, how well do I recall the dismay with which you greeted the prospect of marriage to Preeminence Fal Grizhni. The memory of your tears, your terror, your pathetic pleas, haunts me yet. At the time I did not heed you. Dazzled by the brilliance of the proposed match, I ignored your misgivings. How much better for all concerned had I trusted in my daughter's instincts! For it cannot be denied that events of the

109

past few weeks have proven your fears well justified. Fal
Grizhni is no fit husband for a daughter of the House of Verras, or indeed the daughter of any noble House. I have given
my child into the keeping of a criminal.''

For a moment Verran floundered for a reply. Her glance
wandered about the sitting room of her private suite. She
recalled that she was mistress of vast Grizhni Palace and wife
of the greatest of all savants. When she answered, she spoke
with perfect courtesy, but for the first time addressed her
parent as an adult and an equal. ''You are mistaken, Father.''

''Eh?'' Verras was visibly startled. For a moment he was inclined to chide her impertinence, then recollected her altered
circumstances and held his tongue.

''You are wrong. May I ask why you describe Lord Grizhni
as a criminal?''

Dris Verras's surprise increased. Never before had his
daughter presumed to demand an explanation or a rationale.
Verran was changing. He decided that her elevated status had
gone to her head, but he concealed all trace of annoyance.
''My dear child, I fear I've offended you and such was not my
intent. I've no desire to inflict unnecessary pain. I have already caused injury by means of the cruel marriage forced
upon you at my instigation, and you may be certain I don't
wish to compound my error. As for Lord Grizhni, the man's
pernicious character has surely been demonstrated beyond all
question. The exploitation of Selectic Preeminence for purposes of personal malice, the incessant efforts to augment his
own power at the Duke's expense, and the recent appalling
outrage visited upon a host of innocent Lanthians assembled
on his moorings—these acts reveal Grizhni as a most dangerous criminal, even a traitor—''

''Please stop, Father. You haven't yet heard the truth of it.
People are spreading lies about my husband and they're doing
it very deliberately. *There's* where the true malice lies, not with
Lord Grizhni. Let me tell you what's actually been happening,
or as much of it as I understand. In the first place, as for that
riot on our moorings, you ought to know that the citizens
assembled there were bombarding the palace with rocks, and I
don't doubt for one moment that they'd have killed us if they
could—'' Suddenly it seemed very important to Verran to convince her father of Grizhni's blamelessness, but Dris Verras
was not about to listen.

"Child, I see you are as dutiful a wife as you were dutiful a daughter." He bestowed a pitying paternal smile upon her. "Your loyalty to your lord is commendable, but the truth of your wretched situation is quite apparent. There's no need to maintain pretenses with your father."

"Aren't you at all interested in hearing what actually happened?"

"I already know. The facts have been fully revealed by the League of Patriots."

"Don't tell me you believe those sneaking liars!"

"In light of recent happenings, how can I disbelieve? Terrs Fal Grizhni represents one of the greatest dangers this city has ever faced—a savant of extraordinary abilities determined to pervert his power to malignant ends of self-aggrandizement—"

"You wouldn't dare to say that to his face, Father."

"To be sure, I would not," Dris Verras agreed without rancor. "There are less painful methods of suicide."

"Did you come here for no other purpose than to insult my husband behind his back?"

"Yes, Daughter. I have come to put an end to your unhappiness. I have come to free you from prison."

"What are you talking about?"

"You will abandon Grizhni Palace. One day you may return to my house and your family will welcome you home with joy. At present, however, it is best that this matter be handled with discretion, and therefore I have decided that you must leave Lanthi Ume for a time. Your mother's kin in Gard Lammis will doubtless be willing to—"

"*You* have decided I'll leave Grizhni Palace?" Verran interrupted. She could feel her color rise, and anger quickened her heartbeat. "*You* have decided to exile me from husband and home? Do I have anything to say about this?"

"Child, you must accept the fact that I'm older and far wiser than you, and that I know what's best for you."

"That's just what you said when you married me off against my will."

"I was wrong to do so."

"No you weren't, as it happens. But you're wrong *now*, Father."

"Child, calm yourself and listen to me. You've just cause for anger, certainly. You have been treated with extreme, albeit unintentional, harshness. You were given in marriage to a vicious, unnatural tyrant, and your bitterness is understandable. But now the truth has become apparent, and it's time to put an end to your sufferings. Rest assured that a daughter of the Verras line may rely upon her family to protect her from harm."

"That is very gratifying, Father," Verran replied, and once again Dris Verras was discomfited by the girl's coolness. Had Verran been anything other than the most exemplary of daughters, he might almost have imagined a trace of sarcasm in her voice. "Gratifying and not quite what I would have expected. But Lord Grizhni and I are married. At your insistence I became his wife and that bond cannot be broken, even should I wish to do so. If I left Lord Grizhni and fled to Gard Lammis as you suggest, I'd still be his wife."

"That isn't necessarily true," Dris Verras replied with a promptness that suggested preparation. "In view of the unusual circumstances of your case—your youth, the unwillingness with which you entered into marriage, Grizhni's unnatural vices, and the extreme suffering you have undergone at the hands of such a man—it's not unlikely that a divorce may be obtained. In fact I may tell you in confidence that the Duke favors the suggestion. I've already conferred with his Grace and can almost promise that when the time is ripe, a divorce will be granted, whereupon you will be free to marry again. And this time you will perhaps be permitted a voice in the choosing of your new husband. Think of it, my child," Dris Verras wheedled. "A second wedding—fine new gowns, gifts, balls and parties in your honor, assurance of the Duke's favor, a husband of suitable age and rank—we may even consider young Wate Basef if you so desire. How many women are granted such an opportunity to start anew? Is it not a rare privilege?"

"Rare indeed," Verran replied. "But aren't you overlooking one detail, Father? You're well aware that I carry Lord Grizhni's child. As far as you're concerned, does that count for nothing?"

"It counts for a great deal," Dris Verras returned gravely. "We are speaking of my grandchild, my own flesh and blood. I am concerned for the welfare of my grandchild and of my daughter alike. Therefore I can tell you that you are obliged to leave this place, for the baby's sake if not your own. Come, Daughter—you cannot intend to raise a child in this dreadful palace of horrors? Surely you won't subject a helpless innocent to the dire influence of Terrs Fal Grizhni? The baby will grow to maturity as warped and twisted as Grizhni himself. Maternal duty demands your immediate departure.''

"You speak a great deal of duty, Father. My filial duty. My maternal duty. Your own paternal duty. The word comes very easily to your lips.'' Verran spoke with apparent calmness. Only the rigidity of the hands clasped in her lap betrayed her emotions. "I'm surprised you haven't yet reminded me of my duty to the House of Verras.''

"Do you need to be reminded?''

"Hardly. Recognition of that particular duty ordained my marriage to Lord Grizhni. I suspect you'll now inform me that it's in the best interests of all our House to terminate the marriage.''

"Ah, you recognize that? You are growing wise in the way of the world, Daughter. During these last weeks, Fal Grizhni has utterly discredited himself. He is the hated enemy both of the Duke and of the common citizenry. The Commons cry out against him night and day. The League of Patriots demands his arrest and execution. It has come to such a pass that the Verras alliance with Fal Grizhni dishonors all our House. Our name is blemished, and in the eyes of the populace we are tainted by association. It's unlikely that the situation will improve in the near future. Hence the reputation of the House of Verras may be preserved only at the expense of this most unfortunate connection. It must be severed here and now. Do you understand me, Daughter?''

"You've made yourself very clear, Father. But please explain one point. You've spoken of the accusations against Lord Grizhni—the crimes people believe he's committed, the danger they think he represents. But you've not stopped to consider the question of my husband's actual guilt or innocence. Just because a lot of people are telling stories about him, does that necessarily mean that those stories are true?''

Dris Verras shrugged indifferently. "Possibly not, but that is irrelevant. Fal Grizhni is greatly feared and hated, and that is sufficient to reflect unfavorably upon the kinsmen of Grizhni's wife.'' He ignored his daughter's pained expression. "Already I am eyed askance by many of my peers. Fortunately the Duke remains confident of my personal loyalty, but how long can his Grace continue to trust in the friendship of

his greatest enemy's father-in-law? And if the Duke turns
against us, what then? We are all ruined. Is that what you
seek? No, Daughter. Loyalty to your House requires the immediate dissolution of your disastrous union with Fal
Grizhni.''

"And what does loyalty to my husband demand?''

"You are scarcely more than a child, and you are not responsible. You owe Grizhni no loyalty. All of Lanthi Ume will
applaud your courage in leaving him. You need not fear covert
censure.''

"I don't fear censure, covert or otherwise.'' Her voice was
sharp with something akin to contempt. Dris Verras stiffened
at the sound of it. "It seems I pay less heed to public opinion
than you do, Father. I won't leave Lord Grizhni. In the first
place, I don't at all want to. Even were I not carrying his child,
I should not wish to go. In the second place, you ask me to
break my marriage vows for reasons that are poor, weak, and
shabby.''

"Loyalty to your own House is poor, weak, and shabby?''

"Fear of public opinion and fear of losing the Duke's favor
are your true motives.''

Dris Verras took a deep breath and controlled his temper.
"I've an older, wiser head and I know far more of life than
you ever will. You would do well to be guided by me, for your
lasting happiness is my chiefest concern.''

"That's untrue. My happiness is of no concern to you whatever, and never has been.''

"Don't be insolent. You've risen high, thanks to me, but I
am still your father and I will be treated with respect.''

"As you wish, sir. Is there anything more you care to
discuss?'' Verran inquired with mechanical courtesy.

Dris Verras scowled. "I fear there's little point in attempting to reason with you now. Your newfound eminence has
gone to your head and you won't deign to listen. I ask one
thing of you, however. Do not be so swift to reject my advice.
Give me your promise that you'll take the time to consider all
that I've told you.''

Verran inclined her head. "Very well, but it won't make any
difference. I'll never change my mind, Father.''

"So be it. I've done my best for you, but you scorn my
counsel and I can do nothing more. I have fulfilled my obligation, and your welfare is no longer any responsibility of mine.

Keep our conversation of today in mind, Daughter. Whatever the future may bring, you cannot claim you weren't fairly warned."

Dris Verras rose and took his leave. As he departed her chambers, Verran sighed in mingled relief and exasperation. She profoundly hoped he would not return.

Chapter Ten

꙾꙾꙾꙾꙾

When the Keldhar of Gard Lammis requested the loan of five thousand Lanthian troops to serve Gard Lammis in the Silevian Wars, Duke Povon found it expedient to agree. It was at this time that Preeminence Fal Grizhni further intensified his opposition to the ducal policies. Grizhni carried his suit to the greatest nobles of the city, urging such folk as Cru Beffel, Ro Zanlas, and Dule Parnis to refuse impressment of their bondsmen and slaves. In this he met some success, for the Lanthian aristocrats had little desire to forfeit their servants.

Fal Grizhni was aided in his efforts by Gaerase Vay Nennevay. It was therefore not surprising that the female savant should become a particular target of the League of Patriots. Soon a new broadside was visible all over town. The sheet, obviously calculated to appeal to the worst prejudices of the peasantry, carried a woodcut portrait at once frightening and obscene. Vay Nennevay was shown nude, and the portrait revealed a number of bestial deformities. She carried a dagger, and blood dirtied her mouth and chin. The text beneath the picture read:

The Witch Gaerase Vay Nennevay:
Her Bloody Crimes Disclosed

It has lately been proved that the Witch Nennevay, known Cohort and Accomplice of Fal Grizhni (King of

Demons) is guilty of most abominable Outrages. Let it be known to All that this ancient and loathsome Hag daily seeks out the sweetest Daughters of Lanthi Ume's Commons to make them her Prey. It signifies not who they are, so they be fair and Virgins. These unhappy Maidens are carried to the Witch's Lair, and there she drinks their Blood. When she has by Malice and Magic rendered her Victim helpless, the Witch then flays every Scrap of Skin from the virgin Body. With this white and youthful Flesh she covers o'er her own ghastful and decrepit Form, and so is briefly lent a fair Semblance. In this fleeting Semblance she ventures abroad by Night to practice Harlotry, and her many Dupes little know the hideous Monster they consort with until it is too late.

This Witch's Vileness and Deceit yet flourish, to our Shame. Honor have we None until her Foulness be consum'd in Fire. And so take Heed.

—The League of Patriots

Verran was disgusted when she read it. It was only bad luck that she saw it at all, for she never went out these days. Following the incident on Sandivell Path, Fal Grizhni had given her a choice between confinement to the palace grounds throughout the term of her pregnancy, or immediate deportation to one of the country estates. She had elected to remain, and now spent all her time inside the mansion or wandering the spacious gardens in the company of bodyguards. She had come upon the broadside in the garden. It was wrapped around a rock, which some public-minded citizen had flung over the wall. Verran didn't show the libel to her husband, but suspected that he knew about it already, as he seemed to know about most things. She wondered if Vay Nennevay had seen the wretched object.

Verran had a chance to speak with Nennevay later that week, when the savant visited Grizhni Palace for a conference with, as she put it, "the delegates." It was to be assumed that the Vardruls still lurked close at hand, but the subject was not discussed at the dinner that Verran, Grizhni, and Nennevay enjoyed that evening in the candlelit dining hall of Verran's suite of rooms.

If Nennevay was perturbed, she showed no outward sign. The strong face beneath the hennin was tranquil. Her manner was urbane. She spoke of mundane matters—the impertinence of public dombulmen, Beskot Kor Malifon's latest profligacy, the betrothal of Jinzin Farni's oldest son. She breathed not a word of politics, and Verran was piqued. Evidently Vay Nennevay considered her too young and too ignorant to comprehend anything beyond gossip and housewifery.

When the savant began to describe her method of recording household expenditures, Verran could stand no more. "You might recommend this system to the Duke," she suggested. "Perhaps it would help him manage his debts to Gard Lammis, to Hurba, and to Strell." This was showing off. In reality, Verran had little knowledge of such matters.

Vay Nennevay shot Grizhni a look of amusement. "I had thought this child sequestered here."

"She is by no means devoid of intellect," Grizhni replied.

"Information has a way of flying over the wall," said Verran a little dryly.

"The Duke, my dear, desires my advice no more than he desires that of your husband. He does not relish Selectic interference. Indeed, he's been encouraged to believe that those among us who oppose his decisions conspire to usurp his throne."

Verran nodded. This was more like it. "Does he think that you would be Duchess?"

"It's unlikely that I, an elderly woman, would aspire to the throne. But the Duke might fear that I'd lend support to another, should a coup be attempted."

"And would you?" Verran inquired boldly.

Nennevay's brows lifted.

"I have assured Lady Grizhni that his Grace's worst personal fears have hitherto been groundless," Fal Grizhni remarked. He spoke in his usual impenetrable manner, but Verran discerned a peculiar overtone. Only ears very finely attuned to the sound of his voice could have caught it. She glanced at him sharply. The angular face was expressionless, the mouth firmly set. His eyes were intensely alert—or was it the glint of reflected candle flames in their black depths that made them appear so?

Grizhni felt the pressure of her stare. He turned and their eyes met. In that instant Verran was sure that she had read him right. She faced Nennevay once more. "What would you do?"

"A difficult question, my dear. I think the Duke is leading this city straight to perdition. And yet I could not support the usurpation of his throne by a member of the Select."

"Why not, Madam Nennevay? If he's such a bad ruler—"

"That is not the point," Nennevay told her. "Or at least not the only point. In the first place interference in affairs of state is injurious to the Select as an order, for it perverts our purpose. The savant who neglects Cognition in favor of politics will find that his powers diminish."

"But if it's for the good of the city, wouldn't that sacrifice be worthwhile to the savant?" Verran asked. She noted that Fal Grizhni listened very attentively.

"Perhaps. But there's more to be considered. For example—should the legitimate Duke of Lanthi Ume be deposed by a savant of the Select, what do you imagine the reaction of our sister city-states would be? What would the Keldhar of Gard Lammis make of the event? And how would the Duke of Hurba react?"

"What do you mean, Madam Nennevay?"

"Stop and think. There are organizations corresponding to our Select in all the great cities of Dalyon. Gard Lammis has her Brotherhood, Hurba has the Black Circle, and the Initiates flourish in Rhel. These orders will be regarded with suspicion by the hereditary rulers of their respective cities should it happen that a Lanthian savant deposes his Duke. There would be reprisals."

"Can't the foreign savants look after themselves?" Verran inquired. "That's not our problem, is it?"

"Is it not, my dear young Lady Grizhni? Would you consider war with Hurba to be our problem? Or perhaps a war in which a league of city-states unites in opposition to Lanthi Ume—would that be our problem?"

"Do you think that could actually happen?"

"I'm certain it would. The masters of our sister cities would never countenance Selectic rule of Lanthi Ume—it would set too dangerous an example. It's possible that a very strong savant"—Nennevay's eyes flickered toward Fal Grizhni—"could lead Lanthi Ume to victory in such a war, but only at terrible cost."

"You're persuasive, Madam Nennevay."

"If you remain unconvinced, there's one more argument, perhaps the most important. It's this—human beings should not be ruled by the force of Cognition. Such rule confuses the mind of man, oppresses his heart, and at last breaks his spirit. Men should be governed by others like themselves, not by savants. May the Select enjoy their wisdom, but never occupy the ducal throne! And therefore"—Nennevay regarded Fal Grizhni with a mixture of determination and regret—"Duke Povon would be surprised to know it, but he claims my loyalty."

Shortly thereafter Vay Nennevay departed and Verran sat alone with her husband. Grizhni was silent, and after studying him carefully for a time, Verran asked, "Do you think she's right, my lord? About the danger to the Select, and the war with Hurba?"

"I believe her judgment is quite sound."

"And what about the rest of what she said? Do you think she's right that humans shouldn't be ruled by Cognition?"

"I agree," Grizhni replied after a pause, "that it is not the best thing for them. However, there are far worse alternatives."

Verran continued to contemplate his face, which reminded her of a walled fortress. Grizhni became aware of the scrutiny. "Is there anything you wish to discuss, Madam?"

"No!" She could feel herself start to blush, and was ashamed of the silliness of her own suspicions. "That is—you're very attached to her, aren't you?"

The forbidding expression faded. "I have known Vay Nennevay most of my life. I respect her, and yes, I am attached to her as I am to no other human being—save you, Madam."

"And to our child, in a couple of months," she reminded him, and the rare smile lighted his face. "Things are going to get better and better, my dear lord. Just wait and see."

Gaerase Vay Nennevay didn't know she was being followed. Immersed in thought, she was nearly oblivious to her surroundings. When the hired dombulis docked at South Witlet Pier, she absently overpaid the dombulman and stepped ashore. She certainly did not realize that several caped figures loitering upon the pier had noted her arrival and now ambled unobtrusively in her wake.

Beyond South Witlet Pier lay a twisting maze of alleys and

walkways. One of the oldest neighborhoods of the city, South Witlet housed a number of Lanthi Ume's most renowned artists, philosophers, and alchemists. It was here, amidst the ancient streets with their narrow, old-fashioned houses, that Vay Nennevay had taken lodgings. She lived alone, as did many savants. There was no one to note her comings and goings, no one to know if she did not come home.

The night was coldly moonlit, the street nearly deserted. An early breath of winter stirred Nennevay's robes and she shivered. The wind soon died, but the shivering continued. It was then she realized that men were trailing her. They had been close behind her for some time. A savant of ability had little to fear from common footpads. The men had greater cause to fear her Cognition than she their poniards. Perhaps, she reflected, they weren't following her deliberately. They might live in South Witlet, they might be her neighbors. Nevertheless, Vay Nennevay quickened her pace. Her lodgings were but a few yards distant. Once safely within, she would lock the door behind her, light the candles, and fear no more.

She was almost home. But the men were closing in on her swiftly now. They moved with concerted, almost military precision uncharacteristic of street hooligans. Nennevay turned to confront them and they stopped in their tracks. There were five of them—tall, burly fellows, formidably armed. All of them were masked. The tallest and heaviest among them appeared to be the leader, and she addressed him directly. "I do not think you are thieves. What do you want of me?"

"Your life." His rough voice was elusively familiar.

Nennevay smiled. "Yours to take—if you can. Perhaps you'll find that difficult. Do you know who I am?"

"I know who you are, old woman."

"But do you know what I am? You fear not the vengeance of the Select?"

This threat seemed to alarm one of the men, whose hand leaped to his sword hilt.

The tall leader was unimpressed. "We can deal with witches and magicians, never fear."

"Can you? Yet you hesitate to approach, I see. Why do you wish to harm me?"

"Because the city will be a better place when the sorcerous dung is mucked out of it."

"The city, or the Duke? Did the Duke send you?"

"We've talked long enough. I've no time to listen to an old bitch yapping." He made a gesture to his followers, who instantly drew their swords.

Vay Nennevay spoke softly. One of her attackers cried out, dropped his weapon, clawed at his chest and fell. For a few moments he writhed in torment upon the cobbles while his companions watched helplessly. Presently he uttered a moan and expired.

"I crushed his heart," the savant explained, her manner almost kindly, "as if I held it in hands of iron. For a little while I could feel it struggling to live, then it gave way suddenly and completely. I will do the same to each and every one of you if I must. You!" she commanded the leader of the group. "Unmask."

"You think you've beaten us?"

"I believe I know that voice," Nennevay replied without rancor. "I've remembered at last. Commander Haik Ulf of the Guards, is it not?" No reply was forthcoming. "The masquerade is over, Commander. You may unveil."

He obeyed and tossed the mask aside. Moonlight grayed the heavy features of Haik Ulf, lending him the semblance of a quartz-eyed cadaver. "Think you're clever, do you?"

"Did the Duke send you to murder me, Commander? Or was this your own idea?"

"The Duke knows he can trust me," Ulf replied obliquely. His voice was deliberately casual and his expression was ugly.

"Are you by any chance a member of the League of Patriots? Yes, I've seen the broadsides," she added, correctly reading his face. "Do you constitute the entire membership, or is Saxas Gless Vallage your colleague?"

"That's no concern of yours, witch. Neither is anything else, after tonight."

Vay Nennevay stood tall and straight. "You are a fool, Haik Ulf. How do you propose to murder one who can kill at a distance with a single word?"

"By stopping her mouth." Ulf signaled and a brace of masked Guardsmen sprang suddenly from the shadows behind Vay Nennevay. One of them clapped a hand across her mouth. The other brought forth a narrow leather strap with iron attachments at one end—the garrote of the hired bravo. In an instant the strap encircled the savant's throat. A brutally professional twist cut off her breath, and after that, Vay Nennevay's life was measured in seconds.

She could neither breathe nor speak. Without speech, her power of Cognition could barely manifest itself, as her attackers well knew. Briefly she struggled against the strangling cord, but her most desperate efforts scarcely inconvenienced the Ducal Guards.

Nennevay's hands sketched gestures in the air, wove clutching patterns. The mental discipline of a senior savant of the Select enabled her, even in her dying agony, to attempt a silent Cognition.

Lord Haik Ulf felt a ghostly presence invade his mind. Instinctively his hands rose as if to tear the trespasser from his brain by force. There was a pressure at his throat and he could not draw his breath. His eyes bulged and his face darkened horribly. Without volition, his hands began to follow the gestures of Vay Nennevay, imitating her movement for movement. Pain enfolded him like the wings of a demon. His lungs and throat flamed. Somehow, by means of her accursed sorceries, the witch Nennevay had taken him, had bound him to herself. Now he suffered, dying along with her. Ulf strove to call to his men and could not. His eyes were dimming, but he could still see his own hands duplicate the gestures that were destroying him. He tottered and sprawled forward on his face, body jerking spasmodically.

Haik Ulf would surely have died then and there had his men not intervened. One of the masked Guards grasped Vay Nennevay's wrists and held them motionless. The mental bond was broken and Ulf collapsed. The pressure on his throat was gone and the tortured lungs expanded. Almost simultaneously Vay Nennevay sagged limply in the grasp of her murderer. The Guard released her and she slumped to the ground, dead eyes turned to the moon. With life and intelligence gone, she appeared for the first time as a very old and somewhat frail woman. The Guards regarded her uneasily, and one of them, moved by some impulse he hardly understood, drew the veil of her headdress over her face.

Ulf stirred and groaned. Slowly he sat up, massaging his neck, on which thin red welts were visible. His henchmen watched impassively. It appeared that the Commander was hardly beloved of his Guards. "You—Kronil. Help me up." The voice was painfully hoarse. Kronil complied. Ulf stood unsteadily, but without support. He did not waste a glance at the corpse of his victim.

Kronil was not equally indifferent. "She died game," the

guard observed. "I don't like this sneaking around, and I don't like killing women."

"She was a witch, not a woman. And nobody gives a curse what you like." A sore throat could not prevent Haik Ulf from maintaining discipline.

"What good does this do?"

"It shows Fal Grizhni's followers what they can expect. And it reminds certain upstart magicians that they don't run this city."

"You think the upstart magicians might figure out who did this?"

Ulf replied with an eloquent obscenity. Without further conversation the killers retreated, leaving two corpses behind them.

Late in the morning Verran felt a change in the atmosphere of Grizhni Palace. The air was charged with a force that stirred her hair and set her spine tingling. She might have concluded that a thunderstorm was imminent, but the skies outside were blue and clear. The palace was even more silent than usual. Verran stood up and the embroidery slid unnoticed from her lap. Nothing around her appeared amiss, but the gooseflesh rose on her arms and her sense of foreboding intensified. After a moment's consideration she went in search of her husband.

Fal Grizhni was in the library. On the table before him lay a manuscript which he disregarded. His eyes were fixed expectantly upon . . . nothingness. Verran watched without comprehension. She entered the room and her uneasiness sharpened to fear. The force of the unknown was stronger here, much stronger. Her mouth was sticky dry, but she spoke steadily enough. "Something's wrong. What's happening?"

Grizhni turned to face her. "The Select send a message to me. The method of transmission suggests urgency."

"The air feels all wrong."

"You sense Cognition. Do not fear."

"Where is the message?"

"Watch."

Verran obeyed. Once more her husband's intent frown was trained upon empty space. At the center of the library the air glowed faintly. Seconds passed and the light assumed a ruddy tinge. Swiftly the color deepened and a red mist appeared. The mist thickened, shrank, coalesced to three-dimensional characters of fire that floated at eye level as if borne up by the force of imagination.

The fiery symbols meant nothing to Verran, and she turned to her husband in perplexity. Fal Grizhni was able to read the message with ease, and as he did so his expression changed alarmingly. Verran drew a sharp breath. Her husband's normally impassive face was rigid with pain and grief. Only a blow completely unexpected could have affected him thus. Verran stretched forth a hand, which he did not see. "What is it?" she asked.

Grizhni was silent. His eyes remained fixed on the message until the fiery characters dimmed and faded from view.

"What is it?" Verran repeated.

He answered at last. "Gaerase Vay Nennevay is dead."

"Dead?" Verran was stunned. "But she dined with us only last night and seemed to be in perfect health! Was it her heart?"

"She was murdered," the savant replied flatly. "Strangled."

"Strangled!" Verran whitened. "How . . . why? By thieves?"

"Thieves . . . of life, yes. Gaerase was slain by her enemies —as Rev Beddef was slain."

"What enemies, my lord?"

"When that question has been answered, her death will be avenged."

"But Madam Nennevay was so powerful. She was a great savant, as well as a very good woman. How could anyone hurt her?"

"The matter of 'goodness' is irrelevant, Madam. As for Gaerase's Cognizance—it could not render her invulnerable, 'goodness' notwithstanding. Even a great savant can be taken unawares, and even strong Cognition can exhaust itself. The flesh of savants, like that of other mortals, is subject to the varied influences of steel, cord, and fire."

Verran stared at him, unnerved by the intense bitterness of his tone. "Why should anyone want to murder Madam Nennevay? For what reason?"

It took Fal Grizhni some time to answer, and when he spoke it was with apparent effort. "Gaerase Vay Nennevay was my political ally as well as a personal friend. This double indiscretion drew the attention of my foes and resulted in her death. Similar loyalties were the cause of Rev Beddef's murder. My friendship brings death to the innocent. Surely it is a lethal offering."

"That's not true—you musn't think it!"

"It is quite true. The inferences are clear. Have you no concern for your own safety, Madam?"

"No!" Verran replied vehemently, fearful that he would speak again of sending her away. "And it wasn't *your* fault, my dear lord, that your friends were killed. At most, it can only be said that they died for doing what they thought was right. Surely you wouldn't have had them behave otherwise? It's what you'd do yourself."

"Is it? If so, then not always by inclination. There is a side of my nature, Madam, of which you are happily ignorant. I hope you may remain so. Of late, however, my growing anger threatens to overleap its bounds. Should that occur, then woe to Lanthi Ume—woe to all of Dalyon. For I have it within me to visit such destruction upon my foes and their descendants that this island would bear the scars for all time."

"Destroy the descendants of your enemies?" His expression chilled her. "If you do that, then you'll be hurting completely innocent people."

Grizhni inclined his head minimally.

"My lord, I understand your rage and sorrow. But if you strike at the innocent as well as the guilty, then you choose a very evil path. Only ill will come of it—for yourself and for others."

"Do not distress yourself, Madam. My enmity is habitually suppressed. But if harm comes to you or to our child, I should perhaps give way to it."

"Never for my sake—that's the last thing I'd want."

"I know it."

He took her hand and for a time neither of them spoke. Verran watched him closely, saw the anger drain from his eyes until nothing but grief remained. At last she broke the silence. "Will they ask you to deliver Madam Nennevay's funeral oration?"

"Yes."

"I will attend the ceremony," she told him. "She was my friend too. And I want to be with you then."

Fal Grizhni nodded wordlessly.

• • •

It was thought that the League of Patriots had killed the witch Nennevay, for ensuing broadsides were jubilant. If it was so, had the League committed a crime, or a public service? Lanthian opinion was evenly divided on this score. The body of the masked man remained an unsolved mystery, for those who could have identified it did not speak. The murderers had escaped unscathed, and perhaps it was just as well. Their capture and trial would have posed questions distressing to contemplate.

As for the sorceress, she had no family and it was assumed that her body would be claimed by the Select. She had belonged to the Select, and surely it was incumbent upon them to bury her.

Preeminence Terrs Fal Grizhni, a close friend of the deceased, might have won the approval of the populace at this time with a show of appropriate bereavement. His Preeminence, however, disdained all public displays of emotion. When he spoke at Vay Nennevay's obsequies two days later, it was in so self-contained a manner that his listeners murmured amongst themselves that Fal Grizhni was surely a man of stone —or perhaps not a man at all.

Chapter Eleven

✦✦✦✦✦

Civic discontent increased that winter. Duke Povon had deemed it expedient to impose ruinous new surtaxes upon the estates of his wealthiest subjects in order to finance the construction of a splendid amphitheater of gold and crystal. The aristocrats of Lanthi Ume responded to this demand with an unbecoming lack of patriotism. A conclave of nobles was called, presided over by the lord Terrs Fal Grizhni. The nobles of Lanthi Ume were willing to listen to Fal Grizhni. In addition to Preeminence, he possessed blood regarded as a distillate of the oldest aristocracy. The glittering assemblage voted to refuse payment. Duke Povon would be enraged, certainly; but what could he do about it?

Duke Povon was enraged indeed. There was little he could do to express resentment in the face of the concerted opposition of his wealthiest nobles. Even the Ducal Guards under the command of the redoubtable Haik Ulf would be of little practical use in such a case. Nonetheless, Povon soon succeeded in making his displeasure known. Within days a ducal proclamation announced revisions in the charter of the Select. Henceforth the attendance of ducal representatives at all convocations of the order was to be considered mandatory. No program of Cognitive investigation would be initiated by any member of the Select without prior ducal approval, and periodic reports outlining the progress of such investigations were to be submitted to ducal representatives on a regular basis.

Finally, a permanent garrison of Ducal Guards would be established upon the Victory of Nes. It was to be expected that the savants would react with disapprobation to these innovations. They would, however, realize that the arrogant folly of his Preeminence was the true cause of all difficulties and surely that would sow dissension within their ranks, a consummation always to be wished. With any luck, Povon speculated, they'd kick the bastard as far as the Sea of Ice, and choose themselves a new leader. Someone reasonable. Someone, perhaps, like Gless Vallage.

His Grace's hopes were shared by Gless Vallage. Within the rooms set aside for his very private use in Vallage House, the savant was hard at work on the latest complaint of the League of Patriots. This one was a lengthy diatribe accusing Preeminence Grizhni of necrophilia and cannibalism.

Vallage finished writing and eyed the composition critically. The literary style was execrable, but that was all to the best. It was the crudest and most inflammatory of sentiments that would produce the deepest impression upon the loutish Commons of Lanthi Ume. So much for that. The composition would be delivered to a discreet artist who would create an appropriately horrific portrait of Grizhni. A new broadside would hit the streets within two days.

Gless Vallage, always industrious, turned next to the design for the dressing gown of Living Silk with which he aimed to titillate the Duke. His labors were interrupted by the arrival of a visitor. Cognizance Brenn Wate Basef was announced. Vallage sighed. He found Wate Basef's youthful histrionics tiresome in the extreme, but it was highly politic to tolerate the boy, for now.

Vallage descended to the formal chambers on the second story to greet the visitor. Wate Basef was ushered in and Vallage flashed his useful smile. "My dear Cognizance Basef, thank you for accepting my invitation."

"My pleasure, Cognizance Vallage."

They exchanged neutral courtesies. Vallage noted that his protégé seemed ill at ease. Wate Basef was naturally highstrung, but this went beyond the ordinary. The boy was haggard and jumpy. Poor health? Overwork? Or a guilty conscience—already? Vallage hoped not. He expected a good deal more service out of Basef.

Questioning revealed that Brenn was enjoying his new Cognizance and that his Cognitive investigations were proceeding satisfactorily. A demonstration of the skeletal slaves might be expected in the near future. Yes, the archives of the Nessiva were outstanding. Brenn was most grateful to Gless Vallage and to Cognizance Rom Usine for providing him with such a splendid opportunity.

Vallage nodded benevolently. "It would have been unjust to deny you your chance, my dear Brenn. It is always my pleasure to assist deserving friends."

Brenn stirred uncomfortably. He set his goblet of wine aside untasted.

Vallage noted his guest's uneasiness and silently prayed that it did not portend difficulty, for it was time to get down to business. Might he never be forced to deal with so unstable a personality again! "And now," he inquired pleasantly, "what might you have to report to me?"

The question could hardly have been unexpected, but Brenn's hands jerked sharply. He raised feverish eyes to Vallage's face. "Very little, Cognizance."

Vallage smiled patiently. "Surely there is something? Have you not observed Preeminence Fal Grizhni, as I advised?"

"Yes, I've watched him." Brenn paused, clearly unwilling to continue, and Vallage watched blandly. At last the young man added, "Everyone knows of Grizhni's anger at the Duke's attempt to revise our charter. Now it's rumored that Grizhni may declare complete Selectic independence of ducal authority. It's said that the Victory of Nes could become a separate state within the boundaries of Lanthi Ume."

"That's a fairly widespread rumor, Cognizance Basef. As such, I am already aware of it. I must admit, I'd expected better things of you."

Brenn flushed. "I've done my best."

"Oh, I don't think so. Not really," Gless Vallage returned easily. "If you put your heart into it, I'm confident you could do much better."

"Only if I had Grizhni's personal trust. And I don't."

"Exactly, Brenn. I'm in complete agreement with you. You need to insinuate yourself into Grizhni's confidence. That shouldn't be difficult. You have a great deal of ability and he's bound to respect that. You need only feign agreement with his decisions, and he'll soon come to trust in you as a member of his faction. Then you will be in a position to report on his plans. I foresee no impediment—"

"There is an impediment!" Brenn's veneer of self-possession splintered. Unable to sit still any longer, he rose from his
chair and paced the chamber. "I am the impediment, Cognizance. The subterfuge you suggest is abhorrent to me. I loathe
Fal Grizni and all he stands for—how could I pretend to be
the friend of such a man? I am no liar and I am no spy. I can't
help you. I'm sorry."

Gless Vallage was always in perfect control of his temper.
"I am sorry too," he replied with a masterly blend of disappointment and subtle menace. He paused deliberately to allow
the personal implications of his sorrow to seep into Brenn's
consciousness, then added, "At the time I arranged your admission to the Select, I believed that my efforts on your behalf
would be appreciated."

"They are—I am deeply in your debt."

"I believe you are. Yet the first time I request your assistance, you deny me. I begin to suspect I was mistaken in you,
Master Wate Basef."

The change in address was not lost upon Brenn. "It's not
that I'm ungrateful, Cognizance Vallage. But what you ask is
impossible."

"Impossible? Ah." Vallage nodded gravely. "Yet very little
exceeds the abilities of a true savant. Perhaps your admission
to the Select was premature, Master Wate Basef. Certainly his
Preeminence thought so. Such an error, if it exists, is not ir-
reparable. Your membership status does not become permanent before the expiration of a year's probationary period, as
I'm sure you're aware."

Brenn stared at him. "What are you implying? Permanency
of membership is based on one criterion alone—proven Cognitive ability."

"Is it? Perhaps you're right," Vallage returned lightly.
"Time alone will tell."

For a time there was silence as Brenn roamed nervously
about the room. The young man's increasing pallor was accentuated by the new black robe of a savant. At last he remarked
with an effort, "I will take my leave now, Cognizance. I hope
there is to be no ill will between us, for I acknowledge my great
debt to you." He made for the door.

"One moment." Brenn turned back and Gless Vallage
smiled warmly. Different tactics were required. "I, too, would

regret the demise of our friendship. Before you leave, there's a question I must ask you. We've spoken of Fal Grizhni's possible intention of declaring Selectic autonomy. What do you believe the effect of such a declaration would be?"

Brenn considered the question. "The outcome is difficult to predict. In view of Grizhni's present level of Cognitive power, together with Duke Povon's character and history, I believe his Preeminence might carry it off successfully."

"Then Fal Grizhni becomes monarch of an independent state, while you and I become his subjects." Vallage forbore to mention that a successful coup would put an end once and for all to his own hopes of attaining Preeminence. "Do you wish for that?"

"Never! Such a man is unfit to rule!"

"Then let us say he is not immediately successful. What happens in that event?"

"Conflict, no doubt."

"Correct. It's not unreasonable to expect our Duke to defend himself. That being the case, civil war ensues. Lanthi Ume divides into armed camps, and thousands of lives are lost. During such a juncture, the Keldhar of Gard Lammis might well attempt an invasion. Do you wish for that?"

"Of course not, but—"

"Let's say that the Duke maintains his rights and Fal Grizhni is vanquished. What then?"

"Grizhni is humiliated, and ducal control of the Select increases," Brenn surmised.

"Much worse than that, I fear. The Select as a group would be regarded as traitors. We should lose our charter. We would disband, and the individual savants would be forced to flee. It would mean the end of the Select of Lanthi Ume. Do you wish for that?"

"Cognizance, how can you ask?"

"And yet you refuse to lift a finger to prevent it!" Gless Vallage accused, abandoning his habitually affable manner. "You, Brenn Wate Basef, possess the power to fight this peril, and you will not do it. You alone are marked out as the savior of the Select—and you deny your great destiny! What manner of man are you?"

Brenn was silent. It was difficult to fight destiny. He went to the window and stood staring abstractedly down at the Lureis Canal.

"Surely, my dear Cognizance Wate Basef," Vallage continued in a softened voice, "you understand the absolute necessity of keeping close watch on Preeminence Grizhni? For the sake of the city and the Select!"

Silence, while Brenn agonized. Vallage watched narrowly.

"If I were to unearth evidence of Grizhni's treachery," Brenn inquired at last, "and such evidence is used to bring him down, then what happens to his household members?" He turned abruptly to face Gless Vallage. "To his wife, for example?"

"Dris Verras's daughter?" Vallage asked in surprise. "I hadn't given it any thought." His true intentions regarding Grizhni's household would not have been pleasing to Wate Basef.

"She's a loyal and innocent Lanthian. She was married to Fal Grizhni against her will, and since then he has used Cognition to gain ascendancy over her. She is his helpless victim."

"I see." Vallage scrutinized his guest minutely and nodded in a manner carefully devoid of satire. "Yes, I see. In that case, my dear Brenn, it's up to us as men of honor to rescue the lady. She shall be saved at any cost. Stay and we'll discuss the matter."

After a moment, Brenn resumed his seat.

Chapter Twelve

What next? Verran wondered. She had heard of the Duke's proclamation and she strongly suspected that her husband would not tolerate ducal interference in Selectic affairs. Guardsmen stationed on the Victory of Nes? He would never agree to that—never.

Fal Grizhni was ready to leave. He had called for a congress of the Select to be held in a hidden hall used only in times of emergency. He had not told Verran where it was. Presumably he would be gone the entire day, and perhaps most of the night. Nyd, who had recovered from his wounds, was to accompany the savant.

They stood on Grizhni moorings. Behind them the palace rose somber and splendid. A covered dombulis awaited, its identifying marks carefully obscured. A chilly breeze ruffled the surface of the canal, and the sky was as dull as old iron. All was in readiness for his departure, and nothing remained but to bid him farewell.

Verran could not contain her curiosity. When her husband turned to her she inquired, "Have you decided what you'll do yet, my lord? I know you don't intend to obey his Grace's commands concerning the Select."

"You know nothing, Madam. You surmise, but you do not know." He looked down at her expressionlessly. "In ignorance lies your safety."

"I trust not in ignorance but rather in my husband's power

to protect his wife and his unborn child."

"I am glad of your faith. Will you not trust me, then, to protect you from dangerous knowledge?"

"But knowledge is strength, or so you have often said." She looked up into his unreadable eyes. "I am your wife, my lord. Is Grizhni's wife unworthy of his confidence?"

He studied her thoughtfully and answered at last, "You are young indeed to assume perilous responsibilities."

"But not too young to present you with an heir. I'm your wife, and I ask that you treat me as such."

He inclined his head a fraction. "There is justice in that. We will speak further when I return tonight. Until then, remain here in the company of the guards. In fact, I prefer that you stay within the palace. Do not venture into the garden."

Verran was startled. "Not even into the garden? But why, my lord? Is the danger so great?" He did not reply, and she added, "What of your own safety? You travel forth with only one companion?"

"I am capable of protecting myself. It is unlikely that any direct attempt will be made upon my life today. On the other hand, my enemies realize that the surest way to strike at me is through—" He broke off. "Do not leave the house today, Madam. Farewell."

Grizhni and Nyd boarded the dombulis. Verran stood upon the moorings and watched until her husband's tall, dark-clad figure vanished amidst the mists of morning. Then she slowly trudged inside, and the servants barred the doors behind her.

The day crawled by. Verran spent hours considering arguments and justifications that might persuade her reticent lord to tell her all he could. She considered, too, the implications of a possible declaration of Selectic autonomy in the face of his Grace's intolerable sanctions, and concluded that it would be much to the advantage of Povon Dil Shonnet to dispose of Preeminence Grizhni once and for all. It was not at all unlikely that they would wish to murder him. Suddenly chilled, Verran sat down on the marble hearthstone, heedless of her brocade gown, and stretched out her hands to the fire. Kill Lord Terrs Fal Grizhni? Much easier said than done. Let them try it. He was at least twice as intelligent and three times as powerful as his enemies, and he would surely destroy them. Or so Verran told herself. But as she gazed at the fire, the leaping flames suddenly darkened to blood-crimson. She saw her husband

faintly pictured therein, and his face was the face of a corpse.
Verran snatched her hands back and leaped to her feet. The
fire burned normally. Her mind seemed to be playing her
tricks.

What was he doing, and when would he be home?

She sought the company of the hybrids, and for a while
their croaking fellowship banished the worries from her mind.
But not for long. When would he come home?

The wintry sunset came early, and Verran welcomed it with
gratitude. She had feared the day would never end. Now she
stood by one of the tall, arched windows in the Great Hall and
watched the sky darken to charcoal above the eccentric towers
and domes of Lanthi Ume. Slowly the lights of the city appeared; a few at first, then dozens, then hundreds as lamps
and colored lanterns were lit; torches flared in their brackets
and candlelight glowed through windows of stained glass.
Thousands of colored reflections glinted upon the Sandivell.
Down below, dombuli and sendilli strung with lanterns carried
their fur-swathed passengers from palace to palace. Such craft
were dwarfed by the bulk of Beskot Kor Malifon's jeweled
venerise *Dream of Glory*, anchored alongside Manse Malifon.
Above all thrust Ka Nebbinon Tower, its summit picked out
with ghostly blue lights. Lanthi Ume, as she had always
known it, shone in all its beauty of fire and water. Surely
nothing could change?

The air in the Great Hall was unaccountably cold, despite a
roaring fire. Verran turned to the flames, and in their scarlet
depths she again beheld Fal Grizhni's face, the strong features
twisted in pain. Instinctively her eyes snapped shut. When she
opened them the face was gone. Dreams—visions. She was
breathing hard. Was this what pregnancy did to women—af-
fect their minds? Drive them mad? Surely Nature wouldn't
play so cruel a trick, would it? One thing was certain. She
couldn't tell Fal Grizhni what had happened. If he knew, he'd
pack her off to the country for a long rest, and nothing she
could say or do would change his mind.

Verran pressed a hand to her swollen abdomen. Inside her
the baby kicked. "We're not leaving," she announced.

She stole another glance at the fireplace. No visions came to
disturb her, but her pulse still raced. She wanted the peace and
privacy of her own bedchamber, and thither she turned her
steps.

When Verran entered her apartment she saw the note at once. It lay on the table near the door of her antechamber, and it hadn't been there an hour earlier. No one had approached the house throughout the day—no visitor and no messenger. The note could only have arrived by way of somebody's Cognition. Uneasily she broke the wax seal and read:

Lady Grizhni—

It is necessary to inform you that an attempt has been made this very day upon the life of your husband, noble Fal Grizhni. His Preeminence is gravely wounded and perhaps will not live to see the morning. Even now he lies in a feverish delirium. Often he calls your name and clearly he desires your presence. It is to be hoped you will not deny the request that may be his last.

The allies of Fal Grizhni have removed him to a safe and hidden refuge. At this time his enemies search the city, desirous of completing their fell work. If they discover him in his present helpless state, he is surely a dead man. Hence it is essential to guard the absolute secrecy of his whereabouts.

If you will come to him, then come tonight in stealth and alone, without friend or servant. Take an unmarked dombulis to the Destula Pier, proceed on foot along the embankment as far as the Bridge of Spiteful Cats, then enter the alleyway beneath the arch hung with a green lamp. There you will find friends who will convey you to your husband, whose sufferings must be pitied.

There was no signature.

She went cold all over as she read it, and took an impulsive step toward the door as if she meant to dash straight out of the palace. Then she stopped and recalled the last words addressed to her by her husband. "Do not leave the house today, Madam." Fal Grizhni's counsel was usually worth following, but he couldn't have foreseen this. Now he was wounded, in pain, perhaps even dying, and he wanted her with him. Or did he? Could this be a trap of some kind, designed to lure her into the open? But why should anyone be interested in harming her? And she remembered Grizhni's uncompleted remark, "My enemies realize that the surest way to strike at me is through—'' Through her, he had meant. Through Verran, who carried his child.

She read the note through again and found that her forehead and temples were clammy with cold sweat, as if the tense flutter she experienced when she bet on the Green Octagon had been increased ten-thousandfold.

The pictures in the fire had warned her of disaster, and now the premonition was fulfilled. But the same Cognition that had sent her the note could surely have sent her the pictures. It could so easily be a trap. Verran decided in that instant to obey her husband's commands. And then she thought of him bloodstained, agonized, calling for the wife who did not come to him. She pictured the dark eyes closed in lonely death— without ever having looked on her again.

Almost without volition her hand darted out and yanked the bellpull. During the short time that elapsed before the summons was answered, Verran ran to a pedestal on which reposed a coffer, opened the box and withdrew a jeweled stiletto, a dainty object purchased solely for the sake of its beauty. She had never thought to employ it as a weapon. Now she slid the knife into the pocket of her loose gown. She hurried to a clothespress and chose a plain, dark cloak wherein she wrapped herself warmly. The black folds completely disguised her pregnancy. She pulled the hood well forward over her face.

There was a tap at the door, and Verran opened it. A huge young hybrid named Spryl waited upon the threshold. His hairy countenance reflected mindless good nature. He was not the most dependable of servants, but he was certainly the strongest. The creature croaked inquiringly.

''We are going out,'' Verran announced. ''I've learned that Lord Grizhni may be badly hurt. The report might be totally false, but I can't afford to take that chance.'' Spryl whined anxiously. ''Yes, I know it's dangerous, but what else can I do? What if it's all true? What if I don't go to him tonight, and he *dies*? It's not as if I could enlist the aid of some other savant,'' she continued in response to the question her companion could not formulate, much less express. ''If this note contains the truth, then Lord Grizhni's friends will probably be under surveillance. Anyway, there's no time. He needs me *now*. If he's really hurt, he'll feel happier and stronger if I'm with him, I'm sure of it, so we've got to go.''

The hybrid whined mournfully. He appeared to understand that his master was in danger.

"But . . ." Verran added slowly, "there's a chance this note could be a lie. And therefore you're coming with me, but I don't want you recognized. Pull your hood up." Spryl obeyed. "We're going to the Destula Pier by boat, and the rest of the way on foot. Once we set foot on land, you're to follow me at a distance. Make sure nobody notices you, but don't let me out of your sight for a moment. If you should hear me call to you, be ready to come to my assistance at once. It probably won't be necessary—but be prepared. Do you understand?" Spryl understood perfectly. "Good. Come along, then."

The two muffled figures sped through the halls of Grizhni Palace, out a small side exit, and down onto Grizhni moorings, where a small, private fleet awaited. "That one." Verran indicated a plain black dombulis of no particular distinction, a dombulis that nobody would look at twice. It carried no identifying mark or insignia. Spryl croaked and assisted his mistress to board. Verran stepped down into the boat, lowering her ungainly form with care. The vessel bobbed, and she clutched its polished sides. As her pregnancy progressed, the world became increasingly precarious. The actions that had once come so freely and naturally, now required planning. Not so long ago she had been able to spring from the wharf into a moving boat so lightly that she scarcely shook the vessel, and now—

Spryl loosed the mooring line, jumped in, and took up the oars. The dombulis shot over the water, heading toward Destula Pier.

"Not so fast, Spryl. We'll attract attention." She looked at him worriedly. Spryl was young and impetuous and not too very bright. It would have been a lot better if she could have taken Nyd. Where was Nyd, anyway? The note had not mentioned him. Undoubtedly he would have tried to defend his master. Had he been injured . . . or killed?

They glided under the Bridge of Beggars, where the mendicants congregated to call out to the passing boats. On they went past the image of the Eatchish sorcerer Jun, past the Shonnet Gardens with their sculptured fountains, and into the mouth of Straightwater Canal, a very ancient waterway serving that section of Lanthi Ume known as the Destula.

Traffic was light upon the water now. Few dombuli or sen-

dilli braved the perils of the Destula after dark. Those that did
so traveled swiftly and with minimal illumination. The buildings that loomed along the Straightwater were decrepit, crum-
bling, hideous. For the most part they appeared deserted. The
appearance was deceptive, for the Destula teemed with life.
Those silent buildings housed an assortment of humanity rang-
ing from the pathetic to the unspeakable; from harmless, im-
poverished simpletons, to footpads and cutthroats, on down
to the terrible Expulsions—those embittered savants expelled
from the Select for various offenses, who now concentrated
their powers of Cognition upon elaborate revenge. The presence of an expectant lady of quality in such a district was in-
congruous, and many eyes peering from darkened windows
followed Verran's progress with extreme interest.

She was conscious of danger, but indifferent. Her thoughts
were fixed on her husband. She could not banish from her
mind the image of Fal Grizhni wounded, pain-ridden, deliri-
ous with fever. Grizhni, that proud and powerful savant—
now helpless and hunted, if he yet lived at all. Verran's hands
clenched. "He *must* be alive!"

Spryl listened and croaked. The boat bumped Destula Pier
and the two of them disembarked. The Destula was silent and
shadowy. Spryl carried a lantern, and now he raised it on high
and gazed about him with a puzzled air.

*Proceed on foot along the embankment as far as the Bridge
of Spiteful Cats*, the note had commanded.

"Give me the light," Verran requested, and Spryl did so.
"You remember your orders? Follow behind me and don't let
anyone see you. If you hear me cry out, come *quickly*. You
understand?" He croaked, and she looked at him dubiously.
He sounded too cheerful, too unconcerned. "You're sure?"
He croaked again.

She set out along the embankment and with each step
through that squalid, menacing neighborhood, her fears increased. There were probably cutthroats lurking in every
shadowed doorway, and they would regard her as the falcon
regards the fieldmouse. She would never reach the bridge
alive. And if by chance she did, what then? Would she truly
find friends of Grizhni, or would the place be deserted? She
thought she heard the sound of booted feet upon the cobbles
behind her. Spryl was unshod. She halted, spun around, lifted
the lantern and listened intently. She saw nothing but a few

yards of the empty thoroughfare. Beyond the circle of weak
lantern light, the darkness was absolute. Spryl was invisible, if
he was still there at all. Verran strained her ears, but heard
nothing save the lapping of the waters of Straightwater Canal.
The hand that held the lantern was trembling and the light
jumped. She took a deep breath, set her jaw, and resumed her
journey. On she went, miraculously unmolested.

The Bridge of Spiteful Cats arose before her. Here the feral
strays of Lanthi Ume prowled by the hundreds. Here they had
laired and multiplied for generations, at last attaining strength
of numbers and ferocity so formidable that few humans cared
to disturb them. It was said that in the deep of winter, in times
of greatest famine, the bridge cats had been known to kill and
devour unwary human intruders. It was not difficult to believe.

Verran heard a hiss. She looked down. The ground at her
feet was alive with slinking forms. Dozens of cats barred her
path. So silently had they approached that she had been
unaware of their presence until one of them uttered its sibilant
warning. The lantern light turned their eyes to flame, and Verran gasped. It was clear that trespassers were not to be
tolerated upon the bridge.

Enter the alleyway beneath the arch hung with a green lamp.
The arch that she sought was not far away. Off to the left an
emerald light beckoned through the darkness. Verran took a
step backward, skirted the cats, and moved deliberately away
from the bridge. The cats watched her go, and one yowled in
dissonant triumph.

She paused before the archway, a forlorn figure bathed in
weird green light. Darkness before her. Darkness behind. Not
a sound to be heard. Was Spryl still with her? She did not dare
to call out to him. Were Lord Grizhni's friends close at hand,
as the note had promised? If so, they had hidden themselves
well.

Verran passed cautiously under the archway and found
herself in the meanest and blackest of the Destula's many cul-
de-sacs. Here the rickety buildings were tall and the path was
twisted. Here the fresh breezes never penetrated, and the
heavy air stank of excrement and decay. Lady Verran gagged
violently. In all her sheltered life she had never dreamed that
brilliant Lanthi Ume concealed such foulness. She leaned
against a building and retched. In a moment she would be
sick. Instinctively she grabbed a strand of her own clean-

scented hair and buried her nose in it. It helped. The spasm
passed. Verran pinched her nostrils between thumb and fore-
finger, and took deep breaths of the horrible air into her open
mouth. She was better now. Behind her she heard a quiet footfall—Spryl's, no doubt.

Resolutely she pushed on into the darkness. Twenty paces,
thirty-five . . . She had lost count by the time she rounded
a bend in the alley and encountered a glare of light. Three
cloaked and masked figures stood before her. One of them
carried a flaring torch. They neither moved nor spoke.

Verran stopped at a safe distance. She was customarily
fleet. Pregnancy now encumbered her, but at the first real sign
of danger she would at least try to run. It took her a little while
to find her voice, and when she finally spoke, she sounded
unsteady. "You will take me to Lord Grizhni? You will take
me to my husband?"

The tallest of them answered. "We'll take you." His lips
smiled beneath the mask. She thought she might have heard
his harsh voice somewhere, but couldn't place it.

"He's still alive?" she beseeched.

"He's alive—for now."

He was still smiling, and Verran perceived that here were no
friends of Grizhni's. She had walked into some kind of trap.
Without another word she turned and ran clumsily for the
mouth of the alley. She had scarcely begun to move before
another of the masked men leaped from the shadows behind
her, locked an arm around her throat, and clamped a hand
across her mouth. Verran fought furiously, striking out with
the lantern she still carried, and the arm tightened around her
neck. She could hardly breathe. She saw the other men moving
toward her, and the violence of her struggles increased. The
lantern went flying. Verran bit down hard and felt her teeth
sink into sinewy flesh. She heard an angry exclamation and
then the hand across her mouth was gone and the choking
grip on her throat loosened slightly. She gulped for air and
screamed at the top of her lungs, "Spryl! *Help!*"

Spryl came running in response to her call and three of Verran's assailants sprang to meet him. Their swords were drawn
and the tall one swung his torch. Firelight dazzled the eyes of
the hybrid and confused his judgment. Spryl beheld his lady's
peril, hissed and bounded forward—only to transfix himself
upon the naked blade of one of his foes. The steel pierced his

heart and Spryl hung impaled for a moment. The sword was withdrawn. The hybrid quivered, slumped to his knees and thence to the ground. The men turned to Verran.

The girl jabbed her elbow backward into the belly of her captor. He grunted but did not let go. Her hand flew to the knife in her pocket. She withdrew it and struck blindly. She heard a man's laughter, her wrist was imprisoned, and the weapon was twisted effortlessly from her grasp.

Verran screamed. In the vain hope of drawing rescue she shrieked for help, and the clamor was unearthly. Scream after scream shivered through the noisome winds of the Destula. Many residents heard her, but nobody came to her aid. Her captor attempted to silence her, without success. Verran twisted and fought, shrieking like a lunatic.

The man with the torch spoke irritably. "We'll have half the city down on us. Can't you shut that little hellion up?"

"She bites, sir."

"Little girl's got you scared, eh? Here, hold this." The tall man handed his torch to a cohort and faced Verran. "Here's how it's done." Without further conversation he doubled his large fist and threw a straight right that caught her jaw.

The world exploded in fire and pain, and then there was nothing—nothing at all.

There was no telling how long she had been unconscious. When Verran awoke, she sensed that considerable time had passed. Her jaw ached horribly, she was sore all over, and the world was rocking. She was supine upon a soft surface, and it was pitch dark all around her. At first she lay semi-stupified. Was the world really rocking, or was she just dizzy? Where was she, and how had she come here? She was utterly listless and had no desire to puzzle over difficult questions, but she was awake now. Whether she liked it or not, her mind had resumed operation. What was the last thing she remembered? A mean dark alley, torchlight, fear, masked men, a murdered servant, a flying fist . . . What had she been doing in such a place? There had been a letter of summons, a letter informing her of Lord Grizhni's dire peril. It all came back to her then, and she sat up with a gasp. *Where was she?*

She could see nothing, but somehow she knew she was alone. The world continued to rock, and the Lanthian-born Verran had no difficulty identifying the motion of a ship at anchor. It was a large ship, she thought, and she must be far belowdecks. But what ship? And where?

She sat on a pallet of some kind, which was equipped with a couple of blankets. Slowly and with care, she rose to her feet. She pressed a palm gently to her stomach. There was no sign that the rough handling she'd received had caused any harm to the baby. If those masked men hurt her child, Verran reflected, then somehow she would find out who they were and she would kill them. Unless, came the unbidden thought, they killed her first. Would they dare to do so? Well, they had dared to kidnap her, hadn't they? Moreover, if there had been any truth at all to that note, then it was possible that Grizhni was no longer alive to avenge his wife. Her face tingled, and she clenched her bruised jaw. She couldn't afford to start crying now. Instead, she would employ herself sensibly. She would investigate her surroundings.

There was not much to explore. Verran found herself imprisoned in a small rectangular chamber about five feet wide and seven feet in length. When she stood in the center and stretched out her arms, she could touch the walls on either side. There were no windows. A storage compartment, perhaps? By feeling her way around the walls she managed to locate the door. It was locked, and there was no latch or pull on her side. She ran her hand over the wooden surface, which was very smooth, as if it had been polished. But why would the door of a storage compartment be polished on the inside? Curious.

The chamber contained only two objects. One was the pallet on which she had awakened, and the other was a slop pail. Verran returned to the pallet and sat down. She touched the blankets. They were of very soft, fine wool. Curious again.

It was absolutely dark. By now her pupils must be fully dilated, but she could not see a thing. Verran surmised that outside her prison it was still nighttime. Who could be waiting on the other side of the locked door? Was it possible she might have friends within earshot? Could they hear her if she called? Probably not, but it was worth a try. She lifted her voice in cries for help, but no savior appeared. Her throat was already sore from the abuse inflicted on it earlier in the evening, and she could not yell for long. For a while she tried banging the slop pail against the door, but soon gave it up. Such antics would do no good.

She sat and listened. All she could hear was the creak of timbers. It was horrible sitting alone there in a black prison. There was nothing to see, nowhere to go, and nothing to do but think . . . and think . . . desperate, terrified thoughts that scrabbled around in her head like rabid mice. How long had she been here? Who had done this to her, and why? What were their plans for her? Was Lord Grizhni safe? The note informing her of his danger had obviously been intended to lure her away from the palace, in which case it might well have been a complete fabrication. He might be unharmed. He might be . . .

Another thought struck Verran. If Grizhni was safe and well, then he would use his Cognition to find her. They couldn't expect to conceal her whereabouts from the greatest savant of all time, could they? It would be impossible. In which case—the conclusion was inescapable—they would have little choice but to kill her. So her mind ran, for hour upon torturous hour as she sat alone in the dark.

She was thirsty. Her captors had not provided her with food or water. Her mouth was parched, her throat inflamed. How long could she have been there? It seemed endless.

Verran dozed fitfully and lost all track of time. But surely the hours were passing, for at last a faint line of gray light became visible through the crack under the door. It looked like daylight. The girl got down on hands and knees and tried to peer through the crack. She could see nothing. Miserable as never before, she returned to the pallet and lay down. More than anything else in the world, she longed for complete unconsciousness.

She might have been sleeping very lightly, or her mind might at that moment have been mercifully empty of thought. But something suddenly fired her nerves, jerking her into sharp awareness. Her eyes snapped blindly open. She had felt a slight vibration through the floorboards. She held her breath, listened, and caught the thud of footsteps outside. Somebody was approaching her prison. A rescuer? A murderer? Her pulses leaped and her heart hammered. The footsteps were heavy—a large man's, she guessed. A man with a knife? A man with a strangler's cord?

She jumped from the pallet, ran her hands over the floor, and located the empty slop pail. The pail was of heavy wood with metal bands and handle. It had a very solid feel. The footsteps were close now. They paused outside the door.

There was a scratchy fumbling sound and the rasp of a sliding bolt.

Verran stood near the door. Her muscles were tensed, her weapon ready, and she was prepared to face her executioner, if such he was. Her mind ticked. *There's daylight outside this room, and when the door opens, you'll be blinded. Lower your lids a little and don't face the light directly. You'll probably see the man as a silhouette. Strike at his head. One chance is all you'll get.*

The door opened and a man appeared. He was masked and he carried a tray. Verran swung the pail, felt it collide with flesh. Her victim cursed and staggered. His tray clattered to the floor. The girl shoved him from her path, and he fell heavily.

She sprang from her prison and found herself in a narrow passageway. The place was filled with weak grayish light, painful to her unaccustomed eyes. She squinted, raised a hand to shade her eyes, and threw a quick glance around her. The passage was paneled in dark, beautifully polished wood, and the floor shone. Even in the midst of her terror she was astounded. What sort of a ship could this be?

A few feet away stood a carven, inlaid ladder that seemed to offer the hope of escape. Verran scrambled up the rungs as nimbly as pregnancy would allow. The hatch at the top was locked, or perhaps very heavy. She could not move it. For a few moments she pushed frantically at the barrier, then gave up. She descended and glanced back at the compartment that had lately contained her. Her jailer's legs protruded into the passageway. He lay as he had fallen, but now he was stirring.

She ran along the passage, trying door after door. Behind most of them she discovered small compartments, some empty and some filled with sacks, bales, and barrels.

The floorboards shook and she heard the swift thud of footsteps behind her. Her enemy had recovered himself.

Verran hurried forward another few feet and found herself at the end of the passageway. Before her rose a barred door. On either side of her, blank walls. Behind her, an enraged pursuer. She lifted the bar with an effort, yanked the door open, took a single step forward and paused, staring.

The room beyond was equipped with a couple of portholes through which the daylight entered. It contained three great rectangular blocks resembling biers. Upon each bier lay a man. The men were pitiful—emaciated, pallid, unshaven, exhausted. One turned hopeless eyes toward the door as it opened. The other two were either indifferent or stupefied. White cords bound them to their respective biers. The cords looked soft but strong, and glistened moistly in the dull light of day. They looked alive. They slithered over the floor and walls like pale serpents, hung from the ceiling in fantastic designs, and clung with a will to the recumbent human forms. As Verran watched, the white cords pulsed slowly and one of the prisoners moaned.

The girl stood frozen. The scene before her was as hypnotic as it was inexplicable. But she did not watch for long.

A thunder of footfalls, a muscular arm looped around her from behind, and Verran was swung clear off her feet. There was no point in struggling—her captor was fearfully strong. She twisted her head around to look at him. The man's mask was gone and she beheld a fleshy, brutal face which was not familiar to her. A deep gash marked his forehead and the blood was dripping down his cheek. His eyes were slitted, his expression murderous. She looked away quickly. He half carried, half dragged her back along the passage, and when they reached her dark little cell, he slung her in with a curse.

Verran hit the floor hard and crouched there gasping. The door banged shut and the bolt slid into place. Once again impenetrable darkness pressed upon her.

She was shaking. She made no sound, but the hot tears welled up, forced their way under her tightly closed lids and streamed uncontrollably down her cheeks. Try as she would, she could not stop them.

Chapter Thirteen

Fal Grizhni and Nyd returned home earlier than expected. The meeting of the Council had proven inconclusive. Grizhni's first action upon entering the palace was to request the presence of his wife. The hybrid servants wordlessly informed him of her absence, and the savant's countenance froze in surprised displeasure. "Her destination?" he demanded.

The servants did not know.

"Her purpose?"

No information was available.

"By what means did she travel? Was she accompanied?"

These questions were answered, albeit not to Fal Grizhni's satisfaction. He said nothing, perhaps unwilling to express criticism of his lady before the servants, but the severity of his expression promised that her disobedience to his instructions would not go unreproved. The savant proceeded to his own chambers, and there he scribbled a terse note commanding the presence of Lady Grizhni immediately upon her return. He sealed the missive and summoned Nyd. "Place this in Lady Grizhni's apartment," he ordered, and the hybrid sprang to perform his master's bidding. Fal Grizhni remained seated, staring blackly into the fire. The vertical crease between his brows was unusually pronounced.

Presently Nyd returned, bearing another message which he presented to the savant. It was the letter summoning Verran to her wounded husband's side. Grizhni read, and for once his

face revealed his emotions—terrible rage and apprehension.
Nyd hissed in alarm. He had never dreamed that his omnipotent master could appear so. Grizhni's face was ashen. His
hands were clenched and his entire figure was rigid. His voice,
however, remained cool as he informed Nyd, "Your mistress
has been deliberately deceived, and is perhaps in some danger.
I intend to use Cognitive methods to locate her. You will stand
sentry outside my workroom door and see to it that I am not
interrupted."

Nyd croaked nervously. His facial hair bristled. Had he
been capable of speech, he might have expressed the fear that
his master was ill—quite ill indeed.

Fal Grizhni and his servant hurried to the workroom, and
Grizhni disappeared therein. At least two hours passed. Nyd
stood like a stone, awaiting his master's inevitable triumph.
But when at last the door swung open, Fal Grizhni's lunar
pallor bespoke failure.

"She is hidden from me," the savant remarked calmly. "If
she is still within the city, then she is locked away in some
place shielded from Cognitive observation. I shall penetrate
that shield eventually, but some time may be required to do
so. Therefore I have decided that you will organize your
nestmates into a number of search parties and dispatch them
throughout the city without delay. You will investigate all
streets and alleys, all possibilities. Here are written orders that
must be distributed among the leaders of the various search
parties— they will permit you access to all private dwellings,
boats, and public edifices." Grizhni extended a handful of
warrants that he, as Preeminent, possessed authority to issue.
"Make liberal use of them. The contents of the note you
brought to me suggest that Lady Grizhni embarked for the
Destula Pier. The search party under your immediate command will conduct a thorough examination of that area. Head
for the Bridge of Spiteful Cats, then look for an alley behind
an arch hung with a green lantern. I do not wish you or the
others to return to this palace until you have located your
lady, or until I send for you. While you search, I will continue
my Cognitive efforts here. If you find Lady Grizhni before I
do, escort her home and protect her with your life in the event
of attack or interference. Is all this clear?"

Nyd hissed, and his eyes were scarlet with zeal.

"Begin at once." Fal Grizhni retreated into his workroom,

shutting the door firmly behind him.

Nyd carried out his master's commands with his customary energy and efficiency. Within minutes bands of hooded hybrids were out scouring the darkened byways of Lanthi Ume. Nyd and five of his nestmates rowed for the Destula Pier. Once disembarked, they commenced a laborious search. It was slow work, and in that neighborhood it was dangerous as well. The inhabitants of the Destula did not take kindly to the invasion of their warren, Selectic search warrant notwithstanding. Considerable time elapsed before the hybrids won past the savage felines on the Bridge of Spiteful Cats, passed under an arch bathed in a green glow, and found themselves in a reeking alleyway. There they discovered the corpse of the recently slaughtered Spryl. The body was clothed only in its own wiry hair, for some enterprising local had already made off with the gray robe. The hybrids grieved for the loss of their brother, but realized that they were on the right track. Of their mistress, however, they found not a single trace.

Verran tilted the empty pitcher to her lips in the vain hope of extracting a last drop of water. No use—nothing left. She tossed the pitcher aside, heard a clang as it struck the wall, a clatter as it rolled across the floor. But she saw nothing in the dark, and she wondered if she would ever see again. Many hours had passed since her escape attempt. She had lost all track of time, but she could judge the duration of her captivity by the condition of her mouth and throat.

The jailer she had encountered earlier in the day had carried a tray of food and a pitcher of water. When she struck him, he had dropped the tray and most of the water was lost. Her captors had not seen fit to replenish her supplies, and Verran's thirst raged. Hour by hour her mouth dried out and her discomfort increased. She wanted no food, but had forced herself to consume the meat provided for the sake of its juices. Now all that remained was a small loaf of bread, and there wasn't a suspicion of moisture in it.

Verran wondered if there was anything she might do with the tray and pitcher that had come into her possession. They were made of metal, they were sturdy, and surely they could be of some use—as weapons, perhaps? No. She'd already tried that trick, and her captors would not be caught off guard again. She'd had her chance and failed.

The girl allowed her aching head to rest upon her hands. Her forehead was hot. Feverish, probably. *His Preeminence is gravely wounded and perhaps will not live to see the morning. Even now he lies in a feverish delirium.* The words of the note rang in her mind. Lies, all lies. What a fool she had been to believe them, what an idiot to leave the house in the teeth of her husband's warning! Her husband—did these kidnappers not fear his legendary wrath? For he would use his Cognition to find her, without a doubt. In fact, it was amazing that he had not done so already. Unless the note had been true after all, and he was wounded or dead.

Verran was jolted from her wretched reverie by the sound of a footstep outside her prison. She raised her head. The door opened and a man stood silhouetted there. As soon as her eyes accustomed themselves to the light, she preceived that he was tall, broad, and masked. Even before he spoke, she identified him as the kidnapper whose fist had struck her senseless in the alley. She regarded him warily. He was carrying something in his right hand; a cup or goblet. "And how is our lady doing, eh?" he asked with a thin smile. Her memory itched at the sound of his voice, but she didn't recognize him.

She stood up and faced him squarely. "Who are you and why have you brought me here? If you plan to hold me for ransom, you're a fool. If you're trying to frighten my husband, you're worse than a fool—you're insane."

"Noisy little wench, aren't you?" He laughed shortly and extended the goblet. "This is for you. Drink all of it."

Her eyes slid from his masked face down to the goblet and back again. "What is it?"

"Does it matter? You must be thirsty by now. Well, here's something to drink. Don't waste my time arguing, just take it."

She retreated a step, but there was nowhere to go. "If you plan to kill me, I can't stop you. But I won't cooperate. You can't make me drink poison."

"Can't I? Would you like to place a wager on that, my lady? But this isn't poison, as it happens. It's a sleeping draught and it won't hurt you. One glass of this and you're dead to the world until tomorrow."

"Why do you want me to sleep?"

"Because it'll be less trouble that way for us to transport you."

"Transport me! Where?"

"Look, I didn't come down here to gossip with you. I told you this swill is harmless—"

"I don't believe you."

"Please yourself. But you're going to drink it in any case."

"What if I refuse?"

He advanced a couple of long paces, backing her up against the wall of the tiny room. "I wouldn't refuse, if I were you. If you're that stupid, then you get another clip on the jaw like you got in the alley. It'll be a lot more painful than the sleeping potion, and the end result will be the same."

Verran stared at the goblet. The liquid within was dark and thick. "This isn't necessary. I don't intend to cause any trouble for you," she promised with a fervor her companion appeared to find amusing. "Please don't make me drink that. It might hurt my baby."

"I can think of plenty of things that would hurt your baby a lot worse," he observed significantly. "And me, I think the world would be a lot better off if Grizhni's spawn never saw the light of day." She stiffened, and he grinned. "So make up your mind. Drink up, or take the consequences."

He held the goblet toward her and Verran accepted it reluctantly. She cast a final despairing look around her, then gulped down the potion. The taste was sickeningly sweet, but the liquid soothed her parched throat. She dropped the empty goblet and stared defiantly up at her captor.

"That's a good girl," he remarked. "Fifteen minutes from now you'll be sound asleep. And when you wake—"

"If I wake," she replied in a low voice. She felt nothing as yet.

"Oh, don't worry about that. You're a lot more valuable to us alive than dead, for the moment."

"What do you plan to do with me?"

"You ask too many questions, girl. I don't see how Grizhni stands it." He walked out, locking the door behind him.

Once again it was utterly dark. Verran stood with her eyes wide open and staring. Still she felt no effect of the drug. But soon she'd be asleep and they would take her somewhere—perhaps this boat would carry her over the sea to prison in some foreign land. Even her husband's powers would be insufficient to find her, and she might never see him again. She felt nauseous. Was it the result of the potion, or of panic?

There was no way of knowing, but an idea struck her then.

Verran sank to her knees, ran her hands swiftly over the floor. She soon found what she sought—the slop pail. She placed the pail between her knees, bent over nearly double, and overcoming natural repugnance, thrust a finger down her throat. Her throat contracted and she gagged convulsively. She snatched her hand away and crouched there gasping. It was going to be even more disgusting than she had expected.

She took a deep breath and plunged the finger back down her throat, down as far as it would go, farther than she would have believed possible. This time she was successful. Her stomach churned in outrage and she vomited forth its contents into the pail. For a moment she rested, a foul and acrid taste burning upon her tongue, and then another spasm seized her and the last bitter dregs spewed forth. There was nothing more. The potion—sleeping draught or poison—was out of her system, or nearly so. She felt better, and her mind seemed to be in good working order, for she realized at once that the stench rising from the slop-pail might easily give her away.

Verran crawled to the pallet, grabbed one of the blankets, and folded it into a thick pad. This pad she placed over the open mouth of the pail, which she shoved into a corner. With any luck the cloth would contain the odor—for a little while. The girl returned to the pallet and composed herself as if in slumber. She lay in a relaxed attitude with her back to the door, but her eyes were open and she listened intently. Presently a drowsiness crept along her limbs and her eyelids drooped as if weighted with stone. Some small trace of the drug had found its way into her nerves and muscles, but it could be fought and it could be beaten. She blinked rapidly and bit her lip until it hurt. The pain helped, and she deliberately sank her fingernails deep into the palm of one hand.

Verran's struggle to remain wakeful ended once and for all when she heard voices mumbling outside the door. In an instant all languor fled and she was alert as a cat. There were at least three men out there, and certain of their prisoner's unconsciousness, they spoke freely, albeit in subdued tones. She could catch isolated snatches of conversation.

". . . market day . . . farmers leaving the city at sunset . . ."

". . . cart and horse ready . . . carry her out the southern gate . . . transfer . . . carriage . . . south to . . . all in readiness . . ."

A strong voice belonging to the man who had struck her, the man who had forced her to swallow a drugged draught, spoke derisively. ". . . and keep Fal Grizhni in line for a long time to come . . . particularly when she drops the brat."

Nervous laughter. Then some disagreement or conflict.

". . . if she's still awake?"

"Sleeping like the dead. See for yourself."

The scrape of a lock and the door banged open. Light poured in and Verran shut her eyes. Her breathing was deep and regular.

"There, you see?"

"All right, take her out of there."

Footsteps, and enemies at her side. Someone grabbed her wrists and pinioned them roughly behind her back, then lashed her ankles together. Verran was completely limp. Her breathing remained tranquil, but it was fortunate that no one thought to check her heartbeat. A gag was thrust between her teeth and tied behind her head. With extreme effort she managed to keep still and quiet.

"Now pack her up."

Verran stole a glance under her lashes. Two of the men held an open canvas sack. She shut her eyes quickly. Before she had a chance to wonder what they meant to do, the third man picked her up easily and deposited her in the sack, feet first. Verran allowed her knees to buckle, and she slid down into the waiting bag, which was promptly drawn up over her head. Somebody yanked the drawstrings tightly closed.

"Leave it open. You want her to smother?" It was that hatefully familiar voice.

"No, sir."

The drawstrings were loosened by an unseen hand. A breath of air wafted into the bag. Verran didn't stir. Her eyes were open, but she saw nothing.

"Let's go, then."

"What if we run into someone?"

"Sack of provisions, charity for the poor." This witticism drew no laughter. Someone muttered an uneasy curse.

Verran felt the sack hoisted and slung over a man's broad shoulder. The blood rushed to her hanging head and she blinked dizzily. A fold of canvas lay over her face, but she didn't dare turn her head.

She was carried out of the room, down the passageway a

few paces, then up the ladder. She could hear her porter grunt, and wondered if he might drop her. But he lifted her safely through the hatch, bore her along what must have been another passage, and up yet another ladder.

They were out on the deck in the open air. Verran heard the creak of timbers, the snap of a sail in the breeze, the lapping of water, and most welcome, the familiar shout of a Lanthian raftsman, "Low for dark!", which meant that he was about to shut his floating booth for the night and would now accept unusually low prices for the sake of a last-minute sale. And she heard something else—the music of stringed instruments, music that might have accompanied the most luxurious of banquets. The sound was close, and to Verran it was inexplicable. At that moment she longed to cry out for help, but the gag was tied securely. She might produce a squeal or a moan, but nobody would hear her. Verran's teeth were clenched in frustration, and she noticed that the muscles of her neck and shoulders had tightened. If she weren't careful, her bearer would notice too. Deliberately she forced the muscles to relax.

They set her down on the deck for a moment. The mouth of the sack gaped, and Verran caught a glimpse of the surface on which she lay. She saw bits of polished wood of at least twenty varieties, laid out in intricate patterns. Each tiny piece possessed a beveled edge, perhaps to afford purchase to silk-shod feet in rough weather. What sort of a boat was this?

"Everything's ready on shore, then?" It was the almost-recognizable voice.

"Yes, sir. Cart's loaded and ready to go, with a couple of our men dressed up as yokels to drive it. Vehicles are held for us at all transfer points en route."

"Final destination prepared?"

"Yes, sir. Proof against any wizard's tricks Grizhni might pull, I'm told. Surrounded by a magic shield so strong he'll never see through it."

"He'd better not, or there'll be hell to pay, I can tell you."

It sounded, she thought miserably, as if they planned to lock her up for a long time to come.

Verran's head rested on the deck. With her captors engaged in conversation, she now began very cautiously to push her cheek against the hard surface in the hope of dislodging the gag. It hurt to do so, for her jaw was bruised where she had been struck. She would have persevered despite the pain, had

she not been lifted up, unceremoniously passed from one captor to another, and set down abruptly in a new location. She
turned her face carefully and found that she had a clear view.

They had placed her in a small boat, and evidently planned
to row her to shore. Judging by the conversation she had
overheard, she was to be transferred to a cart, ostensibly a
farmer's cart, which would leave the city along with hundreds
of other such vehicles at the close of a market day. Once clear
of Lanthi Ume, they would transfer her to a fast carriage, one
of a whole series of conveyances intended to carry her . . .
somewhere. Once they got her out of the city, her chances of
rescue were almost nil. With a whole world to search through,
even Fal Grizhni could not hope to find her.

"Lower away."

The boat descended with remarkable speed and smoothness
—so remarkable as to verge on the unnatural, and Verran suspected the working of Cognition. The little craft bore them
swiftly over the water. Verran peeked out of the sack and
beheld a stretch of twilit sky in which the first stars were beginning to appear. Before her loomed a group of warehouses—
shabby and decrepit structures that she did not recognize. The
neighborhood wasn't familiar to her, and she could not identify the canal. It might have been adjacent to the Destula—
there was the same air of sinister poverty, of threatening want.
Quietly she resumed her efforts to loosen the gag, but soon
discovered that any movement forceful enough to accomplish
her purpose was bound to attract the attention of her guards.

They landed, and the sack was unloaded onto the dock. Not
far away waited a cart packed with bulging canvas bags. The
driver looked to be a sturdy rustic, and beside him sat another
of the same ilk. Hitched to the vehicle was a slow-moving
miskin.

Verran felt herself lifted, borne to the cart, and deposited
among the sacks. Someone began piling cargo on top of her,
and the voice she had learned to dread spoke angrily. "Stop
that, you fool! What are you trying to do, suffocate her? We
want that whelp she's carrying born healthy. It'll be worth its
weight in rubies. Get rid of that stuff."

Silence as the weights were removed from her body. Verran
lay as if dead.

"What are you doing with a miskin?" The speaker's annoyance had not abated. "Couldn't you even manage to find a
horse?"

"Most of the farmers use miskins, sir. A horse would be likely to attract attention."

His superior grunted. "If we fall behind schedule, it's your neck."

Verran shifted position slightly. She was lying on her back and her arms were starting to go to sleep. What good did it do to have fooled her captors and maintained consciousness if she couldn't manage to free herself?

Then why not, the thought came, *wait until the cart reaches the southern gate, and reveal yourself to whatever citizens might yet linger there?*

Reveal myself how? I can't speak and I can't move.

Make noise. Thrash around a lot. People will notice. When they see the condition you're in, they'll help.

Oh, will they? Not if the men claim I'm some farmer's runaway harlot of a daughter that they're bringing home. People will just laugh and say I should be given a good whipping and that I'm lucky my father's willing to take me back.

Do you really believe these men would think of telling a story like that? They don't seem very clever.

That tall one is. I don't know about the others. If only my feet were free to run!

Then work on the cord that binds your ankles. But don't be stupid—wait until the cart starts moving, or else they'll notice.

"All right, move on," the hated voice commanded.

Inside the sack, Verran heard and thought, *If I should ever meet you again, I'll know you by that voice.*

The cart creaked on its way. Verran was jounced from side to side. After a couple of minutes she judged it was safe to ease herself into a new position, raise her head a little, and nudge a fold of canvas aside. She could see again. She lay facing the back of the wagon, and through the wooden slats she spied the receding forms of her three erstwhile guards. They did not accompany the cart to the gate, then. For the moment she had been entrusted to the care of the two counterfeit farmers.

She lay quietly. No sense in moving until the cart was out of earshot of the men from the boat. The minutes passed. At last she poked her head cautiously out of the sack and glanced over her shoulder. The two men sat with their backs to her, their eyes fixed on the road ahead. They had no inkling that their charge was awake. Verran drew her ankles up behind her, arched her back, and picked at the cord with her bound hands. She was fortunate. Deeming their prisoner completely helpless, the kidnappers had been careless, and the knots at her ankles were slipshod. Gradually she worked them loose, and at last she pulled her feet free. She looked out again. The street was deserted, the buildings were unfamiliar, and she had no idea where she was—but at least it was still Lanthi Ume. If she could escape for only a few minutes, she might manage to rid herself of the gag and find some citizen who would be moved to help her.

The girl attempted to shift her weight onto her knees. With her wrists bound behind her back, her abdomen protruding, the sack restricting her, and the cart continually bouncing, she could not do it. She squirmed out of the bag on her back, worked her way to the back of the cart, sat up and regarded her captors. They had noticed nothing as yet. With any luck she might even manage to slip from the wagon without attracting their attention. She rose to her knees and then to her feet, swung her legs over the back of the cart, and dropped down to the ground. She landed awkwardly, staggered and fell. Any hope of escaping detection instantly vanished. Despite the rumble of the cart, both guards heard her thud on the cobbles. Verran stood up and took to her heels. She cast a look back over her shoulder as she went, saw the two men spring from their cart, and realized that they could run twice as fast as she.

Verran ducked into a dim side alley, turned at the first intersection she came across, then turned again to lay as confusing a trail as possible. Where should she go? She was completely lost. It was nearly dark, and the streets were empty. There was nobody to help, nobody to unbind her hands or remove the increasingly painful gag. Light shone at a window not far away. It was a narrow, mean dwelling set amidst a clutter of warehouses. Uninviting though it appeared, the place was occupied. Verran ran to the house and kicked at the door. There was no response, and she kicked again. Still no response. She glanced at the lighted window. Through the chinks of the barred shutter she could see the outline of a human form. Someone stood there watching, and Verran longed for the use of her voice. If only she could speak, surely she could persuade that motionless spectator to admit her. As it was, only the violence of her assault upon the unyielding door conveyed her desperation. As she kicked and battered, the figure within finally moved. It stooped, performed some invisible opera tion, and the light in the window disappeared, leaving the house silent and dark. Verran paused, staring in shock. A thin, keening wail of anguish fought its way past her gag.

Her pursuers appeared at the end of the street and spotted her immediately. Verran sprinted around the angle of the house and found herself among the warehouses. She would never find help in such a place. She should have kept to the streets, she realized. In and around the silent buildings she sped in search of a hiding place. Her breath was labored now, and certain internal pains terrified her. For the first time she considered the possibility of miscarriage.

It was hard to run in the long dress. With hands tied behind her, she couldn't pick up the skirts, and the heavy fabric slapped at her ankles with every step. Her pace was slowing and her movements became uncertain. A misstep set her foot down on the hem of her gown, tripped her, sent her sprawling. Verran lay gasping for a moment. Fear and hopelessness tempted her to stay where she was. She clenched her teeth and hauled herself to her feet. Was she not Fal Grizhni's lady?

Around the warehouse she ran, through an open area strewn with bricks, broken glass, and debris, past a tumbledown shack built of cannibalized sendilli. Through an iron gate that swung on screaming hinges, past a row of deserted booths, through another gap amongst the buildings, under an arch, and finally she was back out on the street. Verran paused, gasping for breath. She still had no idea where she was, nor did she know where her pursuers were. When she began to move again, she found she could no longer run. She walked heavily, her feet dragging. Then she heard quick foot falls, wheeled, and beheld the two men, incongruously menacing in their rustic gear. They were not far behind, and they were closing in on her quickly. The buildings rose on either side in an impenetrable phalanx. Before her the road curved sharply. Verran rounded the bend and found herself at the junction of no less than five streets. She chose a direction at random, endeavored to run, and found herself reeling. Her mind continued to function efficiently, but her body no longer obeyed her commands. She could go no farther, and capture was certain unless she could find a hiding place within the next few seconds.

A glint of water ahead, and a shabby little wharf. She stumbled toward it and came upon a stand of empty casks. One of

them might have provided refuge, but she hadn't the strength
to climb in—the barrels were too tall and steep. Verran ducked
behind the casks and there her knees gave way. She sank to the
ground and rested there, cheek pressed to the staves. From
where she knelt she could see out into the street, and very little
time elapsed before she glimpsed her pursuers. Their progress
was slow. Clearly they had no idea where she was. They were
checking every doorway, peering into every shadow, and their
febrile manner communicated a desperation almost equaling
her own. If they did not find her, they would face the wrath of
their superior. Hence they would never give up. They wouldn't
dare.

On they came, and the fugitive held her breath. They had
seen the casks. They were drawing near. There was no chance
they would overlook her and no chance that she could outrun
them. Might she not just as well stand and give herself up? It
would be better than being dragged from her refuge by force.
No, she decided. She would do nothing, nothing whatever, to
make things easy for these people. She peeked out at them,
ridiculously reminded of the hide-and-seek games of her childhood. The men were hunting among the casks only a few feet
away, wrenching the lids off one after another, tossing them
aside with an air of ill-suppressed panic.

And then they were no longer alone. Down the street came a
group of gray-robed, hooded figures, six in all.

The kidnappers suspended their search and stood conferring
in low tones. Verran wasted no time. Calling upon the last
reserves of her strength, reserves she had not known she possessed, the girl forced herself to her feet and staggered toward
the newly arrived party. For all she knew, they could be her
enemies' reinforcements, but they were the only hope she had.
She was still gagged and could not call out to them, but stifled
cries of appeal escaped her.

As Verran showed herself, her pursuers moved to intercept
her. The girl's appearance exerted an immediate effect upon
the hooded strangers, who started toward her at a run. Seeing
this, the kidnappers drew knives from beneath their tunics.

The leader of the gray figures leaped forward with a snarl of
rage. His hood fell back, revealing a fierce and familiar countenance. It was Nyd, at the head of a band of his nestmates.
Verran recognized her husband's servants, and the tears welled
up in her eyes, half blinding her. A moment later the gray
forms surrounded her protectively.

At sight of Nyd, the kidnappers halted. Now the six hybrids advanced en masse, their eyes of flame glinting through the dusk. They bore no weapons and needed none, for their talons took the place of daggers. The two men retreated with reluctance, obviously loath to relinquish their prey. Then, as Nyd hissed and the hybrids launched themselves forward with hoarse shrieks, the men turned and fled cursing. The hybrids would have given chase, but Nyd's imperative snarl halted them. He hissed in summons and his nestmates returned to group themselves as a living shield about their lady.

A couple of strokes of Nyd's razor claws severed the cord that bound Verran's wrists. She lifted her hands and stripped the gag away. Her mouth was very dry and she spoke in a whisper. "Thank you, Nyd. Thank you all." Then the tears came again and she sobbed without restraint while the hybrids clustered around her, croaking in sympathy.

It was a swift and relatively silent journey home by sendillis. Fal Grizhni stood waiting upon the moorings, having ascertained by Cognition that his servants' mission had been accomplished. He greeted Verran with all the affection she desired, and asked no questions. The savant's eyes glittered like torchlit ice as he beheld his young wife's bruised and tearstained face, the marks of the cord upon her wrists, her air of terror and exhaustion; but it was not yet time to discuss these matters. Above all things Verran wanted sleep—natural, undrugged sleep. Numb with weariness, she was scarcely conscious when her husband picked her up, carried her into the palace and through the corridors to the threshold of her own apartment, where he entrusted her to the care of her customary attendants. The servants put her to bed at once.

Fal Grizhni remained at Verran's side until sleep claimed her—a matter of seconds. He then retired to his own chambers, where he sat up far into the night, lost in sinister cogitation.

Verran slept all night and most of the next day. The sun was setting when she finally awakened. She was sore all over and still a little weak, but her spirits were much restored and she was ravenously hungry. She rose, donned a loose dressing gown, ordered a substantial meal, and bade the servants inform their master that she was awake. He joined her at once. Grizhni would not touch the food. He watched her closely as she ate, and Verran saw that he was haggard with sleepless-

ness. His face was set in a grim, almost cruel expression, and
the look in his eyes reminded her that this was the sorcerer
thought to be a son of Ert, the man people called "King of
Demons." She understood now why he inspired superstitious
fear. Verran found herself unable to sustain his gaze. She lowered her eyes and toyed with the food for which she had suddenly lost her appetite. Yet his voice, when he addressed her,
was gentle enough. "Tell me everything that happened."

She described the anonymous note that had lured her from
the palace, the voyage to the Destula Pier, the murder of
Spryl, and her own abduction.

Fal Grizhni's ominous expression intensified as she spoke of
the tall man with the torch, whose blow had struck her unconscious, but he merely inquired, "Did you recognize him?"

"No, he was masked, as they all were. But his voice was
familiar. I'm sure I'd know it if I heard it again. I hope I never
do."

"Do you not desire vengeance, Madam?"

"I desire peace."

"There is no such thing."

"That can't be true, my lord—please don't say it! I don't
want to bring our child into a world of endless strife!"

"It is a little late to think of that," he replied with a slight
smile that somehow managed to emphasize his look of gloom.
"But we digress. Tell me more of the men who assaulted my
wife and slaughtered my servant."

"I—I hardly know what to tell you. The tall one was certainly in command. He issued orders, he was very overbear-
ing, and the others obeyed him without question. In fact, they
addressed him as 'sir.' Whoever he may be, the man hates you
and rejoices in doing you harm." Grizhni nodded. "Do you
know who it was, my lord?"

"I have a suspicion, but as yet no proof."

She looked at him and believed she sensed limitless power.
"Now that I'm back here with you, it seems incredible that
anyone would dare to do such a thing."

"They shall not dare so much a second time. What else do
you recall?"

She told him of the boat with its peculiarly sumptuous appointments, its mysterious music and its pallid prisoners tan-
gled in coils of living rope.

It was the description of the boat that satisfied the last of

Fal Grizhni's doubts and at the same time aroused wrath not the less dangerous for being held carefully in check. "*Sublimity*," he said.

"My lord?"

"You were held aboard Duke Povon's venerise *Sublimity*. All you have said confirms it—the senseless luxury, the music, the exhausted captives whose stolen life-forces power the vessel. It was *Sublimity*, designed and built by Gless Vallage and shielded from surveillance by his Cognition. The Duke's own pleasure craft."

Verran digested this in silence for a time. "Then you believe it possible," she asked at last, "that his Grace may have assisted in my abduction?"

"It is more than possible."

"I can't believe that. It would make his Grace a criminal. And he's ruler of all Lanthi Ume! It can't be true."

"There is more. The masked man who kidnapped and brutalized you—I am quite certain that was Commander Haik Ulf of the Ducal Guards."

"But the Ducal Guards enforce the *law*." Verran could scarcely take it in.

"They enforce only the ducal will, Madam. Have you never realized that?"

"I've never made the distinction. And I don't want to! The Duke is ruler of Lanthi Ume, and Lanthi Ume is our world. If our ruler is corrupt, even criminal—" She stopped, then chose her words with distressful care. "If the law that governs us all is meaningless and there's no justice to be had, then—then nothing makes any sense. There's no . . . order in the world, no reason, nothing to support us and nothing to cling to. There's nothing but . . . chaos."

"Your words are naive, almost childlike. But not the less telling, for all that. Could anything be stated more plainly, clearly, and truly?" Grizhni seemed to speak as much to himself as to her. "Rev Beddef could have written a treatise on the subject, but there is the essence."

"My lord, is there no possibility of error here? I know that the Duke is your enemy, but couldn't it be that this kidnapping took place without his knowledge?"

"There is no error. Our ruler and his cohorts are criminals, liars, and cowards. They are unfit to rule themselves, much less this city. But now, in attacking me and mine, they have committed a blunder for which they will pay dearly. Abduct my innocent wife and her unborn child by force? Hurt her, terrify her, and lock her alone in the dark? They have done an ill night's work, and they will soon know it.''

Verran stared at her husband in wonder. She had never heard him express himself so freely, never dreamed that he would openly display such intensity. He was perfectly composed as always, but very pale, his face set in rigid lines like a carven mask, dark eyes wide and unnaturally blank. When he spoke, his lips scarcely moved. ''I do swear by my life, and by all the powers of my mind, that these deeds will not go unpunished.''

Chapter Fourteen

❧❧❧❧

"Cognizance Vallage, I can't go on with it. I'm sorry to sacrifice your good opinion of me, but I can't help it. It's finished."

"Is that what you came here to tell me, Brenn? Come, come, lad. Don't look so unhappy, it grieves me. I'm sure that somehow, between the two of us, we'll find a solution to the dilemma."

Gless Vallage and Wate Basef sat in the exquisite receiving chamber of Vallage House. Here all was luxury and artistry. One entire wall of the room consisted of a single gigantic, perfectly transparent pane of glass, which could never have been manufactured without Vallage's Cognitive assistance. Through the glass the silver sweep of the Lureis Canal was visible, together with an array of miraculous palaces. The curving walls of the room had been cunningly painted by foreign artisans and displayed a perfect continuation of the actual cityscape, thus creating an illusion that was the current wonder of Lanthi Ume. Brenn Wate Basef found the images confusing, and thus they fulfilled their owner's intent.

Gless Vallage was arrayed in topaz velvet, for he planned to dine with the Duke later in the day. His appearance was effortlessly elegant, as always. Brenn Wate Basef, in his rumpled black robe, with his nervous, unhappy expression, appeared particularly wretched by contrast.

"There is no solution to the dilemma, Cognizance. I can't

continue spying on Preeminence Grizhni for you—"

"For me? No, Brenn. For Lanthi Ume. I had thought we shared common goals, among which might be included the safety and freedom of our city."

"So I thought at first, but now I'm not so sure."

Vallage heaved a patient sigh. "We've been through all this before. What has changed your mind again? Do you fear Grizhni's power so greatly?"

"No. But having falsely established myself as his supporter in the congress of the Select, and having observed him so closely these last several weeks, I'm beginning to suspect that his character and intentions are less malignant than I had been led to believe."

"Then he has exploited your inexperience, and you have been deceived."

"I don't think so," Brenn replied deliberately.

"I see. And what of your concern for Lady Grizhni? Has that vanished?"

"Not at all. But she is his wife now, and perhaps the peril I had imagined doesn't exist."

"And perhaps it does." This made no visible impression, and Vallage inquired gravely, "What of your avowed debt of gratitude to me? Have you forgotten it, or do you simply choose to ignore it?"

"I neither forget nor ignore my debts. I'm grateful for the favor you've shown me. But gratitude may no longer triumph over conscience. I will not play the spy, I'll no longer dishonor myself." Despite his melodramatic choice of words, he was clearly in earnest.

"It hurts me, Brenn—it wounds me deeply—to hear you suggest that I encourage you to dishonorable acts. Your vision is clouded if you don't perceive that what I ask of you is an act of the noblest and most selfless patriotism."

"I can't help my vision, Cognizance. The hypocrisy of my own actions disgusts me, and I'm resolved I will not continue."

"There's nothing I can say to change your mind, my friend?"

"Nothing. Further argument is useless."

"Perhaps you're right," Vallage conceded lightly, without a trace of ill humor.

Brenn looked at him in surprise. He had expected anger,

conflict, recriminations. But his mentor's fine, intelligent face remained genial.

"I cannot bear the thought," Vallage continued warmly, "of inflicting the pangs of a guilty conscience upon my idealistic young colleague. And therefore I have something that may help soothe that same sensitive conscience. I've noted your recent restlessness, hence I'm prepared with a final inducement that may banish your doubts once and for all."

"Inducement? What do you mean?"

"Come and see. It's in the next room."

"Cognizance—" Brenn was embarrassed. "I don't want to waste your valuable time. There's nothing you can show me that's going to make any difference—"

"Humor me. Do as I ask, and then make your final decision. Don't worry about wasting my time. I feel that time devoted to the enrichment of my friends' understanding cannot be wasted. Come along."

Brenn shrugged and followed as Gless Vallage led him out of the receiving chamber, down a corridor paved with tiles of violet stone, and at last to a small door set very inconspicuously in the wall. Vallage opened the door. "In here," he invited.

Brenn took a step forward and paused upon the threshold. "I don't see—" he began. A hand between his shoulder blades and a firm thrust propelled him forcibly into the room. The door slammed shut behind him and he heard the key turn in the lock. He turned and exclaimed furiously, "Vallage, what do you think you're doing? What kind of game is this?"

"There's no cause for alarm, Brenn," came the pleasantly cultivated voice from the other side of the door. "I mean you no harm."

"Open this door at once." He rattled the latch ineffectually.

"All in good time, Brenn."

"Now!" No answer. "You're making a serious mistake, Vallage. In fact, you must be insane if you think you'll get away with this!"

"You are angry and upset, my friend—understandably so. In a little while you'll be calmer, you'll see things more clearly, and you'll realize that I act in your best interests."

"What are you trying to do? What do you want of me?"

"What do I want of you? Why, I want your friendship and loyalty, Brenn. What else have I ever wanted?"

"If you think you can keep me locked up here until I agree to do what you ask, you'll soon find you're mistaken." It seemed to Brenn that it was a very simple matter indeed to open a locked door. What lock could withstand the Cognition of a savant of the Select? The young man folded his arms and regarded the door with concentrated attention. The medallion that he wore around his neck—the medallion that was his favorite and most familiar Cognitive tool—began to glow, softly at first, and then with increasing brilliance. When the metal flashed like a mirror in the sunlight, Brenn spoke in a low voice. For a few moments he proceeded with confidence and authority. Then, very unexpectedly, the medallion produced a searing flash of light and went dark. The young man uttered a cry of intense anguish. He clutched at his skull as if to contain an explosion, tottered dizzily, and crashed to the floor.

From the other side of the door came an easy laugh. "No, Brenn," said Gless Vallage. "I'm afraid that will do you no good."

Brenn raised his head and stared at the door in shock and pain. It was the first time he had ever matched the Cognitive abilities of which he was so proud against the powers of a very experienced senior savant of the Order; a member of the Council, and probably the most accomplished of them all, saving only Preeminence Fal Grizhni. It was the first time he had ever realized the insignificance of his own attainments and the narrow limits of his own power. In the single instant that his mind had met and countered the Cognition of Saxas Gless Vallage, he had realized all at once that he stood in the presence of a force he could not hope to withstand, a force that could crush and destroy him if it chose; something ruthless, determined, and extraordinarily concentrated, which he had never imagined lay beneath the older savant's highly civilized exterior.

Brenn dragged himself slowly to his feet. For the moment the fight had been knocked out of him and his eyes were unwontedly dull. When he spoke, his voice was subdued. "Why have you imprisoned me, and how long do you intend to hold me?"

"Not long, Brenn. Only as long as it takes to convince you to demonstrate the gratitude and allegiance which, as you admit yourself, you owe to me. And I do not think that will take very long," Vallage answered in a voice that smiled.

"How do you plan to convince me?"

"Your suspicions are distressing. Try to believe that I act as your friend in leading you back to the path from which you have so unhappily strayed. In that endeavor, I am assisted."

"By whom?"

"Look around you, Brenn. Search the chamber with your mind."

Brenn looked. It was a plain room devoid of furnishings. Despite the early hour, wax tapers burned in the wall sconces. The artificial illumination was necessary, for there were no windows. Nothing seemed outwardly amiss. But the young man sensed, beyond the range of ordinary human observation, the swift working of Cognition. Deliberately he strove to clear his mind of all conscious thought that might overwhelm the slightest and weakest of signals. It was then he realized that he was not alone.

Somebody—something—was there in the room with him. There was nothing to be seen, and not a breath of air moved, but he had become aware of a strong and distinct identity close at hand. It could hardly be human—there was no hint of rational intelligence. Nor was it a beast, for he would have caught the warmth of a beast's simple passions, and warmth there was none. There was awareness, and there was intention.

Brenn felt the dread awaken within him, and he fought it as best he could. He was no ignorant peasant to be terrified by the Cognition of another savant. "What's the point of this demonstration, Vallage?" he demanded harshly.

No answer.

Still no sound, nothing to be seen, no movement of the still air, but somehow he knew that it was approaching him. Brenn instinctively flattened himself back against the locked door. The unseen presence was inimical, he was certain; and it was powerful. Its intentions were obscure. Perhaps Cognition would enable him to learn more.

Brenn sent his intellect questing, but did not manage to establish contact with the invisible companion. There seemed to be no sense of self within it—not even the rudimentary sense that a plant might own. In place of intelligence, emotion, or even reflex, the young man encountered only a nebulous, imbecile insistence. What it wanted he did not yet know, but determination seemed to be the essential wellspring of its being.

The presence retreated slowly, as if it wandered senselessly
about the room. Brenn could imagine that it moved with a
heavy, shambling gait. Could he succeed in banishing it
altogether?

Once again he attempted to achieve full Cognition. Taking a
deep breath, he moved to the center of the room, where he
stood with head bowed. He spoke, and nothing happened—
nothing at all. He spoke again, with greater effort and resolution. This time his medallion glowed faintly, briefly. The light
faded away, and he heard Gless Vallage laugh.

He was still not alone. His Cognitive exercises had succeeded only in attracting the attention of the unseen companion. It seemed for the first time fully aware of his presence,
and it approached slowly. As it drew very near, the candle
flames wavered and Brenn realized that his vision was slightly
distorted, as if he saw through a wavy glass.

It paused in front of him. Brenn remained perfectly still. At
last he could stand no more, and very slowly stretched forth a
hand and passed it through the air before him. He encountered no resistance, but experienced a sensation of icy coldness. Despite the chill, sweat stood out on his brow. He would
have given his life to know what Gless Vallage had in store for
him.

Contact seemed to act as a signal, and Brenn Wate Basef
felt himself engulfed. The being was around him and within
him, assimilating him, owning him, its very identity merging
with his. And the chill—the bitter, killing coldness—pierced
him to the heart. The room around him darkened, and pain
savaged every nerve. In that instant Brenn knew that he was
dying. His body might live on, but he himself would be gone
or absorbed. He screamed and threw himself at the door,
which remained firmly locked. The alien presence occupied
him now as if his body were a conquered province. He could
feel it in his blood and tissues; soon it would invade his mind,
and Brenn Wate Basef would cease to exist.

He strove to plead with Gless Vallage, who undoubtedly
stood outside, but he could no longer speak. The pain was increasing. When it grew too great to bear, he lost consciousness.

When Brenn regained his senses, he was back in the receiving chamber, slumped in one of the chairs. Opposite him sat

Gless Vallage, looking on with a solicitous air. Brenn's lids lifted slowly and he gazed about in confusion.

"How are you feeling, Brenn?" Vallage inquired anxiously. "You don't look well. Would you like something to drink?"

Brenn answered with an effort. "I'm well enough." Memory returned and he sat up suddenly. "*Where is it?*"

"Where is—ah, the Presence, you mean?"

"The . . . Presence?"

"The Identity, if you prefer. You refer to the colleague to whom I lately introduced you?"

Brenn nodded.

"You alarmed me, my friend. I must confess, I had no idea you'd find the meeting so profoundly moving an experience. You are quite certain you're well?"

"What was it and where is it now?"

"Minor illness hasn't banished your curiosity, I see. That's the sign of a fine intellect, Brenn. But I'd expect no less of a young man whose abilities I respect so greatly." Brenn glared at him in silence, and Vallage smiled warmly. "As for the Presence, it's here with us now. When you are quite yourself again, you'll notice it."

"Here now? In this room?"

"To be sure. Let me show you." Vallage took up a ewer from the table before him, walked to the fireplace, and sprinkled water over the flames. A quantity of smoke and steam arose, billowed out into the room in a great gray cloud. As the mists strayed into the corner, a motionless form became faintly visible in outline. It was a huge hunchbacked shape, monstrous and deformed. It appeared to have the bandy legs of a man; two arms, grotesquely elongated but still approximately human; between the gigantic shoulders, no head was discernible.

Brenn regarded the ghostly form with a mixture of alarm and professional curiosity. "It has no head," he observed.

"Such an appendage would be superfluous. Economy of effort, my friend. Economy of effort is the hallmark of the master."

"What is it?"

"Well, you might call it a reminder, Brenn. Yes, I think a reminder," Vallage replied mildly.

"What do you mean?" The cloud of smoke was already dispersing, and Brenn could scarcely glimpse the still figure.

•

"This Presence was created to act as a reminder of the duty that you owe to your city, to the Select, and to those who have helped you. I am disappointed that such a reminder proves necessary, but you are very young and the young are sometimes injudicious. Assuming responsible behavior on your part from now on, I'm willing to overlook this unfortunate lapse."

"By 'responsible behavior' I suppose you mean the resumption of spying activities?"

"Sometimes, my friend, our obligations are disagreeable. Sometimes they are so disagreeable that we are tempted to disregard them. Hence, for your own good—the reminder."

"It's served its purpose." Brenn cast an uneasy glance toward the corner. The Presence was once again invisible, but it remained there in the room with them. It was amazing how distinctly he sensed its proximity, as if its mindless determination pressed on him with a tangible weight. "You've made your point, now send it away."

"Not yet. Having made your acquaintance, the Presence has developed an affinity for your company. It will remain by your side at all times."

"You mean the reminder is to be perpetual?"

"That remains to be seen. Perhaps one day you'll develop an adequate sense of duty and the Presence may be banished. Until that day, its existence safeguards the best interests of us all."

"Vallage, I can't have this thing following me about everywhere. It's intolerable—"

"You are overly sensitive," Vallage reassured him serenely. "In all probability the Presence will go undetected by all save you. It will not trouble you in any way, provided you refrain from destructive action."

"And if I don't?"

"The consequences might prove unpleasant."

Brenn rose from the chair. Indignation seemed to renew his vigor. "You won't get away with this. The Select won't permit you to visit such indignity upon a fellow savant."

"If we are both discreet, it's unlikely that your predicament will be observed at all. The Presence, after all, is invisible."

"I'll inform the entire membership of the Select."

"Forgive me, but I believe that would be a mistake."

"I'll be the judge of that. And soon." Brenn wheeled and

took a determined step toward the door.

"My dear Brenn, for your own sake I beg you to stop."

Brenn did not bother to respond. As he moved toward the exit he felt a subtle increase in the pressure exerted by the Presence. It was suddenly cold. The air about him was harsh with that uncanny chill he had experienced once before. His eyes traveled uneasily around the room. He saw that Saxas Gless Vallage remained seated, observing him with grave concern. A few feet away he saw the Presence, or rather he felt it, and he beheld a foggy smudge of shadow in the air. This time there was no floating smoke to define its outline. Nonetheless he recognized that misshapen form, faint and vague though it was. The Presence approached him, drifting weightlessly as the mist it resembled. Simultaneously he felt it within him, felt it sink its ghostly talons into his nerves, and knew in the midst of his pain that Vallage's creation had somehow linked itself to him and that he was powerless to set himself free.

Brenn cried out and stopped in his tracks. The pain subsided. He remained still and his discomfort slowly lessened. At the same time the shadow of the Presence faded completely from view.

"My friend, I must beg you to reconsider," Vallage advised. "I cannot bear to see you suffer."

Brenn stared at him speechlessly.

"You must understand that I am your friend. We share identical goals. My actions today, which may seem severe, are only designed to discourage you from committing acts surely harmful to our cause. I urge you to regard me in light of a father, and know that I seek only what is best for you."

Brenn's dark eyes burned in impotent anger.

"Before you leave, my friend, may I have your assurance that you recognize the justice of my argument? I should like to show that I may rely upon your continued cooperation."

"Under the circumstances, I can hardly refuse it."

"I'd like to believe that your assistance is voluntary. After all, Brenn"—Vallage's voice and expression were admonitory —"you must remember who your true friends are. I am your friend. Terrs Fal Grizhni is your enemy—as he is enemy to me, to the Duke, and to the city. You used to know that, but lately you're in danger of forgetting it. Don't quarrel with your allies. Save your anger for your foes, who deserve it. Do you understand me?"

Brenn nodded grudgingly.

"Excellent. Then let us try to forget our differences. You'll continue to report your observations of Fal Grizhni's actions, and we'll both try to forget that this unfortunate quarrel ever divided us. It's for the best, Brenn. I hope you understand that it's all for the best."

Brenn Wate Basef took his leave, looking somewhat dazed. As he went, he sensed the silent, invisible Presence close beside him.

Following the departure of his protégé, Gless Vallage sat alone, his face aglow with benevolence.

Brenn returned to his lodgings in the Shevellin Tower. There in the privacy of his own chambers, he embarked upon a program of experimentation designed to free him of his incubus. His efforts were unsuccessful, and the Presence remained at his side, constant as an unwanted lover.

Chapter Fifteen

﹏﹏﹏

When the Keldhar of Gard Lammis requested temporary use
of the Fortress of Wythe in earnest of timely repayment of the
latest Lanthian loan, Duke Povon found it expedient to agree.
Preeminence Fal Grizhni's objections to this decision seemed
almost perfunctory, and it was thought by some that Grizhni
had lost his old combative spirit. The Duke himself thought as
much, for the Select rarely offered concerted opposition these
days. On the rare occasions that Povon and his former
nemesis encountered one another, Grizhni affected an attitude
of icy contempt tinged with something . . . disquieting. What
that something might be was difficult to judge. Povon would
have guessed that it had something to do with the look in
Grizhni's eyes, were it not for the fact that Grizhni's eyes were
completely expressionless. It was all very unpleasant, but at
least time had finally put an end to the savant's continual complaints and arguments, and that was a step in the right direction. Fal Grizhni was welcome to walk around looking like a
statue of Vengeance come to life if he chose, as long as he did
so in silence!

And speaking of vengeance—was it possible, Povon wondered, that information concerning that disgracefully bungled
affair of young Lady Grizhni's abduction could have reached
the ears of her husband? Impossible. Saxas had assured him
that the entire episode had been suppressed. Even the girl
herself was ignorant of her kidnappers' identities, and thus

there was nothing to fear, nothing at all. Povon shrugged his plump shoulders and strove to think of other things, but found that his accustomed pleasures failed to divert him. Even his dressing gown of Living Silk had begun to pall. Povon needed something new.

The Duke's peace of mind might have suffered had he known what Lady Verran knew.

Verran had begun her last month of pregnancy, and preferred to remain within her own suite of rooms as much as possible. She was nonetheless aware of unusual activity at Grizhni Palace—activity that had continued for some weeks subsequent to her rescue.

There were the visitors. They came at all hours of the day and night, sometimes singly, sometimes in small groups. She was never introduced, but occasionally she glimpsed them at a distance—dignified, dark-robed men with a shared air of consequence. Only once did she spy an intellectual countenance that she recognized—the Cognizant Ches Kilmo, a savant present at the one congress of the Select she had ever attended. It was not extraordinary that her husband should receive visits from his colleagues, but why would they come so stealthily, often in the middle of the night? And why would Fal Grizhni remain closeted with them for hours at a time, sometimes until the break of dawn?

Verran sought an explanation without success. Her husband, ordinarily tolerant of her curiosity, proved completely uncooperative in this case. He informed her only that the meetings dealt with abstruse Selectic matters in which she would find no interest. When she persisted, Grizhni forbade further inquiries.

There were the messages. They arrived by night, carried by masked servants who waited only long enough to receive spoken reply before departing. Verran had never had the chance to peruse any of these notes, for Grizhni invariably consigned them to the fire. He refused to discuss their contents.

There were Grizhni's frequent, unexplained absences from home. Usually he was away for no more than a few hours at a time, but lately his excursions had become more numerous and prolonged. Once he had left the palace around midnight and not returned until afternoon of the following day. He declined to offer any explanation, and firmly discouraged all questions.

Something was going on. Verran didn't know what it was, but she suspected activity both significant and perilous. Whatever was happening, Fal Grizhni did not want her involved, did not want her to know about it at all. But then, when did he ever want her to know about anything? He had forbidden her to leave the palace and he told her nothing. Unjust, she reproached herself. Her husband was only trying to protect her, and would never prevent her from seeking legitimate knowledge. He had brought her to a congress of the Select, he encouraged her to read and to learn, and he clearly took pleasure in her developing intellect. If he withheld information now, then he did so for her own good. But the mystery aroused her most intense curiosity, and she was resolved to solve it if she could. So Verran's thoughts ran as she sat awaiting the appearance of Brenn Wate Basef.

She had not seen or heard from him since the afternoon of their unpleasant encounter upon the Sunburst Float. She had been certain that day that she never wanted to speak to him again. But now Fal Grizhni had entrusted her with certain folios set aside for Wate Basef's use, and the young savant was coming to Grizhni Palace to collect them. Grizhni had been called away on one of his nameless errands, and it remained with Verran to see to it that Brenn received the manuscripts. She might easily have commanded a servant to deal with the visitor, thus avoiding a potentially disagreeable meeting, but she had not set foot outside the palace in weeks and now welcomed company of any kind. Moreover the situation piqued her interest. If her husband loaned Wate Basef articles from his treasured library, then relations between the two savants were obviously friendly. The last time she had seen Brenn, he had expressed hatred of Fal Grizhni. Now something had changed his outlook. What could have caused such a reversal? Brenn was so mercurial, there were a thousand possible explanations. One thing was clear, though. If Brenn was now Grizhni's ally, then Verran wished to make her own peace with him. The prospect cheered her.

She had decided to receive him in her own Audience chamber. It was one of the few times since her marriage that she had elected to use the room. Now she sat in a thronelike chair, with the folios resting on a small table at her side. She wore a loose, very voluminous gown, and her pregnancy was not particularly obvious. A servant appeared on the threshold and in its own fashion announced the arrival of a visitor. Verran nodded, and Brenn Wate Basef was ushered in.

The smile froze on Verran's lips and she repressed an exclamation of dismay. Brenn looked ghastly, so dreadful that only one explanation suggested itself—he must be seriously ill. He had lost considerable weight. He had been lean to begin with, and now he was pitifully thin. His gaunt and colorless face looked tired to death. The dark eyes that had reminded her of Zaniboono's glittered unhealthily in their shadowed sockets. Verran, well acquainted with Brenn's expressions, recognized misery amounting to desperation. There was also something in his eyes she had never seen there before—a hunted look.

"Hello, Verran," he said dully.

Her carefully prepared speech of welcome was forgotten. Any lingering traces of resentment were blotted out.

"Hello, Brenn. I'm glad you came today," she replied uncertainly. "Wouldn't you like to sit down?"

He nodded, and sank exhaustedly into the proffered chair.

"I'll call for some wine."

"No." He shook his head. "I want nothing."

There was silence as she cast about for something to say. She had never had any trouble talking to Brenn Wate Basef before, but she had never seen him like this. "Well," she said at last, "Lord Grizhni was called away unexpectedly and couldn't greet you. He wanted me to make sure you got these manuscripts you've been promised. I gather they contain some information related to your experiments."

"Yes," he replied indifferently. "Drid Gardrid's *Notes on the Infinitely Flexible Bone*. His Preeminence believes this might assist in the development of my skeletal slaves."

"I remember. Is your work going well?"

"I suppose so," he answered with no change of expression. "I've scarce thought of it lately."

"That's strange. You used to be so enthusiastic."

"I've had other concerns on my mind."

"Oh. I see. Nothing unpleasant, I hope?"

"Why do you ask that?"

"I didn't mean to pry. It's just that . . ." She trailed off.

"Well?" he demanded with a touch of his old impatience.

"Don't get angry. It's just that you're not looking very healthy."

"I haven't been sleeping well. It's nothing."

"I believe you're ill, and it worries me."

"Why should it worry you, Lady Grizhni?"

"Of course it does!" she burst out, social conventions forgotten. "Look, Brenn—we've quarreled and there's been ill feeling between the two of us, but I want that to end. You'll always be one of the people in this city that I care about. I want us to be friends, and if there's something wrong, then I want to help you if I possibly can."

"Thank you, Verran. I believe you mean what you say." His variable mood had shifted again, and he spoke with tired gratitude. "I want us to be friends, too, for my feelings toward you are still . . . well, there's no need to go into that. It's true that I'm troubled, but you can't help me. Nobody can."

"But that's where you're wrong. There's no problem that can't be solved. What troubles you? If I can't help, then Lord Grizhni certainly can."

"Ha—Grizhni! If you realized for one moment— Rest assured, Fal Grizhni is the last person in the world to help me."

"I don't know why you say that. Lord Grizhni likes you and thinks well of you. He's lending you these folios, isn't he? He'd never do that if he didn't respect and trust you."

"Respect and trust me?" The young man looked curiously shocked.

"I'm sure of it. Why, if you only knew what store he sets by his manuscripts—but then you do know, don't you? You're a savant of the Select, as Fal Grizhni is. You love knowledge as he does, and you're concerned for the future of Lanthi Ume. In many ways the two of you are much alike. How could he fail to esteem you? You must tell him what's wrong, and he's sure to help."

"No he wouldn't. You don't know— I can't—" Brenn seemed to find it increasingly difficult to speak. He was panting for breath and looked oddly fearful.

"It's easier to talk to Lord Grizhni than you might think. The fact that you came here today proves that your animosity toward my husband has diminished, which makes me truly happy. I'll be happier yet on the day that you and he become

real friends. In the meantime, *I'm* certainly your friend, and
you can talk to me. Tell me what's upsetting you and you're
sure to feel better. Then, if you like, I could talk to Lord
Grizhni about it and ask him to lend his assistance. He's certain to agree, and there are very few problems that he can't
deal with.''

She looked at him, her lips parted and her face alight with
eagerness.

Brenn's haunted eyes closed briefly. "You are generous.
You always were. But you have no idea what's happened to
me . . . what I've got myself into—''

"Then tell me, and perhaps I'll understand.''

He took a deep breath. "You think you know me, but
things aren't always what they seem. I don't want you to think
any worse of me than you can help, so please believe that my
motives were honorable.''

"Motives for what?''

"Not long ago I made the mistake of becoming involved
with—'' Brenn broke off with a gasp. He shuddered profoundly and his hands clenched on the arms of the chair. His
back arched and his face contorted in a grimace of agony. Verran stared, temporarily paralyzed. A groan escaped him, but
the sound was muffled, as if an iron fist had clamped down on
his vocal cords. The young man's breathing was labored and
his hands flew to his throat. For a moment more he struggled
ineffectually to speak, then subsided, utterly preoccupied with
his pain.

Verran sprang from her chair. "What is it?'' she cried.

He could not answer. His eyes were full of anguish, fear,
and some inexplicable hatred. Following his gaze, Verran saw
little. There might have been a faint cloud of smoke hanging in
the air close beside him, but nothing more, nothing to explain
his expression. She ran to the bellpull, yanked it sharply, and
returned to his side. Blood was streaming from his nose and
pinkish froth had appeared upon his lips. He was sprawling,
practically lying in his chair, and the choking sounds he made
were dreadful.

Verran knelt beside him. "Brenn, the servants are coming.
We're going to summon a physician and he'll be here very
soon. Until then we'll do what we can to ease your pain. Lord
Grizhni has devised wonderful restoratives—''

Brenn was still unable to speak, but he shook his head vehemently.

"You must, you need it—"

Slowly the spasm passed and the invisible grip upon his throat loosened. "No medicine," Brenn whispered painfully. "No physician either." He reclined in the chair, his eyes closed.

"But you're very ill—"

"I shall soon recover."

"I wish I could be sure of that."

"Oh, believe me. I'm often subject to attacks of this kind, and they are generally brief."

"How long has this been happening to you?"

"Not long. It came upon me quite suddenly." He opened his eyes and smiled at her drearily.

Two hybrids appeared in the doorway. Verran dismissed the creatures with a gesture, but they seemed disinclined to go. They loitered upon the threshold, their reddish eyes darting uneasily about the chamber, their nostrils distended as if something there disturbed them. Verran repeated her gesture more forcefully, and the servants retired amidst soft whimpers.

Brenn sat up. He seemed more exhausted than ever, but his condition was considerably improved. "I'm leaving."

"You can't do that! You're not well enough to move yet."

"Don't concern yourself, Verran. There's no need."

"I think there is. There's something very wrong, and I want to help. Only let me—"

"If you truly want to help, there's one thing you can do."

"Anything."

"Promise me that you won't breathe a word of this incident to anyone."

"But Lord Grizhni could surely—"

"Speak to no one! Do I have your word?"

"Isn't there anything I can say to persuade you—" His haggard gray countenance frightened her, and she said quickly, "All right, if that's what you really want. You have my word."

He nodded in obvious relief, then slowly dragged himself to his feet.

"I wish you wouldn't go like this, Brenn." He didn't reply, and she added, "If you must go, at least take one of our dombuli. One of the servants will row you—''

"No. Thank you. It isn't necessary. Please stay where you are. I'll find my own way down to canal-level." He plodded toward the exit, moving like a very old or a very sick man.

"Brenn." As she spoke he turned to look at her. "The folios—Lord Grizhni set them aside for you. Do you still want them?"

He nodded, and surprisingly, his pale face flushed. He accepted the books with reluctance. They were not large but they seemed to weigh him down, and he made his way from the room as laboriously as a prisoner dragging iron fetters.

Following Brenn's departure, Verran returned to her chair and sat immersed in anxious thought. At last she sighed, lifted her head, and looked around her. It occurred to her that she had never liked her Audience chamber, and now she liked it less than ever. There was something unpleasant here, and she wasn't the only one to think so. The hybrids had obviously noticed something peculiar. Perhaps the room had bad ventilation. She recalled seeing something like a puff of smoke hanging in the air during Brenn's attack, but there was nothing there now. Probably the fireplace needed cleaning. She dismissed her own qualms, but exited swiftly.

The day passed slowly, as it often did when Fal Grizhni was not about. Verran found herself preoccupied with thoughts of Brenn Wate Basef and his wretched condition. He had looked so sick, so desperate! Certainly his trouble went far beyond mere physical illness. Something was preying horribly on his mind, but she couldn't imagine what it might be. *Please believe that my motives were honorable*, he had begged, which sounded as if he had done something of which he was ashamed. But Brenn was honest and high-minded, and it was hard to believe that he would ever commit a reprehensible deed. If only she could consult Fal Grizhni, he'd surely offer some constructive advice. But Brenn had extracted a promise of silence, and she had given her word not to mention the incident to anyone. The *incident*—that meant only the isolated episode of Brenn's attack of this afternoon. She would not be breaking her promise, Verran thought, if she simply informed her husband that she believed Brenn to be in need of help. If he wanted to know what made her think so, she could explain that it was just a feeling—which was true, as far as it went.

It was late, and the sun was going down. Verran wondered if her husband had come home yet. Sometimes when he had business of particular importance to attend to, he would proceed directly to his workroom, and it was possible that he was there now. If so, he probably would not emerge for hours.

Verran hurried through the endless corridors that had become so familiar. When she arrived at the workroom door, she paused and knocked. There was no answer, and after a moment she entered. The place was empty.

Verran heaved a discontented sigh and wondered for the thousandth time what was taking up so much of Grizhni's time these days; not only Grizhni's time, but that of a number of his colleagues as well. What were they up to—all those savants? Impossible to deduce the answer—she hadn't enough information.

Her husband's prized artifacts surrounded her on all sides—his most treasured volumes, his mysterious instruments, the written records of his experiments, and the myriad small devices used to enhance Cognition. They told her nothing. Verran wandered about the room, examining the contents of the shelves, wondering at the thaumaturgical devices, but touching nothing. In the corner stood a serviceable-looking writing desk, its surface covered with papers arranged in neat piles. She scanned the documents idly. Many of them were written in languages she did not understand, and she quickly lost interest.

Why, she wondered, was she so worried about her husband's activities? Grizhni had vicious enemies, but he was well equipped to defend himself. She experienced a sense of foreboding nonetheless.

What could he be doing? Did he and the others plan renewed resistance to the ducal policies? It was a possibility, but it didn't explain the savant's unwonted discretion. Fal Grizhni had never made a secret of his opposition before. It had to be something more.

Her eyes dropped again to the papers on the desk. One of them, buried under a pile of documents, caught her attention because of its unusual size. She drew it forth and regarded it curiously. She held a very detailed plan of the Ducal Palace, with all sentry posts carefully marked. Attached to the drawing was a smaller sheet bearing a list of names. She read it and recognized a number of savants of the Select, beginning with the Cognizant Jinzin Farni. The list was divided into several groups, each consisting of about half a dozen names. She eyed the two documents for a long time; blankly at first, and then with dawning comprehension. All thoughts of Brenn Wate Basef and his problems fled from her mind. Verran shook her head in instinctive denial. Her imagination was overactive—surely it wasn't possible . . . ? She considered in light of recent events and of everything she had learned of her husband's character since the day of the wedding, and concluded that it was indeed possible.

She heard a footstep behind her and turned to face Fal Grizhni. Verran started guiltily.

He stood watching her inscrutably, and she stared back at him, her eyes enormous. At last he asked, "What are you doing here?"

"I came looking for you. Am I not permitted in your workroom?"

He considered. "Yes, as long as you touch nothing." She was silent, and he added, "*Have* you touched anything?"

"Yes. These." She extended the drawing and the list, and he took them from her.

"You may enter here at will, but you are never again to touch anything without permission. You will give me your word on it." He did not raise his voice, but his expression made her uneasy.

Verran gathered up her courage. "I'd like to know what the drawing is for," she said. "I'd like to know what you and the others are planning."

He looked at her as if she were a stranger. "Is that any concern of yours, Madam?"

"It is," she answered softly. "You're my husband, and everything you do is of concern to me. All the more so if you are in danger."

"You believe me to be in danger?" he asked. She nodded. "Why so?"

"I believe that whatever it is you're doing places you at risk."

"You fear shadows, Madam. I do not want you disturbed at this time, hence I have not made you privy to my plans."

"Shall I never be worthy of Lord Grizhni's trust?"

"I desire your safety. It is not a matter of trust."

"I think it is. But you must trust me now whether you will

or no, for I believe I've discovered what you're about."

"We will not discuss the matter. You will return to your apartment."

She gazed up into eyes that appeared icy and dark as the depths of the sea. The set of his mouth was inflexible. But she had learned to read these eyes and that face, and clearly divined his apprehension. "You and the other savants are planning an insurrection of some kind. I know you've despaired of the Duke's decisions for Lanthi Ume. Now you intend to force him to govern properly. Tell me, haven't I guessed rightly?" His face changed slightly and he was silent. "Won't you answer? My dear lord, can't you see how much it would mean to me to know that I have my husband's confidence? How can we be truly man and wife if I don't?"

He looked at her, and gradually the rigid lines of his face softened. "How did you arrive at your conclusion, Madam?"

"It's been quite obvious for weeks that something strange is going on," she replied eagerly. "Something strange and important, but I hadn't any idea what. Then when I came down here and saw that plan of the palace, with markings for all the guards, and that list of savants attached to it—well, something clicked inside my head and somehow I suddenly knew you were planning something against the Duke. And the only thing I can think of is you're hoping to force him to make some changes, perhaps to get our fortresses back from Gard Lammis. Am I right?"

"Partially correct. Your intuition is good, but not flawless."

"What do you mean?"

"Do you imagine that the Duke can be reeducated—his mind transformed? His tastes, ambitions, and preferences altered?"

"I don't know. Does that matter? If you and the others can force Duke Povon to do the right thing, he doesn't have to *like* it, does he?"

"The right thing? Are you so certain that what I want is right?"

"Of course," she replied instantly.

"Why so?"

"I feel it."

"You answer without thought and without full knowledge of the facts. That is a poor policy."

"May I not believe in you, my lord?"

"Hear all, then judge. Assuming that I force the Duke to do, as you put it, 'the right thing,' then what is his Grace's subsequent attitude toward the Select likely to be?"

"Angry. He'd be your enemy. But he's that already, so where's the difference? What could he do to you? The Select are invulnerable."

"You are naive in thinking so. Consider. Can a man of malignant propensities be forced to govern justly? Can a man devoid of intelligence, strength, and honor govern wisely? Can a weakling, an incompetent, and lately a criminal ever be anything other than a dangerous disgrace to the city-state he governs?"

"If he's that bad, couldn't you use Cognition to change his nature?"

"You do not begin to understand the implications of that suggestion."

"But the Select can do just about anything, can't they?"

"You overrate our abilities. Our powers are considerable, but not unlimited. Suffice it to say we could not and should not attempt to change our ruler's basic nature, and we could not control his actions indefinitely. If we would act in the best interests of Lanthi Ume, what remains to us, Madam?"

Verran thought it over, and her conclusions were unacceptable. "I don't know," she replied uneasily.

"It is not a difficult puzzle."

She wished it had been more difficult. It was only with an effort that she could bring herself to state the unspeakable. "My lord," she asked very slowly, "are you telling me that you and the other savants are planning to kill the Duke?"

"No. He is to be banished."

"Can you actually *do* that?"

"There are obstacles, but they are not insurmountable."

"I can't believe it— I never dreamed—"

"You came close to guessing correctly. It is best that you know the truth, for the reasons you have already specified."

"But—" In her confusion, she could scarcely voice coherent questions. "When is this to happen?"

"In the very near future."

"Isn't it dangerous? The Duke has friends and supporters. What about the Ducal Guards?"

"The Duke's chiefest supporters—Kor Malifon, Dule Parnis, and the like—will be imprisoned or banished along with their master. Amnesty will be granted to those willing to swear allegiance to the new government, with the exception of Haik Ulf. The Commander is to be imprisoned, his property confiscated. As you know, I take particular interest in Haik Ulf," Grizhni concluded expressionlessly.

"You're going to have people swear allegiance to a new government? What new government, my lord? The Duke's eldest son is ten years old and said to be a half-wit. He couldn't possibly rule Lanthi Ume."

"That is true. Therefore, until the boy is competent, a Regent chosen by the Select will govern in his stead."

"And that Regent will be . . . ?"

"In all likelihood I shall be appointed."

"Is that what you want, my lord?"

"I want the Duke removed."

"And you would rule in his place. But for how long? If the Duke and his supporters are banished to some foreign land, won't they raise an army and march against Lanthi Ume?"

"Possibly. I am confident that such an attack could be repelled."

"But a lot of people would die, wouldn't they?"

"Yes. The alternative is to execute the Duke. Such an act would in all probability result in an armed rebellion within the walls of the city."

"And again, many people would die."

"Yes, and they would all be Lanthian."

"Then there's no way to avoid shedding innocent blood? You would have those lives on your conscience."

"I will. The lives that must be lost are a heavy price to pay, but Lanthi Ume will be preserved. Now, Madam," Grizhni remarked with a suspicion of irony, "your curiosity has been assuaged. Lately you expressed your confidence in the justice of my actions. Do you remain confident?"

"I don't know," she answered slowly. "I've come to believe that the Duke is a danger to the city, and I'd be glad if he were gone. But when I think of the resulting warfare—the suffering, destruction, and death—then it almost seems that nothing gained by the Duke's banishment could be worth the price. I don't know."

"I too doubt," he confessed, to her surprise. "I am not a politician. The path that I have chosen is not to my liking."

"Then go no further."

"My decision will not be altered."

She knew better than to argue. "I have another question, then. You recall the words of your friend Madam Vay Nennevay. She said that the Select shouldn't meddle in affairs of state. She said also that human beings shouldn't be ruled by the force of Cognition—that it destroys them. Yet that's what you're planning to do."

"Selectic regency is intended as a temporary measure."

"Many bad things start out as temporary measures." The young girl was unsure of her ground and spoke hesitantly. "And then somehow they become permanent."

"This will not."

"I know you wouldn't plan it that way. But things . . . happen. You've never denied the truth of Madam Nennevay's words. But now, in the name of Lanthi Ume's interests, you're planning something you know full well is apt to harm the citizens."

"Such harm will be kept to a minimum. The Duke must be deposed at any cost."

"At any cost? Then, my lord, I was mistaken. You don't always want what is right. You will succeed, and Lanthi Ume will suffer at your hands."

"It is not my desire to cause suffering."

"You will, though. How can you avoid it, when the people's welfare isn't your chiefest concern?"

"The city's welfare is my chiefest concern."

"Oh? The architecture, my lord? The art? Or the canals? Is that what you mean?"

"Have I then lost your loyalty, Madam?" Fal Grizhni inquired stonily.

"You'll never lose that. It doesn't matter if what you're doing is wrong. Right or wrong, you are my beloved husband and the father of my child. I'll be loyal to you all my life." She looked up and saw that he believed her.

"Then, Madam, let us forget the Duke, for now."

Chapter Sixteen

≈≈≈≈≈

When two officers of Gard Lammis were killed by Lanthian citizens in a brawl outside the Vayno Fortification, the Keldhar demanded a huge indemnification on behalf of his murdered subjects, and Duke Povon found it expedient to agree. The Keldhar, always of a practical bent, did not insist upon lump sum payment of the debt. In order to avoid inconveniencing his "esteemed cousin of Lanthi Ume," the Lammish ruler declared himself willing to accept payment in the form of revenue deriving from a sizable tax imposed upon the profits of certain Lanthian trading ventures. To the surprise of all concerned, Duke Povon offered immediate payment. Those most familiar with the Duke's affairs might have suspected that Povon himself had invested heavily in those selfsame ventures that now claimed the attention of Gard Lammis, but such suspicions were not voiced publicly.

Duke Povon applied to the Duke of Hurba for an immediate loan, which was granted on terms less favorable than those ordinarily offered by Gard Lammis. In order to raise the cash to repay Hurba, whose army was singularly potent, the Duke found it expedient to impose stiff taxes on flour and salted fish, the winter staples of the Lanthian diet.

The volatile citizenry were not slow in making their displeasure known. For a day and a night they demonstrated on the huge gilded moorings below the Ducal Palace, and those attempting to leave the building were pelted with chunks of

salted fish and balls of flour paste. Duke Povon hardly dared
to venture from his own bedchamber. Why, he wondered, did
his people misjudge him so cruelly? Why couldn't they understand? Didn't they know that he could set the Ducal Guards
on them if he wanted? Didn't they realize that Haik Ulf could
chop them to pieces in seconds? The Duke, however, preferred
not to resort to such methods unless goaded, for Povon loved
his people.

The morning of the second day, a change occurred in the demeanor of the crowd. Its enthusiasm abated, and citizens began leaving the scene of the demonstration. Time passed, and
more of the demonstrators departed. By noon the crowd had
disappeared, the moorings were empty, and the beleaguered
inhabitants of the Ducal Palace emerged into the light.

They were gone and Povon couldn't imagine how or why,
until a liveried flunky presented a piece of paper discovered
amidst the litter on the dock. It was a broadside issued by his
anonymous but loyal friends, the League of Patriots. The
broadside bore the customary portrait of a malevolent Fal
Grizhni, with the legend "King of Demons, Author of our
Woes." The text went on to explain Grizhni's personal responsibility for the city's current financial difficulties. Out of
sheer malice, it seemed, his Preeminence had withdrawn Selectic protection of maritime trading routes. The resulting acci-
dents, misfortunes, and disasters involving loss of human life
and property had greatly depleted the city's resources. In addition, it had been proved beyond all question that Fal Grizhni
and his loathsome accomplices, the White Demons of the
Caverns, had engineered a raid upon the city treasury. Hundreds of thousands of silver shorns had been stolen, which
treasure was now secreted in Grizhni Palace. Thus Fal Grizhni
stood revealed as a vampire draining the life's blood of Lanthi
Ume in both a literal and a figurative sense. It was for this
reason that the benevolent Duke Povon, desirous of satisfying
the city's debts of honor, had been unhappily obliged to impose the current taxes upon his subjects. The broadside ended
with a demand for Grizhni's execution.

Povon read in satisfaction and relief. How gratifying it was
to find that some of his subjects remained loyal to their ruler!
The diligence of the League of Patriots restored his faith in
human nature. Perhaps he'd have a chance to thank them one
day.

The Duke decided to travel through the streets by sedan chair to the Parnis Pier, where his beloved *Sublimity* was moored. Once aboard *Sublimity* he would find peace, for the delectable essences so amply provided by Saxas Gless Vallage never failed to delight the spirit. Povon's spirit was greatly in need of delight.

The trip through town took the Duke across the Green. The so-called Green was in reality a granite-paved square. It was the largest square in the city, the site of particularly significant executions and a public meeting place since the days of the city's founding, when the Green had actually been an open field.

Upon reaching the great square, Duke Povon discovered the whereabouts of his erstwhile visitors. A large and angry crowd had assembled there. Why, Povon wondered, did the crowd always have to be angry? Why were they never content? What was it this time?''

They had kindled a tremendous bonfire in the middle of the Green and now they clustered around it, shouting fiercely. Activity of some kind was in progress. As Povon watched through the window of his sedan chair, a human figure was hoisted on sharpened poles high above the flames. It appeared that an illegal execution was taking place, and the Duke was annoyed at the impertinence, yet intrigued. What malefactor was about to meet so painful a death? Some wife caught poisoning her husband? An overly zealous tax collector? If they had to incinerate somebody, couldn't they at least have chosen one of the Duke's personal enemies?

Closer inspection revealed that Povon's wish had been granted, after a fashion. The object of collective wrath was only an effigy—a life-sized dummy stuffed with straw. The effigy was attired in a black robe with a double-headed dragon insignia. It had been given black hair and beard, and a painted face with large black eyes and an open, snarling mouth. Around the figure's neck hung a sign: FAL GRIZHNI, KING OF DEMONS.

So they were burning Grizhni, were they? Too bad it was only an effigy.

The dark figure dropped into the fire, amidst howls of execration. The flames jumped, sparks flew, and the crowd roared.

It was Povon's intention at this time to retire with discretion. *Sublimity* awaited. His desire was thwarted when someone noticed the Dil Shonnet arms blazoned on the sedan chair. New shouts arose, and in an instant the chair was surrounded. The Duke knew an instant's queasy fear. What did these screaming savages intend? If only Haik Ulf were here with his Guards! Or Saxas, with his Cognition!

Saxas was not there, but the mob was not devoid of savants. Not far off stood the Cognizant Jinzin Farni and his companion Ches Kilmo. Both men wore ordinary street garb. Farni, with his deceptively coarse countenance, blended perfectly with the crowd.

Angry cries reached the ears of the Duke.

"Justice, your Grace! Justice for your people!"

It didn't sound as if they meant him harm. Povon swallowed hard, parted the silken curtains that shielded him from the eyes of the multitude, and cautiously poked his head out the window.

Cheers arose, together with renewed pleas for justice.

"What ails my loving subjects?" the Duke inquired unsteadily.

There was silence for a moment, and then a stout, plainly dressed man, a tradesman by the look of him, stepped forward to act as spokesman.

"Your subjects beg for justice, mercy, and deliverance, your Grace."

"You are . . . ?"

"I'm Beldo, a baker, your Grace."

"Well, good Beldo, from what evil do my people seek deliverance?" the Duke inquired with mounting assurance.

"From evil—your Grace has said it! We seek deliverance from evil, from oppression, from tyranny. We seek deliverance from the King of Demons." His companions howled in agreement.

"Do you speak of Preeminence Fal Grizhni?"

Vociferous assent from the crowd.

"My good people, wherein has his Preeminence offended you?"

Fresh howls arose.

Beldo managed to make himself heard. "Your Grace, the Commons of Lanthi Ume aren't blind and we're not asleep. We know the source of evil in this city. We recognize our enemy, we know what he's been up to, and we want him stopped."

"What charges do you bring against his Preeminence?" the Duke inquired. The topic was unexpectedly pleasant, and he was beginning to enjoy the discussion.

"How can I answer a question like that? It's a known fact that he's an enemy of the Commons. He's committed every kind of outrage, most of them not fit to be spoken of. Now he's set such high prices on fish and flour that we're all like to go hungry this winter, while he lives in luxury with his demons. It has to end."

"How do you propose to end it, friend Beldo?" asked the Duke.

"Execute him or lock him up," the baker replied bluntly. "Your Grace is master here." His cohorts applauded.

Povon smilingly inclined his head. "My friends, your loyalty warms my heart. As for his Preeminence—what proofs against him do you bring?"

"The League of Patriots has plenty. The League was formed to protect us from Fal Grizhni. It wouldn't have come into being without a reason, would it?"

"Would any member of the League of Patriots care to step forward and present his proofs?" Povon inquired in a carrying voice. "I am at the service of my people."

Silence fell over the Green. The crowd stirred, but nobody spoke up.

At last Beldo the baker replied, "Your Grace, the membership of the League is secret, and it looks like they want to keep it that way. We've got to respect their wishes—after all they've done for the Commons, it's the least we can do. But what I don't see—and I think most here would agree with me—is how much proof do you need in a case where the criminal's guilt is common knowledge? Does Fal Grizhni get special treatment because he's rich? Or is everyone too scared to stop him?"

"No!" Povon spoke fervently. "Rich or poor, powerful or weak, Preeminence Terrs Fal Grizhni merits exactly the same privileges enjoyed by all other Lanthian citizens—neither more nor less. Thus he is entitled to the protection of our excellent system of laws, under which he is exempt from punishment until such time as he has been proved guilty of a crime." There had been numerous exceptions to this rule, but the Duke chose not to elaborate.

"He's guilty!" Bendo countered, jaw outthrust. "We all know it. Your Grace knows it."

"Then let us prove it," Povon suggested. "The law of Lanthi Ume binds us all—commoners, Duke, and Selectic Preeminence. I cannot take action without proof—action against you, friend Beldo, or your wife and children, or Preeminence Grizhni. But if the accusations against him can be proved, ah, then my people will see me play the tyrant with him. Then my Lanthians will see what a friend to them their Duke can be! Find me the proofs, citizens, and you shall have the justice you desire! For know that I love justice above all things.''

Povon made a sign to his bearers, who picked up the sedan chair and advanced. The crowd parted to permit him passage. There were a few cheers, but most of the citizens stood gaping in confusion. The sedan chair skirted the edge of the fire, in which charred remains of the effigy were visible, and moved across the Green, heading for *Sublimity*.

The Cognizant Jinzin Farni turned to his companion savant Ches Kilmo and observed, ''Grizhni had better move fast.''

Chapter Seventeen

"Hes Perlo, Bor Sovis, Fodin the Younger, and Ril Vennaril. They're all members of the plot." Brenn Wate Basef finished speaking and sat motionless in his chair, seemingly drained. He had revealed everything he knew save one fact. Now Saxas Gless Vallage and Commander Haik Ulf regarded him with very dissimilar expressions.

"I'm proud of you, lad," Gless Vallage declared warmly. "Very, very proud. I knew my faith in you wasn't misplaced."

Brenn said nothing. He found himself unable to meet the cordial eyes of Gless Vallage or the contemptuous ones of Haik Ulf, and therefore gazed out the vast window of the receiving chamber of Vallage House to study the Lureis Canal.

"And I have no doubt," Vallage continued, "that you'll shortly oblige us with the identities of all of Grizhni's co-conspirators. You've provided only four names. We need the others."

The silence lengthened, and at last Brenn replied, "I can't. The faction is divided into small groups and his Preeminence meets separately with each. Fal Grizhni is the only one who knows everybody involved."

"But I'm sure, my dear Brenn, that a young man of your ingenuity will succeed in discovering all."

"It can't be done," Brenn replied. At his side he felt the unseen Presence stir, and he quailed.

"But I expect you to try. Need I remind you—"

"It doesn't matter," Haik Ulf broke in impatiently. "Once we've got Grizhni, we can get all the names we want from him, you can depend on it."

"I wouldn't be so sure, Commander. In fact, I think it quite unlikely you'll extract any information from his Preeminence."

Ulf gave a bark of laughter. "Stick to your magic tricks, and leave the interrogation to me. I'll get anything we want from Grizhni. He's got a pregnant wife, hasn't he?"

Ulf's remark provided unwelcome insight, and Brenn half rose from his chair. "If you think you're going to—" he began incoherently, then broke off as the Presence pressed upon his heart. Ulf's eyes flicked the young man insolently, then slid away as if from an object unworthy of contemplation.

"Really, Commander, your methods are crude," Vallage observed with mild distaste. "Given a little time, I'm sure Brenn will—"

"We don't have time," Ulf told him. "Grizhni isn't going to wait long, if your spy's telling the truth."

Brenn flushed deeply and his eyes blazed. Ulf took no notice.

"Oh, I've good reason to trust in Brenn," Vallage replied, his expression benign. "Then you'll move your Guards today, Commander?"

"What, on an informer's word? You must be joking. I told you what I'd need."

"You require written orders from his Grace?" Vallage inquired. Haik Ulf nodded. "You'll have them within the hour."

Commands were issued, and soon a Vallage factotum shouldered his way past the Guardsmen who waited outside the chamber, entered and presented writing supplies to his master. Gless Vallage swiftly covered a page with elegant script, sealed the missive, and entrusted it to the servant. "Carry this to the Duke," he ordered, "and stay for the written reply. Both coming and going, speed is of the essence. Haste, fellow!"

The factotum bowed briefly and left the chamber at a run. This time the Guards made way to let him pass.

"What makes you so sure the Duke will go along with your plans?" Ulf demanded. "How do you know he'll believe what you have to say?"

"Two reasons. One is that I enjoy his Grace's confidence

and friendship. The Duke knows he may rely on me to guard him against treachery."

"Very pretty. What's the second reason?"

"It's this. Once Grizhni is accused, he'll deny nothing—so great is his arrogance."

"Let's hope so. It would simplify things."

Brenn Wate Basef could stand no more. "Cognizance Vallage, I think you have no further need of me," he said dully. "I'll take my leave."

"By no means, Brenn!" Gless Vallage exclaimed. "I implore you to remain."

"You're not going anywhere," Ulf remarked.

"I've given you what you wanted. What do you need me for now?" Brenn asked.

"We desire your counsel, my friend."

"And I want to keep an eye on you," Ulf replied. "You just stay where you are."

Brenn remained seated, staring blankly out the window. Despite Gless Vallage's professed desire for counsel, the minutes passed silently. Gless Vallage meditated pleasantly, Haik Ulf fidgeted, and Brenn Wate Basef appeared sunk in a daze of misery.

Outside the sky darkened and the embers of a winter sunset warmed the heavy clouds. Subtly the colors of the painted cityscape on the walls altered themselves to match the real world—a testimony to the perfection of Gless Vallage's illusions. One by one, lights began to shine at the windows of the neighboring palaces, and corresponding lights appeared in the painted mansions on the walls. Brenn Wate Basef studied the magical images, and experienced the now familiar sensations of helplessness, confusion, despondency, and shame. What use, he wondered, would Gless Vallage have for him after this? Having fulfilled his purpose, he would probably be discarded. Unless, of course, Vallage had any more dirty work that needed doing. If the world ever knew what a traitor and weakling he was, how he would be despised! He cast his eyes apathetically around the room. In the doorway Guardsmen lounged and gossiped. In the corner he discerned a hovering cloud of mist, almost formless, probably invisible to all save him. The Presence was faint and unthreatening just now, probably placated by its victim's demonstration of loyalty and obedience. Brenn shuddered and turned away, to encounter the affable gaze of Saxas Gless Vallage.

Vallage ordered wine. A pitcher and goblets soon arrived and Brenn gulped his portion thirstily, in the vain hope of thawing what felt like a lump of ice inside him.

The wine loosened Haik Ulf's tongue. "Well, Vallage—" The Commander slouched indolently in his chair. "It looks like things are working out the way you want. Assuming you manage to get rid of Fal Grizhni, what then?"

"Then Lanthi Ume benefits, Commander."

"Always the patriot, eh?"

"I love my city and I strive to serve her."

"What a mealy-mouthed hypocrite you are, Vallage," Ulf observed.

Gless Vallage chose to accept the remark as a joke, and poured himself another glass of wine with a quiet smile. "Well, what do *you* think will happen, Commander?" he inquired. "What will become of Fal Grizhni, for example?"

"You know the answer to that as well as I do. He'll be executed. It'll probably be handled very discreetly. I only hope I get a chance to watch."

"I can almost guarantee it won't be handled discreetly. Quite the contrary. The fate of Fal Grizhni must serve as a deterrent to all potential traitors. I have advised the Duke to submit his Preeminence to a public trial and subsequent public execution, preferably at the stake. I believe his Grace will be favorably inclined to this proposal."

Brenn shot Vallage a look of weary disgust, but said nothing.

"That's not going to look too good for the Select, is it?" Ulf demanded.

"I feel that an example must be made. I believe that his Grace will agree," Vallage replied regretfully.

"And after his Preeminence's public trial and execution, the Select will be all in disarray, won't they?" Ulf observed with a grim smile. "They'll be humiliated, discredited, and the city will be united against them. Eh, Vallage?"

"Unhappily true, Commander. But necessary, I fear—for the sake of Lanthi Ume."

"For Lanthi Ume, certainly. The Select will be greatly in need of a new leader, won't they? Preferably someone who enjoys the Duke's favor. A savant who's in with the Duke could lead the Select out of this mess, and they'll know it. Nice for you."

"A new Preeminence enjoying his Grace's confidence could indeed be of great service to the Order at this time," Vallage replied tranquilly. "It goes without saying, however, that traditional means will be employed to choose Fal Grizhni's successor. That is, the savant possessing the greatest mastery of Cognition will assume Preeminence."

"I suppose that means you."

"It is a possibility that must not be overlooked. It might be of interest to you, Commander, to know that the possibility amounts to a certainty should Fal Grizhni's collection of records, artifacts, Cognitive aids and devices come into my possession."

Brenn stared at his erstwhile mentor in silent disbelief.

"Why should that interest me, Vallage?" Haik Ulf inquired negligently.

"Have I not yet succeeded in convincing you, my friend, that what is good for Vallage is also good for Ulf? You're a man of intelligence and foresight. Surely I need not elaborate?"

"Maybe not. As for these records and artifacts, what's that got to do with me? What are you driving at?"

Vallage rose and strolled to the great window, where he stood gazing off toward the Sandivell Canal. Above the roofs of the adjacent mansions the silver dome of Grizhni Palace was visible, its polished surface glinting red in the light of the setting sun. The savant's back was presented to his visitors and his expression, which they could not see, was unwontedly somber. His eyes, normally alight with quick, if shallow intelligence, were turned inward for once. "Grizhni's house is the most magnificent of Lanthi Ume's palaces," he mused softly. "More than a mere building, it is a monument to the architect's skill, a perfect blending of art, nature, and Cognition. Within are works of art, ancient objects of beauty and historical significance. Such brutal destruction—so much to be lost forever—"

"What are you on about?" Ulf demanded irritably. "I can't hear you."

Gless Vallage took a deep breath. When he replied, his voice was light and easy as ever, but he did not turn around. "Commander, within a very few minutes a messenger will arrive bearing written orders from the Duke authorizing you to place Preeminence Fal Grizhni under arrest. Upon my recommendation you will be given leave to employ whatever means are

necessary to accomplish your purpose. Do you believe that
your men are equal to the task?"

"You can count on my Guards."

"Good. In that case, when you receive your orders, you will
call up additional troops, storm the palace without delay, and
take his Preeminence prisoner—alive, if possible. Is that correct?"

"That's right—if the orders come through."

"Very well. When you have gained access to the palace,
order a couple of your men to remove the contents of Fal
Grizhni's workroom and deliver them to me. There will be
more in the room than you'll be able to carry away, but take as
much as possible. Concentrate particularly on all materials
written in Grizhni's own hand."

"You must be soft in the head, Vallage," Ulf returned
impatiently. "Once we're in that building, we'll have no time
to muck around with magicians' trick books, potions, lucky
charms, and such foolery. Forget about that. We'll have more
important things to do."

"You'll have nothing more important to do. Don't be any
more of a fool than you can help, and don't argue with me.
Just do it, if you know what's good for you," Gless Vallage
snapped disdainfully, as if his customary mask had slipped a
little.

Ulf glanced at him in surprise. "It's not so easy," he replied. "If we loot, somebody's sure to squawk, and it ends up
more trouble than it's worth."

"It won't be noticed that anything's missing if Grizhni
Palace is burned to the ground," Vallage pointed out. "And
there will be no one to accuse you if all the inhabitants die."

Haik Ulf regarded him with increased respect. "More to
you than meets the eye, isn't there, Cognizance? So you're
suggesting that we slaughter—how many people?"

"The servants aren't human. Fal Grizhni's attendants are
those superbly Cognitive hybrids—what some people call 'demons,' " Vallage added, noting Ulf's look of incomprehension. "They are unnatural creatures, and in the unlikely event
that you have qualms about killing them, you needn't worry.
To the best of my knowledge, the only human inhabitant other
than Fal Grizhni himself is Lady Grizhni."

"And her I want alive," Haik Ulf returned promptly.
"Unless we have her, we'll never get the names of Grizhni's
accomplices."

"Getting the records and artifacts out safely and in secret is more important."

"Not to me it isn't."

"Commander, use your head. There's no reason for Fal Grizhni to know that his wife is dead, is there? Once he's in custody, do you intend to tell him? Be assured *I* don't."

Ulf grinned. "Cognizance, you may have solved our problems."

Brenn Wate Basef, who had listened to this exchange with increasing horror, finally found his voice. "Vallage—have you gone mad? You're not actually thinking of murdering Lady Grizhni? It would be criminal—inhuman! She's an innocent young girl." Vallage merely looked at him, and Brenn continued, "I won't believe that any savant of the Select could be so base! It's impossible. Tell this Guardsman that she's not to be harmed!"

Vallage answered gravely, "My friend, I understand your distress. I share it. But sometimes, Brenn, the greater good demands the most painful personal sacrifice, and in this case—"

"Stop there. I don't want to listen," Brenn interrupted. "From the beginning I've done everything you've wanted. For various reasons I've helped to further all your schemes. But not now. At last you've come to such a pass that even I will no longer obey. Cognizance Vallage, I demand that you spare the life of Lady Grizhni. Moreover, she is not to be imprisoned or harmed in any way. Agree to this and I'll continue to cooperate. Otherwise I sever all connection with you here and now, and I think you know what the consequences would be."

"But do *you* know what the consequences would be?" Vallage inquired with a hint of amusement.

"Look Vallage, I'm going to have this idiot locked up in another room. He's getting on my nerves," Ulf complained.

"Softly, Commander. My friend Brenn is under a great deal of strain," Vallage replied gently.

It was true. Even as Gless Vallage spoke, Brenn felt the proximity of the Presence, felt the blood slow to a crawl within his veins and his heart labor as the chill invaded his body, felt the dreadful, icy oppression. He clutched the arms of his chair and forced himself to speak. "It won't do you any good. This time I'm not frightened."

"But you should be, Brenn. You should be."

The pain hit then, and the young man doubled up with a groan. The mist was all around him, the Presence had enveloped him, but through it he could discern the face of Commander Haik Ulf, who watched curiously.

"What's wrong with him?" Ulf demanded.

"My unfortunate friend is subject to occasional attacks of this kind."

"Where's that smoke coming from? He's sitting in a cloud of smoke."

"It will pass. Don't concern yourself, Commander."

"Vallage . . . and you, Ulf," Brenn managed to gasp. "I'll have nothing more to do with your schemes. You sicken me, the two of you—murderers, liars, and traitors. I'll stop you if I can—" He ended on a cry of pain as the Presence sank its daggers of ice into his mind.

"All right, I've had about enough of this spying little weasel with his tragic airs," Ulf declared, rising menacingly from his chair.

"I'll handle this," Gless Vallage forestalled him.

"You don't seem to be doing a very good job."

"I tell you he's no threat to us—"

The discussion was cut short by the reentrance of Vallage's factotum. The man bore a message sealed with the ducal crest, which he presented with a bow to his master. "Leave us," Vallage commanded, and the servant retired. The savant opened the letter, scanned it at a glance, and handed it to Haik Ulf. "Sufficient?" he inquired.

Ulf read laboriously. At last he nodded and stuffed the Duke's instructions into the pocket of his green tunic. "That's it, then. I'm off," he remarked with an air of ferocious satisfaction.

"One moment. I will accompany you. My Cognition will strengthen and preserve your Guards."

"We don't need that."

"Don't be a fool, Ulf. You go to attack the home of Terrs Fal Grizhni. You need the help I offer, and you'll lose men in any event."

Ulf reflected quickly. "All right. You can come." A new thought struck him. "What about the informer?"

Brenn sat petrified with pain. The shadowy Presence hovered above him.

"Don't worry, he can do nothing."

"I'm taking no chances. I'll leave a couple of my men to watch him. And later on you'd better see about housebreaking this lapdog of yours, Vallage. Come on, let's go."

The two men walked out together, and Brenn Wate Basef sat watching them go. For a long time he remained quite still, neither moving nor struggling. At last his docility produced the desired result, and the Presence slowly receded. His blood gradually warmed, the pain was gone, and his mind and thoughts were once more his own. His newfound equilibrium was a precarious thing. Close beside him the Presence lingered, alert to the signs of rebellion. Brenn slumped hopelessly, face buried in his hands, and as he so rested, the Presence withdrew to a corner of the room and its misty form lightened to the point of invisibility. Brenn stood up cautiously. He took a few steps toward the door and discovered how tired he was—tired, weak, and wretched.

At least it was over, he reflected. He had done what was required of him and now there would be no more spying, no more lies and treachery, no more guilt. Wrong, his conscience informed him. There would always be guilt. He would despise himself the rest of his life for what he had done today. Should his deed become generally known, then all the world would scorn him as the betrayer of Fal Grizhni. "But I had no choice," he spoke aloud to the not-quite-empty room. It made no difference. No excuse, no justification could redeem him in the eyes of Lanthi Ume, should his secret be revealed. And it *would* be revealed, unless he maintained himself in the favor of Cognizance Gless Vallage and of the unspeakable Haik Ulf. The strands of Vallage's net held him close and sure. Somehow he had become inextricably entangled, and now he was bound for life. It was even possible, Brenn thought bitterly, that Gless Vallage would consent to relieve him of the Presence. Obviously there was little need for it any more.

He found himself thinking of Verran, and the expression in her blue eyes should she learn the truth. But she would never learn the truth, for Vallage and Ulf intended to kill her and her unborn child. Within hours her dead body would lie in a burning palace, for no crime beyond the misfortune of her marriage.

Verran's image was replaced by that of Preeminence Grizhni, and Brenn found to his surprise that he no longer hated Grizhni, had not hated him for a long time. Finally the young man saw himself as if through the eyes of an outside observer; Brenn Wate Basef, traitor and informer—a puny, ineffectual, contemptible little spy. It was a far cry indeed from the great savant he had imagined himself destined to become. He was Gless Vallage's creature, now and always.

Was there no way out of it? Brenn considered his options, and found them few and depressing. He might defy Vallage, but such an attempt would surely fail. He could flee Lanthi Ume, but that wouldn't undo the harm he had done. In any case, what would life be without Lanthi Ume? He could—and the thought was balm to his mental wounds—he could always escape, cut himself free of the net by putting an end to his own existence. Brenn suddenly felt a lightness, a buoyancy that he had never expected to experience again. There was a way out, after all. It would be easy, clean—but again, it wouldn't undo the harm he had done, and it wouldn't save Verran's life. There was only one way to do that. He must warn Fal Grizhni and the others immediately. He considered quickly. The laundering of his conscience would be a painful and humiliating affair at best; and at worst an impossibility, for the Presence would discourage such gestures. He wondered if the Presence could actually kill him. Beyond a doubt it would try.

Outside the sky was fading swiftly. Brenn made up his mind. He walked to the door, opened it, and found a pair of Guardsmen blocking his way. "Let me pass," he commanded.

They looked at him in surprise and one of them answered, "You're not to leave."

"You understand that I am of the Select?" Brenn asked quietly. "Once again I ask you to let me pass."

His black robe and air of authority perhaps impressed the guards, for they exchanged uneasy glances. They neither answered nor moved.

Brenn spoke softly, and his medallion glowed. He had studied hard and practiced faithfully. With no savant of superior power there to hinder him, he was able to achieve Cognition with relative ease. There were two sharp, distinct cracking sounds. The guards cried out and went down, each with a broken leg. Brenn stepped around the fallen men, hurried along the violet corridor where several servants stared curiously at his chalk-white face as he passed, down the broad central staircase, through the entrance hall and out onto Vallage moorings, with the Presence close beside him.

His first impulse was to commandeer a Vallage dombulis and head for Grizhni Palace, where he could find and warn

Verran. But he paused as he considered the one piece of information that he had successfully withheld from Gless Vallage. Fal Grizhni was abroad this evening. Grizhni had scheduled a meeting at sunset of the small group of conspirators of which Brenn was a member. They would be there now—Perlo, Sovis, Fodin, Vennaril, and Fal Grizhni himself—all of them assembled in the back room of the Savant's Head, an old inn situated on the bank of Parnis Lagoon directly opposite the Victory of Nes. Due to its proximity to the Victory, the Savant's Head enjoyed Selectic custom. The black-robed figures attracted little attention there, and it was for this reason that Fal Grizhni had chosen the inn as a meeting place. The conspirators were assembled there now to settle the last details of the plot, and they probably wondered where Wate Basef was. Well, Wate Basef would be there. His warning would save the lives of his four compatriots; and Terrs Fal Grizhni could undoubtedly look after himself and his own.

Brenn hailed a public dombulis, boarded, and issued instructions to the dombulman. The fellow looked at him queerly and Brenn realized that the Presence was more than ordinarily in evidence. It hovered at his elbow like a corporeal conscience, and the boatman could see something. The young man smiled grimly. If he didn't miss his guess, the Presence would become more noticeable yet, before it was done. At the moment the lethal shadow remained quiescent, but that could not last long.

The dombulman rowed energetically, and Vallage moorings receded. They reached the mouth of the Lureis, and Parnis Lagoon spread out before them, with the Victory of Nes a darkened bulk at its center. Brenn Wate Basef did not look at the island with its looming Nessiva that had once represented the summit of his ambitions. His eyes were fixed on the shore. Not far away he discerned the inn he sought, its painted sign shaped in the image of a man's head with double-headed dragon insignia at the collar.

Suddenly the Presence evinced disquiet, and Brenn felt the familiar, deathly chill. He gasped and his hands clenched involuntarily. The dombulman eyed his passenger with suspicion as they landed. Brenn paid and stepped onto the wharf, almost at the door of the Savant's Head. His step was uncertain and his teeth chattered with cold, although the evening was mild. It was nearly dark now, and lanterns were being lit all over the city. Soon the jeweled reflections would dance on the waters of the lagoon and the lanterns would cast their golden light on Prendivet Saunter. It was quiet there, and Lanthi Ume appeared deceptively tranquil.

Something obscured his vision, and Brenn realized that the Presence now enveloped him. It had thickened like a fog off the sea, cutting him off from all humanity and isolating him in a prison of mist. The cold was intense and growing worse. Pain stirred to vicious life within him, and the imbecile determination of his incubus battered at his will.

The young man attempted to walk toward the Savant's Head, but found movement difficult. The pain grew, and Brenn's steps faltered. How could the Presence know what he intended? Even in the midst of his misery he was moved to grudging admiration. Saxas Gless Vallage was surely a master of his craft. How had he manufactured an entity wholly devoid of intelligence, yet capable of divining an unrealized impulse to rebellion within its victim?

He could barely see. The mist blindfolded him, pain shackled him, and he could feel his determination ebbing. What point in pitting his strength against that of Cognizance Gless Vallage? Through the fog he descried a couple of townsmen who watched with amusement as he lurched and staggered. Brenn addressed them in desperation. "Help me to the Savant's Head." His voice was slow and garbled. "I'm sick."

The men guffawed. "Drunk, more likely," one of them replied, and they departed, still chuckling.

Brenn watched hopelessly. The inn was but a few yards distant, but he feared he would never reach it. The lights beckoned and he struggled forward. There was a tightness in his throat and breathing was difficult—the precursors of the choking spasms that punished attempted indiscretions. He realized that he would be unable to warn the conspirators, for he was no longer capable of speech. No matter. Surely his appearance would alert them to danger.

The Presence squeezed his lungs with frigid fingers. Try as he would, he could not draw a breath of air. He was freezing, nearly sightless, and the alien will bludgeoned his mind mercilessly.

Brenn struck something that gave way before him, and stumbled blindly through the door into the common room of the Savant's Head. For a moment he rested, propped against the wall. Despite the mildness of the weather and the paucity of customers, the innkeeper had provided a generous fire. Perhaps the sudden light and warmth of the place were antipathetic to it, for the Presence subsided somewhat and Brenn's vision cleared a little.

Taking advantage of the temporary respite, he made his way to the rear of the common room, using the wall for support. Those customers who noted the wobbly young fellow in the black robe were duly entertained by the sight of an inebriated savant.

He stumbled down a couple of low steps, through a curtained archway, and into the chamber he sought. As he entered, the five men gathered there turned to stare at him in surprise. Brenn collapsed against the wall, and its support was all that kept him on his feet. He opened his mouth to speak, and produced choking gasps. The fog thickened around him once more, and the room faded from his view.

The five savants exchanged glances of quick understanding. All of them saw the ravening mist that plagued their comrade, all of them knew what it was and guessed what it portended. Ril Vennaril, a husband and the father of four, sprang to his feet and took a step toward the doorway.

Again Brenn strove uselessly to speak. The effort brought a froth of blood to his lips. The monstrous form of the Presence had coalesced nearly to the point of visibility. Terrs Fal Grizhni uttered quiet words and did something with his hands; nobody saw what, for nobody's eyes were upon him. The icy oppression diminished, and the Presence withdrew itself to a corner, where it floated in roiling agitation. It had not been banished altogether, for the Cognition of Saxas Gless Vallage was not to be overcome as easily as that. But for the moment Brenn Wate Basef could breathe and speak.

He chose not to waste words. "I have betrayed you. The Duke knows of the plot and he knows of the involvement of everyone here in this room. Already he has issued orders, and even as I speak, Haik Ulf musters the Guardsmen. All of you must fly to save yourselves or you are surely dead men. Your property will be confiscated, your families imprisoned or enslaved. Do not tarry. Go to your homes, take your wives and children, and escape the city while you may."

For one moment they stared at him, their varying expressions indescribable. Then every eye turned to Fal Grizhni,

whose quick inclination of the head conveyed dismissal and
finality. By some process of instinct or Cognition the men recognized the truth, and no one questioned it. Brenn said nothing more, and there was no time to demand explanations. The
four savants rose and in silence sped from the room, heading
for the dombuli that would carry them to their respective
homes. Only Hes Perlo lingered briefly in the doorway, as if
he would speak. His eyes shone with ineffable contempt as
they rested upon the man who had betrayed them. Apparently
he found no words adequate to express his emotions, for he
turned away and wordlessly followed his compatriots, leaving
Brenn Wate Basef alone with Fal Grizhni.

Fal Grizhni's countenance was unreadable as always, ex-
pressing nothing of hatred, disdain, or alarm. By no external
sign was it evident that the erstwhile mighty master of the
Select had just received the news of his own ruination. He inquired only, "Have you anything more to say, Cognizance
Wate Basef?"

"Yes, Preeminence. Saxas Gless Vallage has engineered
your downfall, and I have been his spy. He aspires to your
place, and for that reason desires your records, artifacts, and
Cognitive tools. Tonight the Ducal Guards attack Grizhni
Palace. In order to conceal the theft of your property, the
building will be burned to the ground and all residents will be
slaughtered—including Lady Grizhni." The minute change in
Grizhni's face escaped Brenn's detection, and the young savant wondered, *Is this a man of stone?* He continued, "They
intend to take you alive. There will be a public trial and a
public execution."

Fal Grizhni exhibited neither anger nor fear. He spoke without haste, as if time, now become his mortal enemy, meant
nothing. "Why did you consent to serve Gless Vallage, Cognizance?"

"There were many reasons," Brenn replied, meeting
Grizhni's eyes steadily. "Resentment, envy, bitterness, ignorance. Later on, a sense of obligation to Vallage. After that—
fear. I regret them all."

"Why have you warned us tonight?"

"I hope to undo some of the damage I've done, and I hope
to save lives."

"You have succeeded."

"I have one more hope—that you will grant me your pardon."

Grizhni studied him for several deliberate seconds, and at last answered gravely, "It is granted, Cognizance."

"Then I have nothing more to say. The Ducal Guards with their swords and torches now hasten toward Grizhni Palace. If you would be there before them, there's no time to lose."

"I shall arrive in time."

"What do you intend to do, Preeminence?"

"Much. I advise you to accompany me." Brenn's expression reflected faint surprise, and Fal Grizhni added, "I have granted you my pardon, but there are others who will not do so. The entity inflicted upon you by Gless Vallage cannot be destroyed save by prolonged application of high Cognition. You have weakened the position of its master and it desires vengeance. Even now it is kept at bay only by my presence. To leave you alone with the entity at this time exposes you to serious danger."

Brenn looked into the corner where the Presence lowered like night waiting to fall. He saw that it had grown much darker, and perhaps even larger. Its outlines were far more distinct. The mists were condensing into a headless shape with vast arms that reached out hungrily toward him. Brenn turned away. "Your control of the Presence which haunts me is maintained at the expense of a portion of your Cognitive energy that you cannot afford to spare now. You are far better off without me. I'll stay here."

"You understand the consequences?"

"Preeminence, I welcome them."

"So be it." Fal Grizhni eyed the young man with perfect comprehension. "I will leave you. Do not commit the error of judging yourself too harshly. As for our common enemies, be assured they will not prevail. They, or else their issue, will pay a heavy price. Farewell, Cognizance Wate Basef." Fal Grizhni departed the chamber, and the unusual length of his strides was his one concession to the swift passage of time.

"Good-bye, Preeminence." Grizhni was already gone. Brenn was alone with the Presence. He turned to face it, and having truly abandoned all hope was free of fear as well and able to watch with oddly detached interest. The end came quickly. The Presence, evidently wrought to a furious pitch of agitation by its victim's defiance and its own subsequent imprisonment, proceeded without restraint. The mists that comprised it swirled and darkened like captive storm clouds. The murky form with its broad, headless trunk was quite visible now, and almost tangible. The nightmare arms groped, encountered resistance, beat at an invisible wall. The Cognitive barrier gave way before the assault and the Presence broke free.

Instantly Brenn was engulfed. The chill paralyzed him and pain smote him more cruelly than ever before. His agony, though intense, was brief. So violent was the attack of the Presence that life fled before it. The young man felt his vitality ebbing, and in those final moments, peace came to him at last. Within seconds, Brenn Wate Basef lay dead upon the floor.

For a little while the entity hovered above the corpse, stupidly awaiting a return of warmth and motion. Its agitation abated rapidly, its color lightened, and its outline softened. Soon it had dwindled to a barely visible cloud, and even this cloud was fading. At last some form of perception alerted the Presence to the demise of its victim. The purpose of its own existence thus ended, Vallage's creation seemed confused. It floated about the room in a lost manner, its awesome determination now unfocused. Time and again it returned to the corpse, but found no self-fulfillment there. Presently it faded completely from view. In this vestigial state it discovered the window, passed from the inn, and was caught by the fresh breezes of Lanthi Ume, which utterly dispersed it.

Chapter Eighteen

✸✸✸✸✸

The shortest and fastest route from the Savant's Head to Grizhni Palace lay over land. Terrs Fal Grizhni hurried through the moonlit streets at a pace approaching a run. Many citizens noticed the tall savant and wondered at his haste, but few recognized him. Despite his fame, Grizhni had always shunned the public eye. Past the walled gardens of the mansions that ringed Parnis Lagoon he sped, past the statues, parks and myriad fountains of Lanthi Ume, and every movement proclaimed dire resolution. His expression was at variance however, for alongside icy anger there was something of doubt, as if Grizhni questioned the wisdom or justice of his own intentions. Ka Nebbinon Bell sounded the hour, and he quickened his steps.

He had left the region of gardens and mansions behind him. Now he traversed the lanes of modest dwellings, the silent market squares with their rows of shuttered merchants' booths, until he came upon a plaza crowded with citizens and orange with firelight. A meeting was in progress, and the square rang with furious voices. Preoccupied with his own concerns, Fal Grizhni scarcely noted them. Then his attention was arrested by a boldly printed sheet tacked up on a post in plain view of the angry crowd. It was the latest and largest of the League of Patriots' offerings. The savant beheld a full-length portrait of himself. The pictured figure bore a great double-bladed sword uplifted in menace and triumph. Both the weapon and the gesture were conventional attributes of Death as personified in Lanthian art. At his feet a family of emaciated commoners crouched in terror. The human figures were superimposed upon a faintly drawn street map of the city, and underneath appeared the legend, "The Great Destroyer." The rest of the text was too small to be read at a distance, but the message of the portrait was clear. Many members of the crowd carried copies of the broadside.

Grizhni automatically paused, and the warm light of the torches colored his pale face. A number of those standing nearby recognized him, and excited cries arose:

"Fal Grizhni—here among us!"

"The Great Destroyer!"

"King of Demons!"

It was neither the time nor place for a confrontation with the Lanthian mob. Fal Grizhni moved to depart, but already it was too late. Rancorous, defiant citizens surrounded him on all sides. The savant surveyed them coldly, as if inwardly debating the necessity of acknowledging their presence. At last he commanded, "Stand aside. I cannot stay."

"You can and you will, Preeminence Grizhni," one of the citizens replied truculently. It was Beldo the baker.

"What do you seek?"

"Some answers, Grizhni. You've been found out by the League, and your game is up. There are scores of accusations against you, and now that you're here, you'll answer them."

Fal Grizhni regarded the tradesman and his companions in icy astonishment. "You citizens forget yourselves. It is not thus that charges are preferred against a member of the Select and a nobleman of Lanthi Ume. I will perhaps consent to answer to a lawfully established tribunal of my peers, but nothing less. Moreover, I do not acknowledge the legitimacy of complaints arising from an anonymous source, as exemplified by the self-described League of Patriots. Such charges are without substance."

"We know you hate the Commons, Preeminence."

"I do not hate the Commons, but I have nothing to say to them at this time. Stand aside."

"Friends," Beldo exclaimed, "Fal Grizhni disdains to reply to the charges. As always, he uses us with utter contempt!"

A growl of anger ran through the crowd, but Grizhni did not heed it.

"We know what you've done, Preeminence, and you're not going anywhere until you've answered our questions."

Fal Grizhni regarded the immovable crowd that hemmed him in and replied, "Thus far will I explain myself to you. I am on an errand of the utmost urgency, and cannot allow myself to be detained. Already I have lost invaluable time. I agree to speak with you another day, should the opportunity arise, but it is not possible now."

Grizhni's answer was not well-received. Indignant muttering rumbled and a few angry shouts arose. Someone called out, "Grizhni says he doesn't have the time!"

"That won't do, Preeminence," Beldo warned. "We're not to be put off. We want answers now."

"My patience is not inexhaustible," Fal Grizhni remarked dispassionately. "I have asked you to stand aside."

So great was the awe in which Terrs Fal Grizhni was held that a few of the citizens actually moved to obey his command. But most of them, finding courage in numbers, pressed in closely upon the savant.

"Better speak up, Preeminence, or there's no telling what might happen."

"Your demons aren't here to help you now!"

"Even your mother Ert won't help you now!"

Although there were so many witnesses, no one was ever certain what Fal Grizhni did next. His use of Cognition possessed a certain quality of misdirection. Some members of the crowd swore afterwards that they had felt the burning touch of evil spirits. Others spoke of a great wind or an incorporeal force. One man even claimed to have been kicked by an invisible horse. Indisputable, however, was the fact that a mysterious agency parted the crowd forcibly, opening up a pathway for Fal Grizhni.

The savant stalked swiftly toward the far side of the square. For a moment there was stunned silence, and then a collective roar of outrage. Grizhni appeared to hear nothing. His iron indifference provoked the mob to new heights of indignation, and they flung curses at him as he passed. One anonymous citizen flung something more. A stone flew through the air and struck Grizhni's back.

The savant gasped, his eyes widened in pure amazement, and he wheeled sharply to face his attacker. Surprise or sudden pain must have shaken his concentration somewhat, for the power holding the crowd at bay weakened. The pathway disappeared and the citizens surged forward. More rocks came flying. One of them grazed the savant's forehead, and blood began to flow.

"He bleeds!" A shout of savage joy. "His magic does not shield him!"

Stones whizzed and some found their mark.

"The Witch Nennevay could be killed by men," some vociferous zealot encouraged his cohorts. "So, too, must her master the King of Demons die, along with his young slut of a wife and the demon-whelp she carries!"

At mention of his wife, Fal Grizhni stopped dead. Very deliberately he turned and sought out the speaker, a capering graybeard with a rock in each hand.

"The evil shall be vanquished!" the graybeard piped up, and launched a rock with unexpected accuracy.

Fal Grizhni spoke. Those near him heard him clearly, despite the frenzied babble of the mob. "You fear the light of knowledge, you fear the light of the future. Darkness you desire, and darkness you shall have."

His next action seemed to contradict this promise. Grizhni spoke again, but this time nobody heard his words. There was a crackle of force and the bearded zealot burst into flames. His hair, beard, and clothing blazed fiercely. For a few seconds the man danced screaming, then collapsed to the ground. So intense were the fires that he died within moments. The ghastly stink of charred flesh filled the air, and black smoke spread out over the square.

Instantly the fury of the crowd gave way to alarm. Those in the vicinity of the victim shrank desperately from the flames. In the resulting press, a number of Lanthians were flung to the ground. Shouts of rage turned to shrieks of fear and pain. The citizens on the fringes of the mob, enjoying relative freedom of movement, wisely fled for their lives.

Not all were similarly affected. The most reckless and bellicose sprang straight at Fal Grizhni. The savant spoke again, two more men ignited explosively, and the crowd panicked. Those able to run did so, and their screams were shrill with unrestrained hysteria. A number of weaker citizens were trampled underfoot as all present retreated in abject terror before the King of Demons. Almost immediately the space around him was clear save for three blackened corpses. The volume of screaming slowly diminished as more and more citizens fled the square.

Fal Grizhni stood quite still, as if to collect his faculties. His stance reflected the fatigue inevitably attendant upon feats of significant Cognition. His white face was full of bitterness, disgust, and hardened purpose. All sign of doubt had vanished. For a moment only he stood there, then continued on his way across the plaza at a quick and steady gait.

Shortly thereafter he arrived at Grizhni Palace. All was quiet. The Ducal Guards were nowhere in evidence, and the windows were unsuspectingly alight. Grizhni permitted himself one look at his home, which took in the entire structure from the great silver dome down to the moorings. He entered, and Nyd came forward to greet him. The creature paused, astonished by his master's bloodstained face and glittering eyes. Despite the uncharacteristic dishevelment, Grizhni issued orders in his accustomed composed and decisive manner. "Secure the door."

He was obeyed, and the huge bar dropped into place.

"Listen. Within minutes, this building will be under attack by the Ducal Guards."

Nyd hissed and his lips drew back over his fangs.

"There will be no direct physical conflict," Grizhni informed his servant dryly, and Nyd's disappointment was plain. "It is my intention to raise a Cognitive barrier that the Guardsmen will be powerless to breach. I foresee no immediate danger to our household, for the palace is equipped to withstand a siege of several months duration. Once the barrier is in place about the building, the only means of entrance or egress will be by way of the tunnel. You may expect to make frequent clandestine excursions, bearing messages to certain colleagues of the Select. It is possible, too, that you may be called upon to escort Lady Grizhni from the premises when I have devised a safe and comfortable means of departure for her—but that is a matter which must be considered with some care. In the meantime, go and communicate the situation to your nestmates. At least three of you will attend Lady Grizhni, that she may not be unduly alarmed by what is about to transpire."

Nyd croaked and departed, leaving Fal Grizhni alone. The savant ascended the great staircase without obvious haste, proceeded to his workroom and immured himself within.

• • •

Shortly thereafter a number of Lanthians—including a large contingent of Ducal Guards under the leadership of Commander Haik Ulf—were treated to a remarkable spectacle. Tremors shook the ground in the vicinity of Grizhni Palace. The surrounding mansions quivered, and the waters of the Lureis Canal foamed violently. Several dombuli capsized, and pedestrians strolling the illuminated Prendivet Saunter were flung face down upon the pebbled path. Even the most prosaic-minded of citizens sensed the action of major Cognition, and public attention focused instinctively upon the dwelling of Fal Grizhni.

It was on the tip of Lord Ulf's tongue to bid his men hurry, but the command was never uttered. Multiple whirlpools indented the surface of the Lureis, and the Guardsmen, along with the rest of the populace, paused to stare. As they stood gaping, the waters of the canal rose up with a mighty roar, rose in a vast fountain, unthinkably high, higher than the topmost pinnacle that crowned the great silver dome of Grizhni Palace. The watching citizens cried out in alarm, while the Guardsmen maintained bleak silence. For the space of perhaps ten minutes the rushing water arched over the palace towers. Then a change occurred in the character of the torrent—its motion gradually slowed and finally stilled. A cold wind scoured the Lureis, and Grizhni Palace stood entirely encased from moorings to cupola in a thick armor of transparent ice that dazzled the eye with its impossible glitter. A diffuse glow escaped the building in those places where ice shielded open windows. In several windows motionless dark figures watched and waited. Whether the sentinels were human or demonic could not be determined, and many a Lanthian spectator prudently retired.

It was hard to get the men moving after that. Lord Ulf was forced to resort to taunts and threats. With difficulty he succeeded in surrounding the frozen palace with Guards and clearing the immediate area of curious citizens. At last, under the lash of their commander's tongue, the men rushed forward in a reluctant body to attack the ice with their blades. For a few moments they hacked and slashed at the obstruction, which proved as impervious as granite. One Guardsman's sword shattered and the fellow stood cursing helplessly. The ice, which appeared to be about two feet thick, showed not a mark. The surface shone flawlessly smooth in the light of torch and lantern.

"Give over," Lord Ulf commanded his baffled minions. "Steel won't do it. What we need here is fire. You, there— Kronil! Take a dozen men, commandeer those sendilli there, break 'em up and get a good blaze going. We'll see how long the ice can stand up to that."

"It won't work, Commander."

"Eh?" Haik Ulf turned in annoyance to face Saxas Gless Vallage, who stood at his elbow. The savant, quiet and deliberately inconspicuous, had removed the dragon insignia of the Select from his dark robe.

"Don't even bother trying," Gless Vallage advised.

"Look, I know what I'm doing. Suppose you just keep out of the way and let me tend to my own business, magician."

"You are wasting my time as well as your own." Vallage's tranquil demeanor gave no hint of the eagerness and impatience that seethed within him. "Cognition raised that barrier, and only Cognition will destroy it. Fire will not help you— yet."

"We'll see about that. Now keep out of my way."

Gless Vallage's lips tightened, but he held his peace.

Swiftly the Guardsmen kindled their great bonfires at the foot of Grizhni Palace. The broken sendilli blazed fiercely, the spectators shouted, black smoke wreathed the banks of the Lureis, and blasts of intense heat assailed the ice-clad palace.

Not a drop of moisture appeared on the gleaming walls. Not the slightest irregularity marred the frozen perfection.

"More wood!" Lord Ulf directed, and soon the flames mounted higher.

The walls stood firm. Fal Grizhni's ice was proof against fire. Presently the sendilli were consumed and the flames began to sink. Ulf looked on in thwarted fury.

"Ready to listen to me now?" the insufferable voice at his elbow inquired. Haik Ulf was silent, and Vallage regarded him sympathetically.

Ulf could not endure it. "A battering ram—" he snapped.

"Useless. Do not exert yourself, Commander. It's only reasonable to expect Fal Grizhni to employ a Cognitive defense. I have not come unprepared. The work before me will take some little time, and during that time I may have need of some assistance. Therefore I must require you to inform your Guardsmen that for the next two hours they are subject to my orders.''

Ulf glowered down at the savant, who met his gaze with bland affability. Their eyes locked briefly, then Ulf turned away with a curse. Vallage smiled to himself and set to work.

Within Grizhni Palace absolute silence reigned. No sound from the city outside made its way past the barrier of ice. It was as if the palace and all its inhabitants had been banished to some quiet limbo. In the midst of that enchanted silence, time had stopped. The danger, now so close at hand, still seemed utterly unreal.

The corridors were deathly cold, but within them the fresh air circulated freely. The Cognition that sheathed the palace in ice spared the lungs of the inhabitants. Most of the hybrids toiled at their accustomed tasks, but a number of them stood watch at the windows, their vigilance belying the spurious atmosphere of normalcy. Several of the creatures attended Lady Verran who, in compliance with the wishes of her husband, remained within her own chambers.

Fal Grizhni did not emerge from his workroom. The diligence of his labors therein suggested that he was entirely conscious of time and of danger, albeit unalarmed by either. The savant sat at his writing desk with a growing pile of correspondence before him. They were letters destined to be delivered by Nyd to various allies of the Select. One such message, the most important of them, was incomplete. It was addressed to the Cognizant Jinzin Farni. Grizhni scanned the last lines he had written:

. . . that a deadlock exists at this time, I am not without hope that sufficient strength remains within our party to accomplish our original purpose, or at the very least, to extract major concessions from the Duke. In order to proceed, it is necessary to marshal the savants of our circle whose names yet remain anonymous, and in this endeavor I shall rely upon your assistance, which I am confident will not be withheld.

In view of the fact that my own part in the affair has been revealed, it is to be hoped that my continued presence in the city may prove sufficiently troublesome to divert the Duke's attention from the activities of our allies, and therefore I will remain. However, I must ef-

fect the removal of my household members within the
next day or so, and in this, too, your assistance will prove
invaluable. . . .

Grizhni dipped his quill and leaned forward. As he bent
over the page, the supernatural silence was broken by a shat-
tering explosion overhead. The savant's hands tightened at the
sound, and a blot of ink smeared across Farni's letter. The
first blast was followed by a grinding rumble and a succession
of crashes. With that, the Cognitive isolation of Grizhni Palace was broken. The splash of canal water was audible, together with shouts and cries arising outside.

Fal Grizhni laid down his quill carefully, rose and walked to
the window, pulled back the shutters. He saw that the ice
enclosing Grizhni Palace was breaking up. Huge chunks were
tearing loose and plummeting from the walls to land in the
canals below. The Lureis resembled the Sea of Ice during a
vernal thaw. The ice that still clung to the palace walls was
melting with unnatural rapidity.

"Vallage." Fal Grizhni spoke aloud. All the brute force of
the Ducal Guards was now backed by the very formidable
Cognition of Saxas Gless Vallage, and the combination was
deadly. Improbable to the point of impossibility that a senior
savant of the Select, a member of the Council itself, should go
so far as to lend Cognition to the enemies of his Preeminence.
In the case of Gless Vallage, however, the act was consistent,
almost predictable.

Fal Grizhni looked down from the window. The space
immediately surrounding the palace was clear, for the Guardsmen and citizens had drawn back to avoid the lethal bombard-
ment of ice. It would not remain clear much longer, for most
of the frozen armor was already gone. The fires of the Ducal
Guards would complete the work that Cognition had begun.
Even as Grizhni watched, a party of Guards arrived, all of
them burdened with firewood.

Quietly he shut the window, returned to the desk, picked up
all the letters and tossed them into the fireplace, where they
were quickly consumed. The respite, the time which he had expected Cognition to provide him, had been stolen. His plans
and hopes, dependent upon that respite, were already dead.
With them died Lanthi Ume's last hope of mercy at his hand.
His subsequent actions would be dictated by a combination of

immediate necessity and ineffable rage.

Fal Grizhni's expression was characteristically remote, but he paused, standing absolutely motionless for some seconds before allowing his hand to touch the bellpull. Nyd and two nestmates answered the summons. The creatures discerned nothing untoward in their master's appearance.

"The Shield of Ice has been broken. We are in great danger," Grizhni informed his servants. "Within moments the Ducal Guards will be upon us. Kevyd," he addressed one of the hybrids, "you will command the defense. Gather all your brethren together and see to it that they are well armed. Seal and barricade all doors and windows. Deploy your followers according to the training you have received. The Guards intend to slaughter all they encounter, so you will be fighting for your lives. Prevent their entrance as long as possible. Go now to your nestmates." The creature croaked and departed.

"Nyd, you will go to your lady. Conduct Lady Grizhni down to the Black Chamber and wait with her there. I shall join you presently. See to it that Lady Grizhni is warmly dressed. I am sending her out of the city tonight, and you will go with her. Hasten." Nyd rushed off toward Verran's apartment.

"Rys," the savant commanded the third hybrid, "you will attend me now." The awestruck hybrid waited while Fal Grizhni scribbled and sealed a brief note. "Bear this at your best speed to the Guardsman Ket Ranzo at Snout's Tavern in Kripnis Alley near the Northern Gate. Go masked and do not call attention to yourself. Entrust the message to none other than Ranzo. Should he have need of your services, you will obey him. And do not return to the Palace tonight. Now go."

Rys croaked and hurried off, leaving Fal Grizhni alone. The savant shut the door firmly. There was much to do and very little time left. Moreover, it was necessary to proceed with caution in order to preserve as much Cognitive energy as possible for the one great and terrible act of vengeance that remained to him. While it was thought by many that the Cognitive force of Preeminence Grizhni was limitless, such was not the case.

Within the space of minutes, messages were dispatched and borne northward on the wings of Cognition to the caverns of the Nazara Sin. Certain treasured records and artifacts were removed from their ironbound caskets and set aside. Many other notebooks, manuscripts, and scrolls were burned then and there, and no one would ever know what the destruction cost their owner. Much remained—more than enough to tickle the cupidity of any ambitious savant—and these things were safeguarded by Cognition, the last that Grizhni could permit himself were he to retain sufficient energy to accomplish his main purpose.

He had finished with the workroom. Fal Grizhni took up the objects set aside for preservation and walked out into the corridor, heading for the subterranean Black Chamber. As he passed the palace entry, where his fierce hybrids waited, he saw smoke gliding in under the door and heard the sound of shouting outside. The barred portal began to quiver beneath the impact of tremendous, repeated blows. The Ducal Guards had brought a battering ram.

Chapter Nineteen

The palace was in flames by the time the Duke's guards finally managed to break the door down. Fire danced in triumph on the wall hangings, the tapestries, the furniture; flickered over the corpses of those slain defending the entry; and sent their clouds of stygian smoke swirling through the corridors, down stone stairways, down as far as the Black Chamber wherein Lady Verran faced her husband defiantly. At ground level Lord Haik Ulf supervised with satisfaction the destruction of his enemy's house. Down below, the sounds of battle and destruction could not yet be heard. Only the faint acridity of smoke in the air presaged disaster.

"I will not leave," Verran repeated, stiff-spined. Her resistance had been strenuous and prolonged. "I will not go."

"I am not accustomed to disobedience," Fal Grizhni replied.

"I am your wife. My place is with you," Verran insisted with uncharacteristic stubbornness. "You dishonor me in suggesting that I go."

"There is no dishonor in obeying your husband's commands, Madam," Fal Grizhni replied, the coldness of his words belied by the gentleness of his voice. "There lies your way." He pointed to an opening in the wall, beyond which lay utter blackness. "Nyd will accompany you as your protector and your guide. When you reach the caves of Nazara Sin, the inhabitants will aid you. There is no more to be said."

"But what of you?" cried Verran. "Do you not come to the caves, my lord?"

Fal Grizhni regarded his young wife. He did not inform her that there was no hope at all for him, that he had already suffered ruin beyond all hope of recovery. If he remained, his death might satisfy his enemies' appetite for blood. If he fled, then Ulf and the others would pursue them both, to the very depths of the Nazara Sin if need be, until the great lord Grizhni, his lady, and unborn child were taken at last. But he could not tell her that.

"There are matters I will stay for," he said brusquely. "I leave when all is prepared."

"I must remain with you until then." She folded her arms.

"You anger me." His arctic tone was one normally reserved for enemies. Verran had never heard it before. She was shocked, and stared up at her husband round-eyed and silent. "Do not try my patience any further. I have expressed my wishes. Obey them."

Accustomed to obedience, Verran could think of no argument. As she struggled with her confusion, her fear and frustration, the tears sprang to her eyes and spilled out over her cheeks. "My lord—husband—don't send me away without you!" she burst out at last. "Come with me. Or if you will not, then stay and fight, but let me stay with you. I'm not afraid—you're greater than all your enemies. No one can defeat you!"

Fal Grizhni did not explain that he had been defeated from the moment that Brenn Wate Basef had betrayed his conspiracy to Saxas Gless Vallage. He merely said, "There are certain risks. Your courage does you credit, but I would not expose you to danger." He raised his hand to forestall her eager rejoinder. "It may be that you carry my son."

Verran pressed her palm to the living bulge beneath her robe. The smell of smoke in the room was growing stronger. The smoke and her tears were causing her vision to blur. Her husband's face seemed indistinct, the black eyes larger and more fiery than possible, the beard a gray-streaked shadow. "Come, the child must be protected, above all else," Fal Grizhni urged. "You please me best by obeying my commands."

Verran nodded desolately. She did not note her husband's relieved intake of breath. "If that is your will. You'll come as soon as you can?"

"Yes—when I can."

"You'll not tarry long?"

"No," he replied grimly. "Not long. Now question me no more, but listen. I am going to send you through the passageway with Nyd. You will let Nyd precede you at all times. There are traps and pitfalls within the passage, and you will therefore move with extreme caution. Remember that. The Duke's men now surround this house. You will pass beneath and beyond them to the far side of the Sandivell Canal, where a boat is moored. If luck holds with you, you will emerge behind the ranks of the Guards and you will not be seen. You will hide beneath the covers you find at the bottom of the boat. Nyd will row you to the city walls, and there you will stop, for the water gates will be down. Present yourself to the sentry, Guardsman Ket Ranzo. He is in my employ and he will help you. All will be in readiness for your overland journey north to the Nazara Sin. The inhabitants of the caverns have been notified. They will provide protection and assistance. Do not let their appearance alarm you—they are your friends. Do you understand all this?"

"Yes, but—"

"Good," Fal Grizhni interrupted. He clapped his hands sharply. "Nyd." Nyd detached himself from the shadows in the corner of the room and advanced to crouch at his master's feet. "You understand what is required of you?"

Nyd croaked and wriggled affirmatively. "Then understand this. Lady Grizhni is depending upon you absolutely. If you fail to guide her safely to her destination, then she dies, the child dies, and all that I hold most precious dies. Therefore take heed, and guard her as you would your own nestmates." Nyd's fervent croaks promised obedience. "One thing more. Certain of my written works must be preserved. You will carry them." The savant produced a package containing a folio volume, a roll of parchment, a leather binder filled with notes, and a thin plaque of gold incised with words and shapes. Nyd accepted them eagerly. "These increase your danger," Grizhni continued. "There are many who would kill for them. But I cannot—I do not choose to destroy the work of a lifetime, and therefore you must carry them. They are of value." For a moment, as he regarded his writings, Fal Grizhni almost seemed to forget where he was. The sting of smoke in his nostrils reminded him. The smoke was quite perceptible now, pushing in under the closed door and building gray clouds in the corners. The Black Chamber was underground, but the atmosphere had grown warm as the fire in the palace above waxed in size and fury.

"Take up a torch," Fal Grizhni commanded. Nyd sprang to the wall, wrenched a blazing torch from its bracket, stood clutching it expectantly. The savant turned back to his wife. "It is time," he told her. "Follow him."

Verran knew the folly of further argument. Quietly and strongly she embraced her husband and even managed a slight smile, as she saw he wished it. "We'll wait for you, my dear lord," she promised. "The child and I." She did not realize as she spoke how like a child she seemed herself.

Fal Grizhni touched her cheek once, very lightly. Then he made a quick gesture, and Nyd leaped forward into the passageway. Grizhni's hands tightened for an instant on his wife's shoulders before he released her and spoke. "Farewell, Verran."

Her eyes still fixed on his, she moved slowly to the opening in the wall, hesitated, then turned and followed her husband's minion into the darkness. A soft scuffle of footsteps and they were both gone.

The savant stood motionless for a moment, and during that time the last traces of softness passed irrevocably from his face until he had assumed the dire, frozen expression that the world knew and dreaded. Calmly he shut the door to the passageway. Once closed, the portal merged invisibly into the surrounding wall. Nonetheless Fal Grizhni pulled a great arras along its rod to mask the spot completely from view. This done, he turned away and stalked to the center of the chamber, where a great map of the universe had been carved into the stone floor. It was a very old and splendid map, rich in detail, depicting the great Serpent bearing its burden the Sun through the heavens, from one edge of the world to the other each day; the stars moving in the complex patterns of their eternal dance; and the mother Moon giving birth to new young stars. Contempt distended Fal Grizhni's nostrils as he observed this evidence of mankind's imperishable ignorance. Disregarding all the rest, he fixed his eyes upon the image of the world, his world, the land of Dalyon lapped on all sides by tiny stone waves, and he spoke aloud. "Darkness you desire, and in darkness you will walk. Let it be so." Quickly he gathered the materials he needed and set to work. The smoke in the room grew so thick that it was difficult to breathe or see. The air was stifling. Fal Grizhni's time had all but run out, but he worked as calmly, as deliberately and unhurriedly as ever he had in the days when the world trembled before him. His instruments, fluids, and powders were prepared. Books he did not need, for the words were committed to memory and the only written record now lay in the package carried by Nyd. Without fear or undue haste he made ready for his last and by far his greatest act of Cognition. Even the most bitter of his enemies would have admired Fal Grizhni now as he stood alone, powerful and terrible even in his downfall, and prepared to work the forces of Nature to his will.

Up above, the fire raged and Lord Ulf grew impatient. He had not come for the minor pleasure of burning an empty building. Fal Grizhni's demons had long since been slain. None of the servants had fled, and all had died. The palace itself and nearly all its contents were doomed. The fire was spreading uncontrollably, mounting to the topmost chambers, eating downward toward the cellars and storerooms. The air was almost unbreathable—hot, smoky, and foul with the stench of burning flesh and hair. But this was not enough.

Lord Ulf, at the head of a party of his best men, ranged through the palace like a starving wolf in search of meat. Dead flesh he found aplenty, both raw and cooked, but it was not the great prey he sought. Room after room he put to the torch, sparing only the workroom, whose contents he ordered removed. The firing of two rooms in particular afforded special satisfaction. One was the library wherein reposed Fal Grizhni's superb collection of manuscripts and printed volumes, assembled over the course of a lifetime. The other was the bedchamber of Lady Grizhni, with its bed hung in pale blue silk and its waiting lace-draped cradle. This violation of his enemy's personal treasures heightened Lord Ulf's triumph, but did not provide adequate compensation for the absence of Fal Grizhni himself.

Ulf's expression bore traces of mingled excitement and frustration as he sped down the winding stairways, his men close behind him. Lower and lower he descended, a few leaps ahead of the fire, until at last by chance he came to a subterranean room whose door was locked against him from within.

"We have him," stated Lord Ulf, and added, "provided he hasn't already finished himself." The prospect of his quarry thus eluding him edged Ulf's voice with urgency as he bade his men break down the door. Although it was strongly built, the door could not long withstand the blows of the mailed Guards and soon gave way. As the portal swung wide, the Guards gave a shout and made a move to rush forward; then stopped, bewildered. The chamber before them was black. It was not the predictable darkness of a smoke-filled underground hiding place. This was a heavy, intense, pitchy blackness with a weight and texture all its own. So dense, so heavy was the darkness that the light from Lord Ulf's torch did not pierce it, but rather, seemed reflected from a solid surface. The darkness bulged from the open door as if to engulf them all, and with one accord the Guards drew back. Ulf, too, automatically recoiled, but soon recovered himself.

"He's in there," he informed his unenthusiastic followers. "I want him. Come on." They made no move to obey. "I said come on!" Ulf shouted angrily. "Get in there!"

The Guards stood still, apparently hypnotized by the unnatural spectacle. The darkness gradually protruded further out into the corridor as they watched. "You must think we're fools," one muttered.

"I don't only think you're fools, but puling cowards as well," Ulf snarled. "You white-blooded mongrels, get in there!"

None of the Guards moved, and Haik Ulf waxed furious. "You call yourselves soldiers? Pah!" He spat on the floor. "You're not soldiers, you're vermin. Afraid of the dark, are you? My own hand-picked Guards? When this is over, I'll throw you all out to beg for your bread or starve. You sniveling cravens, you make me sick!"

Only one of the Guards dared reply. "No one in his right mind would want to go into *that*." He pointed at the yawning midnight.

"Speak for yourself, pigeon-guts," Ulf returned. Torch in one hand and sword in the other, he advanced upon Fal Grizhni's sanctum. The moment he crossed the threshold, the world around him turned dark and hot. It was not the dry heat of the fire above, but a strange, damp swelter. The air was heavy with smoke, and with something more—a peculiar scent as of mold or fungi that caused Lord Ulf to cough and gag. His blazing torch was oddly dim in that atmosphere. Its flame shone red and feeble, illuminating only a small portion of the chamber. He could see a carved octagonal table beside him, a circle of stone floor, and nothing else. The rest lay hidden in impenetrable shadow. There was no obvious sign of the savant, but Ulf sensed a hating presence close at hand that chilled his zeal. He took an involuntary step backward and turned to the door through which he had just entered. The doorway was a foggy gray rectangle, as if the light from beyond stopped short at the threshold. It was crowded with the vague black forms of men.

Haik Ulf realized to his unutterable relief that his men were following him in, no doubt shamed by the accusation of cowardice. Many of them bore torches. The darkness reluctantly retreated a few feet, and Fal Grizhni stood revealed to his attackers. The savant's black robes faded into obscurity, but his pallid face and slender hands gleamed startlingly white. The long fingers were contorted. The eyes in the frozen visage flamed in triumph and disdain. Several of the soldiers gasped. Fal Grizhni stared at them without moving, and no one seeing him thus could have guessed that his recent Cognitive exertions had drained him to the point of exhaustion. Gradually the room lightened to blood-red as more torchbearing Guards entered. The savant's entire form was now visible. He stood with every muscle tensed above the map carved into the floor. For a moment there was silence, and then Fal Grizhni said, "You are too late." It might have meant anything.

The guards gaped at him in superstitious awe. They were not certain they faced a mortal man. Lord Ulf had no such doubts. "You're under arrest," he informed the savant briefly. "You're to come with us. Don't try any of your tricks."

Fal Grizhni's expression was unreadable. "Tricks," he repeated in a voice like a cold desert.

Ulf gestured with his sword toward the door. "Move," he commanded. The savant merely looked at him, as he might have examined a stone, a splinter, a clod of earth. The guards shifted nervously. "D'you hear me, or are you deaf?"

"I will not come," said Fal Grizhni. The Guardsmen stared at him, amazed.

"If you don't walk out of here, then we'll drag you out," Haik Ulf returned. "It'll look as if you were too scared to stand on your own two feet," he jeered in a vain effort to raise his men's spirits. The Guards were badly in need of encouragement. Fal Grizhni's calm power and mighty name unnerved them. The torches and blades in their hands were quivering.

Grizhni did not answer the taunt directly. "Let the darkness be my shroud," he said at last. "I will not leave this room alive."

"Oh yes you will," Ulf replied. "We don't plan to kill you here and now. You don't get out of it that easily. The world is going to see how the Duke deals with traitors. After that it will be a long time before any of your gang of tricksters thinks of treason again."

"With me gone, you have little to fear from the Select," Fal Grizhni told him indifferently. "But I would advise you not to trouble them overmuch. They are capable of defending themselves."

"You're in no position to advise anyone about anything. You've got troubles of your own to worry about. I've waited a long time for this, Grizhni."

"I know it. You are small men, Ulf—you and the others like you. You think and feel and act as small men. But that is of no concern to me now."

"Right," Haik Ulf agreed. "All that concerns you now is what will happen if you don't come along quietly. I don't think you want to find out what will happen."

"What have I to gain by obeying you?"

"Life—for a little while."

"I do not need it," Fal Grizhni replied. "My purpose has already been accomplished."

"What purpose? What are you talking about?"

Fal Grizhni eyed the circle of steel that hemmed him in and answered, "You are too late, and you have lost. My death will not help you. The words have been spoken, Cognition has been achieved."

"What have you done?" demanded the uneasy lord, resolutely banishing all dread from his voice. Beside him, his men fidgeted.

"The darkness that now surrounds you, the blackness that fills this room, will in time cover all the land," the savant promised, his eyes seemingly fixed on the future. "It will be

hot and moist, as you feel it now—blinding and suffocating
you, sapping your strength, your courage, and your will. In
the shadow of that deadly night sickness and madness will
flourish, for it is a darkness malign to humankind. It attacks
your strength here and now. You weaken from moment to
moment."

"That's enough! We're not interested in listening to this
muck," interrupted Ulf with patent untruth. His fearful
Guards were straining to hear every word.

"More than that I do prophesy," Fal Grizhni continued.
"The night whose coming I foretell, dark and destructive to all
men, will be filled with creatures who prey upon you and
yours as you prey upon me now. They will slake their thirst for
conquest with the blood of your descendants. Where darkness
holds sway they will walk in triumph and your sons will give
way before them, losing goods, losing land, losing peace and
rest, and losing life at last. Let it be known that these beings,
rulers in times to come, although inhuman, will yet be mine."

Fal Grizhni paused a moment as if expecting a response, but
there was none. Haik Ulf and his men stood mute. Never had
Fal Grizhni owned greater force and assurance. The threats
that might have been dismissed as the ravings of a madman
bore the weight of absolute conviction, were impossible to
disbelieve. "The shadow," he continued in cold certainty,
"will be born at the heart of the land and will spread outward
from the center toward the sea. Your people will try to arrest
its progress and they will fail, for such darkness cannot be
halted. In the end they will be forced to retreat before it,
retreat even as far as the sea. There upon the shores they will
huddle by the thousands, by the tens of thousands, until at last
they turn upon one another, murderous in their desperation.
The strongest and most ruthless will seize what boats there
may be, and these perhaps will escape. Many will die at the
hands of their brethren. The rest will stay to be overwhelmed
by the darkness—and the beings who inhabit it." Fal Grizhni
spoke calmly, as one stating facts. "Remember my words, let
them be set down in writing and thus preserved against the
coming of the great darkness whose author I am. Such is the
final triumph of my life."

Lord Ulf found his voice. "This is a tale to frighten
children. No one here believes it." Ulf lied. He believed, and
his men believed. It was a matter of instinct.

The Guards milled restively, and one of them barked out, "When? When does this happen?"

"Nothing's going to happen, you fool!" Haik Ulf insisted savagely. "Nothing's going to happen except that this wizard's to be tried and executed. Go on, take him out of here!"

"You will tell the Duke that he has failed."

"You will tell him yourself, just before he passes sentence on you."

"The Duke and I never meet again. But come, no more of this. We have talked long enough."

"I agree. Guardsmen!" Haik Ulf commanded once again. "Take him." Once again he was disobeyed. The naked blades of the Guards stirred like reeds at the first breath of a storm, but no one presumed to move.

"You have asked," remarked Fal Grizhni with the faintest ghost of chill mockery, "when it will begin. You may look for it when a star shines at noon, and a lion gives birth to a dragon."

"What in perdition is he talking about?" a Guard muttered.

"He's talking dreams and trifles. It's nothing. He's trying to scare you," Ulf sneered. "Kronil," he addressed his lieutenant, "if you don't obey your orders right now, I will personally cut your throat on the spot as an example to the others. That promise is gold."

"Couldn't we just lock him up in here and leave him to burn?" Kronil offered miserably.

"The time I speak of may be centuries distant," Fal Grizhni observed. "No matter—rest assured it will come. To quell your doubts, however, I shall give you a taste of what is to be. You will experience it here and now."

The savant spoke and the torch in Lord Ulf's hand flared briefly, then extinguished itself with a hiss. Ulf cursed and dropped it. Fal Grizhni spoke again and other fires leaped, then died. The hot shadows pressed closer in upon them all, and the alarmed Guards recoiled.

"Stop that!" Haik Ulf roared uselessly. *"Get him out of this room!"*

In response to his leader's command Kronil rushed forward, whereupon his torch flared so violently that the Guard's beard and eyebrows were singed before the fire went out.

There was an uproar as the heat waxed, smoke swirled in the dying light, and the men yelled, struggled, and stumbled in confusion. One or two began to choke on the burning, vaporous air. Above it all the voice of Fal Grizhni rang clear and cold as always. "Thus it will be over all of Dalyon," he promised. "A night filled with terror, and a night without end." Another torch winked out. The shadows, close and foul, pressed down on them like iron, while the smoke rioted in their lungs. One of the Guards sank to the floor, overcome. Another let out a high-pitched, almost feminine scream. Cursing viciously under his breath, Lord Ulf leaped toward Grizhni. In the remaining vague and reddish half-light, he could discern another form beside him and knew it to be Kronil. Together the two men threw themselves upon Fal Grizhni, who stood like an image in ice. Swiftly they secured his arms. The savant spoke, a torch went dark.

"Stop his mouth!" gasped Ulf, whose breath was all but gone.

The Guards were in a frenzy. Perceiving the enemy incapacitated, one of them lunged wildly, sending his blade through voluminous black robes deep into Fal Grizhni's side. The steel withdrawn ran wet and red. Grizhni made no sound. He sagged slightly in his captors' grasp, but remained upright.

"Don't kill him!" Ulf cried. "Not here, not now!"

They did not hear him. Another Guard thrust home, and another. Then they were all upon him with their blades, heedless of their leader's raging commands. Fal Grizhni's robes were heavy with blood. He slid slowly to his knees. His head was unbowed, his face the face of a corpse, although he lived still. "You are too late. You have lost," he repeated in a voice so low that they had to bend to hear it. "The darkness comes." Half in terror and half in rage, a Guard made a clumsy pass at Grizhni's throat, and the blade bit in at the juncture of neck and shoulder. The blood spurted in a dark rain. Ulf and Kronil stepped back swiftly. Deprived of their supporting grip, Fal Grizhni pitched face forward to the stone floor, his body and black robes lying like a pall over the carved map of Dalyon. Even in his dying state he managed to whisper the words of power one last time; or perhaps he only spoke them in his mind, for no one heard him. But the two remaining torches in the hands of the Guards extinguished themselves simultaneously, plunging the room into utter darkness, darkness beyond comprehension.

The cries that filled the chamber now were the shrieks and

wails of terrified animals. Several of the Guards sought out the limp body on the floor, stabbing madly at it with their swords in the vain hope that extinction of the last spark of life in the fallen savant would restore normalcy to the world. Most staggered blindly and purposelessly in the dark. The air was unbearable, vile with smoke and that other, indefinable odor that had intensified as the light failed. Three of the Guards fell unconscious. Others stumbled and fell, their outcries subsiding to strangled gasps.

Commander Haik Ulf kept his head. As the last light died and the room went black, he forced himself to stand still. Fighting his own natural impulse to grope and stumble with all the others, he remained where he was and mentally reconstructed the chamber around him as he had last seen it—the location of the map, of Fal Grizhni's body, the table, and the door. When he had fixed that spot in his mind and not before, Haik Ulf moved in what he was fairly certain was the right direction. It was not an easy progress, for he was growing lightheaded from the heat and lack of oxygen. Often his way was blocked by flailing bodies, and these he thrust aside. Once somebody staggered against him, and Ulf struck out with a venomous curse, felt his fist sink into yielding flesh, heard a cry of pain. Teeth clenched, he struggled on. At last he saw the dim gray rectangle that marked the door.

Ulf sprang forward eagerly, only to trip over the body of a prostrate Guardsman. He fell, and as he went down his head hit the edge of the octagonal table. He struck the floor with a crash and lay there aching and partially dazed. He was inexpressibly tired and confused.

But soon the Commander's very well-developed instinct of self-preservation came to his aid and he began to stir. Slowly he raised himself to a sitting position and paused to gather his strength. He was breathless, disoriented, and his head was splitting. The noisome darkness sealed his eyes, and his ears were filled with the cries of panic-stricken men.

Ulf turned in search of the light, but saw nothing. There was a footfall nearby, and a Guardsman blundered violently into his commander. The impact expelled most of the air from Ulf's lungs, but he managed to gasp, "Damn you." His voice was unrecognizable.

The invisible Guardsman set up a loud outcry. "The wizard —he's here! He's alive!"

"Why, you fool—" Ulf began, but got no further. A sharp blade sliced through the darkness and sank into his flesh. Ulf produced a hoarse cry as he felt blood spurt from the cut. At the sound of his cry the blow was repeated, and this time the sword sheared its way into his vitals.

Ulf could no longer speak. He was bathed in blood and the pain was indescribable, but he was still fully conscious and aware of what was happening to him. He groaned and blades struck like blind snakes—several of them, this time. The shouts of the frightened Guardsman had attracted a number of his fellows, and now they hacked, slashed, and stabbed hysterically at the body on the floor until at last it moved and groaned no more, whereupon they abandoned it.

Fate was not kind to Lord Haik Ulf, and his oblivion was brief. He soon awoke to find himself upon the floor in a moribund condition, but aware. He lay, although he did not know it, but a few feet from the corpse of Fal Grizhni. Hideous darkness still reigned, but the killing heat and the dull roar overhead told him that the fire was close at hand. Around him he could hear the agonized cries of a number of his men still unable to find their way out of the Black Chamber. He could not answer them in words, but a single sound escaped him—a sardonic grunt. Crude though he was, Commander Haik Ulf did not lack a sense of irony.

The Guardsman Kronil, now unwittingly in command, finally located the door. "Over here," he called the men. He could manage little more than a hoarse croak, having little breath left. "Here's the way out." A few heard, made their way to his side and joined their voices with his. But they did not dare to wait any longer, for the fire was almost upon them. Kronil and a few of his followers passed through the doorway into the corridor.

The moment they were clear of Fal Grizhni's Black Chamber, courage returned to them. The heat was no less intense, the atmosphere no less strangling, but the panic that reigned in unnatural darkness passed away. A glance informed Kronil that one end of the hall, including the staircase by which he had descended, had become an inferno. The fire was advancing swiftly. The only remaining exit lay at the far end of the corridor, and it would not be open long. Kronil turned back to the gaping door. The darkness still protruded in a great, impossible curve. Beyond it he heard fearful cries and groans. The voices sounded oddly distant. For the last time Kronil called out to the doomed men, but no one answered. Now he and his companions turned and hurried away, leaving flames, darkness, and destruction behind them.

As they went, Kronil mused in frustration, "Those mindless louts! We were supposed to take Fal Grizhni alive. Now we're in for it. When Ulf gets hold of us he'll grind our bums to feed his dogs." He raised his voice. "Does anyone know where the Commander is?" No one knew. "He must already be out. What about Grizhni's household?"

"All dead," replied a Guard who ran beside him. "Put to the sword, burned, or self-slaughtered. Except . . ." He hesitated, as if mildly reluctant to mention it. "Does anyone know what's become of his wife?"

Chapter Twenty

It was fortunate that Nyd knew his way through the secret passage, for Verran could never have survived it alone. Fal Grizhni had constructed the passage for his own use in years gone by. Its existence had enabled him to slip in and out of the palace unobserved, facilitating those clandestine nocturnal sorties that had contributed so greatly to his reputation for omniscience. In his pride he had never dreamed that the route would be used for purposes of escape. Hence the passage, designed to discourage intruders, was filled with dangers of every description.

The torch that Nyd bore illuminated a dry stone floor, arched stone ceiling, and walls with irregularly spaced niches. It looked innocent enough, and Verran was taken completely by surprise shortly after their entrance, when a flock of winged dermati exploded from one of the niches and bore down on the two of them, all fangs and talons and poisonous breath. For a moment the air was wild with beating wings, glaring eyes, and noxious exhalations. Verran screamed and fell back, one hand up to shield her face, the other diving to protect her swollen belly. Nyd's battle cry rose waveringly, and he swung his torch. A spark struck one of the dermati and the creature exploded with a bang as its volatile breath ignited. For a moment a great ball of flame hung in midair, then vanished. Nyd croaked and swung again. Sparks flew and balls of fire bloomed briefly before dying. Enraged dermati bated and shrieked. The floor was littered with bits of their singed flesh and claws. One of the virulent creatures alighted on Nyd's shoulders, driving dagger claws and fangs deep into the hairy neck, blinding him with its skillful wings. In vain the hybrid twisted, struggled, and tore at his tormentor. It was not to be dislodged. At last he thrust the torch backward, catching his enemy's breath in the flame. The resulting explosion burned Nyd's back horribly, from the neck clear down to the sacral spikes. The hybrid hissed and plied his torch wildly. The ferocity of his defense repelled the last of the dermati, who finally retreated to their communal niche. The corrosive reek of their breath lingered in the still air. The attack had begun and ended in seconds.

Nyd turned back to Verran. The girl was crouched on the floor, both arms wrapped around her abdomen. As she perceived the danger past, she rose. "You're hurt, Nyd," she murmured tremulously. "I'm so sorry, my dear. When Lord Grizhni comes, he'll cure you—and he'll be proud of you for what you've done."

Nyd caught the sympathy in her tone and croaked softly. At the mention of Lord Grizhni, his ears twitched. He was hurt far worse than either of them guessed. In wounds left by fang and claw, the poison festered. He retrieved the package he had dropped during the fight, and they continued on their way.

The attack of the dermati was only the first of the dangers from which Nyd's vigilance preserved Lady Verran. It was Nyd who knew the whirling, spinning movement that brought them safely through the region of lavender gaseous fingers that extruded themselves through cracks in the ceiling to clutch at the pair as they passed. It was Nyd who knew where to place his feet to avoid setting off the stone blocks in the floor which would, at the slightest pressure, rise and smash themselves against the ceiling with catapult force. Nyd knew where the acid seethed in glass pits, and where the slime webs lay in wait. He knew where the Living Wires, part metal and part flesh, fed and mated and hung their lethal nooses. He was able to show Verran how to crawl along the floor to avoid explosion in her lord's Abhorrent Vacuum. He brought her safely past the singing nets and the gaping marble jaws. All this proved taxing to them both. Lady Verran, always delicate, was particularly unsuited to endeavor now. It was only the knowledge of her husband's wishes that kept her moving at

all, always three or four paces in the wake of her guide. As for
Nyd, he walked in pain. His burned and poisoned back was a
cruel torment. He was assailed with a sense of lassitude that
his primitive mind could scarce fathom. He did not know why
his muscles rebelled against him, or why he was troubled with
vague foreboding when the obvious danger was past. Nyd
strove to disguise his distress, with some success. The torch he
bore burned steadily, and his leaping gait was undaunted. His
lady followed trustingly.

Verran's fears were manageable. Hadn't Fal Grizhni made
all arrangements for her escape? Hadn't he promised that he
would join her soon? And had he ever been known to fail?
The growing warmth in the tunnel warned her that the palace
above was fully ablaze, but she did not doubt her husband's
victory.

At last Nyd guided his charge safely to the end of the
passageway, its opening masked with bushes and dried weeds.
They emerged cautiously and found themselves beneath the
night sky in a garden on the far side of the Lureis Canal. Verran looked back through the trees, across the canal to her
home, and could not repress a soft exclamation. Grizhni Palace was irrevocably lost, engulfed in greedy fire. The highest
of its vaunting pinnacles had already fallen. Flames shot from
the casements and cast writhing reflections in the beaten silver
that sheathed the huge dome. The carvings were charred, the
fretwork blasted, and even the fog-colored Grizhni banner
that flew so arrogantly over all was burning. The ripples on
the canal reflected a million dancing sparks. The various
moorings were crowded with spectators, and the water was
dotted with a fleet of small boats. The citizens of Lanthi Ume
had turned out in force to view with wonder an unbelievable
event—the downfall of the ancient House of Grizhni. Most of
them gaped in blank incomprehension, as at a happening beyond their ken. But many cheered the triumph of human virtue over the power of the King of Demons. The burning
edifice was completely surrounded by the Ducal Guards,
whose helmets and breastplates flashed like blades in the light
of the fire. All the Guards faced the palace, alert to the capture of fugitives. They did not think to turn back to the canal
or to the garden on its far side.

The boat was moored nearby, as Grizhni had promised. It
was a small, polished dombulis with a high-curved prow, as

light and graceful in the water as a black swan. The seats were covered with painted leather, and down-padded coverlets were folded at the stern. Nyd peered watchfully around him. Although he had extinguished his torch upon leaving the passageway, there was plenty of light; both from the blazing palace and from the lanterns in the boats of the townsmen. All eyes were fixed intently on the conflagration. Nyd beckoned with a jerk of his wiry head. Verran instantly quit her hiding place. As confidently as if she had rehearsed it, she waded to the side of the boat, her hem dragging in the mud and water of the Lureis, clambered in with surprising agility, curled up as best she could at the bottom, and pulled the coverlets over her head. So far events were proceeding as her husband had predicted. Nyd climbed into the boat, allowing his weariness to show now that she could no longer see him. He laid the package aside, took up the carven oars in his singed paws, and began to row.

The black boat performed like an acrobat, springing eagerly through the water as if imbued with its master's desire to deliver them. They attracted no attention from spectators or guards. Nyd kept his shoulders hunched, his head bowed—both from wisdom and weariness. Only once did he raise his eyes to the fiery palace, and a grieving croak escaped him. Animal instinct, stronger than Verran's human reason, told him that Fal Grizhni could not survive. Great blasts of heat rolled over the water at him, clawing at his burned back. The hybrid lowered his head and plied the oars. As he rowed, the night grew gentler and dimmer around him, and the sounds of carnage died away. Nyd found himself rowing along the cool back waterways of Lanthi Ume.

The dombulis skimmed over the waters, through air scented with flowers and perfume, smoke and refuse. Its passengers encountered no obstacle—the eyes of Lanthi Ume did not note them. Presently the boat slid into the vast shadow of the Vayno Fortification. The water gate was flanked by lanterns. It was, as Fal Grizhni had warned, down and barred against them.

Nyd brought the dombulis to the dock and lashed it fast to a slime-coated post. The place seemed deserted. The shabby surrounding buildings were lightless and silent, and the breeze carried the sour stench of poverty. The only sound to be heard was the lapping of canal water. The hybrid climbed out of the boat, set his package down, then helped Verran step to shore.

"There should be someone here," the girl said, her sweet, small voice unsure of itself. "He said there would be."

Nyd lifted his head, sniffed sharply, and swiveled to face the shadows at their right-hand side. A low whistle cut the darkness, and a man stepped out of a doorway wherein he had concealed himself to observe their approach. He was big and young, with a heavy wrestler's build running to fat, wide shoulders, and a fleshy, dissipated face. He wore the uniform of a Ducal Guard. "You're late," he accused without preamble. "I was told you'd be here an hour ago. D'you know what kind of risk I'm running by waiting around here for you?"

"We came as quickly as we could," Verran defended herself. The strange man garbed in the uniform of her husband's foes discomforted her. She consciously strove to disguise her fears. "Are you Guardsman Ranzo?"

"That's right. Look, you'd better know you're in trouble. There's been three separate patrols come around here asking me if I've seen you—" the guard replied, and broke off abruptly as he took his first close look at Nyd. "What's that thing?"

"The guide appointed for me by my husband."

"Looks like a cross between an ape and a sizbar. What happened to its back?"

"He's been hurt. Please," Verran appealed, "please let's be on our way. You'll raise the water gate for us?"

"No, that's not the way you'll be going. I'm letting you out through there." He pointed to a small door, one of many that pierced the huge city wall. "There's a carriage with provisions waiting for you on the other side. I've fixed it all, don't worry. But I'm risking my neck for you, you know that?"

"Fal Grizhni will remember it." She little knew that as she spoke, her husband's body lay in blood and fire.

"Will he now? I'm not depending on it. Do you know what would happen to me if I was caught helping you?" The girl didn't answer, and he added, "Do you know how much it cost me to get that carriage and food for you? And all without a moment's notice?"

She still said nothing, but Nyd snarled softly at the man's hectoring tone. "When I perform that kind of risky service, I have a right to know it's appreciated. It isn't like I'm a servant, you know. I don't have to do this for you."

"Lord Grizhni will appreciate—"

"Lord Grizhni, if you must know, is probably dead by now—"

"That's not true!"

"If he isn't dead yet, then he'll be executed in a few hours. And so would you be if it wasn't for me—"

"That's a lie!" Verran returned so vehemently that the guard was startled. "Lord Grizhni is well!"

Looking down at her white, set face, he decided not to argue the question. "Anyway, the point is I've hardly been paid a servant's wages."

"Well, then?"

"I say I'm not being treated fair," Ranzo declared angrily. "I could be killed, but you wouldn't be interested in a little thing like that, would you, my lady? What I'm doing for you is worth a whole lot more than I've been paid."

"Such arrangements are handled by my husband—"

"Your husband isn't here now. You are. Look, let's not waste time. How much money are you carrying?"

"I don't—I haven't—" Verran stammered.

"You want to get out of this city or don't you? If you do, you'd better play straight with me."

"How much do you want?" asked Verran, holding back her tears with difficulty.

"I said let's not waste time. You wouldn't be running off like this if you weren't carrying something on you, like jewelry. Sewn into your dress somewhere, maybe?" His eyes slid down over her body. "That real?" he demanded with a jerk of his thumb at her belly. "Or have you got something stashed away in there?"

Verran drew back, and the guard's hand descended on her shoulder. Her courage returned all at once. "Take your hands off me," she ordered. "I'll see you caged and sunk by inches in the Great Syan Ooze."

For an instant Ranzo hesitated. Then, looking down at her slight but ungainly figure, and recalling that her lord must surely be dead or taken, he decided he was safe. "Let's see what you've got, then," he demanded, his teeth showing in a grin as he fumbled at her gown.

Before Verran had time enough to scream, Nyd leaped. One paw flung the girl aside. The other swept around the guard's torso and pulled him close—close to the open, snarling mouth with its pointed canines. With a grunt and a heave, Ranzo pushed him off and leapt back, simultaneously drawing a broad dagger from his belt. For a moment the two faced each other at a distance of some feet.

"Nyd—stop it!" Verran pleaded, but her companion ignored her. The hybrid's rasping voice rose in fury, and he charged. Ranzo's knife plunged and blood spouted from Nyd's upper arm. The hybrid hissed in sudden pain, but kept coming. The impetus of the attack slammed Ranzo against the wall of the nearest building. In an instant his face was dripping blood where Nyd's teeth had laid open one cheek. Seizing his dazed enemy by the throat, Nyd hurled him to the ground. The man's head struck on stone with an audible crack, his body jerked, and he lay still.

Verran bound Nyd's wounded arm with her silken scarf, and blood seeped through almost immediately. "Lean on me," she directed. "Let's get away before he wakes up."

The hybrid would not lean on her. Had he been capable of speech, he could have told her that Ranzo would never wake again.

"I'll get the package," Verran offered.

But Nyd insisted on carrying the package himself, evidently regarding his master's property as a sacred burden.

"I hope he was telling the truth about that carriage."

They tried the door in the wall and found it locked. While Verran halted in perplexity, Nyd vainly gnawed at the wooden frame with his teeth. "That won't work," she told him. "It's much too thick. That man must have the key on him. I'll—I'll get it," she said with an effort. "He'd better not wake up."

Verran knelt beside the Guardsman's supine figure. For a brief moment revulsion paralyzed her, and then she very softly detached the leather pouch from his belt. He did not stir, and the first suspicion invaded her mind that he might be dead. She recoiled from the body with a shudder.

The pouch contained a silver shorn; some smaller change; a festillid—an instrument for trapping body pests; a pair of cheap wooden dice; and a key ring with half a dozen keys attached. Verran took the keys and left the rest of the contents. The largest and rustiest key on the ring was the one she needed. It fit the lock, but she couldn't turn it. It took all of Nyd's strength to do that. The door screeched away from them. Darkness lay beyond, with a faint glimmer at the end of it. Verran clasped Nyd's paw tightly, and he croaked his reassurance. Together the two of them passed beneath the sixteen-foot thickness of the city wall. The door at the end of the little corridor had a square grill through which the starlight shone faintly. Nyd pulled the bolt, and this time the door swung easily on its old hinges.

"I hope he told the truth about the carriage!" Verran repeated as they crossed the threshold. He had and he had not. Transportation awaited, but it was not the carriage the Guardsman had described. She beheld an open wooden cart with solid wheels, drawn by a small gray miskin. The miskin—surely the oldest, the sorriest, the most decrepit of its kind—stared at them with bleary eyes and wheezed asthmatically. "This can't be what Lord Grizhni intended!" Verran cried. It was not, indeed. But the money with which Fal Grizhni had long ago supplied Ranzo to procure a comfortable carriage with fast horses and provisions, to be held in readiness at all times, had been lost at the gaming table of the local tavern. At times Verran tended to overlook her husband's human fallibility, but she remembered it now.

She untethered the miskin. The beast's outsized head drooped, and great patches of mange marred its hump. One of its tails was missing. She wondered if it had strength enough to draw the cart, and tried not to think what would happen if it did not. If only she knew one of Fal Grizhni's spells of revivification! But he had never offered to teach her, deeming it unnecessary, and she had never thought to ask. It was too late now.

Verran climbed up to perch uncomfortably on the cart's hard seat. Beside her Nyd handled the reins. Nyd was in greater need of revivification than the miskin, although he strove to hide it. His strength was waning. The dermati poison in his back had ravaged all his system. His wounded arm throbbed and screamed for rest. The hybrid croaked wearily and urged the unwilling miskin out onto the open road.

Behind them towered the Vayno Fortification. Before them stood the few houses and small buildings that clustered at the base of the wall. From thence, the road passed over fields and meadows where the local farmers pastured their sheep, and on around the foot of Morlin Hill. Castle Io Wesha, ancestral home of the Wate Basef family, stood atop Morlin Hill, which on clear days was visible from the walls of Lanthi Ume.

Beyond Io Wesha the road ran by the occasional isolated farm
or cottage until it plunged over the crest of a granite rise
known simply as the Crags, down onto windswept Gravula
Wasteland. There the road as such ended, splintering into
dozens of tiny lanes and paths. The widest of them ran north
to the Nazara Sin, a region not entirely unfrequented by men.
The others were rarely traveled, for they led into the unknown
lands of the interior. The great island of Dalyon was ringed
with seacoast city-states, of which Lanthi Ume was the oldest
and fairest. The interior was largely unexplored and unsettled
by civilized humankind. The inhabitants clearly intended to
keep it that way, and were not apt to extend a welcoming hand
to strangers. Tolerably smooth highways linked the coastal
cities. All other roads were undependable, and in bad weather
often disappeared altogether. It was along such a path that the
plodding miskin now drew Verran and Nyd.

For many hours they traveled through the night. Verran had
time to think, and as she did so, her fears increased. There was
the possibility of pursuit to be considered. Ket Ranzo had
reported that three separate patrols had come searching for
her. How could they have been so fast, so sure? How could
they have guessed which route she would travel, which gate
she would choose? And how, oh how had they managed to arrive there ahead of her? If they could move with that kind of
speed, surely they'd find no difficulty in overtaking her now!
It was a measure of Verran's innocence that it never occurred
to her that Ranzo had lied.

The hours trudged by, and her fancies darkened. What, she
wondered, might become of Fal Grizhni? With her astonished
recollection of her husband's fallibility had come full realiza-
tion of his great danger. Brilliant and powerful he was, but not
omnipotent. No matter, she tried unsuccessfully to convince
herself. Fal Grizhni always triumphed.

Then there was Nyd. The poor creature was in terrible pain,
and he was growing weaker by the hour. It was increasingly
difficult for him to muster the strength to whip the miskin on
its sluggish way. Although in desperate need of rest, he would
not permit Verran to take the reins into her own hands. She
had tried to do so many times during the night, and always it
was the same. In vain she argued and pleaded with him. Nyd
croaked and kept on driving.

Dawn came creeping into the eastern sky, to find Verran

stiff, exhausted, and nauseated. The occasional movements of the child she carried added to her discomfort. Despite her worries, she slipped into a light doze, still sitting upright in the rumbling cart. The pale winter sun was shining in a bright blue sky when the girl awoke. The desolate Gravula Wasteland spread out around her. Sharp, fresh breezes slapped at the grayish hills and stunted bushes; threaded a path among towering blocks of stone. The cart was not moving, for Nyd had fallen asleep. His head was sunk on his breast and the reins had slipped from his paws. The morning sun played full on the ruin of his back, and Verran was torn between pity and horror at the sight. The miskin browsed quietly between the traces, tearing at the scrub vegetation and occasionally nosing the earth in search of the odd worm or beetle.

Verran decided to let Nyd rest awhile longer. She found that she was hungry, and carefully lowered herself into the back of the cart to search for the provisions that Ranzo had promised would be there. She soon discovered the food, which was as stingy and inadequate as the cart itself. Next to Fal Grizhni's package lay a damp canvas sack containing a few loaves of brown bread, some dried biscuits, a small sausage, a rind of cheese, a couple of onions, and a skin of wine. The sight half killed her appetite. Verran struggled unhappily with the stale bread, and longed for her home. The breezes on the Gravula were swift and cold. She shivered some and swallowed a little red wine, which was too thin and weak to warm her.

All around her the grasses and bushes stirred ceaselessly in the wind. Not far away a stand of huge stone blocks—commonly called the Granite Sages—reared themselves skyward in mysterious symmetry. Most of them were gigantic gray prism shapes which could never have occurred in nature. It was said that they marked an entrance to the neither regions. The place was reputed to be haunted, and Verran would not have liked to be there alone at night. She fixed her startled stare on the horizon—did she spy motion there? Perhaps a figure on horseback? A Ducal Guard? No—it was only an animal of some kind leaping among the hillocks. It was time to go. Verran woke Nyd with difficulty. He was alarmingly somnolent. She offered him food, which he refused. She watched the hybrid anxiously as he picked up the reins and shook them. The miskin continued to browse. If it was aware of the desires of its masters, it gave no sign. Nyd snapped the whip and croaked ir-

ritably. A snuffling sound escaped the miskin. It dug its heels
into the stony soil and continued to eat. Nyd's voice climbed
in wavering anger and he brought the whip down across the
miskin's bedraggled flanks repeatedly, with all his remaining
strength. The miskin moved at last. Nyd sank back exhausted,
and this time made no protest when his companion took the
reins from him.

Verran was surprised at the difficulty of driving the cart.
Her inexperienced hands were clumsy on the reins. The miskin
felt the difference and adjusted its willful pace accordingly.
Sometimes it hopped forward briskly, sometimes it slowed to
a crawl. There was little that Verran could do to control the
animal, and they progressed in a series of teeth-rattling starts
and stops. She was grateful when Nyd recovered himself sufficiently to reclaim the reins. In this wise they traveled throughout the day. Nyd would not touch food. When she offered him
wine he accepted eagerly, tasted, and spat it out on the ground
with a croak of disgust. He then sat watching her with a hope-
ful and pathetic expression. Verran felt tears well up at the
sight, but she could not help him.

"Please drink the wine, Nyd," she begged. "It's good for
you. There's no water, my dear. This is all we have, and you
need to drink. I know that Lord Grizhni would want you to
take it."

Nyd's ears twitched weakly. He released his breath in a
mournful gust and shook the reins wearily. He was panting in
a way she did not like to hear. The tongue that protruded from
his open mouth was dry and furred.

Night came and Nyd drove on, sparing neither the miskin
nor himself. His gaze was fixed on the hills lifting before them
under the moon—stark, jagged hills that towered above the
caverns of the Nazara Sin, their destination. The road had become much narrower, the terrain rougher. Around midnight
Verran composed herself for slumber—this time stretched out
uncomfortably on the boards at the back of the cart, her cheek
pillowed on her palm. It was no good asking Nyd to stop and
rest. He was sunk in a kind of torpor and no longer responded
to her voice at all. The last sounds that Verran heard as she
drifted off to sleep were the groaning rumble of heavy wheels,
the creak of wooden joints, and the periodic snap of the whip.

The bright morning came, a duplicate of the one that had

preceded it. Verran awoke stiff and sore in the motionless cart. Nyd was slumped in his seat and the miskin grazed. Gusts of wind teased the grasses and long wisps of cloud raced across the cold sky. Once again Verran sated her hunger on the crude fare provided by Ket Ranzo, and struggled with her growing fears. At last she climbed to the fore to wake Nyd. He did not respond to her call and she was reluctant to disturb the poor creature, who obviously needed his rest. Since they could not afford to linger, Verran decided to drive the cart herself. If she could only get the vehicle moving, then perhaps Nyd might manage a little more sleep. If the miskin misbehaved—she set her jaw—she'd make it sorry. Very quietly, taking great care not to disturb him, the girl bent to pick up the reins where they lay at Nyd's feet. He was motionless, but something impelled her to look quickly up into his face. The hybrid's eyes were shut. His lips had drawn back from his teeth and the pointed canines were chalky and dull in the morning sun. He did not seem to be breathing.

Her own breath caught in her throat. He could not be dead; she refused to believe it. "Nyd, wake up!" she pleaded, and shook him violently. "*Please* wake up! Nyd!" As she shook him, the hybrid toppled from his seat down into the back of the cart, where he lay motionless. Verrran stared for a moment, then stepped down to crouch at his side.

She did her best to make him comfortable. She stretched him out on his side and cleansed his injured back with wine, the only liquid available. The hybrid's wounds were infected, and caked with dried blood intermixed with tatters from the shredded gray robe. They should have been intensely painful, yet when Verran bathed them, Nyd did not stir. When she pressed a hand to his chest, she detected no heartbeat. There was no point in deluding herself—he was dead, or nearly so. The tears came, and Verran dashed them away with the back of her hand.

"Oh, my poor Nyd," she whispered in a shaking voice. "I'm so sorry." Gently she smoothed the rumpled fur on his cheek. "You'll come with me to the Nazara Sin," she told him. "You'll have the best care. But if you don't wake up, you'll lie in honor there. Lord Grizhni himself will sing the Six Stanzas for you when he comes." She knelt beside him, head bowed.

A little while later, with pale face and a heavy heart, Verran

climbed back into the seat, shook the reins and hissed at the
miskin. The animal continued to graze peacefully. Verran
hissed more loudly. The miskin did not raise its head. She tried
cajolery, without result. She took up the whip with reluctance
and brought it down tentatively on the miskin's back, but the
animal took no notice. Next time she struck harder. The
miskin snuffled insolently and kept on eating. Something in
Verran's mind gave way. For the first time in her life she was
overcome with true, white-hot rage. For a moment she was
unaware of her surroundings. Standing up in the cart she
whipped the miskin with all the strength of her slender arm.
She was screaming invective at the animal, beating it with a
fury she had never guessed was in her, hot with wrath and
hatred she had never known before. The miskin hunched its
back under the blows, dug in its heels, and with deliberate per-
versity continued to graze. Verran might whip the brute until
the dust rose from its hide in clouds, but she could not force it
to move.

She threw down the whip. Still raging, and entirely forgetful
of her own condition, she took a careless leap out of the cart;
too careless. She struck the ground heavily, felt the jolt
through her legs and spine. A warning pain stabbed her. Verran clutched the edge of the cart and stood with her eyes
squeezed shut, breathing deeply until the spasm passed. The
miskin regarded her in dull curiosity for a moment, then returned to its grazing. She stepped in front of the animal,
grasped its halter, lifted its head, and pulled with all her
strength. The miskin snuffled and shook its great head, dragging the girl this way and that as she clung to the halter. Verran doubled her small fist and dealt the beast a smashing blow
across the nose. The miskin, annoyed at last, jerked the halter
from her grasp, lowered its head and butted her. Verran went
flying down a short slope and landed on her back, arms laced
protectively around her belly. She made no effort to rise. Pain
stabbed through her again, and all at once the tears she had
fought to suppress burst forth.

Verran lay among the stones and waving grasses of the
Gravula Wasteland and sobbed in anguish, helplessness, and
mounting hysteria. She wailed forth her pain, her fear, her
frustration, her outrage. She shrieked forth her grief for Nyd,
her longing for Fal Grizhni, her hatred of the miskin. She
cried for the loss of Lanthi Ume and the life that she had

known. She beat the ground with her fist and her tears rained down to salt the earth. She wept until her throat was sore, her nose completely stuffed, and her head ached abominably. And when at last she had exhausted and sickened herself, and her outcries had subsided to muted gasps, she lay where she had fallen and it dawned on her that there was no one to sooth her, no one to attend to her. Husband and parents, servants and friends, were all far away or dead. She might cry until the rocks of the Gravula were worn away by her tears, and nobody would hear her—nobody but the miskin, who couldn't have cared less. It was almost inconceivable. Her tears had never gone unnoticed before, and she was struck with disbelief that it should be so now. But the sight of the empty wasteland around her, the indifferent miskin, and the bright, cold sky overhead, convinced her at last—she was on her own, for the first time.

Verran sat up slowly, still sniffling. Time was passing, and each hour might bring pursuit nearer. She could not lie there crying like a child—she could no longer afford that luxury. She rose carefully and returned to the cart. The miskin ignored her, and Verran admitted to herself that she simply did not possess the strength or skill to control the animal. She would have to continue her journey on foot, there was no alternative. But that meant leaving Nyd. Verran studied the motionless hybrid. She didn't know whether he was alive or dead. After all he had suffered for her sake, how could she desert him now? What if he were alive? What if she left him and he awakened to find himself abandoned and in pain, with no help to be had? What a reward for his loyalty and selflessness!

"Please, Nyd," she whispered. "If you're alive, let me know it and I'll stay with you. Move. Breathe. Anything."

There was no response. The hybrid lay, either in a coma or else dead. Verran waited beside him, her eyes fixed on his calm face. An hour went by and she saw no hint of motion. The winds of the Gravula snapped at her in passing and she shivered. At last she reached out, laid her fingers upon Nyd's wrist and then upon his spiky throat. She felt no pulse.

"Nyd, I can't stay here." She spoke slowly and clearly, as if he could hear her. "You know I can't stay. I don't want to leave you, but I must. I'm sorry, but I know you'll understand. When I find the folk of the caverns, I'll send help to you. It won't be long, my dear. I promise it won't be long."

Verran's voice faltered, and she spoke no more. She
descended from the cart with great care.

The cart had stopped at the point where the road broke up
into a tangle of straggling lanes. One of the widest angled up
toward the hills of the Nazara Sin. Verran did not know the
location of the entrance to the caverns—Nyd was to have
brought her there. Now she would have to trust to observation
and luck.

She wondered if she should unhitch the miskin. It could
never fend for itself while harnassed to the cart. Much as she
loathed the beast, she did not wish to inflict the cruelty of starvation upon it. But what if Nyd awoke and wanted to drive?
Verran shook her head. It was time to face reality. Nyd would
never awake. She loosed the miskin. Once free, the animal
gazed stupidly at her for a moment, then dropped its nose to
search for beetles. The girl stepped to the back of the cart to
remove the sack of provisions. Nyd lay at peace. For the last
time she pressed a hand to his heart, and found no sign of life.
She turned to go, and the words of Fal Grizhni rang in her
mind. *Certain of my written works must be preserved. . . . I
will not destroy the work of a lifetime. . . . They are of value.*
Verran reached down and withdrew the package with its book,
parchment, binder, and plaque of gold. She hesitated a moment, then dropped the bundle into the canvas sack to lie with
the cheese and sausage.

"Good-bye, dear friend," she told Nyd softly. He was not
to come with her after all. Verran squared her shoulders and
struck off alone into the wilderness.

It was farther than she had thought. The hills seemed close
at hand, but it took an entire day of walking to reach them.
Verran was not used to walking long distances. Her feet hurt
and her back ached. The sack she carried seemed to grow
heavier with each step—a paradoxical illusion, as the hours
passed and she consumed the contents. Evening found her
toiling up the slopes along a path that could never have accom-
modated the cart. She slept that night in the open air, curled
up under her cloak on the windy hillside.

Morning came and she devoured the last of her provisions.
Grimly she pressed on, wandering among treeless hills as roll-
ing and endless as the waves of the sea. There was no sign of
human presence. Around midday distant movement caught

her attention and she flung herself to the ground to crouch low in the grasses. Hundreds of feet below her rode a party of men attired in the green and gold of the Ducal Guards. Evidently they did not see her. Verran was motionless, and her charcoal robe blended with the hillside. As she lay watching, the Guardsmen paused, then wheeled and trotted off along a path leading toward the sea.

The girl rose reluctantly to continue her random journey. She had no notion where lay the entrance to the caverns of the Nazara Sin, and it was increasingly obvious that she might wander for weeks without ever finding it. Her guide Nyd was probably dead, and the wilderness was inhospitable to the ignorant. Time wore on, and she grew horribly hungry. Her food was gone and the hills offered no sustenance. Frightening pains came and went. The wind blew, chilling her to the bone, and she wondered if she were fated to wander alone and unnoticed until she died of exposure or starvation.

But Verran was mistaken in her perceptions. The hills were by no means uninhabited, and unseen eyes had followed her progress for hours.

She traveled throughout the day in growing fear and confusion. When the wind grew colder and twilight descended, she faced the prospect of another night spent out of doors without food, shelter, or companion. The girl sank despairingly to the ground. She was, although she did not know it, within a few hundred yards of one of the concealed entrances to the caverns.

Then she felt it. A sharp pain shot through her—far more severe than anything she had hitherto experienced. She gave a cry and clutched herself. The pain subsided. Her baby was not due for another three weeks, but she found herself prey to hideous fear. It couldn't be happening! Another pain came and went. And another.

Cold gray evening blanketed the hills, and Verran writhed upon the ground, helpless and in agony. So acute were the pangs of birth that they occupied all her consciousness. There was no room left for fear as she noted that many pale forms had emerged silently from the shadows to cluster about her—crouching, worm-white figures that gleamed in the twilight, faintly luminous.

Chapter Twenty-one

✧❦✧❦✧

The morning skies were appropriately clear over Lanthi Ume. The sun was bright on towers, domes, mansions, and canals. Raftsmen hawked their wares, citizens bustled, and the scene bespoke normalcy. Only the charred and smoking remains of Grizhni Palace told of the carnage of the previous night. It was said that human corpses lay beneath the blackened ruin, but nobody cared to verify the rumor. It was said, too, that the King of Demons had been slain, but the more conservative amongst the Lanthians declared this to be an impossibility. It was far more probable that Fal Grizhni had simply withdrawn himself to the nightmare realm of Ert, there to await a propitious moment to wreak vengeance upon mankind.

Upon that morning of triumph, Saxas Gless Vallage was in the best of spirits, for the future before him was golden. His machinations had been successful at last. Terrs Fal Grizhni had died the traitor's death that he deserved. Gless Vallage, most accomplished remaining savant of the Select and a personal friend of the Duke, was obviously destined for Preeminence. Better yet was the neatness with which this coup had been engineered. No stain or blame could attach itself to the name Vallage. Brenn Wate Basef, whose continued existence might have proved embarrassing, was dead. An additional and unexpected benefit lay in the disappearance and presumable death of Commander Haik Ulf. The only possible accuser whose fate remained a mystery was Lady Grizhni. She, like

Ulf, had disappeared. It was to be hoped that as a dutiful wife she had burned along with her lord, but nobody could state with certainty that such was the case. Vallage shrugged. It didn't really matter. In the unlikely event that Grizhni's wife should reappear to raise her voice against him, he would be well prepared to deal with her.

The savant's footsteps were buoyant as he ascended the stairs to his secluded workroom. His face was bright with anticipation as he unlocked the door and entered. There they were, all of them—four large caskets piled up just as they had been left by the Guardsmen who delivered them. Fal Grizhni's property—Gless Vallage's now.

Vallage opened the smallest casket. Yes—there were the unctions and serums whose ingredients he would now discover; the lenses, charts, artifacts, thaumaturgical devices, Cognitive aids. He recognized an ancient Krunian grel-circle, and there were at least five of the priceless, luminous stones of Woh. Beautiful, all of it—the rarest, the finest, the oldest. With possessions such as these, was it any wonder that Fal Grizhni had been great? Now Gless Vallage would surpass him. He opened another two boxes and found them crammed with treasure; a savant's dream come true.

There were far fewer written records than might have been expected. Only one explanation suggested itself. Somehow Fal Grizhni had found time to destroy the notes before he himself had died. Vallage sighed. It was a great loss, a very great loss indeed. Still, one casket remained unopened, and that one the largest.

It might have been that eagerness and greed dulled Gless Vallage's normally acute power of observation. Accomplished savant though he was, he did not sense the action of Cognition and was therefore utterly unprepared for what confronted him as he raised the lid of the final casket.

A dense black cloud arose. The savant's reflexes were excellent and he slammed the lid of the box down instantly. Swiftly as he had moved, it was already too late, for the black cloud was free of its prison. Vallage took a step backward, breathed deeply, and spoke with authority. He was not unduly alarmed. He felt himself to be at the peak of his powers and there was little doubt in his mind that he would overcome the Cognition of his dead rival. It was therefore with astonishment that he found himself unable to achieve the desired

result. A superior force suppressed his Cognition, much as the
Cognition of Brenn Wate Basef had once been suppressed
under somewhat analogous circumstances. Inexplicable fog
blanketed his mind. He made a second effort, equally unsuccessful, and an ugly expression distorted his customarily pleasant features.

Gless Vallage knew better than to waste his time and energies. It was clear that reinforcements were required to deal
with the sinister visitation, and he walked calmly but quickly
to the exit. The door was locked and his Cognition could not
open it. He was trapped. He turned back to confront the black
cloud.

It was changing. Before his eyes it reformed itself, and a
familiar image took shape. Terrs Fal Grizhni rose before him,
and Gless Vallage realized that he stood in the presence of a
spectral projection of his enemy's emotions and intentions, a
projection a thousand times more powerful than those employed in the Droyle of Nes. Although he fully comprehended
the nature of the thing that faced him, Vallage could not
repress a shudder. The specter of Fal Grizhni was a fearsome
sight, the looming figure composed of opaque vapor that
ranged in tone from white through various shades of gray to
deepest black. The uncannily lifelike eyes burned in a death-
white face. The figure was covered with wounds from which
blood issued in pitchy streams. The slashed throat was black
with it.

As he watched, Vallage became aware of two facts. One
was that he was in extreme danger, and the other was that he
was afraid. A senior savant of the Select, a member of the
Council itself, could ordinarily afford to live free of fear; but
the sensation came back to him now. It would not have become a savant of his standing to give way to terror, and Gless
Vallage did not do so. Once again he spoke, and again Cognition eluded him. His sense of unwonted helplessness was intolerable.

The specter approached. Its face was the face that Grizhni's
enemies had known and feared in life—icy, remorseless, and
relentless. Vallage retreated hastily, beat the door and lifted
his voice in cries for help. His calls were heard by several
servants, who raced to the assistance of their master. Their
efforts were foiled by the sealed portal, which effectively resisted all attack. From within the chamber came the sound of
frenzied activity.

There was nowhere to run. Saxas Gless Vallage watched the specter's unhurried advance and knew himself to be doomed. That death should find him so unexpectedly, at the very hour of his triumph, was a source of additional bitterness. But nothing could change the fact that he *had* triumphed over the great Fal Grizhni. Death itself could not rob him of that victory. He had proved the superiority of the Vallage intellect, the inviolable strength of the Vallage mind. Nothing could destroy those things, and nothing could take them away.

Vallage faced the specter squarely. It was unlikely that the apparition could hear or understand, yet he addressed it aloud. "Mine was the victory, Grizhni. This changes nothing." He stood and watched it come for him.

The black figure slowly extended its hands. Gless Vallage awaited the inevitable grip upon his throat. But it was not for its enemy's throat that Grizhni's specter reached. The white hands with their midnight bloodstains descended upon Vallage's head, one at each temple, and there they rested. Vallage instinctively pulled back, and found that the hands of dead Fal Grizhni were inescapable. Their pressure was inordinate, and he felt his very mind darken beneath it. Awareness was fading away. Intelligence, identity, sanity itself—all were leaving him, and he knew it. Vallage screamed. It was a dreadful sound of rage and anguish. He looked up into the eyes of Grizhni's specter, and terror overcame him. He screamed again, and went on screaming.

The servants gathered outside the workroom heard the unearthly cries and stared at one another in consternation. The cries were followed by a succession of violent crashes. The servants renewed their assault upon the locked door, and this time succeeded in breaking it open. The scene that greeted their entrance was appalling.

Saxas Gless Vallage squatted upon the floor, surrounded by four open caskets and the wreckage of their contents. In one hand he gripped a stone of Woh with which he smashed and beat the delicate devices he had once coveted. Shards of broken glass, bits of twisted metal, spilled powders and fluids were scattered all over the room. He had rent his garments in his fury and they hung on him in tatters. His glaring eyes were innocent of reason.

As the door opened, Gless Vallage looked up and stared at his household domestics without a particle of recognition. A shrill squeal of terror escaped him. Without rising to his feet, he covered the distance from the center of the workroom to one of the corners in a single bound. There he cowered, whimpering piteously, entirely incapable of human speech. When the horrified servants attempted to approach, he struck at them with the glowing rock.

It was naturally assumed that Lord Vallage's unfortunate mental lapse was temporary. Considerable time passed before the permanence of his condition impressed itself upon the world, which came to recognize that the Cognizant Saxas Gless Vallage would remain exactly as he was throughout the many long years of life that yet remained to him.

Chapter Twenty-two

Her eyes opened slowly. She lay on something soft. The air around her was warm, moist, and apparently glowing. Her nostrils were filled with strange odors. Verran had slept deeply for many hours, but now she was awake and confused. Her last recollections were filled with pain and fear. She recalled the parting from her husband, the escape from Lanthi Ume, the flight across the Gravula Wasteland, the loss of Nyd, her wanderings thereafter, and finally the delivery of her baby upon the windswept hillside. She would have died on that hillside had it not been for the help of the white beings. So immersed in pain she had been, she'd scarcely noted the nature of her saviors. She thought of them now, and realized that she had seen them once before in her husband's workroom. They were Vardruls, shy inhabitants of the ancient caves of Dalyon, and they had once sent a delegation to Lanthi Ume under the protection of Terrs Fal Grizhni. These were her husband's allies, known to many as the "White Demons of the Caverns." Demons they might be, but Fal Grizhni had entrusted his wife and unborn child to their care. Inhuman they surely were, but they had saved her life. It was impossible to name the source of their expertise, but they had known how to help her. Perhaps the manner of their own birth was similar to that of human beings. In any event they had known what to do, and her baby had been safely delivered out there on a cold slope of the Nazara Sin. It was a boy, tiny and perfect, with

wisps of dark hair and eyes that would be as black and brilliant as his father's. So much had she seen before exhaustion
overcame her. While she slept they had moved her, and now
she awoke to find herself . . . where?

Where is my baby? All other thoughts were instantly driven
from her mind. Verran sat up with a frightened gasp, and
found she was not alone. Only a few feet distant stood a group
of some half-dozen Vardruls whose presence brightened the
chamber. They glowed. Their flesh was white, hairless, and
quite luminescent. They were unclothed, having little need of
protection in the warm and humid atmosphere of the caverns,
and it was apparent that their bodies were in many ways
similar to those of men, although they clearly were not human. Their eyes, in particular, were alien—immense, colorless
orbs surrounded by multiple ridges of muscle. Their hands did
not terminate in fingers, but rather in short, infinitely flexible
tentacles. They were tall, spare, and angular of figure, lacking
the softened contours of humankind. Upon the wrists of some
rode great brown bats, as falcons ride the wrists of men.

All this Verran noted fleetingly. What occupied her full
attention and froze her with fear was the sight of her baby—
Fal Grizhni's son—cradled in the arms of a tall Vardrul. The
Vardrul bore the baby with extreme care amounting to what
would have seemed reverence in a human being. The other five
white creatures clustered near, studying the infant in obvious
fascination. They warbled softly and melodiously amongst
themselves. The human baby slept.

Verran cried out in alarm. The Vardruls turned to her and
their flesh brightened perceptibly. She could not have imagined it—those luminous bodies, limbs, and faces glowed more
brightly. Those huge, unwinking eyes seemed to pin her to her
bed. Even the bats were staring. Verran moistened her dry
lips. "My baby," she whispered.

At the sound of her voice the Vardrul warblings gave way
to fluting arpeggios. The faces of her hosts were mobile, Verran noted; but their expressions were incomprehensible. "My
baby," she pleaded, extending her arms.

Assuredly the Vardruls did not understand her words, but
the gesture was unmistakable. They advanced, and Verran
repressed her impulse to back away. She sat perfectly still and
watched them. They walked slowly, their heads bowed in what
resembled a human attitude of respect. When they had drawn

very near, they paused and the musical conversation resumed. In the midst of the sung phrases she picked out familiar syllables: "Fal Grizh-Ni." They had spoken the name of Grizhni. She regarded them in amazement.

The tall Vardrul stared into her eyes and spoke very distinctly and deliberately. "Fal Grizh-Ni."

Verran nodded. She had no idea whether the Vardruls would understand the meaning of a nod, but she didn't know what else to do. "Fal Grizhni." She pointed at the baby. "Fal Grizhni," she repeated emphatically.

The Vardruls stirred and voiced their strange melody. The tall one made a mysterious gesture, and gently placed the sleeping baby in its mother's arms. Verran rocked her son. She essayed a tentative smile at the white creatures, and the result was startling. They murmured, and their luminous flesh dimmed and brightened rapidly.

The attention of the Vardruls was diverted by the flutter of leathern wings. A large bat flew into the chamber and alighted on the shoulder of its glowing master. Around its neck the creature wore a collar to which a tiny pouch was attached. The pouch was found to contain an assortment of colored pebbles. Evidently the pebbles held some meaning for the Vardruls, for a musical exchange ensued, at the close of which all the white creatures departed.

Verran watched thoughtfully as they left. She found that she was unafraid. Perhaps exhaustion and listlessness dulled her emotions, and yet—the Vardruls were gentle and considerate, despite their strange appearance. They had proved themselves to be her friends, and she sensed she had nothing to fear from them.

She unlaced the front of her dress and put the baby to her breast. He nursed avidly, and contentment suffused her. She was at peace for the first time since she had left her home. Verran looked down at the tiny dark head. "I'll call you Terrs, after your father. Lord Grizhni is sure to be pleased when he comes." *If he comes.* The unwelcome thought intruded itself, and she rejected at once the threat to her new-found tranquility. "He'll be here within the next few hours," she assured herself, and settled herself more comfortably to take stock of her surroundings.

They had brought her down into the caverns, of that there could be no doubt, but it was not at all what she had expected.

The chamber in which she rested appeared to be of natural formation, and translucent stalactites dripped lavishly from the ceiling. She now saw the source of illumination—it was the stone itself. The rock of the ceiling, walls, and floor produced a steady, faint glow; soft as summer twilight. Red vegetative slime blanketed one wall, and the glow there was ruddy, like firelight. The air was unaccountably warm. It had been Verran's belief that the caves would be dark and cold. She was as yet unaware of the sophisticated heating systems employed by the Vardruls. There was no furniture, but the surface on which she rested was comfortable enough. She examined the woven fiber mat beneath her, and cautiously lifted a corner. Under the mat she beheld a bed of white fungi, somewhat similar to mushrooms. She pressed them, and found the plants to be of a remarkably tough and resilient consistency. Here was the source of one of the peculiar, but not unpleasant odors she had noted. She let the mat fall back into place. On the floor beside her lay Fal Grizhni's package. He would be relieved, she thought, that it had been preserved.

Verran looked down at the nursing baby and marveled at its perfection and at her own intense love for it. At last the child was satisfied, and fell asleep upon her breast. She sighed and lay back, with Terrs cradled in the crook of her arm. She was very tired. Soon she slumbered, and rested undisturbed but not unobserved, for many a Vardrul paused to gaze upon the human girl and her son in silent wonder.

She had no idea how long she slept. In the absence of sunlight or moonlight she had no way of gauging the passage of time, for she had not yet learned the Vardrul methods. She was awakened at last by a harmonious commotion at the entrance to the chamber. She realized that she was feeling much better, much stronger. Now she propped herself up on one elbow to observe the activity of her hosts.

Four of them bore a long, heavy burden. She could not see what it was until they laid it down upon another mat a few feet from her own. Verran beheld a familiar, hairy form. It was Nyd. "Alive," she whispered.

He rested upon his side, and the poisoned wounds on his back had been cleansed, poulticed, and elaborately bandaged with strips of woven fiber.

Verran sat up, then rose to her feet with care. She was a

little unsteady, but reasonably well. As she walked slowly toward Nyd, the Vardruls drew back—warily or shyly, she did not know which. She knelt beside the recumbent figure, noting with gratitude the steady rise and fall of his chest. Nyd was unconscious, but his breathing was deep and regular. She pressed a hand to his chest and detected a strong heartbeat. He was vastly improved and in time he would recover fully. "I'm so glad," she told the sleeping hybrid. "And Lord Grizhni will be so proud of you!" She stroked his cheek lightly. Nyd stirred and croaked in his sleep. At the sound the Vardruls stared and hummed.

One of the white creatures approached, extending a carved stone vessel. Verran threw the Vardrul a startled look, then accepted the bowl. It was filled with thick soup, almost a stew, with herbs and savory vegetable chunks. She realized all at once how very hungry she was. She sniffed, and her appetite sharpened. Did Vardruls eat human food? She lifted the bowl and took a cautious swallow of soup. *Mushrooms*, she thought. It was oddly seasoned, but good, and she drank a great deal before pausing to smile her thanks at the watching Vardruls. Once again she perceived the mysterious, flickering alteration in their luminosity.

The baby awoke and began to cry. Verran returned to the bed, picked up her son, and rocked him until he grew quiet. The Vardruls dimmed and brightened unaccountably. In silence they filed from the chamber, leaving their guests alone.

"They know us, little Terrs," Verran told the baby. "Your father told us we should find friends here, and he was right. He's almost always right, as you will learn." Terrs extended a minute fist and grabbed a strand of her long hair. Verran smiled. "The Vardruls are strange but kindly folk, and the three of us are safe as long as we stay here with them. But that won't be for long, I think. Lord Grizhni will be here very soon, probably within the next couple of hours, and he'll be planning our return to Lanthi Ume. He still has many supporters there, and many of the great savants are on his side— Jinzin Farni, Ches Kilmo, lots of others. I saw the list once, and it was long. And there's Brenn Wate Basef—I believe he'll help too. So you see, it won't be long before you and I, your father and your friend Nyd, all return to Lanthi Ume—return home." She did not as yet realize that she was home.

• • •

"Nyd, you shouldn't be up yet. You're not strong enough," Verran admonished.

Nyd's nostrils flared, and he wriggled. A protesting hiss escaped him.

"No you're not. You still need lots of rest. Believe me."

Nyd fidgeted and stamped the floor impatiently.

"You'll have a relapse if you don't take care. Please lie down now."

Nyd stamped again, and extended his great arms toward the baby.

"You can hold Terrs later, after you've had a nap. Sleep first," Verran insisted. "Then I promise you can hold him. If you're good, I'll let you bathe him," she coaxed.

Nyd hesitated indecisively.

"The most important thing now is for you to recover and build up your strength. You know that's what Lord Grizhni would want you to do." Her throat tightened and her face tingled, the usual precursor of tears. It had been the same for the past couple of weeks, whenever she spoke her husband's name. She tried to ignore the reaction. So far her mind had withstood the assault of her instincts' inferences. Now Verran resorted to her customary litany of self-reassurance. "It's only been a few weeks since we left home, and that's not very long at all." *You don't really know how long it's been. No sun, moon, or stars underground to mark the passage of time. It seems an eternity.* "There are many reasons that could explain Lord Grizhni's absence and silence. He had matters of importance to attend to, he said. He didn't tell me how long it would take to complete them." *And you didn't have the wit to ask.* "He might well have been delayed for one thing or another, or he might have waited a time before joining us in order to lull suspicion." *Suspicion of what? You're talking nonsense.* "He may have sent a message that never reached us. The messenger was taken ill or perhaps the letter was lost." *He'd have known by Cognition if that had happened. Somehow he'd have managed to contact us.* "He may have stayed to help his followers." *If so, he would have sent word.* "In any case, it would be foolish to jump to conclusions. I don't want to think about it yet. I'll wait just a little while longer and he'll be here and it will be all right. Only a little longer."

Nyd's anxious croaks recalled Verran to the problem at

hand. "Please lie down again," she requested gently. "I'll feel much happier if you do."

Nyd withdrew without further argument. He had, as soon as his depleted resources permitted, transferred his sleeping pallet to the corridor outside Verran's chamber. Presumably deference had motivated the move, and none of Verran's arguments or pleas could induce him to return. Noting the odd behavior of their guest, the Vardruls had attempted to install him in a chamber of his own, which Nyd rejected. Eventually the hybrid took up residence in a dry, warm niche in the wall directly opposite the entrance to his lady's lodgings, where he could guard her doorway and hear her if she called. To this niche he now betook himself.

Verran watched as Nyd departed, and then her gaze dropped to the baby asleep in her arms, his face bathed in soft rock-light. Terrs stirred and opened dark eyes so like those of his father that her heart contracted and she had to look away. "Close your eyes, my baby," she whispered. "Close your eyes."

A Vardrul entered the chamber and Verran stiffened in surprise. She had not yet accustomed herself to the spectral silence of her hosts' movements, and wondered if she ever would. The creature bore a tray laden with soup in a two-handled drinking vessel; a salad of mushrooms mixed with wild fremp shoots; and several cakes of a pale, curdlike subtance that Verran could not identify.

The Vardrul set the tray upon the floor beside her, and Verran smiled, then hummed the three briefly sustained syllables that she had learned conveyed appreciation. Although she could produce only an approximation of the appropriate sounds, there was no doubt that her meaning was clear. The Vardrul warbled eloquently in response. His melody was incomprehensible and Verran found it dauntingly alien. It did not seem so to Terrs, who gurgled in delight. The Vardrul's flesh brightened noticeably at the sound, and the warbling notes were repeated. Contractions distorted the muscular ridges that ringed the creature's pale eyes. What the expression was meant to convey Verran could not guess, and alongside her very geniune gratitude she was conscious of confusion and intense homesickness. *A little longer*, she told herself for the thousandth time. *Only a little longer.*

The Vardrul uttered a final throbbing hum, dimmed himself, and retired. The ensuing silence was unwelcome to Terrs, who began to howl.

Verran rocked him and crooned. "Hush, Terrs. Sleep. It's all right, my baby. You'll see." She sang an old lullaby remembered from her own childhood, and her clear, light young voice echoed oddly through the ancient caves of the Nazara Sin, where such a sound had never been heard before. Terrs grew calm and soon dropped off to sleep. Verran continued singing, more softly now. The lullaby was as soothing to her as it was to the infant, and a deep sense of relaxation stole over her. But presently the song died in her throat and she sat silent and motionless as a corpse, for in that unguarded moment the thought she had for so long managed to bar from her mind slipped past her mental barricades and into her consciousness like an assassin. *Lord Grizhni is dead.* She made no further effort to deceive herself. A stroke so swift and crippling was not to be parried; truth so deep and certain was not to be denied.

There were no tears. She felt little as yet; only somewhat dazed, and her mind was very sluggish. There were the words —*Lord Grizhni is dead*—and she suspected she didn't quite understand them, but would comprehend fully very soon. She was cold, despite the humid warmth of the chamber. Her hands were icy and unsteady. Her trembling shook Terrs, who stirred and woke.

Verran looked down into the baby's eyes, saw there the eyes of Terrs Fal Grizhni, and divined her husband's will, which coincided with her own.

"They mustn't escape unscathed." She spoke dully and her face was blank. "If it's true, if Lord Grizhni is dead . . . if it's really true . . ." *It is true. You know it.* "If they've killed him, then they mustn't escape unscathed. Your father is the greatest man in all the world. If they've dared to harm him, then they must pay for it. It's up to us—or to you and yours— to see to it that Lord Grizhni's enemies are punished."

It was the first time she had uttered such sentiments, but it would not be the last. Always she would cry vengeance upon the murderers of her husband, for she had no way of knowing that such pleas were redundant. The dying curse of Terrs Fal Grizhni had already forged a blade that would one day strike Lanthi Ume to the heart.